SINGLE
K.L. SLATER

Bookouture

Published by Bookouture in 2019

An imprint of Storyfire Ltd.
Carmelite House
50 Victoria Embankment
London EC4Y 0DZ

www.bookouture.com

ISBN: 978-1-78681-928-4
eBook ISBN: 978-1-78681-927-7

To my daughter, Francesca

PROLOGUE

Three Years Earlier

The day of the hearing, it was mid-July, scorching hot and I'd dressed in jeans and a thick cable-knit sweater with a roll neck.

I stood, staring at the front door waiting for my social worker, Audrey.

The house was silent, the boys' rooms empty.

Rivulets of sweat ran down my back, pooling at the waistband. The eczema on my hands and neck was the worst it had been, so I'd slipped on a pair of olive-green leather gloves.

I'd wrapped Joel's old striped college scarf around my neck and topped it all off with a pair of red plastic sunglasses I found in the kitchen drawer that I'd got free once with a magazine.

It seemed the right thing to do at the time.

'Have you taken your medication?' Audrey looked me up and down when I opened the front door.

'Yes,' I said.

'Let's go back upstairs and find you something to wear that's a bit more comfortable, shall we?'

'I *am* comfortable,' I said. The thick fabric felt safe and reassuring on my skin, like a coat of armour. It helped keep all the pain inside.

*

Inside the family court, the air-conditioning whirred above our heads.

People stared as I walked through the corridors with Audrey and I wondered if it was because they knew me. Knew everything that had happened and why we were here.

Then I remembered the sunglasses, scarf and gloves.

'This is the room where the judge will hear your case,' Audrey said before we went inside. 'Everyone will already be in there. Sure you're OK and this is what you want?'

'Yes,' I said, thinking about all the meetings, all the talking we'd done in the last few weeks.

Audrey opened the door.

I thought there would be a judge wearing a wig, a witness box and a public gallery but it was just a regular room with regular-looking people sitting in it.

The walls were white and there were two framed prints on the wall of sailboats on water. I stood and stared at them until Audrey tapped me on the shoulder and said I should sit down.

Joel's family were in there and they all sat opposite me and Audrey.

I'd seen them glance at each other when I first walked in. Dave stared with his mouth open until Steph nudged him.

I took off the sunglasses and put them on the table in front of me but I didn't meet their eyes.

A woman with short grey hair and wearing a light grey suit walked in. She sat next to a man wearing navy trousers and a white shirt and striped tie.

'I'm Judge Myra Stevens,' she said, looking at me and then at Joel's parents. 'We're here today to formalise custody arrangements for…' She consulted her paperwork. 'Kane and Harrison Hilton. Is that right?'

'Yes,' Brenda and Leonard said together as if they'd been rehearsing. Their voices rang out loud and clear in the small room.

The judge looked at me and raised an eyebrow.

'Yes,' I whispered, looking down at my gloved hands.

I listened to all that was being said in fits and starts. It was a tsunami of words, all serving to describe my chaotic life, my breakdown, my inability to care for my sons.

I imagined a giant eraser in my head that had the power to make the worst parts of my life disappear.

'Answer the judge, Darcy,' Audrey whispered and I realised everyone was looking at me again.

'I need you to state that you are in full agreement with what has been discussed here.' The judge addressed me directly. 'Your sons' grandparents will assume full custody of the boys with immediate effect. This is because you are unable to care properly for your children yourself. Do you agree?'

'Yes,' I whispered.

'Louder please, so the court can hear.'

'Yes,' I said loudly. 'I agree.'

My boys' faces appeared in my mind. Kane was almost three years old and his hair was wiry whereas seven-year-old Harrison's hair was as soft as silk. Their differences always amazed me. Kane loved broccoli and Harrison hated it so much he once hid some in his shoe and forgot about it and the house stunk to high heaven.

It took us ages to find out what the stench was.

I smiled to myself and when I looked up, I saw the judge was frowning.

More was said then, something about monitoring the boys and the continuation of my own treatment. Truthfully, I didn't pay much attention. I was too busy thinking about how easily some polite talking and a few signatures could take something so precious away from me so swiftly in such an ordinary room.

'Well done,' Audrey whispered, handing me the pen. 'You're doing the right thing for the boys.'

*

Afterwards, everyone stood up together. The chair legs scraped on the floor and hurt my ears.

They all came over to our side of the room. Brenda's face looked sad but up close, I saw the worry had gone and her eyes sparkled again.

She gave me a hug but I just left my arms hanging by my sides.

'We'll look after them while you get yourself well and can cope again,' she said softly in my ear. 'You know that, don't you?'

'And when you're feeling better you can come over any time and see them.' Leonard smiled and I thought, for the first time, how much his incisors looked sort of wolfish, just like Joel's had.

'I'll pop over tomorrow,' Steph said to Audrey. 'Check how she is.'

Then she touched my arm and walked away with Dave.

Audrey led me outside, back into the fierce heat of the day.

Underneath my clothes, every inch of my body felt slick with sweat and I was starting to feel a bit light-headed.

I thought it would be all right, that I'd done the right thing. But the ball of iron in my stomach told me it wasn't going to be all right after all.

I peeled off the gloves and Joel's scarf and let them drop to my feet. I threw the sunglasses on the pavement and crunched them under my boot. When I started to pull my jumper up over my head, Audrey grabbed my arms.

'Not here, Darcy, not in the street. Let's get you home.'

I threw back my head and started to howl.

Much later, when it was dark outside, I woke up in a very quiet, very white room.

There was a machine beside me with red digital figures on a screen and lots of tubes leading over to my bed.

When I tried to move my arms, I found I could not.

The door opened and a nurse came in. She had fair hair up in a bun and she wore a light blue uniform.

'You've woken up,' she said. 'That's good timing because the tea trolley is on its way.'

'Where am I?' I said.

'You're in Edge House Clinic,' she said, smoothing the bed covers with the flat of her hand. 'You're quite safe, there's no need to worry.'

I'd been here before for a couple of weeks, when Joel had just died.

Little did I know back then that this time, I wouldn't come out again for nearly two months.

1

Now

'Can we go on the rope bridge next, Mum?' Harrison asks as his brother, six-year-old Kane, scoots past me towards the simulated rock-climbing face.

'Yes, but wait... Slow down, Kane!' I'm practically yelling as my ears catch the telltale wheeze on my younger son's chest as he runs by. I draw one or two disapproving looks from nearby parents. 'Keep an eye on your brother,' I tell Harrison.

He nods and runs to join his sibling.

'So... have you made a decision about Saturday then?' Steph, the boys' auntie, cranes her head around me to watch as they both race towards the rope-climbing area. 'If you want to come over to mine instead, it's just an informal bring-a-bottle-type supper... just a few close girlfriends.'

I'm slightly irked that she's returned to the subject we were discussing before the kids interrupted us. I was daft enough to mention to her that one of the ladies who attend my yoga class had invited me out on the town on Saturday evening.

'You'll never meet anyone holed up at home all weekend,' the woman had joked.

Steph frowns when I relay this to her. 'I thought you were happy it being just you and the boys right now?'

'I am,' I say quickly, suddenly finding something to root in my bag for. 'And that's what I told her, that I'm happily single.'

She nods. 'Like Dave said the other day, you don't want to go rushing into dating again, Darcy. You've got the boys to consider now.'

'Nice of him to worry about me,' I say tartly, the sarcasm lost on her. I think about Steph and her long-term boyfriend, Dave, who's been *between jobs* for six months now, hunched over a glass of wine discussing me. 'I'm old enough to make my own decisions, you know.'

'Fine.' She stands up straight, squares her shoulders and folds her arms. 'Forget the invite, OK? Subject closed.'

My shoulders drop an inch now the conversation is moving on at last, but Steph looks downcast. I know she's coming from a good place of caring about me and I need her onside. Maybe I was a bit sharp. I try and soften my earlier snappiness, and change the subject.

'Shall we grab a coffee in the café when the kids have finished on the rope bridge? I'm parched.'

She turns and looks at me pleadingly.

'Me, Dave, Mum and Dad… we only want what's best for you and the boys, we always have. Please remember that.'

'I know.'

'I'm fully recovered now but life is far from normal. My late husband's family still sort of run my life, sometimes so subtly, it's hard to explain.

Steph is my late husband Joel's sister and she knows everything about my life. She's like a best friend and auntie to the boys all rolled in one. She and Brenda, Joel's mum, were there to help me pick up the pieces after his death, when I found out the truth of who he really was. Though their support kind of backfired on me, because it became apparent very quickly that their main priority was to sweep the whole distasteful business firmly under the carpet.

In my fragile state, suspended between grief and betrayal, they convinced me not to tell another soul about what I'd discovered.

'For the boys' sake,' they explained. 'That's the only reason. You know how people gossip around here. They'll be so affected by it, might even be bullied at school.'

Having been at the mercy of school bullies myself for years – mainly for the crime of being poor, not having the right brand of trainers, or wearing a skirt that was slightly frayed at the hem – I found the thought of my sons suffering through no fault of their own unbearable.

I decided back then that pushing the truth aside was a price worth paying. What did it matter now that Joel had gone, anyway? That's what I told myself.

But it's been tougher than I thought. As time has passed and I've recovered from the breakdown, I have found it harder and harder not to talk about what happened.

But I've had the boys back for ten months now and although Joel's family watch me like a hawk, the three of us are getting on just fine.

'The three musketeers', Harrison calls our little family unit.

Steph continues, encouraged by my silence. 'I know you've always said your focus will be on the boys for the foreseeable, but—'

'Ahem. What happened to *subject closed*? Look, I'm fine as I am, Steph. I can't even imagine trusting another man again, so it's just me and my boys for now.'

She smiles then, and breathes out what sounds very much like a sigh of relief.

To some people, learning of someone else's stoic determination to remain single is an irresistible enigma that must be challenged. A bit like making a conscious decision not to have children. It's an open invitation for perfect strangers to pass comment. Mere acquaintances will have no problem in bluntly asking what led to you making such a decision, and may even follow up by trying to change your mind. But that's certainly not a problem I have with Joel's family.

I take out my phone and idly check my emails and immediately wish I hadn't.

'Oh, great. That's all I need!'

'What is it?' Steph cranes her neck to look over at the screen.

'Email from the lettings company.' I hand her my phone so she can read the short message. 'The landlord is selling our house.'

'It says here there might be no impact on your tenancy though.' Steph hands me the phone back. 'Sometimes the new buyer wants to keep existing tenants on, don't they?'

'I suppose.' I frown, dropping the phone back into my handbag. 'It's a worry though until they confirm it. It could mean moving in the new year. Nightmare.'

'Oh well, it could take months to sell it. Worst case scenario, there's a spare room at ours... and several at Mum and Dad's,' she says lightly.

Like I said, nightmare, I grumble silently to myself. I'm trying to get a bit more space from Joel's family, not become more enmeshed.

Just as Steph opens her mouth to say something, sounds of collective alarm carry on the air. It sounds a bit like a football crowd's roar of disappointment, heard from a distance. Frantic shouting from the region of the rope bridge quickly follows, and grabs our attention. My worries about our house being sold are instantly forgotten as our heads jerk this way and that, and we frown at each other, trying to work out what's happening.

Without speaking, we start to walk quickly towards the area, our eyes searching out the boys. A staff member rushes by us, her lanyard thrashing in front of her chest.

'A little boy is having an asthma attack in the climbing area!' she shouts over to another uniformed figure up ahead. 'Ambulance is on its way.'

'Kane!' I hear myself say faintly.

Steph and I both start to run towards the area where we know Kane and Harrison are playing. I'm frantic, pushing through the crowd of onlookers, ducking my head this way and that, desperately trying to get a better view of the small figure on the ground.

Kane's asthma has got steadily worse over the last year, and he knows not to push himself too hard physically. He knows when and how to use his inhaler, plus he has his brother with him to help if need be.

Maybe it's not Kane who's in trouble.

Then Harrison is in front of me, wringing his hands, his expression one of dread and panic. 'He just fell on the floor, Mum. I couldn't help him.'

I turn to Steph. Her hands are glued to her mouth as she squeezes her eyes closed against the horror. I look down then and see Kane's stricken little face. Eyes bulging, skin pale and taking on a bluish hue in front of my very eyes. He's lying on his back, clawing at his chest and throat in a desperate bid to drag in air.

Everything slows down as I lurch towards him. My head swims, the faces around me merging into each other and starting to spin. Harrison takes his brother's hand, jiggles his arm as if it might help him recover.

'It's my boy… Somebody help him!' Inside my head, my own voice sounds like a slowed-down record, slurred and deep. I bound forward and everything speeds up again.

I snatch up Kane's small Marvel rucksack from his side and plunge my hand in the front pouch to retrieve the inhaler I packed in there this morning before we left the house. I pull out two toy cars instead.

His inhaler isn't in there.

'He must've taken it back out when he packed his toys.' I look at a frozen Steph, my hands shaking so violently I drop the rucksack.

Steph snaps to life, snatches up the bag and rips open the side pockets, turning it upside down and emptying out his packed lunch. She shakes it until the bag is completely empty of every last item.

'I packed it, I know I did!' I cry out. I look after my boys, I'm a good mum now. This makes me look… negligent.

Steph wraps her arms around Harrison and he buries his face in her side.

Kane's face is properly blue now, his mouth stretching wide as he tries in vain to pull in enough air. I know his windpipe is swollen, closing up. The muscles in his chest have seized up, locking out the oxygen he needs so badly.

I stare down at him, hardly able to breathe myself. My skin feels slick and damp, the voices around me swimming as one through my mind.

My boy is going to die. He's going to *die*.

I let out a wail as I bend forward to cradle his head in my hands.

He's gasping… these are his last breaths. He's slipping away from me. I'm losing him all over again.

'Please… no!' I screech up at the sky. 'Somebody help him.'

The crowd shrinks back slightly, and I recoil in shock as a pair of strong hands grasp my shoulders from behind and push me gently but firmly aside.

'I'm a doctor,' a deep, authoritative voice says in my ear. 'Let me see your boy.'

I collapse back onto my bottom, suddenly unable to keep upright, and sit speechless, making no effort to move. I simply watch as this man, this *guardian angel*, takes command of the situation, and my throat relaxes a touch, allowing my breathing to deepen.

'His name?' the doctor asks me.

'Kane,' I whisper hoarsely.

He doesn't look like your average angel. He is dressed in jeans and an unbuttoned checked shirt with a black T-shirt underneath.

His face and arms are tanned, and he has short brown hair and good teeth. His amber-flecked green eyes are kind when they meet mine.

A pretty girl of about five or six with strawberry-blonde hair shadows him. She steps back and bites her lip, calmly watches the proceedings as if she's seen it all before.

'Sit him up,' the doctor briskly instructs the two members of staff who are hovering around. 'Hold him there; he needs to be upright. That's better.' He turns to the crowd. 'Can someone run for a first-aid kit from the reception? We need a relief inhaler. And someone else get him a hot chocolate or a sweet tea. Hurry!'

As if by magic, people instantly respond to his natural authority. The remaining crowd willingly parts to allow people through, as his orders are followed without question.

I watch, helpless, as he pulls off Kane's grey fleece top and loosens the neck of his T-shirt. His long fingers are slim and nimble; his hands are square. Competent.

'It's going to be fine, Kane,' he murmurs to my son. 'Relax. The air is flowing in now, can you feel it? Breathe in, one, two, three... breathe out, one, two, three. Nice and slow, control it. That's it, champ, you're doing brilliantly. It's going to be OK.'

Minutes later, a breathless park ranger appears at his side with a green backpack featuring a large white cross. 'Spare inhaler.' She hands over the small grey apparatus.

The doctor lifts it to Kane's mouth and my boy pulls in precious air.

A serious-looking young woman in her twenties appears with a steaming plastic cup. 'I put plenty of sugar in it, like you said.'

A few more puffs of the inhaler, and then the doctor brings the cup to Kane's lips.

'It's sweet tea and it's quite hot, but you can take a tiny sip,' he encourages him. 'And another. That's it.'

Kane's eyes are not bulging quite as badly now. He's still very pale, but the blue tinge has given way to a less frightening-looking pallor. A couple more sips of tea and another puff on the inhaler, then he turns to me and gives me a tiny weak smile, and my heart is fit to burst.

A reassuring hum of relief rises in the crowd, and people step aside as two paramedics in green overalls appear.

'Coming through, everyone,' the taller one says as she plonks down her case of equipment. She addresses the doctor. 'We can take it from here, thanks.'

'George Mortimer.' He introduces himself to the paramedics as he gets to his feet. He lowers his voice, but I'm standing close enough to hear. 'Surgeon in urology at the City Hospital.'

The paramedics' demeanour immediately turns deferential, and they briefly confer in hushed voices, glancing down at Kane and nodding as the senior medic advises on his condition.

The doctor turns to me and gives a quick smile. He seems completely unflustered, and waves people away as they step forward to pat him on the back.

'Thank you,' I whisper as he extends a hand to help me to my feet. 'I'll never be able to thank you enough for what you've done today.'

I look into his eyes, and a rush of emotion has me suddenly embracing him a little too zealously, like he's a long-lost friend. He flinches momentarily, and then relaxes into the hug, patting my back.

Totally illogical, I know, but I feel like I never want him to let me go. I feel like I belong there, safe in his arms.

Over his shoulder, Steph takes in my expression and gives me a tight smile. She'll be thinking about the last thing I said to her.

I can't even imagine trusting another man again, so it's just me and my boys for now.

But this is not just *another man*, is it?

This is the man who saved my son's life.

2

I watch from the back of the crowd.

Lots of the people who've gathered here will be willing everything to turn out well for the little boy. But some of them are like a certain type who go to the circus. Their eyes, dark little beads of spitefulness, praying and hoping for the pretty girl to fall and end up a wet, red mess on the floor of the big top.

The mother's plaintive wailing cuts through the noise of the park.

There's a shiver of anticipation when the boy turns blue and the mother starts screeching for help. When the doctor rushes over, strong and focused, barking out orders and saving his life, it's exciting.

When the child begins to breathe again and the blue colour in his face recedes, they start to lose interest. One or two peel off from the sides to resume their park rides.

The way most people can view the lives of others, as if they're watching it through glass, never fails to stun me. The same way we can watch starving children or the atrocities of war and remain quite detached through our television screens…

I'm one of the last ones there. I stay until the paramedics arrive.

I've been following for a long time today but nobody notices me. Nobody asks what I'm doing here. I've worked on my ordinariness: grey and black clothing, beanie hat, pale, uninteresting face cast down towards the floor.

I'm good at keeping my feelings buried deep now, saying and doing all the right things.

I've seen the adoration on the mother's face. I could tell her to be careful, but it won't do any good.

I can see she's already smitten.

More fool her.

3

Finally George Mortimer manages to politely extricate himself from my limpet-like embrace.

Against the embarrassing backdrop of me thanking him incessantly, he reaches for the hand of the small girl and together they melt back into the crowd.

The onlookers are dissipating fast, keen to resume their day at the park now that the drama has passed.

'Your son is going to be fine,' the tall paramedic tells me kindly. 'We'll need to take him to hospital just to get him checked over. You'll be able to take him home when he's been given the all-clear.'

I feel reassured by this. My hands are still trembling from the realisation of how badly today could have turned out. They're going to make absolutely sure my boy is one hundred per cent fine.

'We'll wait for you at home,' Steph murmurs, and with the minimum of fuss, she leads Harrison off to a nearby refreshment stand.

I travel to the City Hospital in the back of the ambulance with one of the paramedics. I hold Kane's hand, never taking my eyes from his pale little face.

He's still got an oxygen mask on and can't really speak, but I make up for that by rabbiting on non-stop about all the great things we're going to do and see and…

'Take a breath, Darcy, or I'll be putting an oxygen mask on you too,' the paramedic jokes, winking at Kane.

'Sorry.' I give her a little smile but feel my cheeks burning.

I've always got through the drama of life by vomiting out words, throwing meaningless promises about the future out there to anyone who'll listen. Fantasising.

I did it when Joel died, even after I found out how he'd deceived us.

In the days after his death, I ran myself ragged planning camping holidays with the boys, a new career, moving away from the area… The list went on as I tried in vain to drown out the noise of the unspeakable truth I had discovered just before he died. All my ridiculous little stories of how everything would be *just fine.*

Looking back, I can see now it was the manic stage before the full meltdown and it didn't work, of course. Didn't make the terrible deeds of the man I'd loved so much go away.

What he did cut so deep, even now, I'm not sure I'll ever quite get over it.

As Kane has arrived at the hospital by ambulance, we skip the chaos of A&E and he's whisked through to see a doctor.

Without the oxygen mask, he's looking a little more like himself. Not quite as pale now, and there's even a ghost of a smile when the doctor jokingly starts to inspect a non-existent foot injury before listening to his chest and taking various observations.

'I don't need to tell you he had a close shave.' The doctor turns to me, releasing his stethoscope to hang around his neck again. 'I think we can safely say this attack was brought on by a combination of too much vigorous exercise, overexcitement and eating a dry biscuit, which brought on a coughing fit.' He wags his finger at Kane in mock disapproval. 'Don't ever leave the house without your inhaler, young man. Even if it means there's no room for your toy car collection. Understand?'

Kane grins and nods, self-consciously patting the arms of the child-size wheelchair he's sitting in.

Once they discharge him, I insist we'll be fine making our own way back to the exit. I just need some space to get my head straight. It's quite a walk, so we keep the wheelchair, and Kane seems to enjoy the novelty of being pushed through the glossy pale-green corridors, the drama of the asthma attack already fading fast.

But the trauma is still very much with me. My heart continues to race too fast and when I used the bathroom on the treatment ward, my cheeks looked bright pink in the mirror and were hot to the touch.

None of that stuff is important now, of course. Kane is fine, and that's all that matters.

George Mortimer's face fills my mind again. His confidence and natural authority were so impressive, and other people there felt it too, eager to carry out his instructions. Aside from that, he was a very attractive man. Although I'd never admit it to Steph, the whole package of this guy adds up to a God-like figure in my mind.

I can never repay him for how he helped my son today. Nothing I could do would come close.

It feels like I've pushed the wheelchair for miles, but finally I spot a sign for the exit.

'I'll call us a cab and we can go straight home, sweetie. You must be exhausted.' I ruffle Kane's short sandy hair, the exact colour and wiry texture as his father's. 'I think an evening of banana milkshake, pizza and a movie might be in order. Is that OK with you?'

He twists his head around and smiles. He's still being very quiet, for Kane, but that's to be expected.

He's experienced breathless episodes before, especially if he's been particularly active or the pollen count is high outside. But a few puffs of his inhaler and he's been good as new. I'll need to take him to our GP to confirm whether the asthma has somehow got even worse without us noticing.

The whole episode at the play park must have scared him witless, as it did the rest of us.

As I steer the wheelchair to the right, following the exit signs, a large arrow and signage to the left catches my eye. In bold black letters are the words *Urology Dept.*

I take a sharp left turn instead.

'The exit is that way, Mum.' Kane points up at the sign and then to the right.

'I know, but the urology department is down here. It's where George Mortimer works, the man who helped you today.'

'But he won't be here *now*,' Kane says patiently. 'He's still at the park with his little girl.'

I know that. I just want to see the place he works, that's all.

'We can bring him in a thank-you card or something. I just need to see where we'll come to drop it off.'

Kane doesn't reply. I know he's exhausted, and I *will* get him home, but a two-minute detour won't do any harm. He's too young to realise just how close he came to disaster today. Too young to fully appreciate what George Mortimer did for him.

But I'm under no such illusions.

Fifty yards later, we stand in front of double doors bearing a large *Urology* sign. I push one open and a passing porter kindly assists us through into the entrance area of the ward.

'Can I help you?' A nurse in her thirties wearing a navy-blue uniform and holding a clipboard turns as we enter.

I tell her briefly what happened at the park with Dr Mortimer, and her face lights up as she winks at Kane.

'Ah, yes, that sounds just like Mr Mortimer. He's a consultant surgeon, you see, so we address him as Mister, not Doctor.'

'I see.' Typical of the man, I think, to understate his status to the paramedics. 'I wanted to know if it would be OK to drop him in a thank-you card, maybe tomorrow. We're so grateful.'

'Of course!' She beams. 'He'll love that, I'm sure. I'm on duty tomorrow, so I might see you then.'

She turns to the secure ward doors and wafts a lanyard in front of the security pad. I manoeuvre the wheelchair back around in the limited space and head towards the exit again.

'Look, Mum, there's Dr George.' Kane points to a row of A4-size photographs on the wall, identifying all the urology ward staff from the senior consultant to the cleaner.

Next to the senior consultant urologist, a Mr Dharval Ratan, is George. He looks so effortlessly handsome in his photograph. Slightly tousled brown hair, strong jaw, and the same easy smile he bestowed on me this afternoon, when I thanked him so profusely.

Under my breath, I whisper his title. 'Mr George Mortimer DM FRCS (Urol.) – Consultant Urologist.'

Impressive. Just like the man himself.

Kane turns around in the wheelchair as I start rooting around in my handbag.

'What are you doing?' he says irritably. 'Can't we just go home now?'

He's tired and I'll have him home in no time. It's just that I have to do something first.

'Yes, in a minute. I just…' I pull out my phone and take a snap of George's photograph before slipping it back in the top pocket of my denim jacket. 'There, all done. Let's go.'

As I wrestle the wheelchair back through the double doors, I feel a warm glow inside my chest.

In a strange way, it feels like I have a little piece of George Mortimer for myself now, right next to my heart.

4

When George had dropped Romy off at her grandparents' for tea and a sleepover, he didn't call Dharval Ratan back as his colleague had requested in his answerphone message. Instead, he went straight home and, before he'd even slipped off his shoes, poured himself a gin. Just the one measure, mind.

Dharval was the senior consultant urologist at the hospital and effectively George's boss. He was due to retire next summer and George was seriously gunning for the job. Dharval knew his opinion counted for a lot with the board, and he was making George earn his brownie points, asking him to take his place at last-minute out-of-hours meetings and giving him problematic case studies that would swallow up all his non-surgical time and more still.

Dharval's thirty years of service at the hospital carried great weight and brought with it a wealth of experience. But the man was like a dinosaur in the sea: so stuck in his ways, he'd need winching out. Team meetings were mind-numbingly boring and served little real purpose. If anyone mentioned new medical research or displayed outside-the-box thinking, their contributions were usually discounted from the off. To top it all, the department budget spend was totally lacking in innovation and desperate for a fresh approach to maximise funds.

Conversely, George was passionate about bringing all this to the table. But his hands were tied until Dharval had finally retired

and he'd managed to win the promotion, which would be no mean
feat given that he was the youngest candidate, with a wealth of
talent and experience snapping at his heels.

That wasn't the only problem facing him.

He slipped his phone out of his pocket and glanced at the list
of at least a half-dozen unopened text messages she'd sent him so
far that day. He pushed the device across the table out of reach
and pulled in a deep breath in an effort to ease his tight chest.

What a day.

He sat there in the dark, staring through the glass doors at the
lit pond beyond. Romy had begged for coloured lights out there,
and he had indulged her. Now the dark pink and green gave the
water an odd, ethereal glow.

It was only 5.30 p.m. and already black as night outside.

George sipped his drink slowly, allowing the astringent gin and
the bitterness of the aromatic tonic water to swill over his tongue
before swallowing.

Finally he'd made good on his promise to take Romy to Farmer's
adventure park, and the day had started well. It had taken a
while, but slowly he'd realised that he was thinking less and less
about work and the promotion and had actually begun to enjoy
meandering around, observing the farm animals.

Even queuing for the small rides had been an unexpected
pleasure, because listening to his daughter's incessant chatter was
a balm to his ever-racing thoughts.

But then the drama, as always, had found him, and on their
way to the climbing frame, he'd stumbled upon the asthmatic boy.

George had done his job, done what any medic would do under
the circumstances. Nothing more, nothing less.

The boy's mother – he hadn't caught her name, but had regis-
tered her attractiveness in a laid-back, natural sort of way – had
been understandably grateful, making all sorts of wild claims that
he'd saved her son's life.

It might have looked that way, but truthfully, the body was astoundingly good at finding ways of staying alive, and as the boy had slipped towards unconsciousness, his throat would have most likely relaxed naturally and allowed in more air. Still, it would have been very frightening for him, and a terrifying experience for his mother, and George was pleased to have been of assistance. As a consultant surgeon, the patients he saw were mostly anaesthetised; aside from a five-minute bedside chat before an operation, carefully managed by his team, he rarely got to see any raw emotion.

It was refreshing, occasionally, to see people close up, and to be able to influence events to turn out well.

Romy had wanted to stay at the park, and he'd somehow managed another thirty minutes, but sadly, the day had been sabotaged. The ruminations and worries had found their way back in, and he'd tempted her away with the promise of a gift from Hamleys when he next visited London.

George often feared he was making a bit of a hash of being a father. It was increasingly hard to tick all the boxes knowing he could never plug the gigantic hole in Romy's life that resulted from not having a mother.

He drained the gin and looked over longingly at the Sheraton drinks cabinet, its warm inlaid satinwood enticing him back. It had been in his late wife's family for generations. Hand-made in the early 1800s, he thought he remembered Lucy telling him once.

But he would not be tempted to have another drink. He couldn't afford to be off his game; there was too much at stake.

He sighed, put down his empty glass and pressed his head back into the soft padding of the armchair.

Things would resolve themselves in time, he felt sure.

He couldn't imagine finding a partner again, someone who would willingly help him weather such a turbulent storm. In just a few weeks' time it would be Christmas, and Romy would feel the absence of her mother even more keenly.

It had been a long time since he'd been able to talk things over with someone who cared enough to listen. Lately, the memory of Lucy seemed to slip a little further from his grasp each day.

Still, as he knew only too well, life could sometimes surprise you. He could but hope.

5

When we get back to the hospital reception with its wall of floor-to-ceiling windows, I see it is already dark outside.

After ordering an Uber, I text Steph and let her know that Kane has been given the all-clear, and say that we'll be home soon. She loves using GIFs and sends back a funny one of a seal clapping excitedly.

I don't know why I feel nervous about what happened today, as if this is all my fault. I packed Kane's inhaler and that's as much as any mother can do.

While we wait for the cab, I sit down on a comfy seat at the end of a row of chairs and park the wheelchair next to me. Within seconds, Kane falls fast asleep. His cheek presses against the side of the wheelchair, pulling his mouth at a funny angle. His eyelids are fluttering and his chest rises and falls dramatically. I wonder if he's reliving the asthma attack. The tightness in his throat, the panic throbbing through his small body.

In his left hand he clutches the inhaler the hospital gave him. If one positive thing comes from today, I pray it will be that he'll always remember to keep one with him from now on.

The attack has really taken it out of him, and I think it might be a couple of days before he's completely back to normal. It's likely I'll keep him off school on Monday, just to make sure his energy levels are back up to where they need to be.

I look out of the large windows at an ambulance pulling up and its back doors flying open. My heart sinks as someone is rushed out on a stretcher to waiting medics.

I shiver, having been too close to disaster myself today. We started off at Farmer's play park and ended up here at the hospital. I find reassurance in routine these days, I've spent enough time on the emotional rollercoaster to last me a lifetime. But the reality is, life can turn on the throw of a coin, and if it hadn't been for George Mortimer… well, I'm absolutely certain things would have panned out very differently. In the worst way possible.

I sit back, stretching my aching neck this way and that as I look around the large reception space.

Nothing is ever still in this place. There are people coming and going all the time, the receptionists simultaneously talking on the phones while tapping at keyboards and then looking up to speak to people who approach the desk to ask a question.

It's only just past teatime, but the light has already seeped from the dense, brooding sky that was threatening rain. I hate these dark winter nights. I think I miss Joel even more, if that were possible.

Just a few days ago, it was Bonfire Night. We attended an organised firework display at a local pub, the Griffin's Claw, with Steph and Dave and my sons' grandparents, Brenda and Leonard.

The boys dashed around in the freezing cold, scoffing mushy peas and pastel-pink marshmallows. Waving sparklers and writing their names in the air, they barely stood still for a second.

Ironically, despite the biting cold and the smoky atmosphere, Kane only needed a couple of puffs of his inhaler when the big bangers went off and filled the air with the caustic tang of gunpowder that caught in the back of our throats. Yet this morning, breathing in nothing but fresh air at the adventure park, his body all but shut down within minutes.

I check the location of the cab on my Uber app and find it's still eight minutes away.

Instead of turning off the screen, my finger hovers above the Facebook icon.

I've managed to keep away from her profile for the last two days. That's got to be some kind of a record.

Steph once told me she'd read somewhere that if you persistently view someone's Facebook profile, someone you aren't yet connected to, you will eventually appear in their 'suggested friends' list that appears on the home page. So logically, you could consider the list to be a way to identify who is silently lurking. Who is viewing your photographs, reading your public posts.

This conversation was the incentive I needed to set up an anonymous profile in the name of Tana Philips, self-proclaimed fashion and beauty guru. Tana has a picture of glossy, sparkly lips as her cover photo, and a vintage Parisian Stockman mannequin as her profile image.

Tana is invaluable to me. She is Facebook friends with Daniela Frost – who accepted her friend request immediately.

It wasn't difficult to mirror most of Daniela's designer and stylist preferences in the new profile. The various pages Daniela followed were set to public view, so Tana liked those too, and I also managed to secure a couple of acceptances for my requests from her existing followers before I friend-requested Daniela herself.

It's surprising how people so readily trust a stranger if a few of their online friends appear to 'know' them already.

My finger taps on the icon and my Facebook feed loads. I scroll down and spot four new photos that were posted just this morning.

This time Daniela is at a posh brasserie with friends. Close-ups of pale frothy lattes held by manicured fingers, and pains aux raisins, glossy with buttery glaze. Perfect bodies pose to their best advantage in each frame. Partial shots of whitened smiles and hair expensively tinted with warm caramel highlights nestle under the status: *Breakfast to celebrate my move!*

Last week there were shots at the gym capturing impressive evidence of the pressing of hefty weights by taut brown legs that already looked pretty much perfect. Maybe she's celebrating losing another half a pound.

I'm suddenly aware of how tight the button on my jeans has become, pressing into the soft paunch of my stomach. I chose a baggy knitted sweater this morning rather than the fitted striped Joules top I wore to death last winter.

I glance at the screen again. Daniela's life looks fabulous, but I'm not stupid. I know as well as the next person that all this social media stuff is staged, the shots cropped and airbrushed.

She's probably got a miserable existence and has grown pale and flabby in real life. I allow myself a little smile at the spiteful thought, and then my satisfaction fades when I catch sight of her radiant face again.

How can she be so happy after what happened? After Joel's death?

We are polar opposites in every way and it only makes me detest her more.

I press a button and the phone screen turns black. Like Steph says, I have to stop doing this. She has no power to take away our happy family memories unless I let her.

'Cab for Hilton?' a harassed, tubby man barks from the entrance.

'Yes! Sorry!' I push my phone guiltily into my handbag and gently rouse Kane from his nap by stroking his arm. I wheel his chair nearer to the door and help him to stand up.

'Can you walk OK, sweetie?' I ask him, and he nods, yawning.

He links his arm in mine and we step outside, our breath escaping like little warm clouds into the frosty air.

I'm so grateful I'm taking my son home. My boys are truly the only thing that matters; I'm so happy I have them back in my life. I don't know why it even occurred to me to look online just now.

I resolve to delete my Facebook account when I get home.

6

When the cab pulls up outside our small terraced house, I have to stop myself from groaning out loud.

'Looks like Grandma and Grandad are already here to see you,' I tell Kane when I spot the blue Volkswagen Golf parked outside. I hope I've managed to disguise the dread I feel inside.

Steph must have already alerted Brenda and Leonard to what happened at the park. An acrid taste fills my mouth and I swallow it down. They're bound to worry, but I could really do without a houseful right now, or a hefty dose of Brenda's advice.

I've done nothing wrong and I'm going to keep that uppermost in my mind. I'm doing my best with the boys and everything has been fine, until today.

I have my key at the ready, but the door springs open before my hand reaches the lock.

'Here he is. Here's our little warrior.' Brenda pulls Kane towards her and envelops him in one of her pincer-like hugs, eyeing me over the top of his head. 'I've just been saying to Len, there must be no feeling worse than being unable to get your breath.'

I stand like a spare part on the doorstep while I wait for Brenda to finish hugging my son.

'Come on, lovey, let's get you inside and get some nourishment inside you.'

The opposite of tall, sporty Harrison, Kane has a naturally slight build paired with a rather poor appetite. Call me paranoid, but I've always felt Brenda attributes this to a failure on my part to feed him up.

After taking a few steps inside, she turns back to me. 'I see he has his inhaler after all. Steph seemed to think he hadn't got it at the play park.'

'The hospital gave him one.' I burn with a quiet fury at Steph's unlicensed blabbing. 'I packed his in his rucksack, but he must have taken it out when—'

'Invaluable to make those last-minute checks before leaving the house, I find.' Brenda pulls Kane closer to her. 'Still, he's here now, and Grandma's going to spoil him rotten until he feels better. Is that all right with you, my cherub?'

Kane grins and nods happily, lapping up the attention.

'Here he is, our little champ!' Leonard's towering, lanky frame strides towards Kane and performs an impromptu shadow-boxing routine in front of him. 'Fighting fit now, he is. Look at him! Told you they'd sort him out at the hospital, Harry boy, didn't I?'

My elder son walks over and presses into my side, watching his brother warily. He seems to sense that any drama isn't good when Brenda and Leonard get involved.

'Will we have to go back and live with Grandma and Grandad, Mum?' he'd once asked me when he'd got a lunchtime detention at school for playing the banned game, Bulldog, in the playground with a bunch of his friends.

I don't know what he picked up, or what he overheard when he lived with his grandparents, but he seems to sense – just like I do – that they're constantly hovering and watching. Waiting for me to put a step wrong.

I squeeze his shoulder. 'Your brother is fine, sweetie. Have you been worried?'

He nods, and Kane ducks out of Brenda's embrace and play-punches his brother in the stomach to show he's back on top form. Then it's smiles all round again.

Steph emerges from the hallway and I throw her a look.

'Thanks for keeping your mum and dad informed,' I say lightly. 'I was going to call them later myself to explain what happened.'

'Mum rang to see how the trip went and Harrison got to the phone first...' Steph falters, and then shrugs. 'I thought they ought to know anyway.'

'Of *course* we needed to know,' Brenda chips in. 'You mustn't be afraid of asking for our help. If you'd only called us when it happened, Darcy, we could have come straight to the park and been of some assistance.'

By doing what, exactly? I feel like snapping back at her, but I manage instead to stretch my face into some semblance of a smile.

It was so much easier, in the dark days after Joel died, for them all to have access to the house. That's why I gave Brenda and Steph a spare key each. They were so good to me back then. Steph minded the boys regularly to give me some space, even doing the food shopping for a few weeks. Brenda would cook nourishing meals while Len ferried two-year-old Harrison back and forth to playgroup.

Then, when my life fell apart to the extent I could no longer carry out the simplest day to day tasks, they applied, with my agreement, for custody of the boys until I had recovered.

There have only been a handful of occasions in the past few years when I've regretted parting with the spare keys, but today is definitely one of them.

But once you've given them out, it's hard to ask for them back without causing offence.

'Home-made shepherd's pie and green beans for tea,' Brenda announces. 'How's that sound?'

Kane looks at me.

'Thanks, Brenda, but I've already promised him pizza and a milkshake,' I say regretfully. 'You know, as a little treat. After the shock of it all.'

She looks at Len as if she's hearing things before turning back to me. 'He needs building up a bit, Darcy love. All that salt and sugar is no good for—'

'It's OK, Mum,' Steph interrupts. 'You and Dad can get off now. I'll help Darcy sort the boys out. I'm sure they all just want to rest.'

I nod gratefully at her. 'Kane fell asleep in the hospital while we waited for the cab, but I had to wake him,' I say. 'We're shattered.'

'But I wanted to hear all about it.' Brenda frowns. 'What they said at the hospital and who that doctor was who came so heroically to his rescue.'

'Could we chat tomorrow?' I say. 'Come over for a cup of tea and a bacon sandwich with us in the morning, if you like.'

'Fine.' Brenda whisks off her apron and stuffs it into her bag.

'Thanks for coming over.' I follow them to the front door, overcompensating as usual. 'Sorry. It's just we're all a bit tired and fractious, and—'

'We'll see you in the morning, then. It's important we get to the bottom of what happened today so we can avoid it in the future.'

We? They're my boys and my responsibility now.

Brenda glances back just before she gets into the car, and I see a look pass between her and Steph before she says, 'I'll leave you two to talk.'

Back in the kitchen I sort out the boys' food and drinks while we sip our coffee and talk about what happened at the park. When I've finished busying around, I realise Steph has gone quiet and seems a bit on edge.

'Is everything all right?' I ask, a curdling feeling starting in my stomach.

Her face drops. 'No. It's not all right at all, really.' She sighs. 'But now is definitely not the time to talk about it. You're exhausted; why don't you go upstairs for a lie-down and I'll—'

'I'm fine,' I say quickly. The boys are already sitting together watching their promised movie with pizza and milkshake in the other room, so if she's got something to say, now is as good a time as any. I'm already rehearsing a defence in my mind for the fact I didn't double-check Kane had his inhaler before leaving the house. 'You might as well tell me what's wrong, or I won't be able to relax at all tonight.'

She thinks for a moment, then nods regretfully.

'You'd better sit down, Darcy,' she says softly. 'There's something you need to know.'

7

The glowing red numbers of the clock inform me it's 6.30. I've been awake for exactly four hours. Long enough to witness the inky black night finally giving way to the weak strains of daylight that lighten my bedroom and herald the beginning of the day.

I got up a few times during the night to check on Kane, but whenever I crept into his bedroom, he was fast asleep. Each time, I stood in the doorway and listened to his breathing, steady and deep. It helped to soothe my restless heart.

After Steph dropped the bombshell last night, she insisted we had a glass of wine together while she tried, unsuccessfully, to convince me that I mustn't fret, that there really was no need to worry.

I excused myself to visit the bathroom. When I got up there, I was sick in the loo and had to take one of my tablets before I came back down.

When she left at about seven o'clock, Kane had his bath and Harrison a shower. They went to bed early without complaint, both of them exhausted after the trauma at the park.

Alone at last, I turned the television and lamps off. Then I poured myself another glass of wine and sat in the chair, staring out blindly at the velvety night sky beyond. Often I don't bother drawing the curtains at night. Our street is a dead end, so people don't use it as a walk-through.

Since I was discharged from the clinic, I've got into the habit of going to bed at the same time as the boys. Far too early for most people, I know, but I like reading in bed or watching something on my iPad. Last night, though, I knew I'd struggle to concentrate on a book or film, so I stayed downstairs later than usual.

For years, I'd heard people say that when you find yourself alone, it's the evenings, the hours when you used to chat about the day with a partner, that get to you. It never meant anything back then, but when Joel died, I found out the hard way that they were absolutely right.

But it's the thoughts, too. What might have been, what you might have done to stop the worst from happening, different decisions you could have made... night after night, it soon wears you down.

With a couple of kids, it's easy to keep busy until they've gone to bed, and then the loneliness that's been crouching in the corner like a black widow spider grabs you by the throat. So going to bed early has been a solution that works for me. It cuts out the empty hours when, despite everything he did, a bone-deep ache blooms for Joel's touch.

But not tonight. Tonight I don't want to infect my room, my safe place, with these unwanted thoughts.

Every so often, a car passes by, its headlights illuminating the houses opposite. The houses on this road are all Victorian terraces, old but with spacious rooms and reasonable-sized gardens. Some are owned but most, like ours, are rented.

We moved here when I fell pregnant with Harrison. Joel insisted on it. Up until then, home had been my draughty one-bed flat, located in an area on the outskirts of town you wouldn't want to walk home in after dark. Joel's preference at the time was to go for a small town house on a new estate being built in Gedling. But I found the properties claustrophobic, built on top of one another with postage-stamp-sized back yards. I couldn't imagine our little one playing out there, a dog running around, so I managed to convince him that Lenton was the perfect place to build our happy home together.

That was before the area became flooded with students. But I got what I wanted, and for years we enjoyed a happy family life with our boys. The strange thing is, when Joel died, despite the dark, cloying grief and denial that I experienced, I still felt blessed for our life together. My gratitude was strong enough to shine through the worst times.

When I found out the truth of who he really was and what he had done – what *she* had done – the gratitude died quickly, like a warm, glowing candle that had been callously snuffed out.

I press the back of my head down into the soft cushions of the sofa and stare up at the ceiling.

Last night, when Steph asked me to sit down, I honestly didn't know what to expect. But I instinctively gathered, from her expression and the tone of her voice, that it wasn't going to be anything related to Kane's asthma attack at the park. And Brenda's pointed look as she left the house added credence to this.

My brain connected these things in a matter of seconds and came up with the past. I did what Steph asked and sat down at the breakfast bar, but my whole body felt heavy and sore.

She leaned against the counter facing me, gripping the edge of it with both hands.

'Listen, Darcy,' she began, biting her lip and avoiding my eyes. 'I realise it's the worst possible time to have to tell you something like this, after the day you've had, I mean. But I want you to hear it from me first. OK?'

'OK.' I swallowed hard. Waited. I tried really hard to keep my face impassive, but my heart felt ready to explode with nerves, and the rattle in my chest told another story altogether.

'Mum got a text message earlier, when we were all still at the park.'

'OK.' I felt my breathing regulate a little when I realised this wasn't to be a blame fest about what happened at Farmer's that day.

'I'm telling you because I think you should be the first to know and because...' She hesitated. 'I think you're strong enough to deal with it now.'

'Let's have it then,' I said quietly, recognising her efforts to delay the moment.

Steph puffed out air, looked at the ceiling, looked at the floor and then fixed her eyes on mine and clenched her jaw.

'It's Daniela Frost,' she said simply. 'I'm so sorry, Darcy... but she's coming back to live here, in Nottingham.'

8

By 8 a.m., I've got the boys up and dressed and they are eating cereal perched on stools at the breakfast bar.

Steph's words are still bouncing around in my head but I just keep batting them back, the way I learned to do in therapy.

'Don't wolf your breakfast down, chew it properly,' I tell the boys, sounding like a broken record. As usual, my instruction falls on deaf ears.

I stand back and consider Kane's appearance for a few seconds. His cheeks have a healthy pink glow again and his eyes are clear and bright. He seems to have recovered brilliantly from his asthma attack, and I feel relief wash over me all over again.

'Has Grandad already finished the train set, or is he still building it?' Harrison asks without looking up from shovelling in his cornflakes.

'I'm not sure.' I pour the boys glasses of fresh orange juice and slide them across the counter. 'Grandma said he was still up in the spare room, so I suppose that means he hasn't finished yet.'

Brenda had called half an hour ago and asked if the boys would like to go over, as Leonard had been clearing out the loft and unearthed the train set Joel had loved and played with as a boy.

'They can stay for Sunday lunch and we'll bring them back at teatime, if that suits?'

It was a rhetorical question. Brenda rarely asks me if she can have the boys; she usually just tells me. Although I took back full-time care of my sons ten months ago now, in some ways, I still feel like Brenda calls the shots. Still, the boys love to go over to their grandparents' big house in Ravenshead, with its gaming room and its half-acre garden that's perfect for all kinds of ball sports.

Brenda and Leonard know exactly how to curry their grandsons' favour. Yet the touching thing is, the boys couldn't wait to come back to live at home again. They were so excited to rediscover their cramped bedrooms and watch movies on our small – compared to their grandparents' at least – television.

'You'd be welcome to come for lunch too, of course.' She hesitates. 'Only... I thought you might appreciate a little time to yourself. A bit of relaxation after yesterday's upset.'

I suspect she means the news Steph gave me about Daniela, rather than what happened to Kane. But Brenda's preference is to tiptoe delicately around a difficult subject rather than face it head on.

I'm so tempted to ask her why she insists on keeping in touch with Daniela, after what Joel did.

A big part of me wants to challenge her to choose: Daniela Frost, or me and the boys.

But I really don't think I'm in a position to make such demands. Brenda and Leonard are still a valuable support in my life and the boys need a full and loving relationship with their grandparents. So instead of voicing my true feelings, I swallow my irritation.

'I think a bit of free time would be perfect. Thanks, Brenda.'

And just like that, an idea pops into my head. I have a yoga class scheduled for 6 p.m., but I'm free all day apart from that. I know the perfect way to push away thoughts of Daniela and utilise my unexpected pocket of free time.

*

The hospital is quieter than yesterday.

I've heard that weekends are the worst time to be ill, because the NHS operates with a skeleton staff, particularly on Sundays.

Some wards, I noticed yesterday as I pushed Kane's wheelchair through the seemingly endless corridors, have all-day visiting. Others operate stricter hours. There don't seem to be as many people wandering around gazing up at the various signs, so I'm guessing I've arrived outside of the bulk of most ward visiting times.

My legwork yesterday is paying off. I navigate the warren of identical pale-green passageways easily, moving ever closer to the urology department, where George Mortimer works – though I'm not expecting him to be here today.

I pass the odd patient or uniformed member of staff, but mostly I seem to be alone, listening to the click-clacking of my own low-heeled shoes on the linoleum floor.

I called at a Tesco Express on the way here and picked up an unfussy thank-you card.

As I draw closer to the area of the hospital I need to be in, I clutch the envelope and a flutter starts up in my belly. This little plan seemed so clever at the time, but now it seems completely stupid and cringeworthy.

I slow down my pace so I can think. There's a run of glass windows to my right, looking out over a small, neglected courtyard with block paving and wooden benches. It must have been a peaceful space to sit at one time, but now the benches are faded and peeling and it's littered with weeds and a collection of discarded sandwich wrappers.

It occurs to me that I don't *have* to go through with this; I could just go back home. After all, I already thanked him profusely before he melted away into the crowd yesterday.

And yet… I'm here now. I've come in on the bus to avoid potential parking problems. I've made the effort; it would be silly to waste that.

Admittedly, it was partly to save me sitting in the house thinking about Daniela bloody Frost and the implications of her coming back here. But still, I feel I have to do something else apart from muttering what feels like an inadequate thank-you to George at the park.

'You OK, love?' A porter stops striding along with his empty trolley in front of me, and I realise I've drifted into the middle of the corridor so he is unable to pass by without brushing against me.

'Sorry, yes.' I give him a wide smile, snapping out of it and stepping aside. 'Just stuff on my mind, you know?'

He nods and presses his lips together in an indication that he knows exactly what I mean. He must see distraught, grieving people every day of the week, and here's me, worrying about looking silly whilst delivering a card.

When the porter has whisked by me, I pick up pace again.

It's just a thank-you card. In which I've written my phone number and email address. And suggested to George that if he can find a spare half-hour at some point, I'd love to treat him to a coffee and a piece of cake. It's meant as a friendly gesture, to offer something slightly more than yesterday's inane words.

I feel my cheeks heat up just thinking about how I wrote it so impulsively, and now… well, I'm squirming at the thought that he might well consider me a bit forward.

But hey, if he doesn't want to take up my offer, that's totally fine. I straighten my shoulders a little as I walk, mentally gathering up a few shreds of pride. I'll probably never lay eyes on him again, but at least I'll know I tried to show my gratitude.

At last I approach the turning for the urology department. I near the double doors that lead to the ward's entrance and notice a woman pacing up and down outside.

She looks to be in her early thirties and has lank light-brown hair parted in the centre and a pale, anxious face. She wears black leggings, a baggy pink T-shirt with a smattering of sparkle on the front, and flat shoes. I can't see a coat or a bag. It's warm in the hospital but freezing outside and she looks painfully thin, not a lot of padding on her bones to ward off the inclement weather.

She chews the inside of her cheek fretfully and alternates checking her wristwatch with gazing down the corridor expectantly.

When she sees me approaching, she stops pacing abruptly and stares straight at me, her expression darkening.

Embarrassed by this sudden and unwarranted blaze of attention, I avert my eyes and slip quickly inside the double doors.

'Hello again!' I spin around at the chirpy voice and recognise the nurse I saw yesterday. She's bending over the desk, tapping through a screen of what looks like medical supply lists. 'How's your son?'

'He's great now, thanks.' I smile. 'You wouldn't know he's been through any trauma at all.'

'So resilient, aren't they, kids? Good at bouncing back. I'm so glad he's feeling better. Must've been awful seeing him like that.'

I notice her name badge for the first time, standing out plainly on her navy uniform: *Sherry Thomas, Ward Manager*. She's obviously a senior member of staff, and I think about mentioning the woman who's hanging around outside. Shouldn't she be aware there's someone strange lurking? Then Steph's voice echoes in my ears: *You and your imagination! You read too many crime novels, Darcy. Chill out.* I decide against saying anything, and instead wave the card in front of me.

'I called in to drop this off for Mr Mortimer. It's just a little thank-you card,' I say sheepishly. 'Can I leave it with you to pass on to him?'

'Course!' Sherry takes it and places it next to her keyboard before hesitating and checking her fob watch. 'If you hang on another five minutes or so, you can give it to him yourself. He's due in at eleven.'

'He's working on a Sunday?'

'He's just popping in for an unexpected patient meeting but he'll swing by the ward to see that everything's OK, he's good like that.'

'Oh!' I take a step back, a whooshing sound starting in my ears. 'No, that's OK, I have to get back home.' The thought of George opening the card in front of me and seeing that I've included my contact details fills me with pure horror.

She tips her head and considers my reaction with amusement.

'No worries, then. I'll make sure he gets it.' She closes the window she's been viewing on the screen, says goodbye and heads back into the ward.

When I emerge from the double doors, the woman is still there. She's stopped pacing now and is leaning against the glossy wall with her arms folded, as if she's been waiting for me to come out.

As soon as she sees me, she pushes back and stands up straight, dropping her arms down but never taking her eyes off me. My Britishness prickles under her bad-mannered stare, and I begin to move, eager to escape her overt gaze. There's something in her expression I can't quite pinpoint… a kind of recognition, but on her part, not mine. I am quite certain I've never seen her before today.

She moves quickly, stepping towards me at an almost alarming pace.

'Are you visiting someone?' Her voice sounds edgy with a brittle desperation. It cuts through the reassuring space between us and I find myself stepping back. 'Is that why you're here?'

I feel half irritated at her forthright enquiry, half unnerved. A cursory glance to the left and then the right tells me there's nobody else out here in the long corridor. Just us two.

That's when it crosses my mind that she might not be well… mentally, I mean. She does look kind of wild-eyed, slightly unhinged, even. And the way she stares so openly is, quite frankly, intimidating.

But she's asked me a perfectly acceptable question and perhaps that's the reason she's waiting here herself, anxiously checking her watch; maybe she's waiting for visiting time.

'No, no. I'm not visiting,' I say lightly. 'I just popped by to drop something off.'

'There's a café here, it's only five minutes' walk,' she says suddenly.

I nod and give her a little smile, spooked by her odd manner.

I turn away from her and start walking back the way I came. When I get to the end of the corridor, I turn around and look back at her.

She's still standing there. Watching me.

9

George opened the patient file and browsed the main facts on the front sheet.

Joseph Hill was a fifty-two-year-old man who was first admitted to the hospital urology unit a month ago. He had recently travelled abroad, on holiday in Europe, and had been bed-ridden for most of the ten days he was there. A private Spanish clinic had treated him for a serious urine infection. The antibiotics he had been given had seemed to help somewhat. Back in the UK, however, his symptoms returned, and two weeks ago, following blood tests, he was rushed into the City Hospital's urology unit on the verge of what looked like kidney failure.

Detailed scans showed extensive damage to his left kidney. But within a day, he was off the drip and walking around. Subsequent scans over the next few days had shown the kidney appearing to repair itself. George himself had been Joseph's consultant, had followed all the correct procedures and sought Dharval's opinion, and no explanation could be found. Despite extensive blood tests, there was no evidence of cancer, no tumours visible on the scans, and the hospital had had no option but to let him return home.

But now Joseph Hill was back. Two days ago, he had been admitted with the same complaint, and this time the damage looked worse than before. The hospital management team were scurrying around like mad ants, praying that the patient survived and desperate to come up with answers as to why he had been released without treatment the first time. Any blot on the hospital's record would more than likely be jumped on and magnified by the press, and in a time when patients were free to choose where they took their treatment, such a development could do untold damage to its reputation as a centre of excellence.

It was a puzzling case that had completely vexed some of the most experienced senior urology consultants, not only at the City Hospital, but the entire East Midlands area, including George's colleague and boss, Dharval. That was what he'd been ringing about when he'd left the voicemail.

'Please review Joseph Hill's file as a matter of urgency for the meeting tomorrow morning,' he'd said without bothering with a greeting. 'If we can crack this one, it will be excellent for the department. There may even be a bit more budget in it for us.'

George had smiled to himself at his boss's choice of phrase: *If we can crack this one.* What he meant was, if George could crack it, then Dharval, as head of the department, would secure himself a blaze of glory and professional accolades before he retired.

So far, the case had been ring-fenced for the eyes of the most senior consultants. Now that they had failed, they had called an annoying, impromptu meeting this morning and were turning to other measures to save face.

It never failed to amuse George how the general public seemed to view medical professionals as being somehow God-like and untainted by the vagaries of everyday life. Yet the stark reality was that working in the hospital was just like being back at school: full of friendship cliques, and rife with one-upmanship and jealousy. Shameless cheating tactics to get ahead were par for the course, even amongst the echelons of the senior consultants.

Yet the most important element, the patients, were often forgotten in the mad scramble up the greasy pole of advancement.

George made a point to remind himself almost daily of the Hippocratic oath, and used it constantly as a yardstick for selecting the correct behaviour.

That was why he'd already given hours of his own time to absorbing the information in Joseph Hill's medical file. A solution to the problem hadn't occurred to him yet, but there was still time.

He got his things together and left for the hospital.

*

Back home after the meeting, he sat quietly in the lounge with his eyes closed and focused on his breath.

The meeting had been difficult. It was taking a turn that he hadn't expected and it ignited a deep rage in him that he hadn't yet been able to solve the mystery of Joseph Hill.

He was a perfectionist and enjoyed the status of being regarded as a dynamic surgeon within the hospital. This case wasn't going to plan at all.

He forced himself to compartmentalise the problem that threatened to take over his thoughts completely. That's how he dealt with the pressure of his job; he shut it away when he had to deal with everyday life.

He stood up and packed away the paperwork and patient files into his briefcase again and spotted the thank-you card that had been delivered to the ward that morning.

'Think you've got yourself an admirer,' Sherry, the ward manager had grinned cheekily. 'What can you expect though, going around saving lives at the park on your day off?'

He slid his finger under the flap of the envelope now, opened it and read the neat handwriting inside.

Hearing the front door being opened earlier than expected, he quickly tucked it under one of the files and allowed himself a small smile.

George covered the distance between his chair and the hallway in four great strides.

'Hello!' He ruffled the top of Romy's head as she slipped off her shoes and coat. 'Did everything go all right at school last week, Maria?' he addressed his housekeeper. She had various additional duties and the school run was one of them. He tried very hard to keep up with everything as Romy's father but sometimes it felt like his job left no space for family matters at all.

'Fine, sir,' Maria answered, taking Romy's coat to hang up.

'Hello, Daddy,' Romy said in her small, contained voice. 'Maria's gout is hurting her again. That's why we had to come back early from the park.'

'Sorry to hear that,' George said. Romy was incredibly fond of the woman.

'It's fine, nothing to worry about.' The housekeeper wafted a hand. 'I'll start the tea, shall I?'

'Nothing for me, thanks. I may be going out.'

Maria bowed her head and disappeared into the kitchen. George was glad to have her around. She served as a mother figure to Romy and also a support to him. She was caring and, importantly, very professional. He'd been unsure when she'd initially approached him about the job but now he was confident he'd made the right choice.

George's own mother had died when he was ten, and his father's solution to coping with a small son and a career as a leading brain surgeon had been to send him to St Mark's boarding school, fifty miles away from his home in Hemel Hempstead.

It had been a childhood filled with the cruellest kinds of bullying and abuse, which he pushed to the back of his mind to this very day. It served no useful purpose to get pulled into the past like that. The important thing was that he had survived his time at St Mark's and had found success in a career he truly loved.

He often told the medical interns that a difficult past could be integral to building a great career. He himself tried to think of his time at school and even his wife's death as experiences that had strengthened his capacity to be an effective surgeon. He liked to think Lucy's death had not been in vain, that he was saving numerous lives each year by employing the emotional distancing techniques he'd learned in his personal life as well as at medical school.

You had to detach yourself from emotional responses to often harrowing problems in order to focus on the patient's medical issue and their subsequent diagnosis and treatment.

Sometimes that response could seep out into his personal life, and people could construe him as possessing a cold nature without empathy. It was true that he had worked on his poker face, as all senior medics did, but it often failed to serve him outside of the hospital when he was aware he could appear cold and distanced from people.

It was hard to strike a balance but he tried.

10

1995

He'd been at the school for only two days when he first tangled with the gang.

A boy called Kelvin Crawley, reputedly the cleverest boy in the class, had been instructed by the form tutor, Mr Sherwin, to take him under his wing.

'Keep an eye on the new lad, Kelvin. Keep him out of trouble and most importantly, show him the ropes. Especially the best ways to keep away from the Panthers,' he'd said meaningfully.

'What did he mean by that?' he'd asked Kelvin when Mr Sherwin had walked away. 'Who are the Panthers?'

'You'll find out soon enough,' Kelvin said. 'Come on, I'll show you Scarrow Point.'

It sounded an interesting place. 'What is it?'

'It's the bell tower and it's peaceful up there. I used to go a lot when I was new and wanted to keep out of the way.'

It had been a Wednesday that day and only ten minutes remained of the lunch break but he followed Kelvin up the steep winding stairs to the top of the bell tower. An ancient wooden door faced them at the top.

'They leave a key here for the maintenance man.' Kelvin lifted the wiry doormat to reveal a long iron key. 'They don't ring the bells regularly any more but they keep them in working order for the term starts and finishes.'

The bell room was tiny and they squeezed either side of two enormous brass casings. The sides of the tower were open to the elements and gave a staggering view of the surrounding countryside and of the school, which seemed miles away now.

He leaned over the side and looked down. Out of the corner of his eye, a mass of swaggering figures in dark clothing approached the middle section of the school field and then headed directly for the bell tower entrance.

'Uh oh,' Kelvin said, his face paling. 'Now we've got trouble. Be respectful, don't say anything silly and... if all else fails... run. You go that way' – he indicated the very bottom of the field – 'and I'll go this way.' He pointed to the school building. 'One of us might get a good pasting but possibly not both of us. If we split quick enough.'

He was about to point out that running to the bottom of the field with no exit probably wasn't the best chance to escape harm but the gang was already much closer.

'You were asking who the Panthers are?' Kelvin whispered, his face drawn and pale. 'Well, you're about to find out.'

The boy narrowed his eyes as the group approached and analysed its make-up.

There were about twelve boys in total, almost all of them older than the two of them. All dressed in varying states of school uniform. The biggest, most aggressive-looking boys stood up front and one of them, a tall, rangy blonde boy with a strong jaw and mean expression, walked a step in front of them all.

The gang was like an animal of sorts. Snorting and posturing and tapering off towards the back like a great beast flicking its tail. All its parts seemed to move in unison as if everyone knew their role, their function.

'Scram, unless you want to be eating dog mess after school,' the tall boy at the front addressed Kelvin directly. He had a monotone, educated voice.

Without a backward glance, Kelvin took off and within seconds was a mere dot in the distance. Would he report what was happening to a teacher, or was that too much to ask? the new boy wondered.

His bowels felt loose suddenly, his skin clammy and crawling but he stood his ground.

'Who said you could come up here?' the tall boy right at the front said. He had black skinny trousers on, a long school shirt, worn out, and his tie was in a loose knot. His blazer was worn around his middle, the arms tied in front. 'I don't recall you asking my permission.'

His dull brown eyes stared relentlessly at the boy, full of hatred. But you had to at least know someone to hate them… didn't you?

'Who said you could even come on to the field?' he repeated.

'I didn't know I needed permission,' the new boy said evenly.

He saw the flash of a hand before a thunderclap exploded in his ear. He staggered back, clutching the side of his head where he'd been slapped.

'I expect a civil answer when I ask a perfectly reasonable question,' the tall boy said pleasantly. 'But I have the measure of you now, I think.' He turned to the others. 'Take him downstairs.'

He felt dizzy, disorientated. His cheek felt raw, as if the skin had been sloughed from it.

The group surged towards him and he found himself carried out of the small room on to the landing area. There, they set him on his feet and shuffled forward, en masse, until he could walk back no further, his back to the stairs.

The group parted and the tall boy appeared, walking quickly through the bodies. He lifted his leg, leaning back for leverage. With the heel of his boot, he kicked the new boy very hard in the bottom of the back, sending him hurling backwards down the stairs.

He must have knocked himself out on the wall on the way down.

When he opened his eyes, his head thumping, he was alone. Lessons must have resumed because he could hear no sounds from the field and, mercifully, all members of Panthers were gone.

Slowly, painfully, he levered himself up to a sitting position. Systematically he checked his body. Scrapes, grazes, lumps and bumps he found. But every joint, each limb, appeared to be intact which seemed like a miracle.

There was, however, a lump as big as an egg on the back of his head where he had obviously taken the impact on the way downstairs.

He tried to get to his feet but his head pounded harder and he began to feel sick. So he stayed put a little while longer.

He looked down and saw large blotches of ink on his white school shirt and smeared over his hands. Where had that come from? He didn't use fresh ink for his schoolwork.

Eventually he managed to get to his feet. He couldn't face shrugging on his rucksack, filled as it was with exercise books and textbooks. Instead, he pulled out one of the long straps and dragged it behind him.

With difficulty, he limped to the exit door.

When he was only a few paces away, he heard feet shuffling outside and someone cough.

He cried out and moved, as quickly as he could, behind a cupboard.

Please God, no. Please let it not be them again.

The raw bite of fear nipped at his throat, making breathing difficult but cancelling out the pain from his bruises and swelling from the fall.

He stood very still and held his breath, waiting.

He heard feet shuffling again, heavy breathing and then someone pushed hard against the door and it flew open.

11

After delivering George's thank-you card to the hospital, I got to the campus transport hub to find it was a ten-minute wait for the next bus back home, but fortunately, I was the only person at the bus stop.

It must be something about hospitals: you can guarantee that if there's someone else waiting, you'll be forced to start a conversation. About which relative you might be visiting, or the ongoing treatment you're having for precisely which ailment.

The bus stop is like a truth bubble; there's something confessional about it. I should know; I had enough of it when Joel was backwards and forwards to the Queen's Medical Centre for treatment and short stays during the last few months of his life.

It was heartbreaking for us all, those final weeks of his illness, when all treatment and medical efforts had been exhausted and it became clear that, this time, he would not prevail. His nemesis – chronic lymphocytic leukaemia – had finally won out. He'd battled bravely for four years, and for much of that time, his prognosis had looked positive. But the last couple of years had been increasingly tough, and the knowledge that he might not make it crept up on us like a thief in the night.

Joel had the chance to go into a hospice, but we wanted him at home, so he could be with his beloved boys. I didn't know he had a choice between two women to make at the time, but now, despite everything, I try to find reassurance that in the end, he chose to be with *us*.

Each night, when our sons had gone to bed and Joel's parents had gone home after visiting him, Joel and I would sit for long hours together just holding hands, talking about all our happy memories. We felt so lucky there were so many; it helped to blur the edges of the awful reality that awaited us.

But then every so often, he would get this intense, troubled look on his face and I'd instinctively back off a little, afraid of what he was thinking.

He'd say, 'Look at me, Darcy,' and he wouldn't be satisfied until I'd looked deep into his eyes – not just a glance; he insisted I held his gaze. 'If you only remember one thing, remember this. No matter what happens when I'm gone, you have to know I've loved you and the boys more than I've loved anyone in my whole life. Do you promise?'

'I know that, Joel, I've never doubted it.' I'd always say it, just like that, and he'd insist: 'Do you promise?'

'Yes, I promise,' I'd whisper, and I'd cry softly into his shoulder as we held each other.

It was a beautiful, sad thing that felt uncomfortable at first, but ultimately, over time, it brought us closer. It happened a lot, and I put it down to Joel's mindset; I thought it was probably a completely natural thing.

Now, it's almost all I think about.

Sometimes, he'd talk more philosophically about life and how his take on it had changed once he found out he was dying.

'Some people say they have no regrets, but I have so many, Darcy.'

'Tell me,' I'd gently press him. 'Share your regrets with me and they'll dissolve into thin air, just you see.'

He'd look so incredibly sad then. 'I wish that were true. I wish I'd been a better man.'

'Well, you shouldn't,' I'd tell him firmly. 'You have brought two beautiful sons into this world and you've given so much love to us, your family. We will never forget you, and nothing else matters, my darling. Nothing.'

Hard to believe now, but I thought of myself as a strong woman back then. I had a handful of friends, mostly whom I'd met back when I worked at the gym. I was a person other people turned to when they needed a chat or some advice.

I wanted to be there for Joel in every way, I didn't get too hung up on the stuff he was saying.

My husband was dying, looking back on his life and finding fault. I told myself that was all it was. We would all of us do that, right? Hindsight is such a perfect science, isn't it?

I remember there was this one particular time, just a few days before he slipped away, when he got the intense look again and gripped my shoulders as he spoke.

'We all make decisions we regret, don't we?'

I hadn't a clue what he was on about at the time, but when I thought about it afterwards, there seemed to be a recurring theme about regrets and a life lived carelessly.

He was feeling so ill, and so I just made all the right noises to try and reassure him.

'Of course everyone makes mistakes, Joel. Don't beat yourself up; you've always done the right thing by us, your family, you've nothing to—'

'Darcy… just listen. Please,' he'd interrupted me, tightening his grip on my shoulders. 'We live our lives like there's always plenty of time to set everything straight, and then the time runs out and it's too late. It's just too late to make it right again.'

His voice broke and his hands fell away from me. He sank back into the pillows and closed his eyes, looking grey and beaten.

'Hey!' I wrapped my arms around him, buried my face in his neck. 'Stop! It's happy memories we need to talk about, not regrets. Deal?'

He nodded, but seemed subdued after that, not wanting to chat much. That suited me fine. I was crumbling on the inside, and every day it was harder to keep it all together for him and the boys.

I never thought anything of that particular conversation. Until after he'd gone.

Then when the life I thought we'd had flipped onto its ugly side, it was *all* I could think about.

It started when I arrived to visit Joel during one of his last hospital stays, just a week before he died.

I stepped into his room and saw, with disappointment, that he was fast asleep.

'You might not get much out of him today, I'm afraid.' The nurse scribbled something on his chart and hooked it back on the end of the bed, popping her pencil into her pocket. 'His last visitor stayed longer than usual. He's really worn out.'

I frowned. We all had our regular visiting times. Steph called in late morning; Brenda and Leonard did the evening shift and often took the boys with them. I always popped in after my afternoon yoga class and left in time to pick Harrison up from school and Kane from nursery.

Our routine gave Joel plenty of time for a nap after lunch.

'Who was visiting? Was it Stephanie, his sister?'

The nurse shook her head.

'Don't think so. There's been a lady coming to see Joel in the afternoons for the last couple of days.' Her eyes flicked towards me, away again. 'Her name is…' She consulted her notes. 'Daniela Frost.'

I frowned. 'I don't recognise the name. I expect it's one of his colleagues.'

Joel had always talked to me a lot about his work as a Microsoft IT consultant, travelling the country troubleshooting software problems for big corporations. He'd never mentioned anyone of that name. He didn't interact with colleagues in the way most other people did, because he hadn't got an office base, but I knew the names of a handful of people he was in regular contact with at the company's HQ.

Once the nurse had left, I sat down beside Joel's bed. There was a packet of Fisherman's Friend lozenges on his over-bed table – our in-joke, because I detested the strong menthol smell on his breath and refused to buy them – and the latest edition of his favourite mountain-biking magazine. He hadn't been in a fit state to go on one of his favoured thirty-mile cycle rides for at least six months.

He'd received his first diagnosis of the condition when Harrison was just two years old. He'd kept it a secret for a week or so. I was furious he'd gone through it all alone, never told me about the appointment with the consultant that had followed several doctor's appointments and blood tests, none of which I'd known about.

Of course, I knew he'd been feeling under the weather. He'd been sweating buckets in the middle of the night in the winter and had been picking up every minor infection going. We'd just put it down to him being a bit run-down.

'Get yourself checked out at the doctor's,' I'd told him on several occasions, but he'd waved my concern away. Or had appeared to. Evidently he *had* made an appointment and the doctor had carried out some tests.

He sat me down one night when Harrison had gone to bed. Told me about the diagnosis.

'It's not as bad as it sounds.' His voice was confident but his face looked pale and drawn, the tiny lines at the edges of his eyes seeming to be etched deeper than ever. 'People live years with it, apparently. Plus, I'm young and strong, and that can only be a good thing.'

He talked about treatment options and how the condition could be managed, and by the end of it, I felt reassured that things might not be as bad as they had first seemed.

Joel was always so skilled at convincing me, I realise now. Or was it that I was just incredibly naïve?

Anyway, that day in his hospital room, there was a glass of water on the side with a small half-moon of pale pink lipstick imprinted on the edge. I held it up to the window, studied the tiny crinkly lines in the sticky gloss.

I read somewhere that everyone's lip print is unique, just like a fingerprint.

I replaced the glass and stared at Joel's face. He looked chronically pale by then and had lost another ten pounds in the past two weeks, but he was still devilishly handsome. The sharp, defined edge of his jaw and his high cheekbones suddenly looked more pronounced, like when we first met.

I glanced away. Couldn't bring myself to think about the horror of what was happening inside him.

His eyelids fluttered periodically, the left-hand side of his full lips twitching every few seconds. I wondered what – or whom – he might be dreaming about.

Me, perhaps? Or our boys?

Looking back, that's the moment it started, I think. My need to know more about her.

While the love of my life slept, I took his phone out of the cupboard next to his bed and searched his emails, and then his Facebook friends list, for a Daniela Frost. There was nobody of that name. I opened Messenger and considered the scant list of communications there. Nothing.

On my own phone, I searched the name generally on Facebook, and a list of relevant profiles popped up. I quickly scrolled down but didn't recognise any of the photographs there – but then why would I? I didn't know anyone of that name.

I remember Joel woke up abruptly then, feeling sick. I called for the nurse and pushed everything else out of my mind.

I told myself that if a female colleague or friend I didn't know about had called in to visit, what did it really matter in the scheme of things?

Just two weeks later, we were holding Joel's funeral. His parents had insisted on organising everything, wouldn't hear of me worrying about a thing. Even though they didn't live that far away, I didn't see much of them as Joel mostly took the boys over there for Sunday football matches. I remember thinking how sweet and caring it was of them to want to protect me from the pain of organising the funeral.

It was a blustery day. Sooty clouds buffeted angrily across the sky, obliterating any chance of the sun breaking through. It was a day when it was all I could do to hold myself together. Everything else became irrelevant.

I had this sense of my life unravelling, spiralling out of control. It had happened so fast: after his initial diagnosis four years ago, there was just six months between Joel becoming desperately ill and then dying.

It was hard to even breathe and Brenda urged me not to go to the funeral.

'You'll end up making yourself ill and the boys need you,' she'd said.

I'd spent my time as a mother reassuring my boys that they were safe and surrounded by the love of their family. How then could I explain *this*, the death of their beloved father?

I tried, I really did try. But none of what I said made sense to them or to me.

In the end, the greatest comfort came from us just holding each other and crying out the grief-laden tears. In the end, there was no need for words at all.

Now, as the bus rattles over the speed bumps on the road, I rub at my damp eyes, refocusing as the streets become familiar. This is what happens if I don't keep my wits about me; I drift back into the past without even noticing.

I don't want to revisit the time after Joel died, not right now. I still can't believe I came out the other side. There were many times I got so low, I thought life was over for me.

The strange thing is, Kane's emergency at the play park, my thankfulness that George stepped in... somehow, it's shaken my life up a bit. I'd been just ticking along, every day very similar and uneventful. And that was fine. But suddenly, I feel a sense of opportunity that's telling me, maybe, just maybe, I'm ready to move on with my life. Baby steps, that's all.

A few minutes later, when I step off the bus, my phone chimes to announce an incoming text message. I pull it out of my handbag to find a notification from an unknown number. When I tap on it, the text message loads.

Hi Darcy, thanks for the card. Are you free for a quick chat if I call you about 4 p.m.? George M.

12

At 3.55 p.m., I'm pacing around the kitchen like a deranged lion.

The boys are still at Brenda and Leonard's and won't be home until after five. My phone sits on the counter, silent and still. I feel like a kid playing the card game snap again. Waiting for the two matching cards to appear, every muscle tense and sprung.

Even though I know the phone is going to ring imminently, I'm like a jack-in-the-box, ready to jump through the roof when I hear the sound.

A chat sounded lovely when I first read his message, but now I can't stop ruminating about what George might be calling to say. In my mind, I've already been through hundreds of possible scenarios, most of them negative.

Maybe he wants to tell me how kind it was of me to invite him out for a coffee before letting me down gently, explaining that he has a wife, a girlfriend, or he's married to his work, or he's gay. I have to face it: he might have saved my son's life but that doesn't mean he wants to see me again, or even talk about it.

Luckily, I have a contingency plan.

I'll explain that the card I left was simply a polite invitation to thank him and there are absolutely no strings attached. At all. Certainly no romantic expectation. I'll laugh as I say it.

George is an attractive man, a surgeon who saves lives on a daily basis. He's probably used to women fawning all over him, and he may naturally assume I'm doing the same.

He wasn't wearing a wedding band, but then that doesn't really mean anything. Yes, I'm single, and I haven't felt that flutter in my belly since I first met Joel in that out-of-town pub all those years ago… but that's irrelevant, because all I'm offering is to buy him a coffee, for goodness' sake!

The dishwasher beeps and I fling open the door too early, hauling out the still-steaming clean dishes onto the worktop and smarting with each scalding touch.

The clink of the cutlery and the clatter of the crockery helps drown out the little voice of my conscience, which is trying to put forward an alternative truth in my head about my real motives.

A vibrating hum suddenly fills the kitchen, swiftly followed by a delicate tinkling sound.

I let out a little shriek as the Orla Kiely mug I'm holding slips from my hand and hits the kitchen counter, the handle breaking clean off.

I leave it where it lands and rush over to my phone. The screen is lit with the same unknown number as before.

I flick my fringe out of my eyes and paste a smile to my face.

'Hello?' I sing out brightly.

'Hello, Darcy? It's George Mortimer here.'

His deep, masterful voice resonates down the line, sending a shiver across the back of my neck.

'George! Thanks for calling!' I don't pause to allow him to refuse my offer of coffee and cake. 'I just wondered if you'd like to meet for a coffee. I just wanted to say thank you again… That was it really, nothing more!'

I clamp my mouth shut and press my fingernails into the soft pad of the palm of my free hand, in an effort to calm myself down, get a handle on things. I'm trying to compensate by being too jolly and upbeat, and it's just making me feel ten times worse, plus I sound like an idiot.

'That's very kind of you. But as I said before, there's no need to keep thanking me. It's no more than any other medic would have done if they'd been there.' His words are unrushed, understated. His tone is kind and I feel my throat relax a touch. 'How is Kane feeling now?'

'He's fine!' I pause and drag in a breath, and my voice drops an octave. 'He's fine. You'd never guess what he'd been through, looking at him scooting around today.'

'Isn't that always the way with kids?' George chuckles. 'Trouble is like water off a duck's back to them.'

'I hope it was OK,' I venture awkwardly. 'Bringing the card into your department, I mean.'

'Of course, it was a lovely thought.' He pauses a moment, and I brace myself for the inevitable *but*. I swear my heart is banging so hard on the wall of my chest I feel certain he must be able to hear it. 'And if the offer's still there, I'm calling to say that I'd love to grab a coffee with you. Maybe even a slice of cake, if my waistband allows it.'

'Of course!' I recall his tan, fit physique and laugh, ridiculously relieved, and exhilarated that he's accepted my offer.

Then, to my surprise, he suggests we meet at six o'clock today.

I hesitate. I know Brenda is planning to bring the boys back around 5.30, but I'm sure she won't mind keeping them a bit later.

George fills my silence. 'Totally understand if it's too short notice for you; it just happens to be one of those rare days when I've actually got home early. But if you'd rather rearrange, that's—'

'No, no,' I interrupt him. 'Six o'clock is fine.'

We arrange to meet at Bru, a small upmarket coffee shop in nearby West Bridgford that I know specialises in fair-trade coffee and home-made cakes to die for.

By the time I get off the phone and call Brenda – who is more than happy to bring the boys back at 7.30, although I don't tell her why – I've only left myself forty minutes to shower and dress before I need to leave the house.

I decide I haven't got time to wash and style my hair, so I pin it up in a French roll and leave a few wisps each side that I curl with the tongs.

Sitting in my underwear – my only remaining matching set now – I apply a tinted moisturiser and just use mascara and a bit of pencil eyeliner. The last thing I want is for George to think I'm making a big deal out of meeting up. Because I'm really not. There's no expectation on my part at all.

I apply a nude lipstick and dab a bit of pink on top, so I don't look too washed out.

'You'll do,' I say out loud after studying my reflection in the dressing table mirror.

It's been a long time since I've applied even a small amount of make-up, so I'm pleasantly surprised when I find I look much brighter wearing it. More like my old self.

I'm wary of overdressing, so just pull on some black jeggings, black patent ankle boots with a low blocky heel, and a fluffy pink sweater I got last month in the Zara sale. After I slip on my short belted black wool coat and a stripy hand-knitted scarf Brenda gave me last Christmas, I'm good to go.

I decide to take the bus as that removes the nightmare parking situation in town. I try and listen to a bit of my audiobook, but the noise in my head drowns out everything that comes through the earbuds. I rewind to the beginning of the chapter three times and then give up.

I'm going for coffee with a man. A very attractive man.

I don't even want to think about what Joel's family would say to that, if they knew. Luckily, they *don't* know.

And I've got no intention of telling them.

13

I step off the bus and fill my lungs with cold air before setting off on the five-minute walk to Bru. Despite the chill, I feel clammy underneath my clothes and my mouth is dry. I'm so out of practice at meeting new people.

It's going to be fine. It's just a coffee, a chat and another thank you from me. That's all there is to it.

I'm a few minutes early. I push open the door to the café and inhale the intense smell of coffee. Inside, it's quite small and dim, but I count four customers, all looking at their phones. Bare light bulbs glare starkly from small steel cages suspended above the reclaimed wood tabletops. Industrial pipework snakes around the edges of the walls and ceiling. It's all very trendy and on point.

George hasn't arrived yet, so I take a table towards the rear of the room without ordering. I haven't a clue what he'll want.

I've literally just slipped off my coat, frowning when I see that pink fluff from my sweater has transferred to my black leggings, when the door opens and in he walks.

He looks dashing, hair slightly damp from the rain, a casual navy Gant jacket worn over his well-cut suit. He runs his hand through his hair and smiles easily when he sees me.

I paste a smile to my own face and hope it doesn't look too forced. I feel… out of practice in meeting someone like this. A man.

All my old insecurities from when I was ill have been beaten back with my therapy stick but I can still feel them there, waiting in the wings. Biding their time for me to make a mess of things.

'I'm not late, am I?' He checks his watch. 'Had to park a few streets away.'

'No, no. I got here a few minutes early.' I stand up, brushing tiny strands of static fluff off my leggings and see my phone has lit up on the table with a couple of notifications. 'What can I get you?'

'Let's see.' He turns towards the counter. 'I'll just have a regular latte, and you can surprise me with the cake.'

I nod and grin and edge past him, scooping up my phone as I pass by. I feel like I'll be sick if I eat anything, but I have to show willing.

There's only a short queue but while I wait, I check my phone. Three notifications now. A missed call, a voicemail and a text message. All from Steph.

Only one person in the queue remains before me now. I decide not to listen to the voicemail but I do check out the text.

Where are you?? Call me asap.

I glance at the door like a guilty schoolkid, about to be caught out when she should be doing homework. I go out alone so rarely, I wouldn't put it past Steph to try and track me down if she can't get hold of me but she'd never think about this place; we've certainly never been here together.

The person in front of me walks away from the counter and I order two lattes and two pieces of cake to eat in. Carrot and red velvet. I'm betting he'll take the red velvet.

The barista says she'll bring them over, so I walk back to the table, noting George's neat but stylish haircut, the back of his broad, tanned neck.

He looks up as I place my phone back on the table and take my seat again.

'So, your little man is back fighting fit already?'

'Yes, you'd never know anything had happened at all now.' I tap my fingernails on the table and avert my eyes as my phone screen lights up again. 'Look, I know you said there's no need, but I just wanted to—'

'Hey, you've thanked me enough, OK?' he says kindly but firmly. 'I'm just pleased I could help. My daughter, Romy, was wildly unimpressed; when it was all over, she bent my ear because the queue for the spinning teacups had got twice as long.'

We both burst out laughing and I feel myself relax a little.

'How old is Romy?'

'She's six.'

I nod. I thought she looked a similar age to Kane, who turned six a month ago.

'Six going on sixteen, I bet?'

'Too right.' George rolls his eyes. 'She keeps me on my toes, for sure, but she's my world.'

I love that he's so openly adoring of his daughter. I glance at his ring-free hand again. Maybe he's a weekend dad – divorced, perhaps, with partial custody?

The barista sets a tray on the table and offloads the coffees and two huge wedges of cake set on quirky hand-painted crockery with tiny silver dessert forks balanced artfully on the side.

'Wow, how did you know?' George licks his lips. 'Carrot cake. My favourite.'

I laugh. 'I had you down as a red velvet man.'

He wrinkles his nose. 'Bit rich for me, red velvet, and all that food colouring, ugh.' Is it my imagination, or does his gaze linger on my face a touch too long? 'I'm a natural sort of guy, not a big fan of artificial additions.'

I feel my cheeks ignite. I look natural all right – bordering on unkempt. But somehow I get the feeling he approves of my pared-down appearance.

'Looks like someone needs to get hold of you.' He nods to my flashing phone, signalling an incoming call. From Steph.

I'm about to reach to turn it off when it suddenly occurs to me... what if it's something about the boys? What if Kane's unwell again?

Concern must show itself on my face because George points to it.

'Don't mind me, answer it if you need to.'

But Steph's text had simply said to call her. She'd definitely have said if Kane was unwell. I slip the phone into my handbag.

14

We sit in silence for a few moments as we sip our coffee. George uses the miniature fork to cut off a piece of cake, and pops it in his mouth, closing his eyes and pulling an 'I'm in heaven' expression.

I grin, poking at the other slice of cake but not eating any. I still feel too tense. Trust Steph to pick now to start badgering me.

'So, tell me a bit about you then, Darcy,' he says, taking another gulp of coffee and laying down his fork. 'You've two boys, right?'

'Yes. Kane has just turned six and Harrison is ten.'

'The pair of them are quite a handful, I expect.' He picks up his fork again and smiles. 'I have my hands more than full with just the one.'

Doesn't *sound* like a part-time dad. I decide to bite the bullet.

'They're both little live wires, but like you said about your daughter, they're my world. I'm lucky, as their auntie and grandparents help me out quite a bit with them.' I hesitate. 'Their father, Joel, passed away when they were just two and six years old. So it's been a difficult journey at times.'

George stares, puts his fork down again.

'I'm so sorry to hear that.' His smooth, tanned forehead creases with concern. 'Sadly, that's something we have in common. Romy's mother died six years ago.'

'Wow,' I breathe. 'So… you get it.'

'Totally,' he agrees.

I'm not sure what I thought taking coffee with a surgeon would be like, but it's not this. He seems so relaxed and is incredibly easy to talk to. I expected him to talk shop and use medical terms I've never even heard of, but he's not like that at all.

He seems so... well, down to earth.

'Your job at the hospital, it must be so demanding. How on earth do you cope as a single dad, working those crazy hours?' I'm always reading in the news about the raw deal hospital doctors have these days, working double shifts, never getting any sleep.

'The ward doctors suffer, but we consultants don't have it too bad. My hours are quite civilised in comparison.' George pushes away his half-eaten cake and picks up his coffee.

I bite my bottom lip, worried I've offended him.

'Sorry, I forgot you're a senior—'

He laughs, holding up his hand in a stop sign. 'Don't worry, the dreaded junior doctor hours are where we all start. It's taken me a long time to claw my way up, and if anything, I appreciate it all the more.'

He traces the rim of his latte glass with a fingertip and falls quiet for a few seconds. It's not an uncomfortable silence, though, and soon he begins to speak in that open, honest way he has.

'Sadly, I don't have family help. It probably sounds a bit odd but my housekeeper, Maria, is very close to Romy and carries out a lot of duties a parent might do, like the school run, babysitting when I'm late home and during the school holidays. That sort of thing. I don't know what I'd do without her.'

'Housekeeper? That sounds grand!' George must have a very different life to me. And big differences in lifestyle aren't always good thing when you're trying to get to know someone.

'You just get through day to day, week to week, you know?' George continues, seemingly not noticing my inferiority complex resurfacing. 'Somehow we single parents manage to scale each hurdle that comes our way. I'm sure you feel the same way.'

I *do*, and he's right: it's terribly hard. It's an important similarity that cancels out the difference in my mind.

'Tell me a bit about your job,' I say, leaning back against the ladder-backed chair. 'It sounds so interesting.'

'Well, there's nothing much to tell really. I'm a consultant surgeon, second in command in the urology department. I've been in the job four years now and it's not nearly as glamorous as people seem to think,' he chuckles.

I glance at his long fingers and broad palms, wondering how many lives they've saved.

'It must be amazing to help so many people,' I say with a flush of admiration.

'You're not going to thank me again, are you?' He leans forward and scowls, then grins, relaxing back into his seat.

'Oops, you rumbled me.' I grin. 'Good job I managed to bite it back.'

'You're funny. Easy to talk to.' He smiles and taps the top of my hand with his index finger. I feel goose bumps spring up on my forearm. 'I'm really enjoying your company, Darcy.'

Our eyes lock and our smiles fade as we study each other briefly.

His eyes are mid brown with tiny golden flecks of light dancing around the irises. His jaw is square and his skin even-toned apart from a tiny nick above his top lip where he must have caught himself shaving this morning. A scatter of freckles straddles the bridge of his slightly crooked nose.

The overall effect of all this is an easy, rugged attractiveness, enhanced by his confident nature.

I look away, embarrassed that I've been staring too long. If I'm honest, I suppose there's an element of not believing my luck.

'It's a while since I've done this,' he says softly, indicating the coffee and cake on the table. 'Met up with someone other than for work purposes, I mean. I forgot how enjoyable it can be.'

I curse my high colouring as I feel another flush in my cheeks. He notices it and smiles.

'Same for me,' I agree, tapping the handle of my tall glass. 'I haven't dated anyone since… I mean, not that this is a date. I meant…'

I will the ground to open and swallow me up. Now the whole café could warm their hands on my face.

George laughs, finishing his coffee. 'Don't worry. I know exactly what you mean, Darcy, and if it helps, I agree.'

My heart flutters when he uses my name. He's got such a great bedside manner, I think cheekily.

'Listen, have you eaten?' He checks his watch. 'I guess we both have to get back to our kids, but could you stay out for another hour, say? There's a little tapas place just opened around the corner from here. I'd love to try it.'

I glance at my watch. Brenda's bringing the kids back at 7.30 and I'll not be able to get home for then. But she has a key, and I can easily text her to say I might be a few minutes late.

'Sounds perfect,' I say. 'I'll just pop to the bathroom before we go.'

When I round the corner, I take out my phone to text Brenda. The screen is full of notifications: text messages, missed calls and voicemail all from Steph.

'This is ridiculous!' I hiss to the empty cubicles just as the phone lights up again with an incoming call. I dab my finger aggressively on the screen and it.

'Steph? What is it?'

'Where the hell are you?' she snaps. 'Mars?'

'I'm out. Your mum has the boys.'

'Out?' I detect her tone is instantly a smidgeon cooler. 'With who?'

I sigh. 'Why are you ringing and texting like a crazy woman?'

'I didn't know you were out, did I?' She sounds petulant, like a snubbed child. 'I wanted to let you know something, that's all. As usual, I was just thinking about you.'

'Go on then,' I sigh. 'What is it?'

'Have you heard anything from the letting agency about your house being sold yet?'

'No.'

'Well I can tell you it's been sold and I know who's bought it.'

'Do you?' I perk up a bit. Maybe we're not going to have to deal with the inconvenience of moving out after all. 'Is it someone you know?'

'It's someone we all know, sadly. Daniela Frost has bought it.'

The phone slips from my hands and the screen fractures on the tiled floor.

15

The tapas restaurant was tucked away down a little side street behind the library. George had heard some of the junior doctors talking about it on the ward a few days ago, otherwise he'd have had no idea it was even here.

As they were shown to a table, he glanced around and saw that it was exactly the sort of place he'd usually take pains to avoid. It had that upmarket feel that always translated to him as pretentious. Small and intimate, it was filled with professional, ambitious types who looked as if they'd just finished working at their plum jobs in trendy advertising agencies. Every time the door opened, they'd glance up and sweep the new diners head to foot, looking to compare for signs of success: a designer suit, an expensive pair of shoes or handbag.

George was irritated but also amused by people who so obviously looked down their nose at others. Probably it was because he worked every day with those great levellers, illness and death. Wealth and status didn't figure as far as they were concerned.

They took their seats at a cramped table for two near the kitchen and ordered drinks.

He glanced at Darcy and saw that she still looked uncomfortable, glancing around her at the well-dressed diners, gulping down the small glass of filtered water the waiter poured.

When she'd finally emerged from the bathroom in the coffee shop she'd looked flustered and her face had flushed a deep pink.

'I dropped my phone.' She'd held it up and showed him the screen with its spider web of cracked glass.

'Is that all that's wrong?' he'd said, helping her on with her jacket. 'You look a bit upset.'

'I'm fine, it's just…'

For a second he'd thought she might burst into tears and had started to wonder if she'd received some bad news in the bathroom. She'd been longer than he'd expected in there and it appeared someone had been trying to call her when he'd first arrived.

'I could do without the cost of getting another iPhone. This is such an old model too, a newer one will cost a fortune.'

She looked genuinely worried at the thought of the extra cost.

'You might get away with just a screen repair,' he suggested and she nodded. 'Let's get out of here, shall we?'

'Hope you don't drink your wine like that,' he murmured drily now, peering at her over the drinks menu.

She laughed, and he loved that she opted immediately for honesty. 'I get thirsty when I'm nervous.'

'Seriously? You're not nervous because of me, are you?' He put down the menu and stared at her. He'd seen her glancing down at her phone several times.

'It's not you,' she said hesitantly. 'I feel very comfortable in your company.'

'I'm glad about that.' He touched her hand briefly and felt a little frisson of electric current there. 'Then why?'

She looked around and shrugged. 'I just feel like everyone here lives a very different life to me, I suppose. You know, successful careers, exciting social lives, that sort of thing. It seems a long time since I've been out in place like this.'

He could almost see the feeling of inferiority creeping through her veins, and it reminded him of Lucy when they'd first met. She'd been beautiful but didn't know it; well-off from the bank of her mum and dad but never flaunted it. He'd adored her honesty and transparency.

'What do you do… as a job, I mean?' he asked, taking a sip of his water.

'I'm a yoga teacher.' Darcy scrunched up her shoulders a little, as if it were an embarrassing fact. 'I haven't got a studio or anything; I just teach a few classes in local venues. I used to teach a lot more, but… well, with one thing and another, I've scaled back quite a bit.'

One thing and another. Interesting, he thought, noticing the furrow in her brow, but it would've been rude to ask so early on, so he stayed quiet.

'Before Joel, before having the kids, I used to manage a successful gym on the outskirts of the city. That's where I became qualified to teach.' Her face brightened.

'Sounds like you enjoyed that.'

She nodded. 'I was full of confidence and fighting fit back then, always looking the part just like these people.' She nodded to the room. 'I loved the variety of my day. Interviewing and appointing staff, brainstorming sales campaigns with the team, regular meetings with senior management visiting from the gym's headquarters in London.' She stopped abruptly. 'Sorry. I'm going on a bit.'

'Not at all. I'm interested.'

She used to frequent places like this tapas bar a couple of times a week at least, she told him. 'I'd barely notice my surroundings, so comfortable was I playing the part, but now, I feel like a bit of an imposter.' She brushed down the sleeves of her fluffy pink sweater and patted her already neat hair down at the back.

'Do you know the last time I came out for drinks after work?' George didn't wait for an answer. 'About four months ago, when someone in my department had a leaving do.' His eyes scanned the room. 'Most of these people are putting on a good show, but they'd rather be at home in their pyjamas watching a box set. Trust me; look at their faces.'

That made her laugh. But she looked around at the other diners and he could see that she saw what he meant: the pasted-on smiles and tired eyes.

'You're right!' she said.

He nodded. 'It's the unavoidable downside to living and breathing a successful career, with little else in your life. So don't envy them, whatever you do.'

'Thanks,' she said, picking up the menu and seeming a little more liberated. 'I feel better already.'

And noting her bright expression and lifted chin, he could see she was telling the truth.

Later, when he got back home, he thanked his housekeeper for agreeing to look after Romy while he was out.

Maria had been with him since Romy was born, when Lucy was still alive. If she was efficient and useful then, she was an absolute godsend now. George and Romy both considered her a member of the family, and she'd proven on several occasions where confidentiality was key that he could trust her implicitly.

When she'd gone home, and with his daughter safe and sound in bed, George poured himself two fingers of Jack Daniel's with ice and just a splash of water. Then he sat down in the lounge, curtains pulled and the lamps on.

He took a sip of the whiskey and closed his eyes, feeling the burn at the back of his throat. It felt like a small punishment, one that he deserved.

There were no two ways about it: he'd made some very, very bad decisions. And the worst one was getting involved with the nightmare that was Opal Vardy.

He'd had a strange feeling about her from their first meeting, but had he listened to it? No. He'd been flattered, seduced, and she'd played him like a fiddle.

He sighed and took another gulp of whiskey.

There was nothing he could do about it now; what was done was done. It was all about damage limitation from this point forward, and that was where he continued to focus his efforts.

Things had been quieter lately, and he could but hope and pray that Opal was losing interest and would leave him alone. He would never give in, and maybe, at long last, she had finally accepted that.

Tonight, while he'd been out, for the first time in a very long time he hadn't thought about Opal Vardy at all. He'd been too enchanted with getting to know Darcy.

It was early days. Just about as early as it could be, after just one date. But it felt right. *She* felt right.

Every day in his job, George had to make life-changing decisions, often on the hoof. Choosing the correct course of action in a split second, sometimes under tremendous pressure, with a patient's life in the balance.

His everyday life, in comparison, was – usually – full of easy decisions, made easier by the fact that he was determined to follow his gut feeling from now on.

Darcy Hilton was funny, quietly beautiful and had an endearing self-deprecating quality that he found adorable. Maybe, just maybe, he'd found a keeper this time.

He knew he would tell her about Opal. If they were to start a relationship, he'd have no choice in the matter, but the time had to be right.

In the meantime, he had one very important job to do.

He must make sure Opal Vardy stayed out of the picture and didn't scare Darcy off.

16

When I get home, I pour myself a weak gin and tonic and sit in the living room with a chillout playlist on and just one lamp lit.

This feels very different to last night, when I couldn't go to bed because my head was full of Daniela Frost and her return to Nottingham. It's easy to see from the check-in locations of her online photographs that she's been living in Manchester. Why couldn't she just stay there? Why has she suddenly got a burning desire to come back here, to magnify all our pain again and, according to Steph, make us effectively homeless?

Before I spoke to Steph in the café when I was out with George, my head felt clear, my thoughts positive and for the first time in a long time, I felt like the old me again. A woman who once thought she deserved to be happy.

Sometimes, it feels like misery follows me around. Maybe it's something to do with the fact I'm an only child and both my parents died before I reached my late twenties.

They had me late in life. They'd tried for a baby for years and finally gave up, accepting it would never happen. Mum was forty when she fell pregnant and Dad was ten years older than her.

Mum went first, a heart attack. And Dad... well, he just seemed to lose the will to live after she'd gone. His death certificate said it was complications caused by the lung disease that had plagued him since his thirties. In my opinion, it was a broken heart.

I've always dreamed of building myself a happy life. Sadly, it hasn't gone to plan so far. It sounds ridiculous, but when I look in George Mortimer's eyes, I see the possibility of a bright future there.

When George asked me to go for food, I texted Brenda and asked if the boys could stay over, and she was fine about it. George texted his *housekeeper*... imagine that! Sounds all *Downton Abbey*.

After our meal, he insisted on waiting with me outside until my Uber arrived. We skipped dessert, but before coffee, we arranged to meet again on Tuesday evening. Just for drinks, as George is working until quite late, but I'm already looking forward to it.

It would've been such a lovely evening if Steph hadn't wrecked it with her news about the house. I don't blame her, of course. I'm grateful she's tipped me off but... I don't know, just as things were looking up, this happens.

I know only too well that the worst thing I can do is to start catastrophising about finding somewhere else to live. I mean, it certainly is a catastrophe that Daniela has quite obviously made a conscious decision to trample on our lives but I know how to talk myself down now.

There are hundreds of places to rent around here and I know Brenda and Leonard wouldn't see us on the street. In fact, they'd probably jump at the chance of having us live there a while so they see the boys every day and night.

But I've fought so long and hard for my independence and the right to care for my sons myself, it would be a definite step back for me to let that happen.

I glance at my phone. It's still limping along but there's what looks like a big grey tear down the middle of the screen now, making it really hard to read anything without squinting. I'll have to see if I can get it repaired at some point.

That's my excuse for not reading Steph's texts anyway and I've ignored another two calls from her. I can't cope with the drama tonight and I don't want my lovely time with George completely tainted.

I plan to ask Brenda if she'll have the boys overnight on Tuesday again. It's nothing new; she and Leonard are both retired, and they often take them for a night's sleepover midweek and drop them off at school the next morning. I'll then be there at the end of the day to bring them home.

Failing that, if Brenda and Leonard happen to have one of their bridge nights organised, then Steph and Dave always jump at an opportunity to have the boys over.

'Dave's like a kid himself. Any excuse to get the PS4 out,' Steph often jokes.

Although George and I got on famously tonight, I have no intention of sharing the fact that I've been on a proper date with anyone yet. After all, even though it felt as if George was keen, it might still come to nothing.

It will be strange keeping the fact that I'm seeing someone from them. Steph and Brenda are integral to my life. When I was recovering from the breakdown, I got into the habit of running everything past them, confiding in them, taking note of their advice.

Once I'd started to feel better and more capable, I tried to back off a bit and make my own decisions. They've never said as much but I've always had the feeling they don't like it, don't take kindly to being held at arm's length. Even now, it often feels like it's a battle to keep completely in charge of myself and the boys.

But there's no ambiguity when it comes to a new relationship. Both Steph and Brenda have made it abundantly clear that dating shouldn't be an option yet.

'It's far too soon,' Brenda is fond of reminding me, although Joel has been gone for four years now.

It actually feels quite nice to keep a little secret to myself. *Secret* is what it feels like, anyway.

I finish the G&T and am debating whether to have another when something catches my eye outside. I squint and shuffle to the edge of the seat cushion, leaning forward to get a better look.

Over the past year, I've noticed my eyes are definitely getting worse for both distance and close-up work, and I keep meaning to go for an eye test. But it's not *too* bad yet and I can enlarge the font on my Kindle so easily, I figured it's not worth investing in reading glasses.

It's dark out there. Anyone would struggle to see.

I put down my empty glass, turn off the table lamp and pad over to the window. There it is, movement again. Then, as my eyes become accustomed to the dark, I see there's a large shadow on the wall behind the lamp post.

I feel a dull ache in my belly.

Is someone out there watching me?

One day I'll make you pay. I promise you that.

It was the last thing Daniela Frost said to me before she left town after Joel died.

But *we* were Joel's family, me and the boys. She was nothing more than a distraction to him.

The shape moves, morphs into something else… a black bin bag fluttering in the light breeze. Now I can see that the edge of it is trapped inside a dark grey wheelie bin.

I breathe out. So much for a sinister crouching figure.

Get a grip, woman, I scold myself.

I decide to give another drink a miss, and after checking that I've locked both the front and back doors, I go upstairs to bed.

I wake about 2 a.m.

I used to sleep really well until Joel died but I don't think I've slept through the night since.

I always feel tired when I go to bed and drop off to sleep OK, but then I wake in the early hours and often lie awake for ages afterwards, sometimes not getting back to sleep at all before the morning alarm sounds.

I visit the bathroom, and then, without really thinking about it, I pick up my phone and open up Facebook.

As I wait for Daniela's profile page to load, I silently berate myself. I had a little blip at the hospital on Saturday, but I refrained from logging in at all on Sunday.

Still, I don't close it down, and my screen fills with photographs of her. There's been no new post since the brunch one on Saturday, but hey, it seems I'm in the mood for a bit of self-torture, and so I take another look.

I use my fingers to expand close-ups of her teeth, her eyes, her flawless skin.

The voice in my head begins its endless criticism.

She's pretty much perfect.

No wonder Joel found her so attractive. You couldn't compete with that.

Her life looks amazing, so why has she decided to barge back into mine?

I close Facebook and force myself to replace my phone on the bedside table.

George and I had such a good time tonight; it really felt like we were getting on well. It's early days, I know that, but do I dare to imagine – to hope – that this could be a fresh start for me and the boys?

He's handsome, kind, generous – everything I thought I'd never get again.

I felt so good about myself a few hours ago, and now… now it's business as usual, and I find myself wondering how I ever believed that someone as good-looking and successful as George Mortimer could possibly be interested in somebody as ordinary as me.

Could I really fit into George's world?

In that split second, I make a deal with myself.

I'll give it everything I have. For once, I'll try and convince myself I can be happy again.

All I have to do is really believe it.

17

The next week seems to fly by.

I contact the company who manage my tenancy.

'We can't discuss the sale of a property with the tenant due to data protection laws,' the receptionist says snootily when I ask if they have a buyer. 'You'll be informed in due course of any changes as per your tenancy agreement.'

Steph came round one evening with a bottle of wine after the boys had gone to bed. 'To cheer you up,' she announced.

'It's going to take more than a couple of glasses of that to come anywhere close.' I grudgingly accepted a glass but all I really wanted was to be alone.

'You've been quiet this week,' she says. 'Is everything OK? You coping all right with the boys?'

It's so irritating when she constantly checks up on me like this. Always presuming the worst, too.

'Yes, I've been working on setting a few more yoga classes up in the area. But maybe I'm wasting my time, I might not be living around here for much longer.'

'You don't know for certain Daniela knows you live in that house,' Steph said. 'It could just be a horrible coincidence.'

'You're right, it could,' I say peevishly. 'But I reckon about a million to one it's not.'

Of all the streets and houses in Nottingham, Daniela has picked ours. She's obviously back to cause as much trouble as she can for me.

At least my plan for Brenda and Leonard to look after the boys comes off perfectly, and George drives us to a lovely traditional pub out in rural Leicestershire.

We share a ploughman's platter and a bottle of wine and talk about our kids and how they're coping without their respective parents. I barely think about my problems closer to home.

'Romy doesn't mention her mum; she was just a baby when Lucy died,' George confides. 'But I always feel she has this... I don't know, this sense of sadness about her, somehow.'

'A sadness at six years old?' I say, feeling my heart prickle for little Romy.

'We had twins, you see,' George explains. 'Identical twins. But Romy's sister died within a week of her birth.'

My hand flies to my mouth. 'Oh no! That's desperately sad. Do you think subconsciously she misses her sister on some level then?'

'As a physician it would be easy to discount the stuff people say about twins and their "shared mind", a sort of extrasensory perception they're meant to possess. But as her father, I have to admit she acts sometimes like she knows something is missing.'

He tops up our glasses with the excellent New Zealand Sauvignon the bartender recommended.

'What about the boys? Do they miss their dad?'

'Kane, not really. He was so young, like Romy. But Harrison, definitely, yes. He keeps Joel's photograph on his bedside table and kisses it every night before he goes to sleep. Joel was a really great dad...' My words tail off. A great dad, but the crappiest partner imaginable, as it turned out.

Before I realise I've decided to, I tell George how Joel died.

'It was cruel and quick in the end.' I stare down at my plate. 'There was a time when we believed he'd beat his illness, but in the end, it wasn't to be.'

George tips his head and looks at me. 'I don't want to make you feel sad, Darcy. We don't have to talk about this stuff.'

'No, it's fine. It's not that I feel sad; it's… well, it's complicated.' I swallow a gulp of wine. 'A conversation for another day, I think.'

He nods. 'For my part, I never saw it coming either. I knew Lucy had been depressed after the death of Romy's twin. It was only to be expected. We got her professional help, though, and when I had to go back to work, her parents were supportive of her, so she was never alone with the baby for long.'

He falls quiet, thinking back. I wait in silence for him to continue.

'One day while I was at work, I got a call from Lucy's dad. They'd found her in the garage of the family's holiday property in North Yorkshire. She'd taken her own life.'

A shiver travels from the back of my head to the bottom of my spine.

'How awful.' I feel truly drained when I hear this. And I thought I had it bad! Poor woman, and poor, poor Romy. 'What about your family in all this? Were you supported?'

'My father retired to Portugal fifteen years ago. I've been out to visit him a couple of times but… I'm not sure he really wants me there, to be honest. He's in his late eighties now, but he was never the affectionate sort. Mum died when I was young.' He says it quickly, as if he wants the words out and done with. I sense it's best not to probe him for more details. Then he reaches for my hand. 'We've both been through it, Darcy. But let's not dwell on the past now; let's look to our future, our children's future.'

I smile and nod, taken aback by him referencing a shared future so early on.

When we get back into the car, ready for the drive home, George turns in his seat, cups my face and we share a long, lingering kiss.

His lips are soft and caress mine with the utmost care and respect. His discreet sandalwood scent and the warmth of his body so close to mine send me into free fall.

When we finally move apart, all I can think about is when I'll see him again.

On Wednesday afternoon, Lady Luck is on my side, as another opportunity seems to fall effortlessly into place.

Steph calls to ask if she and Dave can take the boys bowling on Friday evening.

'They can stay over at ours if that's OK; it'll give you a bit of peace if you want it, what with all your new classes.'

'That's perfect, thanks, Steph. The boys will love it.'

A large room has become available for rent at a village hall just a couple of miles away and I've been busy drafting flyers for a couple of new midweek yoga classes. It's not an ideal environment for a relaxing, calm session, as the facilities are shared with a playgroup and their battalion of toys are stacked around the walls, but it will do for now. And the classes are already two thirds full on pre-bookings, so the extra income will come in handy.

I'm feeling better about myself. It might be early days, but I'm already eating better, and my mood has improved tenfold.

If only Daniela Frost would do one, life would be pretty much perfect right now.

'Cool. Me and Uncle Dave can play *Call of Duty*,' Harrison boasts when I tell them of Steph's offer. He bites back his words when he realises what he's said.

'That game is rated age eighteen and over, isn't it?' I frown.

Harrison shrugs. 'I'm not a baby. It's fine, Mum, everyone in my class plays it. Everyone knows the violence isn't *real*.' He throws his brother a sly glance. 'Auntie Steph says Kane's far too young to play it, though.'

'I don't care, I'll play *Fortnite*,' Kane says tartly, folding his arms. 'Better than all that blood and guts and brains and—'

'That's enough, thank you!' I wrinkle my nose.

I keep reading about the addiction problems with games like *Fortnite* too, though. The boys haven't got a PlayStation at home, just a Nintendo Switch each, but Harrison hardly uses his as he says it's for little kids.

I know I'm going to have to look at getting him something a bit more sophisticated, probably for Christmas. He's growing up so fast and I don't want him to feel left out when his mates have all got the latest gaming paraphernalia. It's so tricky to find a good balance.

I decide I should speak to Steph about what they're exposed to at her house, though. She's a super-cool auntie but she doesn't have any kids of her own, although it's not through lack of trying. She's been trying to get pregnant as a device to force Dave to finally settle down. They've been together for ten years now, but according to Steph, Dave has 'unresolved issues'.

'His mum repeatedly left home when he was a kid and it's left him not trusting women,' is how she flippantly explains his refusal to get married and have children of their own.

But I know it bothers her. She dashes around doing stuff for other people and sometimes I think things like suitability of material just doesn't occur to her when she spends time with her nephews. She just wants them to enjoy their time there. It won't do any harm to make her aware of a few guidelines I'd like observing when the boys visit her house. Not so easy to find a way to say it without offending her.

When George dropped me home on Tuesday evening, we agreed to meet up again on Saturday. But when this child-free option becomes available, although I know he's working until 8 p.m. all week, I decide to be bold and text him to ask if he'd like to come over to my house for supper after work on Friday.

His reply pings back within minutes.

Best offer I've had all day!

My plans for a simple supper seem to take on military levels of planning of their own accord. I scour online recipe websites, leaf through cookbooks I haven't touched for years and finally, in desperation, even think about buying in something posh and ready-made from the small Waitrose in town.

George is bound to have sophisticated tastes. His housekeeper is probably a very skilled cook and this is my chance to impress him.

Eventually I calm myself down and plump for something upmarket but simple: a whole Camembert baked with sprigs of rosemary and thyme and served with slices of crusty bread and a side salad. It's home-made vanilla cheesecake for pudding, a favourite of the boys that I haven't made since last year. *Voilà!*

'This is so good.' George closes his eyes and, I can't help but notice, speaks with his mouth full. I tell the boys off for doing the same thing, but tonight, I don't care. I have melted cheese, chilled white wine and a gorgeous man. Nothing else matters.

'Glad you like it,' I say laconically, sipping my wine and thinking how much blood, sweat and tears went into just choosing which dish to serve him.

'Oh yes, I could definitely get used to this.' He winks at me, sending a little shiver of goose bumps down my back, as if he's actually traced my spine with his fingertips.

'It's not always this easy to get time off being a mum.' I grin. 'I've just been lucky that Joel's family have offered me lots of help this week.'

George nods and breaks off another piece of bread before dunking it into the cheese. 'What are they like, your in-laws?'

I hesitate, wondering how much to tell him. I don't want to get into the whole 'Joel and his betrayal' thing. My instinct is to keep it brief and polite, but George and I are getting to know each other. And you can really only do that if you take a risk and open up a little.

'They've been fantastic to me and the boys since Joel died. I don't know what I'd have done without them,' I say honestly.

George looks at me, his eyes twinkling. 'Do I sense a "but" coming?'

'Not really.' I trace the rim of my glass with a fingertip. 'But…'

'Ha! I knew it was there somewhere.'

I laugh. 'OK, you got me. They've been amazing, but now I'm ready for a bit more space, and it's starting to feel awkward. Hiding *us*, I mean.'

'They'll take it badly?'

'Not necessarily. Steph, that's Joel's sister, and his mum, Brenda… Well, they've always made it clear that it's too early for me to start rebuilding my life. In terms of dating again, I mean.'

'That sounds entirely unreasonable to me and a bit controlling, if I'm honest. It's been four years now, after all.'

'Hmm. They do like things to be on their own terms,' I sigh. 'They're so used to being involved in every area of my life, I think they'll be floored when I tell them I've met someone special.'

I think about the time they had to take over custody of my sons because I was a complete dysfunctional wreck and I feel a shaming heat rush up to my face.

George picks up his wine and leans back in his chair, watching me.

'Brenda and Leonard adore Kane and Harrison; they spend a lot of time with them. As Joel's family, I think they might feel a bit strange when they know there's another man in the boys' lives, that's all.'

How did I end up saying all this personal stuff? I've got ahead of myself, it's too much for our very new relationship.

'I mean… I'm not saying you're in their lives yet. That's ridiculous, it's far too soon! I just meant…'

George reaches for my hand, envelops it in his own.

'I know exactly what you mean, Darcy,' he says softly. 'You should start to take control of your own life again ready for when you do tell them about us. Their primary concern is bound to be the effect our relationship has on their grandsons. But hey' – he squeezes my hand again – 'don't look so worried. They're all just going to have to suck it up, right?'

'Right.' I laugh, but my heart is heavy when I think about what their reaction might be.

Then the full of the implication of his words dawns on me. He fully expects our relationship to get serious.

And probably quite soon.

18

1995

If he thought his ordeal was behind him when he came back to school three weeks later, he soon realised he was sadly mistaken.

After his 'fall', which is how both his father and the school referred to it now, he'd told the janitor who found him at the bottom of the bell tower that he had lost his balance and although the man had looked sceptical, the school seemed happy to accept his explanation without further questions.

'Could I go to a local school now?' He'd asked his father. 'There are people from the village and I'd be closer to home and—'

'Impossible.' His father had blustered. 'I work away too much and there's nobody here to look after you.'

'I'm thirteen.' He protested. 'I don't need looking after.'

'Not up for negotiation. It's inconveniencing me enough you're back now.'

It took some time before his injuries had healed to the extent he could return to St Mark's. After breaking his right leg and fracturing his left arm, he was still on crutches.

His father sent his luggage to school separately at the weekend and he got the six o'clock train back down on the Monday morning, preferring to do that as opposed to arriving the night before to get 're-accustomed', as his father had suggested.

There were still four months to go until the end of the academic year so he was sent back to the same class as before the accident, Form 3A.

On that first morning back and after registering at the school office, he hobbled into the classroom and felt cheered that the first person he saw was Kelvin. Even better, there was a spare seat next to where Kelvin now sat.

As he made his way across the classroom, the hum of conversation dropped and all eyes focused on him. When he was a few steps away, Kelvin picked his bag up from under the desk and placed it on the vacant chair next to him.

At that moment Mr Sherwin came into the class and instructed a boy at the front to vacate his seat.

'Now you don't have as far to limp,' the teacher said in a jolly manner.

At break time, he made sure he stuck close to Kelvin when the class emptied. He moved much slower because of his leg and tapped Kelvin on the shoulder.

'What do you want?' Kelvin snapped when he turned around.

'I just… I just wondered if you were around at lunchtime?'

Kelvin looked around the busy corridor and swallowed.

'No,' he said. 'I'm not around during break time or lunch time or any time for that matter. Get it?'

He nodded, flabbergasted. Kelvin walked away but after a few paces, he turned around again, his angry expression now regretful.

'The Panthers gave me a choice,' he said in a low voice, his eyes darting around to check who might be watching. 'I took the coward's way out. I'm sorry.'

And then he was gone.

*

During the first couple of weeks back, he slowly caught up with his schoolwork again. Mr Sherwin had sent work home throughout his time off and that had helped him ease back into his lessons again.

In fact, lesson time was easy. Breaks and lunchtimes and the evenings were by far the worst.

He had spotted the Panthers gang marauding around the school grounds and he knew, from their shouts and nudges, that they had spotted him, too.

It was exhausting, constantly being on one's guard. He never relaxed, not even at night when he slept in a dorm quite apart from where the Panthers and the other older boys boarded.

But their reach was long.

One night he climbed into bed, his body aching and heavy, longing for the temporary release of sleep, to find his bed soaking wet. When the other boys started laughing and someone snapped on the lights, he saw his saturated sheet was stained yellow. The urine had soaked through to the mattress.

During the day he was on high alert, never walking anywhere before checking out the surroundings. Once he was out in the open, journeys took three times as long, a combination of his injured leg and the fact he stopped often to check behind him and all around him, especially in places where people could easily hide.

This constant surveillance, paired with his physical injuries, exhausted him.

Despite this vigilance, on his third day back, the Panthers ambushed him when he turned the corner into the quad.

'You really must be more careful and watch where you're going,' one boy said, standing so close their shoulders touched. 'Clumsy oaf, falling down the stairs like that.'

Sniggers from the rest of the group.

His heart pounded harder when the tall, blonde boy pushed his way to the front.

'I want to know why you came back at all.' He pushed his face closer. 'Why didn't you just curl up and die, or run away like a coward… like your mother?'

He lifted his chin in disdain and for a moment, the boy braced himself to throw his body weight back, certain he was about to be headbutted.

But after a guttural noise, a large blob of gob hit his left cheek, just below his eye.

Every day after that, the tall boy spat on him, sometimes without saying a word. As the first couple of weeks went on, he found himself relieved at the act because he knew, after that, he could get on with his day.

But at the end of lessons, anxiety gripped him like an icy hand around his throat the second the bell sounded. He felt sure that on several occasions, he'd seen Kelvin glance sympathetically in his direction.

It was difficult, on crutches, to skulk around until most people were back in lessons and to use the longest routes around the school to avoid the busiest areas. At the end of his first week back, he was last out of history class. He made his way steadily down the corridor, keeping his eyes on the double doors at the end. The corridor was dim and his crutch made a tapping nose on the tiled floor.

As he drew closer to the exit, he suddenly felt disorientated, unsure of which way to walk. He stopped and leaned against the wall, shaking, gasping for air. His crutch fell to the floor with a clatter as his heart hammered with sickening irregularity against the wall of his chest.

It was his first panic attack and one of many. That night he telephoned his father.

'I'm struggling, Father. They're giving me a hard time here.'

He heard his father speak to someone in the background.

'Sorry, I'm still at the office. What did you say?'

'Could I come home, find another school? I'm struggling here, not quite fitting in, I'm afraid.'

His father's laugh was hard and hacking.

'The school maketh the man, mark my words. If you give up when the going gets tough you'll achieve precisely nothing in life.'

Someone spoke again at his father's end.

'It's just… I didn't tell you everything, about the accident, I mean. It wasn't really what I said… a fall, I mean.'

'My meeting's about to start,' his father interrupted. 'Look, you're due for an interim home visit in a weeks' time. We can chat then.'

It was true the principal had agreed he could take a few weekend home visits for a while, to help ease him back into the routine following his long absence.

'Bye, Dad,' he said faintly but the silence told him his father had already ended the call.

Things did improve slightly when he discovered a surprising oasis in the middle of all the danger; he found a new passion for the library.

His previous aversion to reading disappeared almost overnight when he began to devour books, his favourite being in the non-fiction genre, during the difficult lunchtime period and often after school.

He found he was particularly enthralled by books about World War II, in which he knew his great-grandad, an army doctor, had served his country. He sat for many hours in the relative peace and warmth, feeling safe amongst the myriad of bookshelves.

Mrs Dunmore, the school librarian, soon got to know him by name and made a point of setting aside any new books she thought might pique his interest.

One day, he spotted a book on Mrs Dunmore's desk. He stared at the title. Still in its plastic shrink wrapping, it had been marked for immediate return to the publisher. An elastic band secured a white note that bore Mrs Dunmore's handwritten words: 'Unsuitable for this age group. Do not resend.'

While she was stamping and categorising new books over the other side, he sauntered by the desk and slipped the book inside his rucksack.

He'd been skipping eating tea in the main hall for a few days now. He soon got used to the hunger pangs and he didn't mind the solitude. At home, he'd been used to his father retiring to his study until late – no interruptions allowed, his father always said, 'unless your hair is on fire' – he sat alone, in the lamplight of the lounge and read the book from cover to cover.

19

The boys are getting ready to go over for a kickabout in the garden later with Leonard, but Brenda calls me first thing.

'I'd like to ask the boys something, if you don't mind, Darcy,' she says.

I put the call on to loudspeaker. She often talks to them directly like this, and it's usually to propose something nice, so I have no problem motivating them to gather around the telephone.

'Harrison, Kane... are you there?' Brenda's voice calls out.

'Yes, Grandma,' they chime in unison, their faces alight with anticipation.

'Grandad's been offered late tickets to go the Nottingham Forest footie game and he wants to know if you'd like to go with him and then come back here for a picnic tea and a camp-out overnight in the playroom?'

Sure enough, there are whoops of delight and squeals of approval. During the finer weather, Leonard often pitches a tent in their large garden, and in the winter, it moves into the playroom.

I've never understood why the boys prefer to sleep on the floor in a tent rather than in the comfy bunk beds they have at their grandparents' house, but there you go. That's kids for you.

'I'll take that as a yes then, shall I?' Brenda laughs.

'Thanks, Brenda,' I say, genuinely thrilled that my boys are so happy.

'Nonsense,' she says brightly. 'We love having them, as you know. What are you going to do with yourself? If you want to come over, you and I can—'

'Honestly, I've got lots to do,' I say quickly. 'There's paperwork from my new classes to sort out, and it'll be quite nice to have a bath and read a book or something. Thanks for the offer, though.'

'Well, if you change your mind, you've only to say. I expect you've been worrying about the house sale.'

Harrison looks at me, alarmed.

'The boys are still in the room, Brenda,' I say meaningfully. 'Probably best we speak about it some other time.'

'Of course.' She pauses, then, 'Len and I just want you to know, if you do need to move, there's always space here for you all so don't think you'd be—'

'Thanks Brenda, I appreciate that. Must dash.'

The boys call out their goodbyes and when the call has finished, Harrison sidles up to me.

'Why did Grandma say we might have to move house?'

'Oh, it was to do with something Auntie Steph said the other day. Nothing for you to worry about, pudding.'

I gather together a few discarded items of clothing from the sofa and chair and head for the stairs. But Harrison is not to be dissuaded.

'I like living here in this house,' he says firmly. 'Dad used to live here, too, and I don't want to move away.'

'I don't either,' Kane echoes from the Lego tower he's currently building.

'I hear you both,' I say, non-committally.

Try telling that to Daniela Frost.

'I'll come and pick you up,' George says. 'I wanted to ask…'

'Yes?'

'There's no pressure whatsoever, but if you'd like to' – he sounds uncharacteristically awkward – 'you can stay over. At mine. Or not… that's absolutely fine too.'

I'm silent for a moment, and then we both burst out laughing, which feels like a relief.

'I made a bit of a mess of that, didn't I?' I can imagine him cringing at the end of the line.

'No! It's fine.'

'Really? I wanted to ask, but if you feel it's too soon, or—'

'I'd love to,' I say quickly before I can talk myself out of it.

'You would?'

'Yes, I would.'

'That's amazing.' He blows out air. 'Pack an overnight bag and I'll be there to pick you up at eleven.'

I put the phone down and immediately start to feel sick. I wish I'd lost a bit more weight before he sees me naked. Have I got any razors to defuzz… and what about decent underwear? And I'm so pale! The ancient bottle of Fake Bake wedged at the back of the cupboard is bound to have gone off.

I push the negative thoughts from my mind and focus on getting the boys ready.

I'm relieved when Leonard turns up at 10 a.m., bang on time as usual. He's carrying a large brown box.

'This was on your doorstep.' He sets it down on the floor. 'Organic vegetables with the looks of it. Very healthy!'

I frown and pull out the delivery note attached to the top.

Welcome to the family. Thank you for subscribing. This first delivery is FREE!

I shake my head. 'I haven't ordered this,' I say.

'They must have got it wrong,' Leonard shrugs. 'Sent it to the wrong address.'

But my name is on the address panel, too. I push the box away with my foot.

'Have a lovely, lovely time at the football,' I tell them all. 'Hope Forest win.'

The boys kiss me and troop outside eagerly, but Leonard hovers at the door.

'Bren and I were just saying, love, we haven't seen much of you recently.' He looks sheepish, and I wonder if Brenda has put him up to questioning me. 'Is everything all right? Are you coping? We heard about... the house problem.'

'Yes, fine!' I say, a bit too brightly, ignoring the reference to my inadequate parenting skills again. I'm conscious of little ears listening in. 'Everything is fine, Len. Just busy, you know?'

'Busy. Yes, of course.' He turns to follow the boys, and then looks back at me. 'Brenda told me about Daniela coming back. She's...' He seems to be choosing his words carefully. 'She's worried this will set you back again, you know... make you ill again, like before.'

I stand stock still and stare at him.

'I was grieving, Len. Trying to deal with betrayal, too, if you remember.'

'I know you were grieving, love. We all were.'

He's been well schooled by Brenda in the art of skirting around any unpalatable references to Joel's abhorrent behaviour.

'There'll always be a place for you in our family, Darcy,' he continues. He hesitates before sticking the knife in. 'But we do feel for Daniela too.'

I bite down on my back teeth, but there's no stopping the words that rush forward.

'Well you shouldn't be sympathising with her at all,' I say in a low voice. 'Joel belonged to us, me and our sons, not to her. You'd do well to remember that.'

He opens his mouth to say something, but I hold up my hand, signalling that I don't want to hear it.

Silently he turns, pale-faced, to follow his grandsons outside, and I swallow down a bitter bile that rises in my throat.

I stand there in the kitchen and glare at the brown box at my feet. Another job on my list to sort out. Had someone played a trick on me? If so, it was a stupid thing to do.

If so, whoever it was knew my name and full address.

Something dark and predatory slinks through my guts.

20

When the boys had gone outside to play, Leonard walked into the kitchen and saw immediately that his wife had been crying.

He felt a twist of guilt knowing he could have spared her this pain, but he'd decided that honesty was the best policy. Brenda needed to be aware what was at stake here. If things became unpleasant, it was crucial his soft-centred wife was onside.

'Come here, love.' He held out his arms and she fell into them, pressing her face against his chest.

He kissed the top of her head and inhaled the scent of her, the heady mix of white lavender and jasmine he loved. She'd smelled the same since the day he met her when she'd been the prettiest girl on his A level English course at Nottingham College.

Leonard himself had been muscular and strapping, whilst Brenda had been slightly built and curvaceous. They'd both changed over the years; age came to everyone, didn't it? That was just life.

They took the view that reaching their late sixties was a bonus to be celebrated. Too many people these days fought against it, putting their energies into chasing the elusive fountain of youth. Meddling with their faces and bodies surgically instead of just enjoying life. Enjoying *family*.

Without physical work though, Leonard's muscles had deserted him. Now, when he looked at his reflection in the bedroom mirror in his boxer shorts, he looked pale and stringy, with pigmented patches all over his skin. 'A bit like a runner bean past its best,' he'd suggested to his giggling wife only last week. At least they could still laugh about getting older.

Brenda had filled out into her womanly shape and had a little too much padding here and there, as she always complained. But to Leonard, she was perfect. Just as beautiful, in his eyes, as the day he'd met her.

They loved each other deeply and had always been loyal and true in their long marriage.

They had loved their son even more, if that were possible, and when he had died, it had ripped a piece from both of their hearts. Those wounds would remain raw until the day they met their own maker and were reconciled at last with their boy, Joel. They held on to that.

But Leonard and Brenda's saving grace, their reason for living in the early months after Joel's death, had been the love and joy their grandsons brought to their lives. Every time they saw them – which, thankfully, was frequently – each lad grew a little more like his father in different ways.

Young Kane had Joel's physical characteristics – the hair, eyes and mouth – and Harrison had inherited his father's build and sporting prowess. Looking at those boys felt like Leonard and Brenda's own future looking back at them, and nothing and nobody could be allowed to get in the way of that. That's what he'd explained to his wife before he told her of the plans that were afoot.

Brenda had sniffed and leaned into him.

'If you're right, and she's purposely distancing herself from us, we can't risk losing the boys, Len,' she murmured, on the verge of tears again. 'I'd rather die than let her keep us from seeing them.'

Leonard stroked her hair. 'That's not going to happen, Bren. I'll never let it happen, you know that.'

'But you can't stop her! I read about it all the time in my magazines: grandparents becoming estranged from their own flesh and blood.' Brenda pulled away from his embrace, her eyes flashing. 'It's our responsibility to ensure they're safe. Sometimes, I wish we'd never agreed she could take them back.'

'We did what we thought was right for the lads,' Leonard remarked.

'I worry, though. She seems of sound mind but still can't accept the reality of what happened. However crazy Darcy is, she's their mother and we'd do well to remember that. Whatever happens, we have to carry on. We can't let the mask slip.'

'Leave it to me and Steph, Bren. Trust us to sort this out… if it even comes to that. Perhaps we're worrying needlessly.' Leonard stared over his wife's head and watched his two grandsons, both wearing their red and white football scarves and gloves Brenda had bought them from the market yesterday. They were chasing each other around the garden, their breath leaving a frosty trail in their wake. 'Under the circumstances, Daniela coming back here might just be the best thing that could happen.'

21

An hour after Leonard takes the boys, I make sure I've turned everything off and locked the back door, then I pick up my overnight bag and handbag and step outside. I pull the front door closed behind me and walk down the path to George's gleaming black Audi.

He gets out and meets me at the car, taking the large bag to stow in the boot. He's wearing jeans and a thick knitted navy sweater that looks brand new. He smells of soap, and the ends of his hair are still damp from the shower.

'You look gorgeous as usual,' he says, planting a kiss on my lips.

I'd hardly call it gorgeous exactly, but I have made an effort, wearing my new denim skinny jeans and knee-length flat black riding boots. A simple knitted mustard sweater and an old leather jacket from the back of the wardrobe that sponged up decently complete the look I'm aiming for. Casual but well put together, I hope.

I washed and dried my shoulder-length brown hair before the boys left, so had time to style it with the curling tongs to show off my new caramel balayage.

'Did the boys get off OK?' he asks.

I nod, pushing away thoughts of my disagreeable exchange with Leonard. 'Did Romy?'

'Oh yes, although I had to call her back for a kiss and a hug before she left.' He grins.

Romy has gone to a play park for the day with a little friend and her family. 'They're extending it into a sleepover,' George told me when he called earlier.

We get in the car and he leans over for another kiss.

'And you know what they say. While the cats are away…'

My stomach churns, and I pray it won't start gurgling the way it can sometimes do when I haven't eaten for a while. I'm so out of practice with this dating game, I'm bound to embarrass myself in some way.

George lives in Papplewick, a village around a half an hour's drive from the city centre.

We chat amicably about this and that on the way there. Then, out of the blue, George ups the ante.

'Are you happy to stay put for the day, seeing as we have time to ourselves?' he asks. 'I plan to pan-fry us a couple of rib-eyes later, rather than eat out, if that's OK with you?'

'Sounds perfect,' I say happily.

We chat about this and that and in what seems no time at all, the car is slowing. George points a fob at a single wide wrought-iron gate and it begins to slide open. The car sweeps up a short driveway and comes to a stop outside an imposing stone house complete with a small turret at one end.

'Wow, you didn't say you lived in a castle,' I joke lightly when I get out of the car, but suddenly I do feel quite small and insignificant.

'Hardly.' He grins. 'It might look sixteenth century, but it was only built about fifteen years ago.'

There he goes again, with that humble, easy manner, making me feel I'm good enough, when the old 'less than' feelings stir inside.

Inside, the house is immaculate, not a thing out of place. I look around the spacious hallway as I slip off my shoes.

'Oh!' I start as a figure appears at the bottom of the stairs.

'This is Maria, my housekeeper,' George says. 'Maria, this is Darcy.'

She is a handsome middle-aged woman with short dyed hair, tall and broad shouldered. She wears a dark dress and a white full apron.

'Hello, Maria, pleased to meet you.' I offer my hand and she takes it.

'Welcome to the house,' she says rather formally. 'I'm just leaving for the day but I hope to see you again soon.'

'She looks like a proper housekeeper,' I remark to George when Maria leaves.

'She's a godsend,' George says. 'Housekeeper, nanny, cook and cleaner all rolled into one. She's a member of the family.'

'How sweet,' I tease him and he slaps my backside lightly.

He reaches behind me and hands me a small white bag with the Apple company logo on it. 'So you can read my text messages properly.'

I open it up and peer inside. A brand new iPhone and the latest model no less.

'George! I can't believe it!' I lift out the box and stare at it. 'This must've cost a fortune. Are you sure?'

'Do you like it?'

'I love it! Thank you.' I kiss his cheek.

'That's all that matters then. Now,' he takes the bag and places it back on the hall table behind me, 'fancy a drink?'

'Give me a guided tour first, please,' I say brightly, as if the grandeur doesn't phase me. 'I want to see every room!'

We start downstairs.

'Kitchen is hand-made and the floors downstairs are all reclaimed wood.' George is matter-of-fact; there's not a hint of a brag about him as he shows me around the cream Shaker-style units and the huge island with a sink and induction hob in the centre of the room.

'Heated, too,' I murmur, pressing my socked feet into the solid warmth beneath them.

He opens a heavy oak door and I step inside a large, bright room with an enormous log burner. At the far end, an oversized wooden table with chairs and a matching bench sits before bifold doors that lead out to a large deck.

'Living room, dining room,' George says, already leading me back into the hallway, where he opens another door. 'Games room.'

'What?' My mouth falls open at the sight of a full-size table tennis set up and a big television screen on the wall complete with a gaming console equipment shelf underneath it and scattered bean bags. 'You realise that when the boys see this room, you'll have made friends for life, whether you want them or not?'

He laughs, disappearing out of the room. I rush after him.

'Downstairs loo.' He points to a door and starts to climb the stairs.

He shows me several bedrooms and an enormous bathroom with a whirlpool bath, and then leads me into a huge bedroom overlooking the garden.

'And this is the master bedroom,' he announces, sweeping his arm low as I follow him in. 'This is where the magic happens.'

He bursts out laughing, and I do the same, even though my stomach does a little flip when I see the super-king-size bed with its padded floor-to-ceiling headboard. It's very impressive, but after years without intimacy, I'm not sure I'll be able to live up to a room like this.

George points out the en suite and dressing room as we walk back out to the landing. 'And that's it,' he says, as if it was all no big deal.

I think this is where I'm supposed to pretend it's all no big deal too, but it is. It's a very big deal. I don't say another word, but under my clothes, my skin crawls. I don't even know how to act.

George reaches out and pulls me to him, and we kiss, there on the light airy landing. Our kiss begins gently and quickly progresses to become passionate and wild. In the space of a few seconds, my entire body is burning from the inside out.

He takes my hand and leads me back into the bedroom. He presses a button on the wall, and the window blind closes and a soundtrack begins to play.

I look into his eyes and I see my future looking back at me.

But you don't belong here, the voice in my head insists.

I peel off my sweater, and George pulls me over to the bed.

22

'Daddy, why aren't there any pictures of Mummy up on the walls?'
Romy said, brushing the violet tail of her My Little Pony toy. 'Like
there are at Sophie's house, I mean?'

George looked up from his case file, stunned. He felt the muscles
in his face tighten. Sophie was Romy's little friend at school who
was being raised by her father but also partly by her aunt. Her
mother had died just last year and Romy had visited her aunt's
house for tea for the first time yesterday.

Aware that his daughter's eyes were still on him, he wiggled
his taut jaw and smiled.

'But we have so many nice pictures up there already, darling.
Ones we've both chosen.' He turned and looked to his right at the
longest wall in the lounge. 'There's the woodpecker print that you
chose from the craft fair last year, remember? And then we have
that nice painting of the church in the village where you sang in
the school carol service last Christmas.'

'Yes, but there are none of Mummy! Sophie's aunt has lots of
her mum up in the house.'

George nodded, biting his tongue. He'd made the mistake of
visiting Lucy's parents' house in France just after her death. Martha
and Colin's house was like a shrine to Lucy. Totally understandable
on the one hand. She had been their adored, only daughter, after all.

But George had always felt there was also something about it that stopped life moving on in a healthy way... it felt morbid, having the walls so completely swamped with Lucy's image at the expense of anything else at all.

Starting at the front door, the images showed Lucy as a baby, Lucy winning the egg and spoon on her school sports day, Lucy accepting a reading prize at senior school. Then the photos tracked, via the slightly claustrophobic hallway, her journey through college, university and finally her graduation with a 2:1 in the History of Art at Newcastle outside the lounge door.

George had pondered before if their entire wedding album was represented in the rooms of the house: up on the walls, in solid silver frames and on the digital photo slideshows that Martha had installed in every room, upstairs and down.

They had tried, in the early days, to get him to agree to Romy staying in France with them during the school holidays but he had soon put paid to that. His daughter was generally happy and settled and their morbid attitude would be a bad thing to inflict on her.

They'd visited the house a couple of times last year but contact had dropped off to a bare minimum now as both suffered from various health complaints.

'You have a lovely picture on your chest of drawers of you and Mummy holding you, don't forget, darling.' George reached for something comforting to say as he thought about one of the rare photographs he'd taken of Lucy holding newborn Romy. 'She watches over you every night as you sleep.'

Romy put down her pony and folded her arms, looking out of the window.

'When I told Maria, she said you have lots of pictures of Mummy packed away in boxes and that really, they should be on the walls,' Romy said archly. 'Then we could see her every day in all the rooms and it would be like she was still here, with us.'

Maria was sharp and George knew that nothing escaped her eagle eye. Usually, the housekeeper kept herself in check admirably but he might have to have a word with her about this photograph business. She had her feet firmly under the table here and it wouldn't hurt to remind her who was in charge.

Romy spent a lot of time with Maria and recently it had been more than usual because of him seeing Darcy. George had passed it off to Maria as a need to attend departmental meetings at work about the possible effect of Brexit on medical services and supplies. Everything else seemed to be being blamed on Brexit these days, why shouldn't he join the doom-mongers?

Anyway, Maria had seemed to think it a worthy excuse and hadn't batted an eyelid. He felt certain she believed that's how he was spending his time without Romy. Now he'd introduced Darcy to her, however, she would probably realise why he'd been absent more than usual.

Maybe her comments to Romy were her way of showing her displeasure at having another woman around.

Tough luck on Maria if so because George was thoroughly enjoying Darcy's company. She'd been a bit starry-eyed when she visited the house for the first time a couple of days ago, wanted to look around all the rooms. She'd oohed and ahhed in all the right places, it was quite sweet really.

George didn't really see the house itself any more but he supposed it was quite a special home. He'd had such wonderful plans to settle down with his family there at one time…

Darcy told him she'd just found out the house she rented had been sold and, as yet, the management company hadn't told her whether this would bring her tenancy to an end. She'd put on a brave face, maintained she wasn't too worried about it but George saw the shadow that passed over her face. A big upheaval was always a worry when you had kids to consider.

Once she'd had a bit of a tour around the house, Darcy seemed to completely forget the grandness and, for all the interest she took, they could have been in a grubby little bedsit, holed up together. And George had loved that, appreciated her lack of materiality.

Lucy, for all she was a wonderfully caring wife and mother, was the opposite. She coveted new and beautiful possessions almost constantly.

If George bought her a beautiful bracelet as a gift, she immediately had her eye on the matching necklace. If they refurbished a room in the house – new carpets, the latest furnishings and colour scheme – before the paint was even dry, she'd be planning the next area of the house to needlessly improve.

George had taken it all in his stride. It wasn't Lucy's fault, she'd been brought up that way. Always given the best, taught that if something hadn't got a designer label attached and cost the earth, it wasn't worth having.

Worst of all, Martha and Colin had cursed their daughter as a child with the deeply held belief that material possessions brought happiness and the more of them you amassed, the happier you'd be.

Heartbreakingly, Lucy had found out far too late, at the end of her life, that this was a fallacy. When little Esther – Romy's twin – died, Lucy was blind to every single item she'd worshipped before

'Can we get the boxes out then, Daddy?' Romy brightened and stood up. 'Can we look at the pictures of Mummy and Esther together?'

'Of course, darling,' he said, although there were no photographs of little Esther. He closed the case file he'd been working on and patted his knee. Romy skipped over and perched there for a moment.

George kissed the top of her head, sniffed in the scent of fruit shampoo.

Everything he wanted was just a hair's breadth away from him.

He wouldn't let anyone ruin it this time.

23

Over the coming weeks, George and I enjoy movie dates at the Broadway cinema, and I'm delighted to discover he loves independent films just as much as I do. We see *The Mousetrap* at the Theatre Royal, and George, who knows the manager, arranges for us to meet the cast afterwards as a surprise.

Our dates are a welcome distraction from the impending house move. If Daniela really has purchased our home – without even viewing it, it seems – then we'll be moving out, simple as. Even if the lettings company tells me we can stay, I've no intention of giving her the chance to wield power over me and my sons.

I've been looking at Rightmove and set an alert up for suitable properties coming up to let in this and surrounding areas. There doesn't seem to be much about at the moment, probably too near to Christmas. I'm sure I'll have better luck in the new year though.

I'd be far more worried if I hadn't met George and was sitting at home dwelling on the situation, worrying about our fate. As it is, we've been seeing each other every couple of days or so.

Sometimes meeting up means grabbing a quick coffee or a Pret sandwich in between dashing around during everyday life, just so we can continue to touch base. Occasionally we manage to spend a night together when our childcare synchronises.

We've been able to schedule in a couple of dinners while our respective families babysit, citing work reasons for being late home. I don't feel bad for the little fibs, it's better than the alternative. I will tell Joel's family about George but it will be when I'm ready.

Before long, the inevitable subject is raised.

'Let's tell our kids at least,' George says, his face open and hopeful. 'We should be enjoying time together, not sneaking off when they're out of the way.'

'I agree, it does feel a bit like that,' I say. 'But people would say it's still early days, wouldn't they? I mean, we haven't been seeing each other for long.'

'Who cares what other people say or think?' George frowns. 'Look, it's Christmas in a matter of weeks. Why don't we spend it all together?'

My throat begins to ache. Without fail, the boys and I go to Brenda and Leonard's every year, Christmas Eve through to Boxing Day. Steph and Dave are there too, and Brenda always places Joel's photograph on the table. 'So Daddy is here with us too,' she tells the boys.

This year, she hasn't even asked if we're going over there for Christmas, she's simply assumed that's the case. She's mentioned one or two things to me in passing, like her menu choices, and the presents she's considering buying for the boys.

It's gone way past mentioning that we're thinking of doing something else this year.

To be fair, over the past few years we've had nowhere else to go and I've been very grateful that Joel's family make a big effort to make Christmas a fun time for Kane and Harrison.

For me, it's always an ordeal. Those three days seem to drag on and on. Joel's name is centre stage, and Brenda gets out all the photographs and takes the kids through Daddy's childhood once again, with every hint and trace of what he did to us neatly airbrushed out of the conversation.

George takes in my expression.

'I suppose you and the boys usually go to your in-laws for Christmas?'

I nod. 'I can't imagine Brenda's face if I just announce out of the blue that we won't be there. She started planning it in early September.'

George laughs, but grows serious again when he sees my expression.

'Look, I don't want you to worry about it. Let's not discuss it for now. I've flagged it up, so just have a think.' He sighs. 'We're doing nothing wrong here, Darcy, don't forget that. Your in-laws have been caring and kind, but now we have a chance to make a fresh start together. All five of us.'

'And I do want that,' I whisper. 'More than anything.'

'Then we have to make it a priority, even if people's feelings may be hurt initially. Trust me, they'll handle it.' George speaks gently, and I know he's right.

True to his word, he changes the subject, and after a quick discussion, we decide it's definitely a good time to introduce our kids to each other. After a lengthy debate about what they might enjoy the most, Bounce, an indoor trampoline park attached to a local leisure centre, wins out.

'Cool,' Harrison says when I tell him. 'Who did you say we're going with?'

'Just my friend George and his little girl, Romy. She's the same age as Kane.'

Harrison looks up from organising his football stickers and wrinkles his nose. 'A *girl?*'

I bite back a smile, amused that he's immediately picked up on Romy but not batted an eyelid about my 'friend' George.

'Is it Dr George who helped me at the park, Mum?' Kane pipes up. 'The one you took a thank-you card to?'

'That's right.' I nod, impressed by his perception. 'We've got to know each other a bit since then, and we thought it might be nice to all go out together. For our kids to meet each other.'

'But how have you got to know him?' Harrison asks distractedly, staring at the television. 'You haven't seen him since we were at the park.'

Kane looks at me, full of mischief. 'He's not your *boyfriend*, is he, Mum?'

Here it is, the moment I've been worrying about. Once I tell them, I can't very well ask them to lie to their auntie and grandparents.

But do I come clean right away and tell the truth, or let them meet George first and see how nice he is before I break the news that we're in a relationship? Kane was really young when his daddy died, but Harrison remembers Joel well and often asks me stuff about him plus Joel's family talk about him non-stop whenever the boys go over there. It's a sensitive subject.

'We're good friends and we think you guys will get along together really well too,' I say lightly. 'It's just a nice day out for us all. That's OK, isn't it?'

'Suppose so.' Harrison shrugs, seemingly not quite as enthusiastic all of a sudden.

I chivvy the boys along into my little Fiat and we arrive at the leisure centre. As we park up, I spot George and Romy standing at the entrance. They're deep in conversation, Romy looking up at her dad and George nodding and using his hands as he explains something to her. He's mentioned many times that she is quite the chatterbox, naturally inquisitive about the world around her and bright as a button too, by all accounts.

It makes me wonder what her mother, Lucy, was like. He's spoken about her a little, as I have about Joel. Our focus is on each other and our children for now, rather than our pasts, and although I know there will come a time for me to tell George about everything that happened after Joel's death, I feel instinctively that we haven't yet reached that moment.

'There he is.' Kane points at George. 'There's the doctor who helped me at the park.'

'That's right.' I smile at him. 'But he's just our friend George now, so you don't have to call him Doctor or anything like that.'

I glance at Harrison. He's not looking over at George and Romy but staring down at the pavement in front of him, scraping at the ground with the toe of his new training shoe.

'Don't do that, Harry, you'll ruin them.'

He ignores me and carries on.

George spots us and waves. He takes Romy's hand and says something to her, and she presses shyly into his side as they walk towards us.

'Here they are!' He smiles at the boys. 'Kane and Harrison… have I got that right?'

'Yes, you helped me to breathe again at the park,' Kane states simply.

'Well, you did most of that yourself.' George winks at him. 'You were a tough little soldier.'

Kane grins up at me.

'Your brother gave us quite a scare, didn't he, Harry?' I squeeze my elder son's hand, and he nods but doesn't look up.

George holds out his hand. 'I'm George.'

Harrison reluctantly shakes hands, and his eyes dart quickly over George's face before he studies the floor again.

'And this is my daughter, Romy. Say hi, Romy.'

'Hi,' Romy says shyly. She smiles, and dimples spring up at the edges of her mouth. She is adorable, all dark blonde curls and big blue eyes with a peaches-and-cream complexion.

I haven't yet seen a photograph of George's late wife. It's a bit strange he hasn't got any photographs up in the house but I suppose everyone has their own way of dealing with things. As George is dark-haired with brown eyes, I'm betting that Romy has inherited her mother's colouring. No doubt she was a very attractive woman, I think miserably.

Inside, we queue for our tickets and the children take off their shoes, as it's socks only on the apparatus. They sit side by side, saying absolutely nothing to each other as they fiddle with buckles and laces. I feel the muscles in my neck start to pinch.

'Hey, relax.' George touches my cheek. 'It's bound to be a bit awkward at first, but you wait and see, we'll all be best mates by the end of today.'

I nod and smile, wanting to believe him.

Romy is a little nervous when we reach our designated trampoline. 'Don't worry, princess,' George tells her. 'Harrison will take good care of you. I'm betting he's going to be great at this, right, Harry?'

Harrison gives a curt nod and reluctantly takes Romy's hand as she struggles to keep her balance on the trampoline. And then the most amazing thing happens. Within minutes, he transforms into the perfect big brother, patiently helping Kane and Romy with their bouncing technique while showing off his own fancy double somersaults that I had no idea he could do.

He shrugs off our compliments at the end of the session. 'We have trampolines in the sports hall at school.' But I can see he's secretly pleased with the attention.

Afterwards, in the café, we have burgers and milkshakes, and George makes the kids laugh with stories from when he was an A&E doctor in the early part of his career.

'He had a baby's *potty* stuck on his head?' Kane howls theatrically and mimes falling off his chair.

Harrison snorts and almost chokes on his milkshake.

'It's true!' George insisted. 'He'd had a few beers and was dancing around the living room trying to keep his kids entertained. The potty got stuck fast because of an unusual suction effect, and his wife had to drive him to the hospital.'

Afterwards, when we're getting ready to leave, Kane and Romy are busy chatting about their favourite game on Nintendo Switch, and Harrison is deep in conversation with George about the best way to train for performing an advanced back flip.

I hang back a little and savour the sight. And I realise that for the first time since Joel died, I don't feel quite so hollow inside.

The boys say goodbye to George and Romy and I give Kane the remote control to open the car while I have a few last words with him.

'It's been a lovely day, I couldn't have wished for it to go any better.'

'The kids get on just as well as we do,' he agrees as Romy climbs into the Audi, waving to me.

'I've decided something while we've been here, today.' I take a breath. 'I'm going to tell Joel's family about us. Now the boys have met you and Romy, it's probably only a matter of time before they say something that gets Steph or Brenda's ears burning anyway.'

'That's great news.' He beams.

I feel exhilarated, like we've reached a really important landmark in our relationship.

We both turn, the moment ruined by yells of outrage from the boys.

'Ugh, look what someone's done to our car, Mum!' Kane rushes up, clamping his hand over his mouth.

George locks Romy in the car for safety and rushes past the seven or eight parked cars between our vehicles. When he reaches my Fiat, he stops dead.

'What is it?' I call, catching up with him. 'Oh!'

'What's that stuff all over it, Mum?' Harrison pulls a face and sticks out his tongue in disgust.

The car bonnet is covered in what looks like oozing, bloody bits of flesh. It looks like I've hit an animal. I'm too shocked to speak for a moment but George steps forward, bends down to scrutinise and, to shrieking outrage from the boys, wipes some up with his fingers and brings it up to his nose to sniff it.

'Tomatoes,' he murmurs. 'Rotten, squashed tomatoes, that's all it is.'

'That's all it is? It still shouldn't be all over my car... who would do this?' But I'm answering my own question before George can speculate.

I spin around and scour the car park and the leisure centre entrance for any sign of Daniela Frost. Who else could it be?

I turn to George, burning with fury rather than fear now. But mindful of the boys listening, I pull back the curses about to trip off my tongue.

'What is it, George?'

He looks like he's seen a ghost. His face is pale, his mouth a short, tight line.

'Nothing.' He seems to collect himself. 'I... it's just a shock that someone would do this.'

'Too right. If I'd have caught them doing it I'd have rubbed their nasty little face in it.' I think about Daniela's perfect make-up and how satisfying it might be to carry out the threat.

'It's probably just local kids,' George remarks.

'Strange it's completely isolated to my car though,' I add, feeling another spike of heat inside. There's not so much as a speck of tomato on the vehicles parked either side of mine. 'You're right though, whoever's done this is immature and pathetic.'

George nods. Shifts his weight from one foot to the other.

If I didn't know better, I'd think there was something he's keeping from me.

24

She doesn't realise it, of course, but I'm actually trying to help. Trying to stop all this nonsense before it's too late.

I follow them everywhere. I could show you spreadsheets with all the details: when, where, time and length of stay… I'm sure a small part of them would secretly be impressed if they knew.

You might wonder why I go to the trouble of logging their every movement? I shall tell you. The details might not mean much in themselves, but put them all together and you have a story. A narrative which clearly tells the tale of how and where they met, how their relationship grew so rapidly, how their children are being affected.

When I finally face her, I'll have all the evidence I need to illustrate that my actions are justified.

The simple fact of the matter is that she doesn't belong with him. She's getting in the way and acting so selfishly.

Her two sons are just pawns in the game. Defenceless boys who are being dragged along against their will.

Someone has got to help those children. Even if one of them gets hurt in the process.

Collateral damage… that's what they call it, isn't it?

25

'You're like a different person,' Steph says, watching me intently through narrowed eyes while I busy myself around the kitchen. 'You laugh more, you look... I don't know, *brighter*. Are you on a new vitamin supplement or something?'

Brenda nods encouragingly, and I laugh but feel a spike of nerves when I think about what I have to tell them both today: that I've been seeing someone and in fact am now in a full-blown serious relationship. Admitting that it's the doctor who saved Kane's life at the adventure park is just plain embarrassing.

Yet Steph is right. I *am* feeling much brighter and I *do* laugh more. I've started eating smaller portions and making healthier food choices, and as a result, I've lost five pounds. I've had my hair done and purchased a few new make-up items – a highlighter and a smoky eye pencil – and updated my look with the help of some YouTube 'how to' videos. Plus, I've found renewed enthusiasm for my yoga classes.

It's not much, but it's made a great deal of difference to my outlook. I keep catching myself thinking about the future in a positive light and it still feels like a novelty.

'I just feel... better than I've done for a while,' I say mildly.

'Are you coping all right, Darcy?' Brenda asks. 'With the boys?'

'Yes, Brenda,' I reply shortly. 'Oddly enough I am. Everything is fine.'

Brenda and Steph's exchanged pointed glance doesn't escape me but I ignore it.

I take the vegetable lasagne I made earlier out of the oven and place it next to a bowl of mixed salad. I carry a glass jug of sparkling water with ice and sliced lemon over to the kitchen table, too.

'Well, this looks like a lovely, healthy lunch.' Brenda beams as we take our seats. 'It's so nice to see you cooking again, Darcy. I'm glad you're feeling a bit brighter; it's been a long time coming.'

I glance at Brenda. Although she's being friendly enough, her words sound a bit stilted, as if she's over-thinking everything she says. They both seem slightly on edge.

When Joel was alive, cooking was my go-to activity. Not only for family necessity, but also as a way to wind down and relax. If I felt stressed, I'd make a batch of scones. If I wanted to take my mind off work, I'd bake a date and walnut loaf. Joel was always grateful and very complimentary about my culinary efforts, seeming to genuinely appreciate the effort I put in to creating every meal from scratch.

Occasionally, Brenda and Leonard would come over for tea when the boys were small, so she knows just how much I used to love cooking. But when Joel died, my enjoyment of it disappeared overnight – along with every other interest I had, come to think of it.

My nerves are jangling in my stomach now and the smell of the melted cheese from the steaming lasagne makes me feel a bit queasy. I don't feel remotely hungry, but I sit down and gulp half my glass of water, though my mouth still feels dry.

I've had to make a real effort to get myself looking decent this morning. I've barely slept, rehearsing endless ways in my mind of broaching the issue. My relationship with George is getting serious; I really can't put that fact off any longer.

'You've got quite a thirst on.' Steph points at my half-empty glass. 'Want me to serve the lasagne?'

I smile and hand over the large spatula. She stands up and wields it above the earthenware dish.

'It was a lovely surprise when you suggested lunch,' Brenda says. 'It seems a long time since we did this.'

It *is* a long time, I think a little guiltily. The three of us used to meet at Brenda's house about once a fortnight and share a light lunch. But the closer I've grown to George, the less I've wanted to do that sort of thing, largely because I haven't told them anything about my new relationship and it's easier to keep shtum when I don't have to see them. But also, since I've started to feel a little better about my life, their interfering nature has been harder to ignore.

Steph serves a large square of lasagne onto Brenda's plate and I slide the salad bowl over to her.

Brenda clears her throat.

'To be truthful, Darcy, I've been a little worried about you lately. You're fine today, of course but you've seemed so quiet and withdrawn – not yourself at all. Goodness, we've barely seen anything of you.'

She and Steph glance at each other before a slab of lasagne appears on my plate. It's true, I haven't called on Brenda as much and Steph hasn't had the boys at her house since the time I was supposed to have a word with her about watching what computer games they're playing. I never did get around to that conversation.

'On the plus side, you do look great!' Steph remarks cheerfully. 'You've lost weight, and your skin and hair are so healthy.' She pauses. 'Obviously benefitting from the extra time Mum and Dad have been looking after the boys.'

Irritation snatches at my throat at the obvious jibe. Things have changed for me, and I've taken a step back from Joel's family to get a healthier balance. But Steph and Brenda are used to telling it like it is, passing uncensored comment on my appearance and my life. Doling out advice without being asked.

It used to be OK; I even used to think of it as them showing me affection, reasoning that they cared about me and were just trying to help. Treating me like one of the family. But now I want my door keys back and I want a bit of space between us, like normal families have. The trouble is, I can hardly just come out and say all that in one go.

First things first.

'Cheers to our little get-together.' Brenda regards me as she raises her glass of sparkling water and takes a sip. 'This lunch is very well timed, actually. I want to run possible desserts for Christmas past you both. I'm thinking of getting one of those posh Christmassy creations from Marks and Spencer. The boys will like that.'

I take a sip of my own drink and the bubbles feel like razor blades when I swallow. I take a breath and begin to speak before she can hijack the discussion with her Christmas lunch plans.

'It's brilliant to get together again, but I asked you here because there's something I want to tell you.' My voice comes out bolder than I intended, and both Steph and Brenda look up in mild alarm.

'Is everything all right?' Steph ventures. 'Are the boys—'

'The boys are fine.' I say from behind gritted teeth.

'Darcy, what is it?' Brenda says faintly. 'You're not… ill again, are you?'

'No. I'm not ill, it's nothing like that.' I put down my fork and clear my throat. 'I wanted to let you know that I've met someone. I'm… well, I've been seeing someone. For a while now.'

26

My words echo in my ears, bouncing off the walls with nowhere to land. Brenda's mouth drops open and she stares at Steph.

'But you told me you weren't remotely interested in dating!' Steph exclaims.

'Things change,' I say gently. 'It wasn't planned.'

'Is this relationship *serious*?' Brenda asks nervously, as if she can't handle an affirmative reply.

'How long have you been dating?' Steph demands before I can answer.

A flare of resentment burns inside my chest. Why do I feel as if I'm talking to my big sister and my mother? I only wish I *had* got my own family to confide in then I wouldn't have had to rely on them so much.

'I've been seeing him a few weeks, that's all. And yes, I'd say it's quite serious.'

I take another gulp of water so I don't have to look at Steph's horrified expression.

'And does he have a name, this *boyfriend* of yours?' Brenda presses me.

'His name is George.'

'George,' she repeats thoughtfully. 'Where did you meet him?'

I open my mouth and close it again. I didn't expect the Spanish Inquisition. I knew they'd be taken aback, but I feel like I'm fighting them off. It's ridiculous.

'I didn't meet him online, if that's what you were thinking.' Every time Brenda reads a story in the news about someone who's come to a nasty end at the hands of a psychopath she's met online, she calls me and reads it out like a cautionary tale.

I see realisation dawn on Steph's face.

She snorts. 'Don't tell me... it's not George the doctor, from the play park?'

'As a matter of fact, yes. It's George the doctor.' I press my fingers down on the table and keep my voice calm and level. Inside, my innards feel like a churning stew, and I can feel my face burning.

'Who is George the doctor?' Brenda frowns, completely lost now.

'You remember, Mum, he treated Kane at the park when he had his asthma attack.' Steph doesn't take her eyes off me as she speaks. 'Darcy was embarrassingly smitten by him from the moment she saw him.'

I let out a high-pitched laugh, but she's hit a nerve. 'I was very grateful to him, if that's what you mean.'

I wish I could make my own voice a little frostier when Steph barks out a question, but every time I try, a slew of moving pictures fills my mind: Brenda comforting me at the hospital on the day Joel died; Steph postponing going out with her friends after work so she could mind the boys while I pulled the blankets over my head and hid away from the world.

These two women have been my rock when I needed them, but inadvertently over the past few years I've given them the impression they have the right to exert control over my life and influence the decisions I make.

I find myself wishing they'd just finish their lunch and go home. But I'm in waist deep, so I might as well get it over with now their hackles are up.

'He's a surgeon at the City Hospital, Brenda, and he lives in Papplewick village.' I'm babbling, trying to make amends for my uncharitable thoughts. 'I think you'll both really like him.'

Papplewick is an affluent village and is actually located close to Ravenshead, where Brenda and Leonard live, but I doubt that's any comfort.

'And have the boys met this *George*?' Brenda says his name like it's a tricky word she's never pronounced before. 'I mean, other than that day at the park?'

I nod. 'And they've met his little girl, Romy, too. She's the same age as Kane.'

'But they never mentioned anything about meeting your new boyfriend when I saw them yesterday.' Brenda raises an eyebrow.

'I didn't introduce him as my boyfriend per se,' I mumble. 'I just said he was my *friend*.'

'I see.' Steph's voice is thick with judgement. 'You've decided not to tell them the truth, then? Because if there's one thing we need to be absolutely clear on, it's that the boys' wellbeing is not negotiable. They've had enough upheaval as it is when Mum and Dad had to take them in to save them from foster care.'

I release my fork onto my plate with a clatter. 'I invited you here to tell you because I care about you both and I've hated keeping this from you. But I can do without the sarcasm, Steph, and I resent you implying I'd do anything that was detrimental to my sons.'

'Well, it's very good of you to come clean to us.' She turns on me, her eyes sparking. 'But I'm just wondering how many times Mum or I have put ourselves out to look after the boys when you're "busy" or "stressed", and actually you've just been out with your fancy man… your *surgeon*.'

'Steph!' Brenda reprimands her. 'No need for that.'

'We're idiots, though, Mum. I told you she's been acting weird for ages now.'

'I don't need your permission to date, Steph, and much as I value what you've all done for me, I'm not your responsibility.' As I say the words, I feel an unexpected rush of relief that spurs me on. 'I have every right to start a relationship without asking for your permission.'

'I thought we were friends!' Steph snarls. 'We've always talked about everything together, like sisters. But now you've obviously had your use out of me and Mum and have managed to get yourself into a full-blown relationship without saying a word to us.'

'It wasn't like that. I—'

'You're entitled to a personal life, Darcy,' Brenda says kindly. 'No need to apologise for that.'

'Not while we're putting our own lives on hold to mind her kids she's not!'

I glance at Steph and see that her eyes are blazing, full of disapproval. I've felt nervous about telling her today – I knew she wouldn't like it – but I didn't expect such a vitriolic reaction. It's shocked me to the core.

'Let's just all calm down a bit, shall we?' Brenda gives Steph a hard stare and then turns her gaze to me. 'If you've found someone you can be happy with, then I'm pleased for you, Darcy. But – and I have to ask this – do you feel well enough to deal with a new relationship yet?'

Here we go again!

'I feel *fine*. I've never felt better.'

Brenda smiles; patronisingly, I feel.

'Let me rephrase, Darcy, dear. I'm not just talking about your breakdown. You had some *confusion* after Joel died, we know that. It's been difficult for you to accept certain things, and I understand. We all understand.'

I'm close to boiling point, but I force myself to speak slowly and clearly. I'm not going to give her the chance to say I'm unhinged.

'There's no confusion, and I'm not ill any more, Brenda. Joel betrayed me and lied to me and I was very, very upset about that. Still am.'

'I've got news for you: you weren't the only one,' Steph says.
I ignore her.

Brenda smiles tightly. 'If that's how you've chosen to reframe it, Darcy, then—'

I bite down on my back teeth and pull air in through my nose. I can't let them get to me like this. 'All that has no bearing on my relationship with George, and that's why I wanted to tell you about him today. I didn't tell you before because I didn't know if it would come to anything but… well, we're close. Our relationship has become serious quite quickly.'

'Tell me about it,' Steph murmurs slyly.

Brenda's sudden maudlin expression, the sad cast to her vacant stare, pulls at my heartstrings and my anger evaporates. This bickering is doing none of us any good. It's obvious she must be thinking about Joel and the fact I'm moving on. And I understand that, to a degree, the fact that I'm dating someone else might feel like a betrayal of Joel's memory.

Then she surprises me.

'Darcy, I wonder if… Would it be possible for me and Len to meet George?' she asks tentatively, ignoring Steph's thunderous glare. 'It would be nice to get to know him, if he's to be part of yours and the boys' lives.'

'Of course, I'd love that.' I'm touched by her request. It doesn't feel like she is asking to approve my choice of boyfriend; she sounds more concerned with staying part of our lives, and that's completely natural. The boys are her only link to Joel now. 'We'll sort out a time we can all get together. You and Dave too, if you like, Steph.' I feel the tendons in my neck give a little as it seems we've all come to a bit of an understanding at last. 'Now, shall we tuck into our lunch?'

'No thanks.' Steph pushes her plate away. 'Strangely, I don't feel hungry any more.'

27

1995

A week after stealing the book, he had read through it, digested its grim content five or six times.

Entitled *The Suicide Diaries*, the book spoke to him. Its stories and descriptions filled his mind, had this way of making him feel less alone… there were other people who felt this way, people who felt as wretched as he did!

Even when he wasn't reading it, somehow it seemed to soak up all the available space in his head. He barely noticed his classmates' sniggers now, the way they turned their backs when he walked by and sometimes lingered, hoping, on occasion, to join in with a conversation or two. The way he felt so completely and utterly alone.

Since the accident, as he'd come to conveniently think of it, he'd been unable to sleep more than an hour or two before waking in the early hours bathed in sweat, his heart pounding. His clothes all hung from his newly skinny frame – which he'd disguised thus far with the use of belts and baggy shirts and sweaters.

Worst of all was the lack of interest in everything he used to enjoy. Watching sport on television with his father was one of the rare occasions they spent any time together on his weekend visits home but eventually, after numerous excuses, his father had now stopped asking.

He couldn't get excited about anything any more. He'd wondered endlessly what was wrong with him. He hadn't a clue... until he read the stolen book.

Then, and only then, did he realise he was not alone and moreover, he controlled his own destiny.

The book taught him that many people secretly felt this way. He had arrived at the swift realisation that there was, in fact, a way out his living hell after all.

One Friday evening, just minutes after he'd arrived home for one of his short visits, he mustered the courage to tap on the door of his father's office.

There was a brief silent pause before his father bellowed, 'What is it?'

He opened the door a crack, enough to crane his head around.

'Sorry to interrupt you but... I wondered if I could borrow your library card?'

The furrows in his father's forehead dissolved.

'Oh, is that all?' He opened his desk drawer, dug around and brought out what looked like a plastic credit card. 'Interested in reading now, are you? A late developer, huh?'

His father's tone was mocking as he picked up the heavy cut-glass tumbler and took a draft of whisky from it.

When the boy's mother had been alive, that same tone, that same whisky, had often pre-empted one of his father's violent episodes, causing his mother, with her silent coded look, to send him up to his room immediately.

He'd lie on his bed with his pillows over his head and hum loudly but it still did not stop the sounds of his mother's pain. He had felt useless, terrified and he had hated him. Had hated himself for his inability to save her.

Yet in that moment, at the office door, he suddenly wanted with all his heart to impress his father.

'I've been reading books about World War II,' the boy said quickly, stepping into the room. 'The history is interesting and I know that Grandad—'

'Just take it, haven't used it in years.' His father held out the library card. The skin on his knuckles looked red and raw. 'Close the door on your way out.'

The next day, free of his crutch at last, he'd caught a bus and called in at the large library in town.

He approached the librarian who most closely resembled Mrs Dunmore and gave her what he hoped was a winning smile.

'Hello, I'm a student at St Mark's,' he began, watching as the private school connection worked its magic. Her slightly suspicious expression gave way to a friendly smile. 'I'm doing a project about suicide, methods used and reasons people do it. Very sad it is, harrowing. But I wondered if you could help me find possible titles on the subject?'

Within ten minutes he had borrowed two books and the librarian had ordered him in three more to collect on his next visit home.

28

Brenda and Steph don't stay long after my big revelation. They don't even finish their lunch.

I clear the table and tidy up in the kitchen, and then take a coffee into the living room and stare out of the window at the frosty hedge.

I feel so knotted up inside. Completely unsettled.

I don't know why they keep asking if I'm unwell. I feel perfectly fine. And as I keep telling them, grief and anger aren't illnesses. I had good reason to feel all the emotions I did, regardless of their own denial about Joel.

What is it about mental illness that makes you feel as if you can never put it behind you? A bad day, a low mood, vegging out and eating junk food in front of the TV… perfectly natural occurrences for most people but for Joel's family, these are all signals that I might not be well. Worse, perhaps even signs I could be neglecting my parental responsibilities.

This puts pressure on me. Pressure for me to keep smiling through problems, pressure for me to accept their interference and not to challenge their advice. To be the perfect mum twenty-four-seven.

It's enough to drive me back to pulling the covers over my head and staying put in bed for the whole day… or the whole week, as was the case at my lowest ebb.

They assumed custody of the boys back then for all the right reasons and I'm so grateful they got us through that awful time. I just don't need to be reminded of it on a weekly basis.

It's true the doctor prescribed me some sedatives even after I'd recovered from the breakdown as quality sleep remained elusive, but I wasn't on them for long, just a month or so. He also gave me some antidepressants. Non-addictive, he said.

They made me feel as if I was watching life from behind glass. I still remember that feeling, and I don't mind admitting I quite liked it at the time. It was a relief, a sort of buffer from the pain.

That was when I confided in Steph about my online activities. She and Brenda had taken the boys to the park one day and she came back unexpectedly after a few minutes for Kane's gloves. I jumped like a startled deer when she let herself into the house.

It was obvious I was up to something, so I just came out with it and told her I was monitoring Daniela's activities online.

'What… you mean like *cyber-stalking* her?' She seemed shocked, but my embarrassment was blunted by the medication, and I simply laughed and showed her the fake profile I was using to snoop anonymously.

Steph didn't mention it again, and I found that strange. I think it really worried her and she decided she would rather not know.

I was fine with that; it suited me not to talk about it. In fact, I never really gave it another thought. But on reflection, I wish I hadn't told her. I always feel she judged me and found me wanting after that, and now that she's obviously miffed about George, I regret confiding in her.

Life felt so much simpler and easier to deal with when, metaphorically, I sat a few steps away from all the drama and heartbreak.

When I'd finished the course of medication, I didn't go back to the doctor, despite Steph and Brenda urging me to do so.

'I don't think you're strong enough to deal with what happened yet.' I remember Brenda saying it as if Joel's double life was somehow partly my fault.

Someone beeps a car horn further down the street and I break my vacant stare.

I don't know how long I've been sitting here, but my coffee is lukewarm when I eventually take a sip. I can't drink it like that – I like it red hot – so I rest it on my thigh and close my eyes. When the letter box rattles, I jump involuntarily and spill cool coffee on my jeans.

I put the mug down and pull a tissue from my sleeve, dabbing at the mocha stain before scooping up the three envelopes on the floor.

It's fairly obvious that the two small letters are bills of some sort, so when I sit down again, I turn my attention to the large envelope. It's one of those reinforced ones with a sheet of cardboard inserted on one side.

My name and full address, including postcode, are printed neatly on the front.

I pull it open and extract the contents. Three photographs, but no letter.

I hold up the first one and study it. Just a load of kids at some kind of play area.

'Oh!' I drop the envelope and press my fingers to my lips as I peer closer at the colour image. Then I snatch up the other two pictures and study those.

The photographs have been taken at Bounce, the trampoline centre. There are kids I don't know in them, but Kane, Harrison and Romy are on one of the trampolines, and sitting on the right-hand side are me and George, chatting and laughing. In the final photograph, he's kissing me on the cheek.

Someone is trying to send me a message here. Someone wants me to know they are watching us.

And there's only one person I can think of who would get off on making me feel threatened and vulnerable.

Daniela Frost.

I change out of my jeans and stick them in the wash with a pair of Harrison's mud-spattered tracky bottoms. Then I take my laptop into the living room and open up Instagram.

Daniela has an open profile on Insta; anyone can look at it. But I still use my false identity to browse, just in case I click on a post by mistake and inadvertently 'like' it.

Her latest post is a selfie in front of one of the lions in the Old Market Square in the centre of the city. She's obviously back in Nottingham already.

A worrying thought occurs to me: what if Steph has mentioned my online snooping activities to Daniela? I've always trusted Steph like a sister, believed she wants the best for me and the boys. But her reaction to my news about George is so out of character, I'm not sure whether I've been naïve and gullible in that regard.

I log into Facebook next and wait for Daniela's profile to load. More photographs on here: she's shopping in Nottingham, drinking Glühwein and eating mince pies at the Christmas market. A smutty joke about the size of the bratwursts on the German food stall…

Perhaps she's heard on the local grapevine that I've found happiness again and has taken to watching me, waiting to see how she can wreck my life. It sounds extreme, but then people hold grudges for years, don't they?

After what happened with my car, I realise I'll have to speak to George about the photographs and confide in him about the awful events I so desperately want to leave in the past. My heart is heavy, but I can't escape the truth, and the longer I try, the worse it will sound when he does find out. I need to explain who Daniela is and why she seems so obsessed with getting even, to the extent she's going to the trouble of buying the house I'm renting!

But before I get the chance to call him, he sends me a link to a beautiful log cabin park on the North Yorkshire coast.

Fancy wrapping up warm and taking the kids to this wonderland for Christmas?

Far from worrying about what Brenda might have to say about it, my heart soars when I think about getting away from here.

There looks to be so much to do for the kids. An indoor heated swimming pool, cycle hire, and Christmas festivities with plenty of entertainment and family games.

There are bound to be lots of opportunities, when the kids are being entertained, for me to speak to George about Joel and Daniela Frost.

Before I can change my mind, I send him a message back by return.

Looks perfect. Let's do it!!

Mid-afternoon, George calls me, flustered after a short phone call from the hospital.

'Apparently there's another emergency meeting been called over this chap Joseph Hill, the patient with the failing kidneys. The powers that be want me there but it's Maria's day off and I'm picking up Romy.'

'You must go,' I tell him. 'I can pick her up, no problem. The boys are at after-school clubs but she can go back with me to collect them later. I'll give her tea at my house.'

'Are you sure? That would be perfect.'

'Of course I'm sure,' I laugh. 'It's no big deal and it will give me chance to get to know Romy a little better.'

George calls the school and lets them know I'll be picking her up.

When the classroom doors open out on to the playground, I walk up to the young teacher to introduce myself and she calls Romy over.

'Someone new to collect you today, Romy!' She beams.

Romy freezes and stares at me.

'It's OK, Romy, Daddy has had to go into work for a meeting. So me and you are going to have a little bit of girlie time now, how's that sound?'

The teacher crouches down at her level.

'Everything OK, sweetie?'

One or two of the other parents glance over as I stand there, feeling like a child-snatcher.

I hold out my hand. 'Ready to go, Romy? Thought we'd treat ourselves to a hot chocolate before heading home.'

She blinks and the faintest smile plays around her lips.

'That's better!' The teacher stands up again and Romy takes my hand.

'Can I have whipped cream and a flake in mine?' she says.

At the café, we huddle together over our hot chocolates at a small table at the back.

'Sometimes Maria brings me for treats after school but we don't say anything to Daddy,' she says, loading her teaspoon with whipped cream and popping it in her mouth.

'Is that so?' I smile to myself. The formal housekeeper has got a soft side after all, then.

'She reads me stories and plays snakes and ladders with me. I love Maria.'

'That's very sweet,' I say, touched by her openness. 'I hope we can become good friends too, in time.'

She nods and shovels in more cream and I imagine myself in the future, married to George with our three children. Romy is only six, young enough that I could be a proper mother to her and so she doesn't have to rely on the housekeeper for maternal affection.

I feel a growing hope that, if George and I get closer, she will fully accept me as such. Is that too much to ask?

When George calls at the house later to pick up Romy, he looks bright and happy. 'I've booked the lodge! I got a last-minute deal and ten per cent extra discount too, as they had just two cabins left.' He hesitates and then, in an apologetic tone, says, 'I'm afraid this means it's time to tell your in-laws that you and the boys won't be spending Christmas with them.'

When they've left, I steel myself and call Brenda.

'Are you free this weekend?' I ask nervously. 'I could bring the boys over, and George too… if you'd like to meet him?'

'That would be perfect! Could we make it Saturday afternoon?' I'm encouraged when Brenda sounds upbeat. 'Leonard and I are going to one of those turkey and tinsel events on Sunday.'

Just the mention of Christmas has me stammering.

'Great. We… we'll see you then, let's say about three?'

I put down the phone and take a breath.

It looks like I'm really going to go through with this.

29

George Mortimer walked into the room and Steph's heart did a little flip. She'd barely looked at him at the park that day, busy keeping Harrison distracted, and had quite forgotten how good-looking he actually was: textbook handsome, but with a relaxed and modest manner about him, and seemingly completely unaware of his own attractiveness.

His slightly wavy thick brown hair was immaculate but looked as if he'd combed it through with his fingers rather than grooming it with a comb or using products. A hint of stubble grazed his jawline and chin, and his soulful brown eyes – in Steph's opinion the *pièce de résistance* – were fixed on her beneath his thick, defined eyebrows.

When Darcy had confessed her secret dating a few days ago, Steph had googled him. Although Darcy hadn't mentioned his surname and Steph couldn't recall it, she did remember he said he worked in urology at the City Hospital.

His details had popped straight up then and when she clicked on the images tab, his photograph had been the first one.

'Urology surgeon?' Dave had said disparagingly, from over her shoulder. 'Mending prostates and bladders for a living… rather him than me.'

'I'm sure he earns a ton,' Steph had said drily. 'How's your job hunt going by the way?'

Predictably, Dave had mumbled something about his bad back and disappeared into the kitchen.

Dave swaggered over to George now, his tracksuit bottoms riding low below his muffin top.

'All right, mate? Welcome to the madhouse.' He offered his hand and George shook it and began to make small talk. Dave seemed distracted, looking everywhere but directly at George, and Steph had to bite back a snarl instructing him to sit down. He looked like a complete mess next to the other man's groomed appearance.

She glanced over at a smiling Darcy and felt a twinge of envy.

Brenda laid a hand on her chest. 'Welcome to our humble abode, George. I'm Brenda, and this' – she indicated Leonard, who was looming at her shoulder – 'is my husband, Leonard.'

'Pleased to meet you, George.' Leonard offered his hand cautiously. As soon as he'd shaken hands with George, he stepped back again.

Brenda made a fuss of the children and tried to strike up a chat with George's daughter. But the child kept dodging behind Harrison and would barely say a word.

Steph looked across at her mother and stifled a grin. There was life in the old dog yet, she thought mischievously, noting Brenda's wide eyes and slightly flushing cheeks.

But then she saw that her father looked concerned, and she remembered that this personable, intelligent man might be a threat to the plans she and Leonard had been discussing recently.

While the kids disappeared up to the playroom, the adults sat down on the comfy sofas, and Brenda buzzed around them serving drinks and nibbles.

Leonard asked George about his job at the hospital, and Steph wanted to know all about the operations he'd carried out.

'I'm a bit of a *Grey's Anatomy* addict,' she confessed.

George obliged with a litany of anecdotal stories, causing Brenda and Darcy to wince at several rather colourful descriptions of bladder operations. But when he announced that he'd signed the petition to stop the new housing estate on the outskirts of the village, he really hit the jackpot.

A slightly reluctant Brenda appeared to transform into his biggest fan.

She patted the seat cushion next to her. 'Come sit here next to me, George, and tell me what you think of our wonderful grandchildren. Your daughter… Romy, is it? She's adorable.'

Steph watched Darcy carefully and smiled. Her hands were balled into loose fists and she kept nibbling at her bottom lip. It was obvious she was feeling insecure. Perhaps this new life of hers wouldn't be so perfect after all. Surely a more confident career-type woman would be more George Mortimer's type?

Then, just as Steph began to think this was a relationship that probably wouldn't last, Darcy dropped a bombshell.

'There's no easy way to say this, Brenda and Leonard, and I do apologise in advance, but…' Her foot bounced incessantly on the floor. 'I've decided to take the kids away for Christmas this year. Just for a few days.'

There was a terrible silence for several seconds as they all took it in. George took a swig of his gin and the ice cubes clinked together like a clash of swords.

'But I've ordered the turkey now,' Brenda said. 'And the boys… they've never been away from us at Christmas time.'

'I'm sorry it's such short notice, Brenda,' George said kindly, seeing that Darcy was faltering. 'It was entirely my suggestion. I just feel we need some time together, the five of us. We're trying to make a fresh start here, and of course, we want you involved in that, as Kane and Harrison's grandparents, but—'

'It's fine,' Leonard interjected, ending George's slightly awkward speech. He touched Brenda's arm. 'It'll be fine, Bren. We'll see the boys before and after the big day, I'm sure.'

'Of course,' Darcy said quickly. 'You can have them over before we go, and then again after Boxing Day.'

Brenda sniffed into a hanky but gave a little smile and nod, and Steph watched the relief flood over Darcy's face. She really thought everything was settled. She really thought her new life would just fall into place as easy as that.

But Steph knew everything about Darcy, and she'd bet her bottom dollar George knew next to nothing.

The Darcy he was making his fresh start with bore no resemblance to the version Steph was accustomed to.

Perhaps someone ought to enlighten him.

30

'Phew!' When we all leave Brenda and Leonard's house and get back in the car, George wipes his brow. 'I got out alive.'

I laugh. 'Oh come on, they weren't that bad. I think you won Brenda over within minutes, and Steph seemed very interested in what you had to say.'

'Dave and Leonard didn't seem that impressed, though,' George remarked.

'Can't win 'em all.' I grin. 'I thought it went rather well, considering.'

'Considering what?'

'I dunno. Considering they all think I shouldn't even look at another man.'

George glances at me. 'Really?'

'That's what it feels like.' I shrug, and turn to look in the back at the kids. Romy's already asleep; Kane and Harry are poring over the Nintendo Switch. I lower my voice. 'I got a package of photos through the mail the other day.'

'Oh yeah?' George stares ahead, his hands on the wheel.

'Yes. Pictures of the five of us at Bounce. No letter or anything, just photos of us in there.'

George frowns and glances at me briefly before looking back at the road. 'How weird. Maybe they've got an official photographer there?'

'But how would they know my address! Besides, they have to have permission to take photographs; they can't just go around clandestinely snapping pictures of kids. And anyway, it's highly unlikely they'd be sending them out as freebies. No. Someone took those photos and then sent them expressly to show me they were there. Watching us.'

'Who'd do that?'

I don't reply.

'Darcy?'

'I'm not sure. Have you got any ideas?'

He sticks out his bottom lip. 'Can't think of anyone.'

The car is a neutral place, making it great to talk and this is the perfect time to broach the subject of Daniela before we get home.

But when I open my mouth to begin speaking, I find there are no words there at all.

*

The days leading up to our Christmas break at the lodge are a whirlwind.

We decide, in the end, to take most of our food with us, although Christmas lunch is laid on at a nearby pub, thank goodness. But ensuring all the presents are wrapped and tagged and that we've all got adequate warm clothing… I soon start to doubt our sanity in making such an immense last-minute decision.

From the moment we arrive, though, I know it was completely the right thing to do.

The park is nestled in the middle of a forest and the whole campus is festooned with white fairy lights and fake snow – to make up for the fact that real snow hasn't been forecast.

At the check-in desk, Romy and Kane are speechless with glee at the news that Santa will most definitely be stopping off here.

'You have to listen *really* carefully for the reindeer bells so you can run out of the cabin and wave, OK?' the young blonde receptionist, dressed in a short red and green elf dress, tells them enthusiastically.

Romy and Kane both nod vigorously, but Harrison looks a little more cynical. Still, he seems happy enough to play along.

I only realise during the check-in process that George has paid an extortionate premium to stay in one of the biggest and best lodges.

'I thought you said it was one of the last ones left?' I challenge him playfully.

'And that was the truth,' he says defensively. 'I just failed to mention that the reason it hadn't been booked was because nobody had been daft enough to pay a small fortune for it. Until I came along, that is.'

The cabin is stunning. Four double bedrooms, an enormous lounge complete with log burner and glass doors that lead directly out into the forest, plus a fully equipped dining kitchen. George laughs when I insist on taking a few snaps before we mess it up.

The kids' faces are a picture when they see the hot tub on the decking outside.

They disappear outside to take a look, squealing with excitement and at that moment, a text pings through on my phone.

It makes me smile and warms my heart. I feel both relieved and touched she wants to get back on an even keel again.

Sorry for being such a grump lately. Hope we can have lunch when you get back. Happy Christmas! Love, Steph.

I tap out a quick reply, attaching it to one of the snaps I took of the lodge.

Would love to! Lodge is amazing... Merry Christmas!

I turn off my phone then and drop it into my handbag before stepping closer to George.

'I have a feeling this is going to be the best Christmas ever,' I say, kissing him.

'I have a feeling you're right,' he replies, pulling me closer.

'Our kids are so lucky; they're going to love it here.' I look up at him. 'Is this what your childhood was like?'

'How do you mean?' He draws back a little.

'I mean that as far as childhoods go, mine was happy enough, but there wasn't much money spare. We never went anywhere like this.'

A shadow passes over his face, and his smile falters. 'No. I never did anything like this either.'

I'm worried that I've said something to upset him. 'George?'

'I'm fine.' He sniffs. 'My childhood was… well, I try not to think about it, to be honest. Put it this way, it wasn't the stuff of fairy tales.'

'I see. Sorry… Forget I said anything.' But my interest is piqued. George doesn't talk much about his past, and I suppose I'm equally reticent. But I'd always assumed, because of what he's achieved, that he must have had quite a privileged upbringing, with no shortage of money… or love, for that matter.

I want to feel I know him on a deeper level, and finding out about his life – as I know he'll want to know more about mine – is unavoidable.

One day soon perhaps he'll tell me more, but for now, I let it go.

I inhale his clean, subtle scent and bury my face in his shoulder. My whole body prickles with desire. I can't wait to get the kids to bed later and to spend some time snuggled up together on that big comfy couch—

'Mum! Mum!' Harrison runs in, breathless and alarmed. 'There's somebody out there in the woods… They tried to take Romy!'

George moves fast, and within seconds he's outside, combing the fringes of the trees.

'What happened, darling?' I pull Romy to me, but she clams up, her face startled and pale. She won't say a word.

'Kane was over there with Romy – they were standing by the wood,' Harrison tells me, understandably shaken. 'I saw someone moving in the trees right near them, and when I ran over, Romy started to cry.'

'Romy, what happened?' George says, a little breathless from his frantic search. He crouches down in front of his daughter, but she won't look at him. 'Kane, can you tell us?'

'You're not in any trouble, sweetie,' I reassure him. 'Just tell us what you saw.'

'We were collecting pine cones by the trees and a woman called us over,' Kane says, looking at George warily. 'She opened her handbag and said, "Hey, look at this." I tried to stop Romy going, but the woman held out her hand.'

'What did this woman look like?' I feel hot, and my mouth is bone dry.

'She had a hoodie on, but it was definitely a lady because she had nail varnish and I heard her voice,' Harry offered. 'She was about the same height as you.'

'I couldn't see her face,' Kane chipped in, 'because of her hood. But Romy looked at her.'

'Romy?' I turn back to her, but she is staring at her hands. 'This lady, can you describe her to me? What colour were her eyes?'

I suddenly realise I could show her a picture of Daniela Frost. Could Daniela have followed us here? Would she do that – be so desperate to ruin my chances with George that she'd try and abduct his daughter?

If I've put the kids in danger by coming here, I'll never forgive myself.

'Everyone inside,' George says grimly before I can question them any more. He takes Romy's hand and we shepherd the boys back in. 'We'll need to report this to the management.'

'Never mind the management, we should ring the police!' I say quickly. 'I dread to think what could've happened here if we hadn't got outside so quickly.' I take a breath and pause before speaking. 'There's something I need to talk to you about, George.

I should have told you before… It could have a bearing on what just happened out there.'

But George seems distracted and doesn't reply. He locks the doors, and digs out cookies for the kids from the food box. Then he calls me through to our bedroom.

I open my mouth to speak, but he puts up a hand to stop me.

'My turn to come clean first,' he says, his face a mask of tension and dread. 'I thought I had plenty of time to tell you, but it seems things have taken a turn for the worse.'

Then, with the kids safely tucked up watching TV in the other room, he begins to explain the nightmare situation to me.

31

George started with the sucker punch. There was no other way to do it.

'There's someone I need to tell you about, Darcy. A woman.'

'A woman?' she repeated faintly, shrinking away from him.

George sighed, pinched the skin at the top of his nose before looking at her again.

'I'm sorry, I really am. I should have told you all this before we got so involved. But I thought it would scare you off and—'

'Just tell me now,' she said. 'Tell me everything.'

So he told her. She listened, saying nothing, and he could tell she was trying her hardest not to seem shocked while all this *stuff,* this awful detail, spewed out of him.

'Her name is Opal Vardy.' He felt his mouth twist slightly. He could barely stand the name on his lips. 'I met her about eighteen months ago and she's tried to ruin my life ever since.'

'OK,' Darcy whispered, somehow managing to sound calm and unflustered, though George knew the probability was that inside her chest, her heart was galloping nineteen to the dozen. She looked as if she might throw up any second.

'Like you, I'd resigned myself to staying single for the foreseeable,' he explained. 'After the heartache of losing my wife, it felt like a positive decision, if you know what I mean. My life felt full enough with Romy and my career. It just seemed simpler not to bring anything or anyone else in to disrupt that.'

She nodded.

'Anyway, one night, after consuming a bottle of red wine by myself and feeling low, I ended up on an online forum for medical staff, just a way of like-minded people having a moan really. Folks can often get a bit political on there, and in hindsight, it was too close to home. In my senior position, I should've never done it.' He sighed. 'But I got chatting to a few people about shared concerns we had: funding problems and the never-ending cuts to NHS services. Then Opal sent me a private message asking if I was the same George Mortimer who worked at the City Hospital.'

'She already knew you?'

George nodded. 'I was shocked. Like an idiot, I hadn't realised my messages would appear under my real name.' He rolled his eyes at his own naïvety. 'I signed off the forum conversation then but ended up talking to Opal on private messenger. She was on the temporary staff roster, worked in the City Hospital archives and knew of me, but I didn't know her.'

He hoped Darcy could see how that might be possible. The consultants were very high-profile and respected throughout the hospital. They were right at the top of the medical staff hierarchy and visible to all staff.

'We chatted online for two or three nights that week, and it turned out Opal had been single for three years. We got on so well, I ended up asking her out for a drink. And it all went downhill from there.'

'So what happened?' Darcy swallowed. 'Are you trying to tell me that you're still involved with her in some way?'

'No!' He raised his voice, then softened it again. 'No. After that initial meeting, we went out several times, maybe four or five. We got on well, but it was just a casual thing. For me, anyway.

She was quite full-on, pushing me all the time to see her more. I explained my situation and was honest about the fact that I didn't feel ready for a full-on relationship.'

'And she was happy with that?'

'Seemed to be.' He hesitated. 'She said she felt the same way.'

Darcy wrinkled her nose, no doubt disapproving of the obvious 'friends with benefits' sort of arrangement he'd just described.

'Then one day, she came over to Urology to see me, and as she was hospital staff, they let her straight through. I didn't realise she was standing outside my office door. I was talking on the phone to another consultant, senior to me. Between us, we'd carried out a very difficult and lengthy procedure on a patient, and sadly the man had died on the operating table.'

He looked at Darcy to check she was following, and she nodded. But her guarded expression told another story, like she was wondering exactly where this was going.

'My colleague asked me, off the record, to tell him exactly what steps I had taken before I'd handed over to him, and I admitted I'd been forced to make a call about a certain course of action and it had turned out to be the wrong one.' George sighed. 'I didn't know Opal was listening. She could only hear my side of the conversation, of course; couldn't hear my colleague sympathising that such things happened and were part of the job and advising me to say nothing to the family.'

A few minutes after he'd finished the phone call, she'd tapped on the door and asked to see him.

'She said she'd had second thoughts and wanted us to carry on seeing each other but in a more formal relationship. I told her it would be nice to have a drink together sometime but that I thought our connection had come to a natural end and we should just try to get along as friends.'

Darcy recognised the obvious let-down line and George saw her cringe a little.

'And how did she take that?' she asked.

'Fine! She seemed to take it OK and her contract finished, so she left the hospital soon afterwards. That's when it all started going wrong.'

Darcy waited for him to continue.

'At first it was just little things I barely noticed: I'd turn up somewhere and she'd be there. Or I'd take Romy to a pizza restaurant and Opal would walk by the window and end up coming in to chat to us.'

He ran his fingers through his hair, shifted around in his seat.

'This went on for a few months, but there were long breaks in between incidents so I really didn't think anything of it. Then other stuff began to happen. Deliveries would come to the department for my attention that I hadn't ordered. I had a two-day conference in Scotland organised, and when I got to the airport, I found my flight had been cancelled without my authorisation. Annoying, inconvenient things like that.'

'And you think all this was Opal's doing?'

'Oh, I'm certain of it. I called her, asked if we could meet for a chat, but she was having none of it.' He laughed bitterly 'She actually accused me of bothering *her*. Said that we'd agreed to call it a day and I shouldn't be calling her!

'Then it shifted up a notch. Maria, my housekeeper, called me at work one day, said a woman had come to the door claiming to be my girlfriend. She wanted to collect some things I needed that I'd apparently sent her to get. She was quite insistent about gaining entry, but Maria had the sense not to allow her in, thank goodness. When I asked her to describe the woman, it was quite obviously Opal, and when I showed her a photo on my phone, she confirmed it.'

32

I stand up abruptly, suddenly dizzy with worry. 'You think it was Opal outside just now? It was her lurking in the woods?'

'No!' Then, 'I don't know, Darcy. But the kids are safe now. We're all inside.'

'That's hardly the point! Other families might be in danger if she's unhinged.'

'If it's her, I can assure you it's just me she's interested in. Nobody else.' George sighs. 'Please, Darcy, just sit down so I can finish. This will only take a few more minutes.'

I think about refusing and then sit down anyway. I feel a tiny flash of relief that it's not Daniela out there and I might not have to come clean to George after all. But that selfish thought is immediately superseded by concern about what he is telling me, concern for the safety of our children.

'As you can imagine, the fact Opal had tried to gain entry to the house while I was at work really spooked me, and I contacted the police. Just for some advice. It soon became clear that I had next to no evidence, and although her meddling was annoying and inconvenient, it wasn't endangering myself or Romy and she still hadn't threatened us in any way.' George shakes his head in frustration. 'It seems when a man is stalked by a woman – the officer I spoke to insisted on referring to it as me being "hounded" – it's received very differently. I wasn't *scared* by Opal, you see. Just annoyed.'

He pauses for a few moments and frowns.

'Like lots of people, I used to be a bit scornful of stalking complaints, used to think it was as simple as getting a court injunction against the culprit. But it turns out it's nowhere near that simple. Opal was so clever about it. She never showed up regularly or did the same thing twice so that other people noticed. The police told me they'd still have an informal word with her, if it would help, but I said not to bother. It wouldn't have done any good. And then she seemed to go quiet and I thought it was over.'

'I told you about those photographs at the trampoline centre… do you think that could be her? And the mess on my car?'

'I'd bet my life she's behind it, and I agree that it's creepy and it annoys the hell out of me. But again, there's no cast-iron proof it's her, and as far as the police are concerned, it's hardly life-threatening.'

I give him a hard look. 'Why did you try and pass those things off as being something innocent, George? You must have known how unnerved I felt but you came up with some excuse for both of them.'

George looks sheepish. 'I'm sorry. I suppose I panicked a bit because I had to explain all this in the right way. I couldn't just come out and say that I have a stalker; you'd have run a mile and I kept telling myself there could well be another excuse. That it wasn't her.'

He has a point. I have my own secret that I need to tell him about, but it's easier to put it off than bite the bullet.

'I'm sorry I didn't tell you what was happening before now, Darcy.' He hangs his head. 'I did think about it, several times. I swear. But nothing has happened for weeks or so I thought, until the photos and the car. I thought she'd finally got fed up, and I didn't want to scare you off.'

I hesitate. 'I've noticed other strange things happening over the last few weeks, George. Stuff I can't put my finger on and so I've not mentioned them to you.'

His forehead creases with concern. 'Like what, exactly?'

'I keep feeling like I'm being watched. During routine tasks like dropping the boys off at school, or once it happened at the supermarket: I felt certain someone was shadowing me, but when I turned around, there was nobody there and' – I laugh because it just seems so petty – 'someone signed me up to an organic veg box company.'

But George doesn't laugh.

'Sounds like Opal's signature all right. A couple of months ago, there was a slew of anonymous patient complaints about me at the hospital. Fortunately, there were no hard facts, just information anyone could have found out, and the administration board decided to discount them.' He shakes his head. 'I knew exactly who was behind them, but I couldn't tell the board what was happening.'

'Why not? If Opal is making a nuisance of herself, your employers ought to know.'

He looks pained. 'Nobody knows, and it has to stay that way. If they challenge her, she'll probably come right out and tell them about the complication in the operating theatre, which would be devastating for my career.'

'But you can't let this keep happening; our kids might be at risk. I think you should speak to your bosses, George, take her power away.'

His expression darkens.

'You have to trust me, Darcy. The hospital board like to appear very visible in supporting staff, but privately they'd be thinking, "How on earth did he get himself into this mess?" They'd start asking questions about my personal life, question whether I can be trusted in a more senior position. That's if they even believe me; after all, it doesn't sound like much when I say it out loud, does it? A woman walking past a restaurant window, or texting me when we're no longer seeing each other.'

'No, but trying to gain entry to your house when you're not there and attempting to abduct your daughter outside just now sound pretty worrying.'

'We don't know it's definitely her out there. And anyway, I can't drag the hospital into this, Darcy. I've worked too hard for too long and my big chance of promotion is coming up very soon. Surgeons are supposed to be immune to scandal of any kind; that's a well-known fact, even if it's never actually stated.'

I think he's probably right. The management of professional organisations are well known for raising a collective eyebrow if someone in a senior position becomes embroiled in a personal scandal. But still… what price is he willing to pay for his promotion?

'Can I see the picture of her?' George's expression is blank. 'Opal, I mean? So I know what she looks like if she… Well, you know, if she's hanging around here.'

He shakes his head. 'I can't bear to talk about the woman, never mind keep her photograph to hand. I've got one on my phone somewhere, probably take me ages to find it. But we can talk about all this later and I'll find out a picture of her. There's nothing for you to worry about, Darcy, it's me she wants to annoy. Any problems, let me know, but the last thing I want is for you to involve yourself.'

'If it's her who's hanging around in the woods trying to tempt our kids away, I'd say it's a bit more than just an annoyance.' A thought occurs to me. 'Let's get Romy in here and show her Opal's photograph if you can find it. That will clear up any ambiguity once and for all.'

George looks at me and presses his lips together, and I almost feel like taking out my phone and looking her up online right now.

'Let's just leave Romy to recover for a while. She clams up when stuff bothers her, and sometimes it can last days. That's not going to make for a very happy Christmas.'

I feel boxed in at every turn. Some of what George is saying just doesn't add up, but the last thing I want to do is have a massive row when we've just got here. If it is Opal out there, nothing would make her happier than ruining our Christmas.

'I know I should have warned you before, should've come clean so you had all the facts, and I'm sorry about that.' George touches my arm. 'But I thought Opal had stopped all this nonsense, truly I did, and… you and the boys are the best thing that has happened to me in a long, long time. I didn't want to scare you off. But I'll understand if you want out.'

A tangled ball of emotion begins to unravel inside me. I feel hot and tearful and I reach forward and grasp George's hand.

'I'm in it for the long haul,' I say. 'It will take more than Opal Vardy's silly little games to put me off, but I can't just ignore the fact that she might be out there.' I look fearfully out of the window. 'I'd feel better speaking to someone in charge here at least, so they're aware of what just happened. I have the boys to think about, George. She might try and get to you through them.'

'Look, I'll go and speak to the management now, OK? If anything else happens, I promise we'll go straight to the police, but she's probably long gone now and hey, it's Christmas! I want more than anything for us all to have a lovely time. I don't want the shadow of that woman spoiling our family time and I don't want the kids nervy and scared.' He hesitates. 'We're only here for a few days; let's make it count. After all, we can't be certain it *was* Opal out there.'

Daniela's face flits into my mind's eye and a dull ache starts up in the bottom of my stomach. Maybe it's *her* out there and I haven't said a word about that possibility to George.

He lets out a long breath and squeezes my hand when I nod.

'Thank you,' he says. 'Now. I'll make you and the kids a hot chocolate and then I'll go and speak to the manager. OK?'

'OK,' I say quietly, but the tightness in my throat tells me it's not OK at all.

33

Steph glanced at her watch and frowned. They had arranged to meet at ten o'clock but the person she was meeting was already ten minutes late.

She turned as the door to the coffee shop opened and an attractive, well-groomed woman wearing a black leather look mac and tight leggings with heels tottered in, heading straight for her table.

'Hi, Steph, sorry I'm late, my Uber didn't turn up, I had to order another one.'

'That's OK, shall we skip coffee and get going right away?' She laid a hand on the woman's arm. 'It's good to see you again, Daniela, you're looking great.'

They walked down the road together and turned into a side street. Steph took the key out of her pocket and thirty seconds later they were in Darcy's house.

'Bit of a dump, isn't it?' Daniela wrinkled her nose. 'You said it was a nice little Victorian terrace.'

'It is! Well, sort of. It's a Victorian terrace and it's small,' Steph remarked. 'Let's face it, you're not planning on living here, are you? Soon as you've got her out you can flog it again.'

'Seems like a whole lot of trouble just to get even.' Daniela pulled a face. 'I wouldn't have even looked at a place like this as a sound investment.'

Steph's mouth felt dry. The last thing they needed was Daniela losing interest. It would be so much harder to achieve their aim if she did so. When Darcy had told her the landlord was selling the house, she immediately thought of Daniela who'd told Brenda she'd bought one or two buy-to-let properties in the Manchester area.

'If Darcy struggles to get somewhere else, Mum can put her up. That way we can make sure the boys are OK, see if she's coping.' Steph hesitated. 'You said yourself you'd get revenge on her one way or another, after Joel.'

She still didn't seem that keen. Perhaps it was time to avail Daniela of Darcy's troubling pastime.

'There's something you ought to see,' Steph said, walking into the kitchen. Daniela followed. 'I wasn't going to show you but… well, I think you should know.'

Steph opened a wide narrow drawer and pulled out Darcy's laptop. She opened it up on the kitchen counter and keyed in some numbers. 'Password is Harry's birthday.' She smirked.

Daniela looked uncomfortable. 'Are you sure she's out of town? If she comes back and catches us—'

'No fear of that. I told you, she's in North Yorkshire, playing happy families with her new boyfriend and his kid.' One side of Steph's mouth twisted down as she opened the photo of the lodge that Darcy had sent her on her phone and slid it over for Daniela to see. 'She couldn't resist boasting, of course. Those poor boys will be calling him "Dad" soon and my brother's memory will be non-existent. Mark my words.'

Daniela looked at her, sliding the phone back. 'As you know, there are parts of Joel's memory I'm quite happy to let fade into oblivion.'

'Hmm. Well let's keep focused on the job in hand,' Steph said hastily just as the computer screen leapt into life. 'The best way to avenge the past is to stay on the path we've agreed.'

Daniela glanced at the clock on the wall. 'I haven't got long and I want to see the rest of this dump before I instruct my solicitor to go ahead with the purchase.'

'And you will. But first, look at this.' Steph turned the laptop so Daniela could clearly see the screen.

Steph smiled when Daniela took a sharp intake of breath.

'I haven't touched anything.' Steph held her hands in the air. 'I opened it up and your profile was the last thing she looked at.'

'That's impossible.' Daniela frowned. 'My Facebook account is locked down and I'm certainly not friends with her.'

'You're not friends with Darcy Hilton, but you're friends with this person… who is also Darcy Hilton.'

Steph double-clicked on the image of a pair of glossy lips and Daniela's mouth fell open.

'Meet Tana Philips, aka Darcy Hilton. She's used a false profile for years,' Steph told her. 'She got drunk one night and told me she spends most of her waking hours tracking your every move online.'

'That's crazy!' Daniela's face fell. 'And actually quite sad.'

'Don't go feeling too sorry for her,' Steph remarked. 'She used to watch your house before you moved to Manchester. And take a look at this.'

Steph tapped around the keyboard and Darcy's photos loaded. 'Look, you even have your own album, tagged with your initials.'

Daniela bent forward, squinting her eyes in disbelief when Steph double-clicked on the album entitled 'DF' and hundreds of Daniela's photographs downloaded from her social media accounts filled the screen.

'But why?' Daniela shook her head. 'Why would she even do that?'

'Because – and I'm sorry to be so blunt – she hates your guts, Daniela. She blames you for everything and at the same time is obsessed with you.'

'She blames me? What about Joel? What about her own behaviour?'

'You don't have to convince me.' Steph shut the laptop, eager to get the subject away from Joel and back to the reason for her asking Daniela over here. 'The point is, she's obviously unstable and we've got the evidence of that right here. You've seen how obsessed she is with you and it will only get worse. Who knows what she might do?'

Daniela swallowed and hugged her shoulder bag closer.

'We've got a chance to stop all this now, Daniela. You've seen for yourself that she's not right and there have been signs recently that she's slipping back into her old ways. She's been distancing herself from us and lying to cover up why she's not around to care for Kane and Harrison. She's not fit to look after the boys and what she's been doing to you, basically stalking you online, it's got to stop.'

Daniela raised an eyebrow. 'Let's hope it all works out as you have so meticulously planned.'

'We just need to push her a bit, that's all.' Steph's voice brightened. 'The boys need stability and routine and you need your privacy and a sense of justice done. I'll show you around the house and then you can get cracking with the purchase.'

34

True to his word, after making hot drinks, George shrugs on his big padded jacket and pulls on his wellies before leaving to go to the lodge park reception. I lock the door behind him, and while he's away, I go back twice to check it's still secure. Then, while the kids watch a bit of television, I sit by the window and wait.

When he returns, he looks relieved.

'I spoke to the manager, a Mr Romano, and he says the children might have been entirely mistaken,' he says as he slips off his wellies at the door. 'He says there are actors in costume all over the park to entertain the kids, pretending to be characters.'

I frown. 'This was a woman was in a hoodie. Hardly a Disney character!'

'Well, anyway, I explained the situation, said the children were adamant, and he's sent an army of security guards to comb the wooded area immediately. He's also assured me that there's twenty-four-hour security in the park, including on Christmas Day, and he's arranging for a nominated officer to hang around our lodge in particular.'

'That's good of him,' I say, relieved. 'Did you tell him about Opal?'

'I didn't go into detail.' George walks over to the couch and sits down. 'He didn't ask. When he saw how concerned I was, he offered the extra support.'

I feel like a weight has been lifted off my chest, reassured that George has taken action. I stand up and peer out of the glass sliding doors to the wood beyond. I can't see any security officers out there, but nonetheless, I feel comforted.

We turn the television off and all have a game of snakes and ladders, and I'm pleased that the children seem relaxed. I think the excitement of Christmas and a visit from Father Christmas is overriding any anxiety over what happened out there.

When they are snuggled up in bed and George and I are alone at last, he mixes two gin and tonics and brings them through to the lounge.

'Peace at last,' he says, taking a big gulp of his drink. 'It's quite nice here when there are no kids around,' he quips.

'You're so good with them, always making them laugh, like that story of the potty getting stuck on your patient's head you told them at the trampoline place.'

He gives me a strange look as if I'm simple. 'Obviously that wasn't true, Darcy.'

'What? You said—'

'I'm know what I said, but that was just for effect!' He shakes his head. 'Honestly. What are you like?'

I might be gullible but I believed him! And actually, I'd never lie to the boys like that, even if it was just light-hearted fun.

I try and push my irritation away. I'm being over-sensitive, I'm stupid to have believed his silly story. And anyway, there's something niggling at me. Something I need to get out of the way, because it feels like the right moment.

Just do it, the voice in my head says.

'George, I've been waiting to tell you something since before we came away.'

'OK.' He puts his drink down and looks at me. 'I'm all ears.'

'Before you told me about Opal Vardy, I thought the person lurking around in the woods might have something to do with me. Someone who has an axe to grind.'

He pulls down the corners of his mouth, surprised.

'Go on,' he says, edging forward a little on his seat.

'During Joel's last days in hospital, the nurse let on that there'd been a woman visiting him. Someone called Daniela Frost.' Just saying her name out loud makes me shiver. 'I'd never heard of her and Joel had certainly never mentioned her. But after he died, it became apparent that he'd been living a double life.'

'What?' He looks genuinely shocked. 'You mean like one of those men who have two families on the go? I've read articles about that before, couldn't quite believe the wife never smelled a rat!'

I give him a hard look, and he looks a bit sheepish, realising he's spoken out of turn.

'Turns out Joel was effectively living half the week with me and half with her. His real family was me and the boys, of course. She didn't have any children with him, had no right to be with him.'

'That's terrible, Darcy,' he says, his tone softer now. 'I can't imagine how you dealt with that.'

I didn't, I feel like saying. I still haven't dealt with it. Not really. Then I explain that Daniela has returned to Nottingham.

'The news has made me feel… I don't know, unsafe, I suppose. Like the ground is shifting beneath my feet. I hoped never to set eyes on her again.'

'Totally understandable, I'd say.' He thinks for a moment. 'Neither of you knew about the other? He deceived you both?'

'She claimed she didn't know, but I'm sure she'd have done anything to keep him.' I feel heat rising through my neck and into my face. 'We had children together; she was nothing more than a distraction for him.'

'Do you know when he started the affair with her? How long had you two been married?'

I feel sick at the mere thought of it now. 'There's still a lot I don't know, but he wasn't having an affair; it was far more serious than that. He was living with us both, sharing his life completely. There's a hell of a difference.'

George nods. 'I'm sorry,' he says.

'I just thought you needed to know,' I say. 'It's important we're honest with each other.'

'Agreed,' he says. 'And I appreciate it.'

'Then you won't mind returning the favour?'

He visibly tenses. 'In what way?'

'I want to see a photograph of Opal, George. I want to know what my enemy looks like, if she comes near me or my children.'

'I've told you, she's not dangerous or—'

'I know what you've told me, but I still want to see a photograph of her.' I put down my glass with a thud. 'Right now.'

A shadow passes over his face, but I'm adamant. I'm sick of looking out of the window and feeling vulnerable, seeking out anyone who might be acting suspicious.

He picks up his phone, his jaw set and eyes hooded. I'm forcing him to face something he absolutely wants to ignore, and I know how *that* feels. But I have to think of my sons' safety here.

He seems to spend ages scrolling through photos. Finally he turns the screen to face me.

'There she is. Satisfied?'

The room seems to swirl for a moment and I'm glad to be sitting down. I gasp as I take in the face he's showing me. Then I sit back and stare into those slightly vacant eyes again, and shiver as the realisation dawns on me. I've definitely met Opal Vardy before.

The same shoulder-length brown hair, dark eyes, pale skin… She's smiling here, looks bright and lively, but there's no mistaking it's her.

'I've met this woman, George,' I whisper. 'She was at the hospital, outside the urology ward, the day I dropped off your thank-you card.' He looks aghast. 'She was acting weird, pacing around and staring at me. When I came out, she asked if I was visiting someone.'

'Did she threaten you?'

I shake my head. 'No, but it was all very odd. I felt uncomfortable being alone with her.'

'You should have told me this before,' he says grimly. 'I'll have a word with the ward manager, Sherry. She'll keep an eye out in future.'

I'm dumbfounded for a moment, waiting for his outrage, his concern for my safety. But it doesn't come.

'This proves we need to go to the police,' I state simply. 'She's obviously obsessed with you.'

The words seem to wobble there, at the end of my tongue. But George doesn't look at me. He doesn't say anything at all.

'It's gone too far now, you must see that. I'm scared what she might do next.'

'Look, let's not jump to conclusions. We don't know for certain it was Opal in the woods; it could've been Joel's other—' He catches himself. 'Sorry. I'll speak to the ward manager when I get back to work. She'll soon stop to anybody hanging around outside.'

'But we can explain to the police that I've seen her at the hospital and that she's probably here too.' I glance outside again, get up and draw the curtains. 'I think you should alert your bosses at the hospital.'

'I'd need to be sure. This could damage my career... it would never recover.' He reaches for my hand. 'I will sort this out, but it's Christmas Eve and I refuse to ruin it with a visit from the police. The kids would be so alarmed.'

I don't answer him and I don't pull my hand away, but I can't shake the feeling that something about his attitude feels odd. It also stings that he's so ready to trivialise my assertion that I have seen Opal before.

George is extremely ambitious; he's in line for a very big promotion and he's nervous that Opal could cause problems for him at work. That I can accept.

What I can't accept is that he would willingly put his career before our children's safety. He's such a caring, logical guy, but he simply will not acknowledge that Opal could be a risk to them. I shudder when I think what might have happened to Romy out there if Harrison hadn't thought on his feet and rushed in to alert us.

He needs to get something legal in place, a restraining order or similar.

Despite everything George has told me, the whole situation feels like a jigsaw that has a bunch of key pieces missing right in the middle. It's making me feel increasingly uncomfortable that I can't get a handle on the whole picture.

Could there be there something he isn't telling me?

In the interests of us enjoying our Christmas break, I decide to keep that concern to myself... for now.

35

Harrison, Kane and Romy troop through from the television room.

'*The Simpsons* has just finished,' Harrison says. 'Can we go outside?'

'Perfect timing!' George claps his hands. 'Who's up for going in the hot tub?'

'Me!' three excited voices chorus.

It's a bit of an ordeal getting ready for the hot tub. The strap on Romy's one-piece snaps, but I easily remedy that with a safety pin. Kane, possibly still a bit nervous, decides he doesn't want to go outside after all and has to be persuaded by the rest of us.

I slip my own swimsuit on and look critically at myself in the full-length mirror in the bedroom. I wish I'd invested in a new one with better support and a flattering cut instead of recycling this old one. I bought it about ten years ago, when I was considerably younger and leaner around the hips; now, the high-cut legs aren't doing me any favours.

George, however, raises an appreciative eyebrow as I lower myself self-consciously into the tub. The kids are bubbling with excitement, but I feel stiff and uptight as I scan the trees in front of us. The light is already starting to fade.

'Hey.'

I look over at George.

'Relax,' he says. 'Everything is fine.'

I nod and make a big effort to focus on the children instead of the awful possibility that someone is still out there. I'm yet to see a security officer patrolling around our lodge but I know George will object if I suggest he pays another visit to reception.

There's an outdoor speaker on the patio, and George has set a jolly Christmas playlist going. 'Rudolph the Red-Nosed Reindeer' and 'Santa Baby' have us all singing along in no time.

The hot tub does what it says on the box. It's relaxing, fun and lovely and warm. The kids gasp as all around us tiny fairy lights suddenly spring to life, illuminating the trees and patio. The fake snow glitters on the ground, and the scene is instantly transformed from slightly eerie to wonderfully festive.

George reaches down behind the tub and hands me a glass of mulled wine. As I sink lower in my seat and allow the jets to massage my tense neck and shoulders, I actually start to feel like this might not turn out to be such a bad Christmas after all.

Christmas morning has to rank as one of the best the boys and I have ever had.

The kids are all up at 6 a.m., and although George tries in vain to get them back in bed for another hour, he's outvoted and we open presents.

Romy is delighted with her Disney princess outfit from me, and Kane and Harry jump up and down with glee when they unwrap the latest Nottingham Forest football strip from George and Romy.

I've also brought a few presents for the boys, and George has done the same for Romy. The rest of them they'll get when we return home.

We enjoy watching the children open their gifts, and then George and I exchange presents.

He seems genuinely pleased with the Paul Smith shirt and Trent Bridge cricket membership I've got him.

He hands me a small, exquisitely wrapped flat box. All eyes are on me as, with bated breath, I pull open the scarlet velvet double bow and peel off the expensive silver paper to reveal the pale gold box inside.

I have butterflies in my stomach when I remove the box lid to reveal the most beautiful diamond tennis bracelet I've ever seen.

'It's... sublime. Truly, George, I've never owned anything so stunning.'

The children all gasp in admiration and George laughs as I continue to stare, open-mouthed. He reaches over and takes out the bracelet, slipping it around my wrist before fastening it.

He sits back to admire it glinting on my arm. 'Truly elegant and graceful, like its new owner.'

I lean forward and kiss him on the lips. 'Thank you. I love you.'

'Love you too,' he whispers.

'Yuck!' Harrison exclaims. 'Get a room.'

'Hey, cheeky!' I playfully scold him. We both burst out laughing and Harrison grins, but there's a tinge of sadness playing around his eyes. Sometimes he really surprises me; shows me he's growing up.

At 10 a.m., after breakfast, the staff, dressed as elves and reindeer, visit all the lodges, bringing warm cranberry juice for the kids and Buck's Fizz for the adults.

Romy and Kane in particular were mesmerised late last night when we heard jingling bells and ran outside to see real reindeer pulling Santa Claus in a gloriously authentic sleigh through the park. All the kids at the neighbouring lodges were out in their pyjamas, and everyone waved and said hello to each other. I glanced at the trees I'd been so wary of earlier in the day, and felt reassured that we were safe here now that George had taken the necessary steps.

There has been no sign at all of anything or anyone untoward and earlier, I did spot an official in uniform walking close to the lodge which could indicate the security presence the manager promised is now in place.

Now I glance over at George and see he looks a little mesmerised himself at the young blonde elf we met on reception when we first arrived, but I push it out of my mind. She's very lovely and he's only sneaking a crafty glimpse.

Besides, she's accompanied by a couple of strapping Santa's helpers, and now I don't feel too bad checking out the biceps on show.

Before long, it's time to get dressed and go out for lunch, and we enjoy a superb meal, great quality and traditional in every way, surpassing all our expectations.

Later in the afternoon, the kids are all fast asleep in the TV room and George and I finally get a little time alone.

We kiss and snuggle together, watching the flames flicker in the log burner. I'm beginning to doze myself when George speaks up.

'Darcy, there's something I want to ask you. But I'm worried you might not appreciate it.'

I smile, eyes closed as I listen to the smooth tones of Michael Bublé emanating discreetly from the sound system. Reaching up, I touch George's cheek, feel the bristles under the softness of my fingertips.

'Just say it,' I whisper, my heart beating harder. When I open my eyes, I see he looks troubled and I'm not sure if it's a good or a bad thing he's about to say.

'I wondered if… Would you and the boys like to move in with us? I mean, it doesn't have to be right now, but soon… that's if you don't feel we're rushing things.'

In a flash, the long years of struggling as a single parent whoosh through my mind. Our small cramped house; crying myself to sleep when I'd put the boys to bed at night; finding out Joel wasn't the man I thought I knew, but protecting his memory for the boys' sake.

And now George is giving me the chance to start again, living as a family in his lovely house and garden, playing games with the kids, cooking meals together. I think about how the boys are already comfortable in George's company and treat Romy like the sister they never had.

It's the perfect solution to scupper any plans Daniela might have to evict us on her terms, too. It couldn't be better timing.

But what will Joel's family say? They're bound to have an opinion on how quickly our relationship is developing.

'Darcy? Say something... even if it's no.'

It's definitely rushing things, there are no two ways about that. And they'll be sure to make their feelings known.

But then so what? I suddenly feel a certainty that dispels my doubts.

We're not love-struck teenagers; we've seen a lot of life, both of us surviving tragedy. We know what we like and what we don't like.

No matter what people might say – what other people might think – do I really want to pass up this chance of happiness for the sake of appearances and some dated idea of how long people ought to get to know each other before making a serious commitment?

I look at George, register his guarded expression as he seems to steel himself for a knock-back.

'The answer is yes,' I say, my words breaking with emotion. 'Me and the boys would love to move in with you and Romy.'

He grabs me, holds me tightly.

'I love you so much,' he whispers, grasping my hair and kissing my lips, cheeks, eyelids.

I've got this bubbly, hopeful feeling in my chest that I hope lasts forever. And it's all I want to focus on right now.

I push the other, shadowy stuff to the back of my mind. I refuse to let anything spoil our happiness.

36

When we arrive back home after our wonderful Christmas break, I feel rejuvenated and so positive for our future together as a new family.

Steph calls me the day we return and invites herself over.

'I'll bring a bottle of wine over tomorrow night. I want to hear all about your break and see the pics. It'll do us good to have a catch-up and get back on track after our disagreement.'

There was no *disagreement* about it. I told her I was dating again and she couldn't handle it.

'We'll catch up soon, I promise,' I say, thinking on my feet. 'I've got a ton to do and really want to see you but the next few days are swallowed up with chasing up jobs after the Christmas break.' As I expected, she greets this news with a frosty silence. 'Let me look at the diary and we'll sort something out, I promise.'

I feel bad when she ends the call abruptly but my news about moving in with George has to be given properly. I owe Brenda and Leonard the courtesy of telling them face to face and Steph knows me too well. I'd never be able to conceal the news if we meet up. Sensing I was holding back, she'd hound me until I cracked.

The following week, it's back to business as usual: shopping for bits of school uniform, updating my new year yoga classes on the website. We're already spending lots more time at George's house and I've started clandestinely packing boxes upstairs.

'It's better for the boys to get used to the house gradually over the next few weeks,' George sensibly suggested. 'Bring them over as often as you like.'

I nod, appearing to take it all in my stride but privately, I crumble a bit when I think of telling Joel's family about my decision to move in with George. Still, I arrange with Brenda we'll go over for a family tea on Sunday.

Saturday morning, I drop the boys off with Brenda and Leonard, and drive over to George's. He's suggested we speak to Maria today about me and the boys moving in.

'She's not working today but I've asked her to pop in for half an hour and she's offered to take Romy to the park. You don't have to tell her today but I'm guessing you might want to reduce her working hours once you get into the swing of things here.'

I gulp a bit at that. I hadn't thought about the practical measures of moving in with George and part of me feels guilty for having a negative impact on Maria's position.

I've made an effort to look a bit smarter than I usually would at the weekend, wearing a fitted top and black trousers instead of my preferred jeans. I want to feel I match up to Lucy in Maria's eyes, when we tell her of our plans.

Typically, George and Romy are upstairs, getting her stuff together, when Maria arrives. I call up to George but Romy has the television on in her bedroom and he doesn't hear. I steel myself and open the door.

'Maria, hello again!' I offer her a big smile when I open the door to save her using her key.

She looks slightly taken aback to see me but nods and gives me a small smile. She's a tall woman with well-preserved skin. But there's a faded air about her, diluted, almost. I find myself wondering if she has her own family.

I take a few steps back so she can come inside, but she hovers around in the porch, seemingly a bit nervous in my company.

'Would you like to come through, Maria? I can make us some tea while Romy's getting ready, and there's an artisan mince pie from the lodge park hamper going spare if you fancy it.'

'No!' she says quickly, and then seems to catch herself. 'Thank you, Darcy, but I've eaten quite enough recently to last me through the next month at least.' She pats her tummy and I laugh.

'I know how that feels!'

I'm hoping we've broken the ice, but she falls silent again. Shifts her weight from one foot to the other. She spends so much time in this house and yet she's acting like a stranger in my presence.

'Romy!' I call up the stairs, over my shoulder. 'Maria's here.'

'Did you... did you all have a nice time at the lodge?' She watches me intently.

'We did. It was really wonderful.' Our conversation is so stilted, I find myself grasping for something interesting to say. 'George bought me this; it was a lovely surprise.'

I hold up my wrist, and the diamond bracelet sparkles under the crystal chandelier in the hallway.

Maria lets out a little gasp, and her hand flies to her throat.

I feel the smile melt from my lips.

'What's wrong?' I take a step towards her, but she backs off. 'Maria, are you OK?'

She shakes her head. 'It's just that...' She falters, and I hold my breath, thinking she's about to open up to me about something.

Then I hear the sound of feet thundering down the stairs.

'Maria!' Romy jumps off the bottom two steps, skips across the hall and barrels into the housekeeper's arms. I marvel at how relaxed she seems compared to her usual restrained mood when we're around.

'You were saying, Maria?' I prompt her to continue, but her eyes flicker to the stairs, to where George now stands.

'Hello, Maria,' he says.

'It was nothing important.' Maria gives me a weak smile. 'I'm just glad you all had a nice time.'

'Romy, pop back upstairs and get your scarf and gloves,' George says. 'We just need a little chat with Maria.'

We all go into the lounge and I see Maria's fingers are fidgeting against her leg.

'Nothing to worry about, Maria,' I say. 'We just wanted to let you know about our plans.'

We sit down and George speaks.

'Darcy and her two sons will be moving in here with us shortly and we wanted you to know, that's all.'

Maria stares at him.

'Are my services no longer required?' Her lip quivers and I wish I knew her better so I felt able to put a comforting arm around her.

'Of course we still want you to come in,' I say quickly, anxious to reassure her.

'Although Darcy may, in time, need to tweak your duties and hours,' George adds.

Silence.

Romy thunders downstairs and into the lounge waving her scarf and gloves in the air. Maria stands up slowly as if she's afraid she might keel over.

'Thank you for telling me,' she says and pats Romy's head. 'Get your coat on, little one. Time for us to get off to the park.'

I follow them out to the hallway and help Romy with her outerwear.

'Thanks, Maria,' I say as they walk to the door hand-in-hand. 'I'm sure we're all going to get on just fine.'

Romy drops a glove and I bend to pick it up but instead of looking down, I lift my chin to smile at Maria and stifle a gasp at the expression of pure hatred on her face.

'Is there something wrong? Something you want to say?' I stand up and fix her with a stare that belies my nervousness.

Her face breaks into a smile. 'Not at all,' she says softly. 'I'm sure everything will work out for the best. One way or another.'

*

When Maria has left and George is dealing with some paperwork in his office, I open up the Google homepage and in the search bar I type: *Opal Vardy*.

Then I press enter.

Predictably, there are hundreds of thousands of results. The first couple I click on take me to details of Opal Vardys all over the world, so I refine the search by adding in *Nottingham*. This time it's better, but still nothing leaps out at me.

I open up Facebook and select the fake profile I use to get closer to Daniela and retain my anonymity. To my surprise, not one profile in Opal's name comes up. There are near misses and plenty of Opals and Vardys, but no exact combination of her name. This is highly unusual, though I only have to look at my own fake profile to understand what she is probably doing.

Over on Twitter, it's a similar story. There are two people named Opal Vardy. One has no profile picture and has only two followers. The other one is an American teenager who hasn't posted or retweeted anything for over a year.

Over on Instagram, there are two profiles with the name Opal Vardy. One has no followers, no posts and is following precisely no one. The other profile is private with no profile picture. I put in a follow request to this account.

It seems I've hit the proverbial brick wall, but it will take more than this to put me off. The obsessed mind is clever, canny… She's out there somewhere; it's just a matter of finding that one less obvious link. It's here somewhere, I can feel it.

I return to Google and scan down the search results, aware that it's like looking for a needle in a haystack. Then something George mentioned pushes its way into my mind.

She used to work in the hospital archives.

In the search bar, I type: *Opal Vardy City Hospital*.

My heart sinks a little as nothing interesting loads. I click on the images tab and the screen splits into photographic tiles. The third one along forces me to take a sharp intake of breath. I click on it and it fills the screen.

The photograph forms part of a local hospital magazine article from two years ago. Underneath the narrative are the words: *Employee Opal Vardy was awarded Temporary Staff Member of the Year at the Nottingham University Hospitals NHS Trust awards presentation at the East Midlands Conference Centre.*

I take a screen shot of the photo and crop it so that Opal is the only one in the picture. She looks younger and happier than the woman I saw in the hospital, but you can clearly see it's her.

When Maria brings Romy back from the park, she watches her to the door from halfway down the drive. It's obvious she doesn't want to speak to me again.

When I've helped her off with her coat and scarf, I bring the photo up on my phone and show it to her.

'Is this the lady who tried to speak to you in the woods at the lodge park, Romy?'

She stares at the screen. Doesn't blink, doesn't say a word.

'You won't get into trouble if you tell me. I just need to know so we can keep you super safe, OK?'

Her eyes are still fixed on the photograph, but I can't tell if that's because she recognises Opal or if she's trying to recall the woman in the woods.

'Have you seen this lady before, Romy?' I press her, nervous in case George pads softly downstairs without me hearing.

She nods, and my heart seems to jump up into my throat.

'She's my friend,' Romy says, and looks away.

I feel breathless, trying to make sense of why she'd say that. Has George been secretly seeing Opal? Is he doing the exact same thing with another woman that Joel did to me?

My voice catches in my throat and I cough before speaking.

'Do you see her often? Does Daddy take you to see her?'

She shakes her head and I feel a flood of relief in my chest.

'How do you know she's your friend then?'

'Because I saw Maria talking to her and she said she was,' Romy says.

37

When Brenda had gone up to bed, Leonard sat in his armchair nursing a brandy. He wasn't a drinking man, had never over-indulged on that score. Nevertheless, he had to admit there were times you needed a little boost that only a stiff drink could bring.

Darcy and the boys had been over for tea and everyone had been looking forward to hearing all about their trip to the log cabin. He and Brenda, especially, had missed the boys terribly over the Christmas period. It had been the first Christmas day since the boys' births that they hadn't spent it with them.

Brenda had done all the usual festive things. Set the table so beautifully, planned a feast fit for kings and Joel's photograph had sat pride of place as always. Yet without the upbeat energy of their grandsons, Joel's handsome face had added a sadness to the proceedings. Rather than feeling he was there with them, watching over the family, they all felt his loss so much more keenly.

So when Darcy agreed to come over for tea – she made some excuse about George being too busy to come – Brenda had taken heart and got all the boys' favourite foods in.

From the moment Darcy appeared, they all knew something was wrong. She seemed jumpy, on edge. It was worrying as they'd witnessed this behaviour before when she'd spent time in the clinic.

She was a very persuasive person, good at putting on an act that fooled most people but they all knew her too well, now. Knew that she often imagined things, conjured up imaginary situations in her head which she then convinced herself had actually happened.

In the kitchen, while Darcy sat talking to Dave in the living room, they'd all congregated and agreed that something was wrong.

'Maybe they've had a fall-out,' Brenda said hopefully. 'Maybe George is off the scene.'

Sadly, there *was* something Darcy was nervous of telling them, but it wasn't that.

When Brenda called everyone to the table and, before they touched a morsel of the food she'd so lovingly prepared, Darcy spoke up.

'I've something to tell you all.'

Leonard saw the knowing look Brenda shot Steph. Here it was, he'd thought to himself, the big news that the relationship was off. They'd all make the expected sympathetic noises but when she'd gone home, they'd be celebrating. Leonard thought he might even open the bottle of Moët he'd had in the fridge for a few months, waiting for a special occasion.

'Me and the boys, we're moving in with George next month.'

Brenda's colour had drained and Leonard had stood up to get her a glass of water.

'It's a bit soon, Darcy, love,' he'd said in the absence of everyone else's stunned silence.

'You don't always need months or years to make an important decision, Leonard,' Darcy had told him tartly. 'Sometimes you just know.'

'And what about the boys?' Steph had asked, turning to her nephews. 'What do you two think about going to live with George?'

'It'll be fun,' Kane said lightly, helping himself to another cheese sandwich.

But Harrison looked at his plate and his face crumbled. Tears began to fall.

'Oh lovey, come here.' Brenda's voice cracked as she rushed over to her elder grandson and pressed his head to her. 'That's it, let it all out. It's all right, my darling. It's going to be just fine, you'll see.'

It tore Leonard apart to see his family in pieces and he looked at Darcy in expectation.

'I've chatted about this,' Darcy said, watching Harrison with alarm. 'They're fine about it. It's probably just being here, in front of you all. He feels torn.'

'Torn?' Steph gave a harsh laugh. 'He doesn't look torn to me. He looks devastated, like moving in with George is the last thing he wants.'

They didn't stay for tea after all. Darcy bundled them up and rushed them out to the car, refusing to discuss the situation further.

When Brenda went up for a lie-down, Steph and Leonard had a chat.

'If there's any good that's come out of this, it's that it's proved it is definitely time, Dad,' she said grimly. 'We have to put our plans into action soon. For the sake of the family.'

And Leonard knew she was right.

He drained his glass of the last of his brandy and turned off the lights. In the morning, he would set the ball rolling.

38

It's another six weeks before we're ready to move in with George.

Six weeks might sound like a long time, but it's gone in a flash, with everything that has to be done.

It feels particularly sweet when I draft out the email to the lettings company informing them we're vacating the house. I'm on a month-to-month contract so only need to give four weeks' notice. In view of the new owner, of whom I've heard nothing about yet from the company, I don't intend giving her the courtesy of a day more than I have to. Nothing would give me greater pleasure than to think of Daniela having to foot the mortgage bill while she finds new tenants.

I can't find out any more about what's happening on the house front because Steph isn't speaking to me any more. The boys are still going over to their grandparents' house but our contact is polite and minimal. If that's how they want to play it, then so be it.

I sit down with the boys and ask them how they feel about moving in with George and Romy.

Kane is buzzing with excitement about the move but Harrison is a little more reticent.

'Are we leaving here forever?' he asks quietly. 'Someone else will live here, where our Dad was?'

A physical pain grips my chest and I reach for my boy, kiss his forehead.

'It would mean us leaving this house, yes,' I tell him. 'But the memories of your dad and the fun times you had with him? They go with us. And they'll always be with you; nobody can take them away, Harry.'

'Keep them in here.' Kane taps the side of his head. 'Then you can get them out and look at Dad's face, even in the middle of the night.'

I bite down hard on my back teeth. If I'm not careful, I'm going to burst into tears and ruin my chance to discuss the move properly with the two of them.

'Will we have to call George "Dad" if we go to live with him?' Harry asks, scratching at the seam of his jeans.

'Absolutely not! He's just George to you; you already have a dad, right?'

He nods, seeming to be relieved.

At the end of our chat, both boys seem happier, and as far as I'm concerned, that's the really tough bit out of the way. Sorting out their admission to Papplewick primary school, giving the landlord notice that we'll be moving out and everything else that moving entails is straightforward by comparison.

Halfway through February, the big day arrives, the day we've all been waiting for, when the boys and I finally make the momentous move into George's house to create a new whole family from our two halves.

Why, then, is my stomach roiling? I can't eat breakfast, or sit still for any length of time.

Romy and Kane have been like effervescent balls of excitement about the move, but I had a little blip yesterday with Harrison.

He wouldn't come down from his bedroom for tea, and when I went up there, he was sitting on his bed with his photograph of Joel in his hands, fat tears splashing down onto the glass. I sat next to him and took his hand.

'Your dad will always be with you, sweetie,' I said softly. 'Remember what Grandma told you? He's looking down on you all the time, and he wants you to be happy.'

Harry sniffed and nodded, then laid his head on my arm.

The boys stayed over at Brenda and Leonard's last night. For once, Brenda seemed to understand that I had a lot on with the move.

'It must be very stressful, leaving your home,' she said when she called yesterday afternoon. 'How about we pick the boys up from school and then tomorrow we can bring them back.' She paused for a moment. 'We can even bring them to the new house, if that helps.'

Despite my efforts to hold out the olive branch, Steph still doesn't seem as happy for us. But I get the feeling Brenda is intent on worming her way into our new life until she's got the same kind of involvement as with our old. I'm afraid that's not going to happen.

'Well that might be a bit tricky,' I said lightly. 'I'll be here for the first part of the morning, but after that, I'll be back and forth.'

'Leonard can bring them back in the morning before the removals arrive.' She sounded quite upbeat. 'How would that work?'

'Thanks, Brenda.' I breathed a sigh of relief that I hadn't offended her and began to relish the thought of a clear evening ahead to make a start on the hundred and one jobs that needed doing before I handed the keys back to the management company.

I haven't heard anything from Steph since the day before yesterday. To be fair, she has come round a bit from her sulk and done some useful things to help: informing the utility companies, the local council, time-consuming tasks like that. But something between us has changed for good. I can just feel it.

I know that if the boys and I were moving to another rented house alone, she'd be virtually camped out here, helping me every step of the way. She would have insisted on it.

There's no doubt about it: Joel's family have been wounded by my unexpected and rapidly progressing relationship with George. Moving in with him is a step too far in their opinion. I feel regretful that I've contributed to their sadness, but I understand it. Yet I wouldn't renege on this chance of happiness for myself and my sons and they've really got no choice but to accept my decision.

I stand in the living room and look around. Everything has been packed into boxes now, and our local Oxfam shop sent a lorry to take away the sofas and other large items of furniture we don't need to take with us.

The result is a long bare wall with squares of clean magnolia paint. The biscuit-coloured carpet still looks fresh and new close to the walls, but in the middle of the room it is flat and faded and marred with dents from the newly removed furniture. Everything is grubby and in need of an overhaul, where once it seemed to be our perfect place. A place we could be happy together.

I can remember standing in this exact spot with Joel all those years ago, deciding how to furnish what would be an important space in the house for our growing family. He slid his arm around my shoulders and I leaned into him affectionately.

'I think we should definitely go for cosy, but not too fussy,' I suggested. 'Lots of blankets, a basket of logs even though it's a gas stove, plenty of cushions.'

'A warm den for us all to snuggle up in together,' Joel agreed, grinning. 'Oh, and a big TV on that wall.'

I laughed and rolled my eyes.

'Not just for the footie!' he protested, nudging me playfully. 'I mean for family movies and pizza nights, holed up together against the great British weather. That's the only kind of entertainment I'm interested in now.'

He kissed the top of my head, and I still remember the feeling of utter contentment that settled over me like a comforter.

Eighteen months later, and the sad reality was that Joel was hardly ever home to watch movies with us. He was far too busy driving around the country on jobs, building his customer database of I.T. contacts. At least that's what he led me to believe. On the nights he didn't stay overnight somewhere, when he told me he was up north or down south, he hardly ever got back home until the boys had gone to bed.

I shake myself now, stretch my arms above my head and give myself a little talking-to in an effort to pull myself out of the doldrums. We're on the threshold of a new life with George and Romy; why spend time mired in painful memories, when I can look to the future with renewed optimism and hope?

We arrive at George's house just before eleven.

The electric gates are already open as we approach. I glance in the rear-view mirror and see the removals lorry is right behind me.

I flick on the indicator and swing the car into the driveway, parking over on the far side of the gravelled frontage.

The front door opens and George steps out onto the tiled front porch. Kane jumps out of the car and races over to him. Harrison ambles over, hands in his pockets, head lowered. I watch, my eyes prickling, as George gathers them to him, one in each arm, regardless of Harry's lack of enthusiasm.

'Welcome to your new home!' he announces just before the diesel rumble of the removals lorry drowns out any further hope of hearing anything.

George looks behind him and little Romy inches past them, clutching a huge bunch of lilies in her arms. She smiles and says something, but I don't catch it as the roller shutter on the side of the lorry is being lifted.

'Thank you, Romy,' I half yell as I take the beautiful bouquet from her arms.

I dip my head and inhale the pungent scent of the lilies, several of which are in bloom. 'Thank you,' I mouth to George.

The boys wriggle free of George's hug and disappear into the house with Romy. He slides his arm around my shoulders and speaks directly into my ear, his discreet spicy aftershave filling my nostrils and giving me a little shiver of pleasure.

'Thought the flowers were a nice touch,' he says cheekily. 'Starting as I mean to go on.'

'Sounds like a good plan.' I grin.

'We're ready to start, love,' barks the grizzled removal guy, checking his watch. 'All in through the front door?'

'Best to come around the back way,' George answers. 'The bifold doors are open and I've cleared a space for the boxes. Just leave them all there.'

'Champion.' The man's expression brightens as he realises they're not required to traipse up and down stairs delivering the marked boxes to each room.

'Come on.' George leads me down the side of the house. 'I've something to show you.'

The narrow walkway opens out into the mature back garden. I gasp when George points to the large expanse of grass, where two sets of bright shiny goalposts have been installed.

The upstairs window opens and Harrison and Kane appear there, whooping and calling down their delighted thanks to George. I'm so heartened to see Harrison has perked up.

'They're permanent goalposts and really good-quality ones too,' he says. 'We're going to have some cracking matches out here, you just wait and see.'

'George, I...' I sniff and wipe my eyes with the back of my hand. 'Thank you. This will mean the world to them.'

He nods and takes my hand as the removals men emerge from the side of the house, laden with boxes.

'And this... is for you.'

On the other side of the garden, behind the cluster of apple trees, a new, small patio area has been laid. On it is a set of beautiful, modern outdoor furniture consisting of a dark wooden corner suite with pristine cream cushions, and two matching chairs. There's also a glass-topped table on which stands a bottle of champagne in an ice bucket and two glasses.

'I had to put the furniture out for effect' – George grins – 'but we'll freeze to death if we try and use it today.'

'George, I…'

I'm speechless. That with his mega-busy life, he would even think about doing this for us.

'It's your own peaceful reading spot, Darcy.' He tucks his fingers under my chin and moves my face gently towards his, planting a soft kiss on my lips. 'You deserve it, and I want you to feel relaxed and have your own space in our home together.'

'Thank you,' I whisper, bewildered, as he pops the cork on the champagne and pours us two glasses. 'All this… It's wonderful you've done this for us, George. I love you.'

'I love you too,' he says, handing me a glass. 'To us all.'

'To us all,' I echo, and our glasses chime prettily as we toast our new beginning. I take a sip of the pink fizz, enjoying the pop of the bubbles across my tongue.

'Oh no!' George exclaims, and pulls a jokey expression of horror as our three kids suddenly tumble out of the open doors into the garden, screeching and hollering with delight. 'Looks like our romantic moment just got hijacked.' He grins.

'And I couldn't be happier,' I say, my heart full of the hope and happiness I thought I'd never find again.

39

Despite my worries about it being far too cold and there being far too much to do, the three kids and George pull on gloves and scarves and head out to the garden for a knockabout between the new goalposts.

I roll my eyes and grumble, to their delight, but secretly I love the fact that George is doing this. It's what the boys have been missing in their young lives: a fun father figure who isn't nearly as sensible as me. I'm forever warning them about catching a chill, or nagging them to eat properly and tidy their rooms. But sometimes they don't need that. They need someone who's there to remind them how to enjoy themselves again.

I check my phone and see I've got a missed call from Steph. I stare at the notification. I've tried to keep in touch and suggested meeting up to talk through everything but she's snubbed me so far, not returning calls or texts.

There are a thousand things I need to do right now and I think she and the rest of Joel's family have treated me unfairly. Brenda and Leonard keep in contact just enough so they can arrange to have the boys but there's no love lost there, either. But they'll always be my sons' family so I have a responsibility to maintain communications. I press a key to call her back and Steph answers right away.

'Sorry I missed you,' I say as friendly as I can manage.

'Hi, Darcy, thanks for calling back. I hope your move is going well.' Her tone is on the cool side. 'I called because this is just silly, I feel like we're avoiding each other. You've made a decision and that's your business. It doesn't stop us meeting up now and again for a quick coffee, does it?'

The way she says it, it's like I'm the one who has broken contact. Typical Steph.

'I agree,' I say magnanimously. 'Let's put something in the diary.'

And we do. For the next day, even though I could keep ridiculously busy unpacking boxes for at least the next week.

But I do feel a bit uneasy when we've ended the call. Although there's nothing worse than a niggling worry at the back of your mind that there's an unresolved disagreement with a family member, I don't want to slip back into doing everything Steph asks. I feel in some ways I'm sending out the wrong message in agreeing to meet up like we used to do.

While George and the kids are still outside, I capitalise on the undisturbed time I have and start tackling some of the boxes he's brought through to the hallway.

I'm unpacking our shoes and shaking out coats before storing them in the large under-stairs cupboard with George and Romy's outdoor things when the doorbell rings.

I smile as I approach the front door with its ornate panes of coloured glass. Someone is standing there with a huge bunch of flowers. When I open the door, a cheery delivery driver hands me the bouquet and wishes me a nice day before disappearing away in his van.

The flowers are gorgeous. Roses, gypsophila and lilies, hand-tied in their own gold presentation box. Romy already presented me with flowers when we arrived, so someone else must be wishing us well in settling in. After Steph's call, I find myself hoping they're from Joel's family, a peace offering of sorts, but the smile melts from my face when I pull out the small, sombre card inside.

In silver script against the backdrop of a black rose are the words: *With Deepest Sympathy*.

A small gasp of surprise escapes my mouth, and I drop the bouquet. It lands on the floor with a dull thud just as George walks into the hallway.

The smile on his face disappears.

'Opal,' I whisper.

40

She knew all about George's new girlfriend way before Darcy Hilton was even aware that Opal existed.

She knew where she taught her yoga classes and she knew all about her two boys, too.

It was imperative she made it her business to track George's life to the nth degree. It was the only way she was ever going achieve her ambition. And achieve it she would. No matter what he or his new little Rottweiler did to try and shake her off, one day Opal knew she would get what she wanted.

Or die trying. That was how serious it was for her.

It was surprisingly easy to track someone's every move. The secret to it was recording data. She kept detailed spreadsheets on their movements, along with photographs and video footage taken on her phone. She imagined that police or security officers might be tricky subjects, but ordinary people like George and Darcy were so wrapped up in their own lives, they barely looked further than the ends of their very own noses.

Nobody ever seemed to do one thing at a time any more. To look around them or take notice of the small things and the strangers who constantly hovered around them within inches of their most precious assets.

Their trust in others was staggering, so secure were they of their own infallibility. They really believed they were the masters of their own universe.

Until somebody came along and showed them otherwise.

It was all too easy to write someone like Opal off as crazy, a stalker, a nutball… and a thousand other insults. She'd heard them all, but she was none of those things.

She was organised and focused and, most importantly, she felt a love that could not be shaken by anyone.

What she was doing was powerful and right. Noble, even. No matter what anyone thought or said, her intent was pure.

She had given George so many chances to sit down and talk things through with her, to put the past behind them and make a new start, but of course he had denied her every time. He had often been scathing and unnecessarily cruel in his dismissals too.

Once, when she'd pleaded with him to admit they had something special together, he'd looked at her as if she was crazy.

'Special? We have nothing together, Opal. We've never had anything more than a bit of fun.'

All she'd wanted was to make him understand on some level what torture it was to live life without the person you adored more than anything in the world. She wanted to explain how it ripped her apart to see the one she loved with another woman every day.

But George would have none of it. Since he'd met Darcy Hilton, he wouldn't even acknowledge Opal now, much less speak to her. And that made her angry.

It made her very angry indeed.

She suspected he had instructed Darcy to ignore her. He had liked to pretend Opal did not exist for a long time now. But that simply wasn't going to work any more.

'Let's see how easily Darcy Hilton can ignore me when I get friendly with her boys,' she murmured to herself, smiling into the mirror.

41

The next day, I sit in the middle of the café, feeling a bit hemmed in by the cloying hot bodies and the noise level. It's busy, but I quickly satisfy myself that she's not in here. It's comforting to know that if Opal Vardy wanted to confront me, she'd have to do it here, in front of all these witnesses.

'You seem really quiet. A bit jumpy, even.' Steph puts two lattes on the table and sits down, unhooking her handbag from her shoulder. 'Did everything go well with the move?' She studies my face but I lift my cup to my mouth so I feel less scrutinised.

'Yes thanks, everything went fine. George made a real effort to make us feel welcome; he's put up goalposts for the boys as a surprise. They were delighted.'

I swear her face drops but she manages what, to me, seems like a rather disingenuous smile.

'They're also both getting on fine at their new school, Harry's already been picked for the football team.'

It doesn't seem to be the sort of thing she wants to hear.

'And how are *you* feeling? I know you get stressed easily and the boys will no doubt pick up on that.' She sips her coffee smugly and I feel like standing up and telling her it was a mistake to meet up.

My body feels heavy and tired and I can't think of anything to say. I feel a bit sad as Steph has been my main confidant, my only friend, really. If it was a few months ago, I'd be telling her all about Opal and all the weird things that are happening and she'd be advising me and coming up with good ideas of what to do about her, no doubt.

But to tell her this stuff now feels like I'd be arming her with evidence to whine on about the boys' welfare and how I should never have got involved in a serious relationship so quickly. So I stay silent and keep my worries to myself.

'I can see you're not happy with me, Darcy, but it's important you understand I just feel protective of you and the boys. That's all it is,' she says. 'Nothing's changed; we're still best mates.'

But I know things *have* changed and deep down, she knows it too.

'Everything is fine,' I'm forced to say after taking a sip of coffee. 'It's just a lot of change to deal with in a short space of time but at least it's scuppered Daniela's plans to buy our home.'

Steph seems to be her usual caring self, but I can't help but feel that for some reason she's trying to get as much information out of me as she can. I think if I told her the truth about how worried I am about the Opal Vardy situation, I suspect she'd combust with pleasure. But she can pass on my gleeful comment to Daniela with my blessing.

'Mum was saying it must be difficult for you right now. Everything new and happening so quickly.' Steph's voice has softened into a sympathetic tone that doesn't ring true. 'She wants us to go over to the house for lunch on Thursday. Just you, me and her, when Dad's at golf. Like the old times. What do you say?'

Steph knows my yoga class schedule. I can't use that as an excuse as we still share a diary on Outlook. It's been so difficult to knock these things on the head without upsetting her. With our recent tensions, refusing her access to the diary would be akin to terminating someone as a Facebook friend and it would just make a bad situation even worse. So I've solved the dilemma by putting new appointments relating to me and George in a separate diary.

'That sounds nice,' I say non-committally.

She starts telling me something about the summer holiday Brenda and Leonard are planning, and I zone her voice out, taking the opportunity to scan the coffee shop again for any sign of Opal. There are people coming in and out all the time, so she could easily slip in without me being aware. Observe me from a table on the other side of the room.

I can't shake the feeling she's out there somewhere, watching me. She seems to know our movements and what we're doing, like the fact my car would be parked undisturbed for a couple of hours at the trampoline centre and arranging for funeral flowers to be delivered on the exact day we moved in.

She probably knows I'm here with Steph right now… and frankly, it creeps me out.

I pick up my cup and try to focus on what Steph is saying.

'You seem… different,' Steph remarks. 'Sort of uptight.'

I take a bite of the complimentary shortbread biscuit on my saucer. I'd dearly love to confide in her about Opal, dissect everything George has told me and discuss what I have in mind. But that can't happen. George would be furious if I told anyone else about the situation; he's adamant he's in control of it. But I'm really not so sure.

I might struggle with Joel's family at times, but I can't deny them their role in the boys' lives. Sadly, that's in direct conflict with the fact that George and I need to try and move on without them having too much influence on our own affairs.

There's literally no guidance to be had on this situation. No self-help manuals on what to do when your spouse dies and his family are a great support and then you finally move on and their goodwill disappears.

What's supposed to happen then? How does this stuff work?

I become aware of Steph's voice again, changing the subject.

'Mum and Dad were wondering…' She sounds hesitant. 'If you still want us to pick the boys up when you're busy and stuff…

perhaps you can get us a key cut for George's place? If he doesn't mind, that is.'

'That won't be possible,' I say quickly, before I get cold feet. 'George would never agree to it.'

Steph's helpful expression turns sour. 'Then how are we going to see the boys when we want to, or help you out with childcare now you're holed up in his mansion?'

It's an interesting comment. I gave Brenda George's address for emergency contact purposes and they've obviously checked the property out from the road.

'We can make our arrangements week to week,' I say, choosing not to rise to the bait. 'It won't be a problem.'

What I really want to say is that we can have a normal, healthy arrangement that other families enjoy, where Steph and her parents don't just turn up when they feel like it.

She's off talking about something else now, but I can see by her tight mouth she's miffed at my reaction. I nod here and there to make it look as if I'm still listening, while discreetly flipping my phone over in my handbag on the chair next to me and taking a quick look at the screen to see if George has texted about getting the cinema tickets for tonight.

There's nothing from George, but there's an Instagram notification informing me that DanDan_Frost93 has added a new post. I get that unwelcome feeling in my chest again. Part nausea, part excitement.

'Are you even listening to me?' Steph grumbles, draining the last of her coffee and pushing away her cup and saucer. 'Just tell me if I'm boring the pants off you.'

I can hear the slight edge to her words. Nobody enjoys being ignored, after all.

'Sorry. I am listening; just got distracted by my phone.' I reach down and close my handbag. 'You're doing really well with your fitness plan. How much have you lost again?'

'Ten pounds in five weeks.' She narrows her eyes slightly, obviously irritated at repeating herself. 'You know, you were looking good too, Darcy, but now you look a bit peaky. You feeling OK?'

I nod, then blurt out, 'Have you heard anything else about *her*? About what she's up to?'

As soon as the words are out of my mouth, I wish I'd never said anything. Meeting George has helped me push Daniela to the back of my mind, but the knowledge that she's back in Nottingham now and plans are afoot for her to buy the house we were renting, makes it so much harder to tuck everything away, to rewrite the story of what happened.

Steph's face freezes for a moment. Then she sits up a little straighter, seeming to steel herself.

'Mum is meeting up with her tomorrow. Just for a coffee and a chat.' She sees my face and rushes to explain. 'She just needs to ask her a few questions about Joel. Stuff she's always wondered about and never got to ask, what with her rushing to move to Manchester so quickly. It's no disrespect to you at all; just something Mum needs to do for her own peace of mind, and now that you've obviously moved on—'

I push my cup away and stand up, scooping up my handbag. The people sitting on the next table stop talking and stare.

'I can't handle this,' I say, my voice shaking. 'I can't deal with you embracing her into the family again.'

'It's nothing of the sort. It's just a chat. Don't go,' Steph pleads. 'I don't want this to come between us.'

'Neither do I. But it's time you and your family remembered that *I'm* the mother of Joel's sons, not Daniela. I'm the one you should be sympathising with. She was probably planning to evict us, before we moved in with George.'

Steph glances at the other customers who are taking an interest. 'Darcy, you can't carry on like this. It's not healthy.'

'I've got to go,' I say shortly, marvelling at the way she always manages to turn everything back on to me so effortlessly. I shove my chair under the table and see the elderly woman next to us grimace as it scrapes the floor tiles noisily. 'I'm sorry, Steph. I can't talk about this right now.'

42

I step outside just in time to see a figure dart behind a couple walking towards me.

Before I met George, I'd probably think nothing of it at all, assuming, as there are several people around nearby, it's someone just messing around and dodging a friend. But this is now. And every suspicious thing, no matter how small, boils down to one name in my mind: Opal.

I stand there a moment, almost turning around and going back into the safety of the café but that's ridiculous because I don't know it's her. The odds are surely stacked against it.

But if it is, if that person *is* Opal, what can she do, really? She could stab me in the street, attack me, but this constant fear, watching out for her, is driving me insane.

The couple are chatting, laughing about something together, and the figure is walking directly behind them. Advancing closer to me by the second.

And then all at once, they're right in front of me and the figure behind them is revealed. Opal Vardy.

She looks wild-eyed and desperate, as if she's searching for something but isn't quite sure what. There's no sign of the shiny hair, the sparkling eyes and wide smile of the woman in George's photograph. I might not have even realised they were the same woman if we'd just passed in the street. But this person is definitely the one I met briefly outside the urology ward. She has that same neediness emanating from her like steam.

'Stop following me around!' I yell, the frustrations of my conversation with Steph fuelling my indignation. 'Sort out your own life and leave us alone!'

The sound of my own voice almost makes me jump out of my skin. The couple falter as the woman nudges the man and they look at me warily as they pass by.

Then all of a sudden, it's just me and Opal. We stand in silence, two women squaring up to each other. Face to face, eye to eye. Like two boxers waiting for the bell. And I do feel as if I am fighting, for both the safety of my children and for my right to be with George without her interference.

George has been adamant on one point, and that is that I must have no contact with her.

'She's like poison, Darcy. One drop and she's into your bloodstream, corrupting everything that's good. She thrives on attention, so don't give her any.'

I break the stare, turn and walk briskly back up the road the way I came.

'Darcy, wait!' I shudder at the sound of her shrill voice uttering my name, but I don't turn around.

I feel rigid, like a robot, as I stride forth, focusing on putting one foot in front of the other, my mind racing. I clock the vehicles coming past, praying for a vacant cab. She's still calling to me, following me, when at last I spot one. I put out my arm and it slows, pulling up so two wheels are on the pavement.

As I rush towards it, a hand clutches at my upper arm. I pull away and spin around, expecting to face her fury.

Yet there are no devil horns on her head, she brandishes no weapons, nor are there vitriolic words spat in my face. Just eyes that aren't as much wild now as tired and sad, and a pale, slightly puffy face.

'Darcy, please. Just give me five minutes. Listen to what I have to say and then you can make up your mind about—'

'Take your hands off me,' I yell, and pull open the cab door, sliding in and locking it. I feel breathless with adrenalin, but I just about manage to tell the driver my home address before sinking back into the seat. My heart hammers on my chest wall, making me feel nauseous.

Relief floods through me, but as the cab pulls away, Opal hammers on the window. I sit bolt upright and she presses her face up close, calling out words I can no longer hear.

'Blimey, she's got an axe to grind, hasn't she, love?' The driver laughs, putting his foot down and leaving Opal behind us. 'Bye bye, crazy woman.'

I don't answer him; I can't. I just want to get home and sort this mess out once and for all with George.

After today's confrontation, I've made up my mind.

I'm going to the police whether he likes it or not.

Typically, George is working late tonight. He sees his private patients on a Tuesday and Wednesday evening until 9 p.m. I have a few hours to myself before the kids get back. They've all got clubs straight after school, so I have some time to think about the idea that has been constantly circling in my mind since George told me how Opal is making his life a misery.

I make a coffee and sit quietly in the living room. I'm already developing favourite spots in my new home, and this is definitely one of them. It's situated at the back of the house where wide French doors lead out onto a small patio and the long-grassed lawn.

Romy is such a well-behaved child, you would never guess a little one lived here. She has a quiet nature, and although she'll giggle at the boys when they ape about, she rarely joins in, preferring to tuck herself into a corner and observe proceedings.

I hope that with time, I'll win her trust. When I try and show her affection, or pull her close, she stiffens and can't wait to escape my embrace. That saddens me, as I have a lot of love to give.

I sip my coffee, certain that the boys will eventually manage to introduce her to the joys of football and cricket. My eyes alight on the glossy new goalposts on the lawn, a symbol of George's kindness and thoughtfulness.

I want to believe George is invested in us and wants the best for us all, I do. But I'm afraid because once, I believed with all my heart that Joel was devoted to our little family and look what happened.

But George is not Joel and Opal is not Daniela. The situation is completely different. This is the present and that's the past.

I feel a little calmer now, and force my thoughts back to the problem in hand. George is bound to feel protective and has tried to shield me from Opal's toxicity but it's obviously not working. We've been given this wonderful opportunity of making a new family, and I feel a dull rage inside when I think about anyone trying to scupper that.

George is so busy with his career, it makes sense for him to push the problem away and convince himself that Opal will tire of her games. When she sent that awful death bouquet, he took the flowers from my arms and dumped them unceremoniously in the wheelie bin.

'Don't give it another thought,' he said as he closed the door and gave me a bright smile. It was as though he believed that by removing the blooms from sight, he'd made the problem go away. George might be a skilled and brilliant surgeon with a detailed knowledge of the human body, but he has very little understanding of an obsessed mind.

A cramp of hypocrisy makes itself known in my lower abdomen as Daniela's perfect face drifts into my mind's eye.

Thankfully, I've never had the urge to send her funeral flowers or disturb her in restaurants, as George has had to put up with.

But, before she moved away to Manchester, I did drive to her house on several occasions and just sat in the car, staring up at the softly lit windows where Joel spent so many nights, when I believed he was working to make a better life for me and the boys.

In the early days, just after his death, when Daniela first ran off to Manchester, I contacted her several times under the cover of a false profile, saying, I'm ashamed to admit, some not very nice things. And shockingly, up until I met George, I'd been regularly and obsessively monitoring her life and activities online, to the extent that I'd look at the clock and be shocked to find I'd been sitting there for over an hour, while the boys watched television, utterly absorbed in my snooping.

I hated her for what she did to us, truly hated her. It blinded me, negated every step I tried to take to move on with my life.

Yet I've never approached anyone she knows or tried to directly push myself into her life. Daniela hasn't got children, although when I grilled a reluctant Steph, she said it wasn't through lack of trying. Daniela just never managed to fall pregnant. Joel obviously knew the problem wasn't him because he was father to our two perfect sons! I'm not sure Steph told me the full story but it sounded close enough.

Daniela has been a drug. That's the only way I can adequately describe it. A drug I hated but once needed, one I've been unable to wean myself off. Even now, I still check her online profiles periodically although that's far, far less than it used to be.

Never did I think any good could possibly come out of this sad and shameful period in my life, but after today's confrontation, I've had a bit of an epiphany: I'm probably expertly qualified to understand the workings of Opal's mind. Far better than logically minded, academic George could possibly do.

The time has come to stop listening to his advice on dealing with the problem. I love him, and although his reasons for letting her carry on with her disturbing campaign are valid, they don't make enough sense for me to continue to put my boys at risk.

I take another sip of my coffee and grimace when I find I've been so embroiled in my thoughts, it's gone cold. But I don't make another. I reach for my phone instead, and before I get cold feet, I call the non-emergency number to speak to a police officer.

43

'Let me get this straight, madam. This woman is stalking your partner, not yourself?' says the slightly bored-sounding officer on the end of the line.

I've explained the situation as clearly as I can, but the police operator still seems not to be getting it.

'She started off stalking him, but the situation has now escalated. I've already explained this. If we hadn't gone outside during the lodge incident I've just described, one of our children might well have been abducted.'

'But you said you weren't able to obtain visual identification of the suspect.'

'My partner's daughter did though.'

'And how old is she?'

'She's six.'

Silence on the other end of the line.

'Well who else could it be?' I snap and then I'm immediately contrite. 'Sorry, I didn't mean to snap. It's just so frustrating. We have every reason to believe it was her, and the lodge park management must have thought so too, because they put on additional security.'

It's just like the brick wall George said he came up against when he went to the police himself. Everything Opal does affects our life tremendously but leaves no trace of any proof.

'What about the coffee shop incident?' I say.

'As far as I can ascertain from what you've told me, the woman asked to speak to you,' the operator stated. 'She didn't attack you, or threaten you?'

'No, but… What do I need in order for you to speak to this person, warn her off our family? Do you really want to wait until she takes one of our kids? The papers would be very interested in the fact that I tried to get police help beforehand.'

It's a low blow, and worse, it doesn't work.

'As it's your partner who seems to be at the centre of this situation, and for some time before meeting you, so I suggest you ask him to contact his local police station with full details including dates, times and any other relevant information.'

Great! I can just imagine George's reaction to me telling him this.

'Whatever happened to the new stalking act I read about a while ago?'

'The Protection of Freedoms Act 2012 is in place, but incidences of stalking can't be taken in isolation. There needs to be a clear record kept over time, and that's why I'm suggesting that you—'

'Fine. Thanks. You've been very helpful – *not!*'

I slam down the phone, my throat and face burning. They were absolutely useless, just like George said. I've questioned his lack of action so many times, and yet here I am, in exactly the same predicament myself. I wouldn't bother calling for advice again.

Yet a part of me knows that what the operator said makes perfect sense. We need to keep Opal's antics logged, so the police can see there's a clear record of incidents. I know George has never kept one, so we'd have to start from scratch, and it would take forever to compile a case that reflects how awful the reality of the situation is.

But if she's to be stopped and we're to keep our children safe, then I guess that's exactly what needs to be done. It occurs to me that I might start by calling the council to try and trace the cab driver who picked me up earlier. He witnessed Opal's unstable and aggressive behaviour.

George and I could also sit down and try to remember dates and times of the incidents that have happened recently, even those that can't be proven to be Opal's doing like the funeral flowers, the mess on my car. That would give us a good start.

Then, out of nowhere, my mind lights up with another idea that might just help convince the police there's a problem. I could contact the management of the lodge park and asked them to confirm details of the Christmas Eve incident in an email. That's the kind of evidence the police will take seriously.

I pull up the lodge website on my phone and click on the telephone link. After a couple of rings, the call is answered. I explain that we recently visited and had a concern, and that I need to speak to the manager.

'Hold the line, please, I'll just put you through.' Awful tinny muzak rattles my ear until a polite male voice with an accent interrupts and ends the torture.

'Good afternoon, Antony Romano speaking. How may I help you today?'

Romano! I distinctly remember George mentioning that was the name of the man he spoke to. For once, something is on my side.

I give him my name, and George's as the lead booking contact, and explain again that we stayed over the Christmas period in one of the two Woodland Supreme lodges.

'Excellent. Let me pull your reservation details up on screen for that period... Ah yes, I have you here. Two adults, three children in a Woodland Supreme, booked in the name of George Mortimer.'

'That's right. There was an incident not long after our arrival when a woman lurking in the woods tried to communicate with our children.' I take a breath, aware that I'm talking too fast. 'George reported it and you agreed to provide additional security around our lodge.'

A moment of silence. Then, 'Who was it exactly that your partner spoke to, madam?'

I frown. 'It was you. When he came back, he told me he'd spoken to the manager, a Mr Romano.'

I suppose he speaks to a lot of people in his job and might not instantly recall a conversation. But when he replies, he doesn't sound confused at all.

'It wasn't me, I'm certain of that. I'd taken holiday leave and didn't come back to work until the twenty-seventh of December. Your partner must have spoken to the duty manager working that day, but it's very strange…' I hear him tapping the keyboard. 'There's no note of the report on the reservation.'

'Perhaps they forgot to do it, I'm sure it's a very busy period.'

'No,' he says firmly. 'Absolutely all formal communications with guests must be logged, and something of this nature… It would definitely have been filed, and reported to the police as well.'

I bite down on my tongue. What is he saying? That I'm *lying*?

'I am not doubting what you say,' he adds hurriedly, breaking the terse silence. 'Just that I will need to investigate this issue further with my colleagues.'

He asks me to put everything in an email and send it to him personally.

When I end the call, I sit for a moment with my head in my hands. My first thought is that I've hit yet another brick wall but it's swiftly followed by a far more troubling conclusion.

If George didn't in fact speak to Mr Romano as he'd said, then did he actually care enough about our children's safety to report the incident at all?

44

George gets home later than expected. Something about him makes me take pause. He has a sort of confidence, a swagger that I haven't noticed before.

His manner reminds me of how Joel used to act on occasion. He'd say he'd had a good day at work but of course, with hindsight, I know now he'd probably been with his 'other' woman.

'You look very pleased with yourself,' I say lightly.

'I've had a good day.' He beams. 'Confirmation of my interview for the promotion for starters and then an interesting meeting after work with a colleague. My kind of day!'

It's a shame I'm about to wipe the smile off his face but I can't waste time fretting about that. Some things just have to be said.

'I've been busy myself today.'

'Oh yes? What've you been up to?'

And so I tell him about the altercation with Opal outside the café.

'What the hell were you thinking of?' George puts down his glass of wine with a hard clunk and tiny drops of the thick red liquid within leap up towards the rim. 'I told you not to have any contact at all with her.'

'I know what you *told* me, but I came out of the café and she accosted me! I barely said a word to her.' I feel the tears stacking up behind my eyes. This feels so frustrating and unfair. 'Something's got to be done here. She's making our lives a misery.' The first tears plop down my cheeks and I try to sniff the others back.

George claps his hand to his forehead. 'Sorry. I'm sorry I snapped at you. It's just… I could do without it, Darcy. If this interview goes well, I'm on the cusp of being offered the job, and Opal could go off on one and completely ruin it for me.'

'I know your job is important to you, but you seem to have lost sight of everything else… stuff that's far more important than work – our kids' safety!'

'The children aren't at risk. I don't know how many times I need to tell you that.'

'Is that why you didn't report the incident at the lodge park to the manager?'

A beat of silence, and I swear the room temperature drops a degree.

'What are you talking about?' He stares at me, baffled.

Now I've no choice but to come clean. Even though I feel my actions are thoroughly reasonable, I still feel a bit of a weasel for not telling him what I intended doing.

'I rang the police to ask advice about the situation,' I say.

'Please tell me you're joking.'

But this is no joking matter. I feel a resolve growing inside. I did the right thing, despite what George says.

'I rang the non-emergency number, that's all. You won't discuss the situation and I'm beside myself, constantly on edge and watchful of the kids.'

'And what happened? Absolutely nothing, I expect. They weren't interested when I approached them, I already told you that.'

'They said we need to keep an incident log. It makes sense when you think about it.'

He stares at the wall and doesn't comment, but I'm undaunted.

'So I thought it might be a good idea to ask the lodge park manager to send over an email confirming your report of an intruder.' I'm trying to keep my voice level, but his continued lack of response is getting to me. 'I spoke to Mr Romano, the manager you said you reported it to, and he told me he was on annual leave at the time. Plus there's no record of the incident on the park's computer system.'

He turns and looks at me then, his eyes full of disappointment.

'And so your instant conclusion was that I'm a liar, is that it?' He looks down at his hands, clasped in front of him between his knees, and shakes his head slowly.

'What was I supposed to think?' I cry out. 'You won't discuss Opal with me, you don't seem to care that our children might be in danger. I'm at the end of my tether with it all.'

I'm suddenly both afraid of losing him but determined to push him on the issue, whatever the outcome might be.

His reaction is calm and considered.

'I asked to speak to Mr Romano because his picture was up in reception as the general manager. And I did speak to a man, but I never thought to ask, "Are you Mr Romano?" I was worrying about getting back to the lodge to make sure you were all safe. I'm sorry if you think I misled you.'

'I… It's just he said there was no record of it on the computer, and—'

'The place was in chaos when I got over there!' George objects. 'Santa Claus outside on his sleigh waiting to get the all-clear, elves and reindeer hanging around the place… They didn't know whether they were coming or going.'

I press my lips together. It would be hilarious if it wasn't so serious. But George has put his point over well. Maybe there is a chance his chat with the manager was overlooked.

'I understand it's a massive dilemma for you, George, hoping Opal will just give up so your career isn't affected, but this has gone on for too long. Things have escalated and I think it's a good time to take her power away.' I keep my voice level, trying to appeal to his logical nature. 'Look, I know this will probably sound crazy to you, but have you considered coming clean about the operation?'

'What operation? What are you talking about?' He stands up quickly.

I stare at him steadily. 'The operation where you made an error of judgement and a man died?' I say, deadpan. 'I thought that's what she was holding over you?'

He's pacing up and down. I've never seen him this flustered. 'I don't know, Darcy. I can't think straight at the moment.'

'Is there something else, George? Something you're not telling me? Because I—'

'No!' He spins around and faces me, his eyes wild. 'There's nothing else, I swear. Just leave it, can't you?'

I stand up. 'No, actually. I can't leave it. I care too much about my boys and I care too much about Romy, too. You've lost sight of what's important here, George. It's time to stand up to her.'

'Don't lecture me about what's important. I've spent my whole life standing up to people who've tried to put me down from as far back as my schooldays, and now it seems you've joined their ranks.'

'What? Don't be ridiculous. I'm on your side... *our* side!'

'Are you, Darcy? Are you really?' He stands still and whips around to glare at me. 'Maybe you have secrets of your own.'

'What do you mean by that?' My armpits flood with perspiration. My heart feels like a battering ram in my chest as I push away the stuff that fills my head.

He stands there silently for a moment, as if he's deciding whether to answer me or not.

'I suppose what I'm saying is that sometimes it feels like you're playing a part on the outside.' He fixes me with a look. 'As if you're not quite the same person on the inside.'

Before I can reply, he strides across the room and slams the door behind him.

I sit aghast, staring out of the window. And I don't move when George gets into his car and zooms off, scattering gravel everywhere.

The most shocking thing to me is that I think he might know about the one thing I'm so desperate to keep hidden. But how?

45

They'd been laughing so hard playing the board game that Kane had ended up having a coughing fit. Harrison waited to make sure his brother didn't need his inhaler. When he was sure he was OK, he left the room.

'Stay here, I'll go get us some juice,' Harrison said.

They were having a great time here at Grandma and Grandad's house. It felt like being at home now, seeing as their old home, where his dad had lived with them, had been left behind.

George's house was really nice and the garden was even bigger than his grandparents'. George had put in some really cool goalposts to make them feel welcome, which had been kind of him, but it still didn't feel like it was *their* garden.

Maria looked after them quite a bit now. She was kind and easy to fool; she didn't seem to mind how much television they watched and didn't impose a thirty-minute gaming slot like their mum did. She spent a lot of time doing crafts with Romy.

Harrison felt certain something weird had happened between the adults, but nobody discussed it with them. In a way, it felt like he and his brother had been forgotten about.

Even his bedroom felt as if it belonged to someone else, but his mum had said it would make a big difference when it was decorated the way he wanted it.

Some things had gotten better, though, since they'd moved in with George and Romy.

For one thing, his mum didn't sit for hours staring at her laptop now. Harrison had peeked over her shoulder a couple of times, and it was always the same woman's photos she was staring at.

She went out more and smiled more and had started teaching more yoga classes, which seemed to make her happy. He was glad. He wanted his mum to be happy.

As he neared the bottom of the stairs, he heard lowered voices coming from the kitchen. Instinctively he lightened his footfall and crept down the rest of the way quietly.

One thing he'd learned was that when adults tucked themselves away and lowered their voices, they were usually talking about something that wasn't meant for the ears of kids.

Which obviously meant it was going to be interesting.

He sidestepped the giveaway creaking middle bit of the third step from the bottom, and finally his socked feet reached the smooth polished floorboards of the hallway.

Padding up to the kitchen door, which was ajar, Harrison stopped to listen. He could hear the faint sound of the ride-on mower, which meant his grandad was still up at the top end of the garden, so there was little risk of being caught eavesdropping here.

He relaxed a little and leaned his head on the door frame, listening to Grandma and Aunt Steph's hoarse whispers.

'But I know she thinks the world of those boys,' he heard his grandma say. Her voice sounded sad.

'I know, but that's not the issue, Mum. The concern is how competent she is to look after them.' That was Aunt Steph. 'She's clearly still in denial and I doubt that's going to change now. We haven't helped matters, playing along with her delusion all this time.'

'I told you, if it means seeing the kids, I'll keep doing it.'

Harrison frowned. It sounded like they were talking about him and Kane, but *who* was in denial? And *competent to look after the kids*… what did that even mean?

'George seems like a lovely man; she's struck gold there. Perhaps he'll have a positive influence on her.' Grandma again, still sounding troubled.

'Maybe, but he isn't their father, is he? *We're* their flesh and blood, the closest thing to Joel they've got left. It's down to us to protect his memory.'

They were talking about George, his mum and even their dad. It felt to Harrison like his mum should be here, included in the conversation.

Aunt Steph sounded like she didn't really like George, and that gave Harrison a strange sort of satisfaction, because even though George had been kind and welcoming to them, it was true what she said: he wasn't their dad. He never would be.

But he got a slight tummy ache when he thought they might be saying bad things about his mum.

Harrison couldn't be sure they were, because they were talking in that weird code that adults sometimes used amongst themselves. They seemed to just understand each other without saying everything in full detail. It was a bit like a riddle.

He heard his Aunt Steph sigh.

'Anyway, you're meeting Dani for coffee tomorrow morning. I think that might be the best way to sort the whole sorry mess out. And when Darcy comes over for lunch, we'll tell her then.'

Danny… who was *he*? Aunt Steph's boyfriend was called Dave. What if… Harrison frowned. It was all getting too confusing but Harrison thought he might mention what he'd overheard to his mum. She had a right to know they'd been whispering about her, right?

He heard feet shuffling in the kitchen and dashed back to the stairs.

When the door opened and Aunt Steph came out, he was just jumping off the bottom step.

'I've come to get juice,' he said hurriedly.

'Everything OK, champ?' She grinned, high-fiving him as he passed.

'Yes thanks, Aunt Steph,' he said, more brightly than he felt. 'Everything is fine.'

46

As agreed with Steph, I drive over to Brenda's house for lunch. I park up and reach the front door, and I'm surprised when it opens and Leonard appears.

'Oh, hello.' I smile. 'I thought you were playing golf today.'

Leonard's attempt as a smile falls short and his lips stretch into a grimace.

'We've had... there's been a change of plan,' he mumbles, tapping his fingertips on the door frame.

'Is everything all right, Leonard?' The more I look at him, the more jumpy I see he is. There are dark shadows under his eyes, and he looks a bit of a strange colour.

'Everything is fine. I've got this, Dad.' Steph appears from behind him. 'Come through, Darcy.'

Something's wrong. Steph's acting a bit formal and Leonard's just being plain weird. As Steph closes the front door, I walk into the kitchen to find Brenda standing by the open window, drawing in great breaths of cold air. To top it all, when Steph returns from the hallway, I see that Dave is with her. It's a full house. Unheard of.

'What's this? Some kind of family meeting?' I laugh, although I feel a bit miffed. It's not the casual girlie lunch Steph told me it was going to be. Anyway, there's no sign of any food and the kitchen table isn't set.

Nobody else joins in with my light-hearted banter.

'We've been concerned about you for a long time now, Darcy,' Steph begins, obviously the appointed spokesperson. 'But it seems now that things are getting worse.'

'We're all worried about Kane and Harrison,' Dave pipes up, earning himself a hard stare from Steph, which he appears to ignore. 'They seem quieter than usual, and we wondered if you meeting George and moving in with him so fast has been the best thing for them in the circumstances.'

I look at him, incredulous. This man, who barely shifts his gaze from the television if I pop round to Steph's, has said more words to me in the last five seconds than he usually does in a whole month.

'I never realised you took so much interest in the boys, Dave. I'm impressed.'

His face reddens and he opens his mouth to say something else.

'Dave. Don't,' Steph says through her teeth.

I look at them then, in turn. 'You're actually all *worried*? You don't think they're well-adjusted enough to cope with me having a new relationship?'

They all have the grace to look away from my laser stare.

'You think I've just torn them from their old home without properly discussing their feelings on the matter?'

'Is it true the children were nearly abducted at Christmas by someone lurking in the woods near your lodge?' Brenda's voice is strained, and she moves away from the window and sits down heavily on a small wooden stool in the corner of the kitchen. 'Harrison told us all about it. Apparently there was some woman hanging around. He even thought he'd seen someone watching him in the school playground. Is all this true, Darcy?'

'Sounds like stalking to me,' Steph remarks.

My heart begins to pound. George and I have obviously been speaking far too openly in front of the boys. I feel sick at the thought that Opal might have been at their school, though. Why on earth didn't Harrison say anything to me?

'The lodge park management assured us nothing was amiss, and the park had full security.' I'm trying to strike a balance between being affronted and reassuring them, but it's not working. My words sound forced and an octave too high. 'There was no evidence to suggest someone was targeting our kids.'

'Well, Harrison still sounded nervous about it,' Brenda says, and I kick myself for not having sat down properly and talked to him about it. 'He says that all kinds of strange things have been happening. That you received some flowers that George dumped in the bin, and that you told George some woman had accosted you outside a café.'

I've underestimated Harrison's ability to understand stuff that's happening. He's nearly eleven years old, not a baby any more. I should have explained things to him so he wasn't unnerved; it might have avoided a situation like this.

'Right, well if you've all finished passing judgement, I'll get off.' I turn around to leave, but Dave blocks my exit. 'Excuse me,' I say icily.

'Take this with you then.' He pushes a thick white envelope towards me. I stare at it, bemused.

'Take it!' Steph glowers.

They're closing in on me like pack rats. I feel my chest tighten, and my breathing becomes faster, shallower.

I realise Leonard is standing back from the others and hasn't said a word.

'Leonard,' I say, my voice rising. 'What the hell is this?'

'Just take it, Darcy,' he says, sounding worn out. 'It's for the best.'

Dave waves the envelope in front of me again, and then Steph snatches it from him and shoves it into my open handbag.

'We're applying for custody of the boys, permanently this time,' Brenda says, gently, almost regretfully. 'You're not in a fit state to take care of them, Darcy.'

'What?' I laugh, but inside I feel like my insides have just liquidated.

'We know what you've been up to, stalking Daniela online and even going to her house when Joel died! All these years you've been an obsessive stalker yourself.' Brenda shakes her head and I turn to glare at Steph, but she won't meet my eyes. 'And now there's some crazy woman shadowing the family. This *can't* be good for the boys. You must see that.'

'They've already lost their dad, love,' Leonard chips in, his tone regretful. 'They need some stability in their life.'

Something sparks inside me.

'They were never used to having their dad around full-time anyway, because as you know, your son turned out to be a liar and a cheating rat of the worst order. So don't worry yourselves too much about that; they're probably better off without him.'

Brenda yelps as if my words have speared her.

I push past Dave and stride outside, slamming the front door behind me.

I don't look back. I get in the car and pull away immediately.

When I reach the top of the street, I breathe out. If the papers in my bag really are a legal bid for custody of my sons, I've got another massive problem to deal with.

But that final altercation and those things I said about Joel?

After years of keeping my mouth shut, all that felt so good.

47

When my mobile phone rings, I snatch it up. It's three hours since I left the message for George.

'Just to let you know I'll be on my way in ten minutes. I saw your text message. Is everything OK?'

His casual tone annoys me.

'No. Everything is not OK! Didn't you check your messages before now? It was important, George. I needed to speak to you. I've got big problems with Joel's family.'

'Sorry.' He sounds tired. 'It's been a long, tough shift. Two life-saving operations and we lost a patient.'

I'm momentarily shamed into silence.

'Sorry. That must have been awful for you.' Is it me, or does he always find a way of making me feel guilty for complaining? 'And I know you sometimes can't get back to your locker to check your phone, but this was really important.'

'Don't worry, you weren't to know. Tell me now, what's up?'

'It's complicated. Just get yourself home safely. The kids want to watch some movie on Netflix after their baths, so we should get some time to talk then.'

Thirty minutes later, I hear George's Audi pull up on the gravelled area outside the front door. The kids are all clean and in their pyjamas; they're fed and watered and watching their movie in the television room.

I should be feeling content and looking forward to a nice evening ahead, but my heart is in my mouth. Tonight feels like a bit of a watershed. I've asked Maria to give us a little privacy in the lounge and, judging by the sour look on her face, she isn't used to being told any of the house is off limits to her.

'Well, this is nice.' George beams, kissing me on the cheek, and glancing at the two glasses of red I've placed on the coffee table. 'I could get used to a welcome like this every night.'

He's loaded down with his briefcase in one hand and a stack of folders under his other arm. I take the briefcase and he dumps the files on the hall table. I see from the name stickers and hospital stamp that they are patient records.

'I'll just take a quick shower,' he says, jutting his chin forward and loosening his tie. 'Then you can tell me what's on your mind.'

'OK,' I mumble, wondering how long I can keep it all to myself. I walk into the kitchen, pleased that Maria is in the utility room doing the laundry.

A few minutes later, I hear the low growling noise that signals the en suite shower is running upstairs.

I take the platter I prepared earlier out of the fridge and look over the artfully arranged Italian meats, olives, sun-dried tomatoes and artichokes. I add some mozzarella and pecorino, and a spoonful of chilli jam at the side. Then I grab the cutting board and slice half a French stick, layering it neatly on a wooden board that matches the platter.

Everything looks so perfect here. It *should* be perfect. But my heart is heavy and my head feels so full of problems, part of me feels like running away instead of facing up to things. And getting George to face up to things too. Just lately it feels nigh impossible.

'This looks nice.' He appears in the doorway and strides over to the sofa, kissing me on the top of the head as he walks behind me. He sits down and picks up his wine, and before I can clink glasses with him, he gulps down a deep slug. 'Beats coming home to one of Maria's cheese sandwiches.'

I hold up my glass without much enthusiasm.

'It's been a tough day,' he sighs. Our glasses chime and George puts down his wine and pops an olive into his mouth. 'Before we eat, why don't you tell me what's up?'

You're not in a fit state to take care of them, Darcy. Brenda's voice echoes in my head. It's true that things have moved fast with me and George, but the boys are always my priority.

'Darcy?' He plucks a sun-dried tomato off the platter with his fingers, and a drop of oil falls onto the dark grey sweatpants he's changed into. I hand him a small side plate and a napkin. 'Thanks. So, what have Joel's family done to upset you?'

I take the papers out of the envelope, flatten them out and place them on the table. He doesn't pick them up. Instead, he butters a piece of bread.

'They got me over there on false pretences – supposedly a lunch with Steph and Brenda, but instead they gave me this.' My sinuses start to sting. 'They say they're going to apply for sole custody of the boys. They've been plotting against me. All of them.' A sob rises in my throat.

He stops chewing and looks at me. 'Well they won't get it. No court is going to hand kids over to their grandparents without exceptional circumstances. What reason do they give?'

You're not in a fit state to take care of them, Darcy.

'They say it's because of Opal Vardy. Harrison's told them some of the stuff that's been happening.' I wipe away the tears. 'They think I'm not looking after the boys properly because I've had my head turned by you too quickly.'

George puts down his glass and looks at me. 'That's ridiculous! Our problems with Opal are none of their business, and our relationship certainly isn't either.'

'It's the fact that my children are living here that worries them. If Opal decides to do something like she did in the woods at Christmas, or scares the boys by challenging them in the street like she did me…'

'You're all quite safe here,' he says, spearing some prosciutto. He loads his fork with meat and mozzarella and pops it into his mouth, chewing thoughtfully.

'She's not going to go away, George. We have to deal with it.'

'*We're* not dealing with anything, Darcy. *I* am. It's my problem and I *will* deal with it… with her. But it's going to take time. She'll lose interest eventually, and as you now know, that's our best bet, because the police have zero interest.' He lays down his fork and looks at me.

I nibble on an olive and its bitter taste floods my mouth. I put it down on my plate and it rolls off onto my lap. I'm making such a mess of everything.

'The police have asked us to get an incident log together. There are things we can do: contact the cab driver who witnessed her causing a scene outside the café, pursue the complaint you made at the lodge park… It's inconvenient, but if we put our minds to it, we can start to make life difficult for her.'

'She's *irritating*, not dangerous, Darcy.'

'No! She approached the kids at the lodge park, she felt she had a right to confront me outside the café! For goodness' sake, what has she really got on you, George?'

I bang my glass down on the table and the stem snaps, cutting my finger. Red wine sprays everywhere.

George rushes into the kitchen for the first aid box, checks my finger for glass and expertly applies a small bandage. Then he gently lifts my chin so I'm looking right at him.

'Stop worrying. It's you, me and the kids now, and that's all that's important.'

'No. I can't stand it any more, George. I could lose the boys over your refusal to tackle that… that crazy bitch!'

'For the final time, Darcy, *stop*. Opal Vardy is nothing to us and she can't spoil our happiness together unless we let her. I love you, I love the boys, and that's all you need to be thinking about from now on. Why can't you trust me on this?'

I stand up. My legs feel shaky and my body is aching as if I'm coming down with a bad cold, but it has to be said.

'I'm sorry, George, I just can't do this any more.' My voice is barely a whisper. 'I've tried everything to make you see that you're deluded about Opal, but the time has come.'

He sighs. 'The time has come for what, exactly?'

'You have to choose. Deal with Opal, or me and the boys are moving out. There's no room for us all in your life.'

48

George grasps my hands in his. 'I hear what you're saying, how you feel. Let me think about it all. Please, Darcy, give me a little time.'

I don't answer him. It's not the response I was hoping for, and let's face it, he's had all the time in the world to sort this out – from long before I met him.

I should have given him an ultimatum before now, I've let this whole Opal situation go on far too long. But I can't move out immediately, that's not logical. In some ways it could cause more problems than it solves. Joel's family's case would be strengthened if I move the boys again, so soon.

I have to give George a little time as he asks. So long as he understands I absolutely meant what I said.

While George finishes up some paperwork in his office, I clear up our supper dishes.

'I can do this, madam,' Maria says, making me jump as I carry in the supper dishes. She closes the utility room door behind her, shutting out the noise of the washing machine.

'It's fine, thanks, Maria, I honestly don't mind.' She backs off without saying anything else and I wonder if she thinks I'm trying to take over her duties. I place the dishes on the side. 'If you don't mind then, I'll let you take these and I'll look in on the children.'

'I just did and they're fine.'

I turn around and she holds my stare.

'Well, I'll look in on them anyway,' I say firmly.

Upstairs, I check on little Romy first. I push open her door a little wider and tiptoe in. The soft glow from her night light illuminates the pink canopy that hangs around the top of her bed.

Her entire room is princess-themed, and having two boys, I find it fascinating to see the difference in their chosen decorations. Romy's white wardrobe and dressing table are beautifully hand-painted with glowing stars and flowers. I'm certain so many little girls would describe this as their dream bedroom.

I pad closer to the bed, my eyes adjusting to the dimness now. Her plump, flushed cheek twitches in the midst of a dream, the skin smooth and unblemished like a peach. I reach down and gently smooth back the wisps of dark blonde hair splayed across her face, and her long dark eyelashes flutter as though she knows on some level that I'm here.

My heart fills with affection for this tiny, loveable girl who lost her mummy and her twin sister so cruelly. I'd never try and take Lucy's place; it would be impossible. But I can make sure I'm the best stepmother that I can be to her, and provide all the love and guidance her own mummy would have done if her life hadn't been cut so tragically short.

I bend forward and kiss her cheek before creeping out to check on the boys further down the hall. George's deep voice carries upstairs as he potters around in the kitchen, chatting to Maria.

I push open Harrison's door, and smile to myself. The boys shared a room in our old house, and when I did my last check on them before bed, the sight of them asleep never failed to amuse me. Harrison – just as he is now – was always splayed across the bed, covers thrown awry, limbs dangling carelessly off the mattress. Kane, on the other hand, is a neat sleeper. Usually cocooned in his quilt, or a sheet if it's warmer, he looks like a little dormouse, snug and content in his resting hours.

I gently rearrange Harry's arms and legs so they're back on the bed, and kiss him before popping next door to Kane, who is wrapped up neatly as usual. From his pillow I pick up a bright green spotted Tyrannosaurus rex, whose tail is threatening to poke him in the eye, and place it on the floor.

The boys' rooms are still quite plain, painted cream with beige carpet, but they have big plans. Harrison, who is football mad, is currently trying to convince George that a Nottingham Forest theme would look brilliant in here, while Kane is debating dinosaur or superhero wallpaper.

Decisions, decisions.

I kiss Kane gently and leave the room. Only yesterday, I'd felt so grateful that my boys were safe and happy in their new home and now I'm worrying about leaving George and Joel's family taking them away from me.

George won't tell me the full story of why he seems so nervous of doing anything about Opal Vardy. When it comes to her, he just seems to roll over and blindly accept her attempts to control our lives. It has to be more than the fact that it could ruin his promotion prospects; that's just not a good enough excuse when his family's safety is on the line.

I decide here and now it leaves only one viable solution.

It's down to me to find out what's really going on.

Back downstairs, I glance into the lounge to see George sitting in there with a drink. I walk into the kitchen and stand in the doorway for a moment, watching Maria busying around. I glance at the wall clock and see she should have left twenty minutes ago.

She's the sort of person who just never stops. I've walked in the house lots of times and she's been unaware of my presence at first because she's working hard at some household task.

I'm pretty sure most folks, myself included, would be tempted to slack off just a touch now and again if my employers weren't around. But not Maria, it seems. She works like she's doing it for her own benefit.

'Oh, madam! I didn't see you there.' She lays her palm flat on her chest like I gave her a fright.

'Sorry if I startled you, Maria, but please, call me Darcy.' I push the kitchen door closed behind me. 'None of this "madam" business. You should get off, it's way past your home time.'

She nods, smiles a little tightly. 'Can I get you anything… *Darcy*? A tea, perhaps?'

'No, no. Thank you, I'm fine.' She doesn't look in any rush to get home, so I pull out a stool and sit at the breakfast bar. 'We've been here a little while now and you and I, we've had no chance to chat at all.'

Maria stops wiping down the work surfaces and looks at me. 'Chat… about what?'

Her body looks tense all of a sudden and every few seconds, the side of her mouth twitches, very slightly.

The last thing I want to do is upset Maria. She's so mild-mannered and kind to the children, George would not be impressed if he thought I was prying. Am I prying? Not exactly, just making conversation… you never know what might come up.

'Please don't look so worried, Maria!' I laugh. 'I just meant it would be nice to get to know you a little. I know George thinks a great deal of you and you've been with him for a long time, I think.'

She nods but her shoulders still look stiff.

'I think Mr Mortimer values what I do here.'

'I know he does. How did you come to work for him?'

She picks up her cloth again and rubs distractedly at a mark on the counter.

'Mr Mortimer put an advert in the village newsletter,' she says. 'My daughter told me about it and I applied. Of course, I instantly fell in love with little Romy.'

Her face softens a touch.

'Who wouldn't?' I smile. 'She's a delight and I know she really cares about you, too. Did you… did you know George's late wife, Lucy?'

She doesn't answer for a moment but turns to the sink and turns the tap on full pelt. I shift on my stool, wondering if I've upset her by mentioning Lucy. Although she's never been anything but pleasant to me, I've always felt held at arm's length from getting to know her.

'I knew Mrs Mortimer for a little while, that's all. Then she had Romy and died. It was all very sad. My heart broke for little Romy, growing up without a mother.'

I strain to hear what Maria's saying through the noise of the tap and I hope she turns it off in a moment.

George must have brought Maria on board to help when there were just the two of them here, before Romy was born. From what I've heard, Lucy had quite a privileged upbringing and was probably used to having some domestic help in the house.

'I hope I can be a mother of sorts to Romy,' I say, smiling to myself as I think about how we're getting closer now and how I'm slowly gaining the little girl's trust. 'She's young enough, I think, that eventually, I can play a full role in her life and—'

Maria turns off the tap and whips around to confront me, her face red and twisted.

'You will never be her mother! We were managing just fine before *you* came along.'

The change in her mood happens in a split second. Such is the strength of her reaction, I find myself slipping off the stool and taking a step back, reeling from the vitriol that's suddenly rolling off her in waves.

I open my mouth, feel my cheeks burning with the shock. Surely in a moment, she'll be begging for me to accept her apology.

Maria wrings the dishcloth hard, between her hands. She looks mad enough to do the same thing with my neck if she gets close enough.

'You've ruined everything with your interfering. *Everything!*' She juts her chin forward, speaks in a hissing whisper. 'You haven't a clue what you're getting into here.'

'Maria! For goodness' sake, calm down… what on earth's brought this outburst on? What do you mean, "what I'm getting into"?'

She shakes her head, biting down hard on her back teeth so I can see the muscles working in her jaw.

'Don't say I didn't warn you. If you mention this to Mr Mortimer, I'll deny everything and we both know who he'll be inclined to trust.' She glares at me as I fight and fail to respond with a suitably cutting reply. 'Now, if you don't mind, I have to get on.'

And with that she dumps the dishcloth in the sink and storms out of the room. I hear the door to the small cloakroom click across the hall.

I just sit there, on the kitchen stool, in shock. Five minutes pass and I hear Maria let herself out of the front door. I walk to the lounge and stand in the doorway. She passes in front of the window as she heads down the drive to the bus stop just down the road from the front gate.

I feel a bit shaky, so unexpected was her reaction. She must have been harbouring ill feelings towards me since I arrived here… since I first met George.

If she can keep her true feelings so well hidden, it makes me wonder if she really is as fond of my boys as she appears to be. Should someone who can act so volatile on the turn of a coin be left in sole charge of our children?

George becomes aware I'm standing there and turns around in his chair.

'Want to watch something on TV? Or shall we just have a drink and chat?'

'Yes please,' I say, forcing myself to remain calm. 'A drink and chat would be perfect.'

He disappears into the kitchen and returns with two gin and tonics. 'I thought we'd try the rhubarb and ginger one tonight. Someone I work with has recommended—'

'George, something happened just now, in the kitchen, with Maria,' I say in one breath. 'She attacked me… verbally, I mean. She said I'm interfering and ruining everything. She said I don't know what I'm getting into, here with you!'

'What?' George's hand freezes halfway to lifting his glass to his mouth.

'That's what she said. I just asked how long she'd worked for you and suggested I can soon take on more duties with Romy. I was making conversation, that's all, and then she just turned into this crazy woman.'

He takes a sip of his drink and puts his glass on to the coffee table, his brow furrowing. He doesn't say anything.

'You don't believe me, do you?' A whooshing sound starts in my ears. 'She was… like a different person. Aggressive and bitter in the space of a few seconds. I don't think she should be around our kids.'

'Maria's been with me a long time, Darcy,' he says softly.

'I know she has. But she has a big problem with me living here, George. I'm not sure there's room for both of us in this house.'

I wait for him to start defending Maria, to tell me it's all in my head or that I must be mistaken but he does none of those things.

'That must have been unnerving for you,' he says. 'I hadn't realised how territorial she's obviously become. I've probably given her more licence to run things in the home than I ought to have done.'

I nod, relieved he's taking me seriously.

'She seemed to flip when I said I'd like to do more in the house and play a full role in Romy's life.'

'I don't know what's got into her but you shouldn't have to put up with that,' George says grimly. 'I'll speak to her tomorrow.'

49

1995

The day after his crutches went was the day his problems really started again at school.

Instead of choosing the long route to the library at lunchtime, he picked a more direct way, though it was still much quieter than the main drag across the quad where everyone gathered. Walking slowly, he turned a corner and ran straight into the Panthers.

'We wait in the shadows until our prey appears... and then we pounce!' one of the older boys hissed, jumping in front of him like a warrior.

He stopped short, almost lost his balance. While he struggled to right himself and catch his breath, the tallest boy, the boy who had pushed him from the tower, stepped forward.

'So,' he sneered. 'Looks like you survived.'

He did not reply but stared straight ahead, feeling the weight of his books in the rucksack on his back. He began to run through the chapters in his mind, trying not to think about the tightness in his chest or the bone-deep ache in his legs.

The tall boy carried on talking, his sneering face seeming to move in and out of the younger boy's blurred vision. But the words of the book played in his head like an audio and he couldn't stop it, couldn't focus on what was being said to him.

His rucksack was pulled roughly from behind and he toppled over backwards, landing on the hard, cracked concrete. He heard himself yell out in pain, felt his bones crunching, his muscles snapping.

He tried to grab the shoulder straps, tried to hang onto the bag with its precious contents, but it was too late. One more tug and it came away, the books spilling out onto the floor.

Four very special hardback books.

'Well, well.' The tall boy crouched down and picked one of them up. 'Now this *is* interesting.'

50

The next day, George doesn't have an early-morning departmental meeting for once, so the five of us have breakfast together.

The kitchen is nice and big. George explained that around seven years ago, they had an extension built and installed a living area and the bifold doors that open out on to a wide expanse of composite decking.

'Lucy's original idea was for us to start the day with fresh air by taking al fresco breakfasts.' He grinned. 'But of course, the weather soon put paid to that. I think we might have managed it a handful of times that summer.'

George doesn't say much about Lucy and their life together, but piecing together the odd mention, I get the feeling she was a gentle, caring person. Certainly someone Maria thought highly of, anyway.

Perhaps someone I might have got on well with under different circumstances.

We've not spoken about Maria's outburst since last night, but I don't feel as if George doubts what I've said. It makes me wonder if he's witnessed her temper before.

I'm going to bide my time and see what comes of it before I demand Maria apologises or, even better, leaves her position. After our conversation about Opal, I don't want it to seem as if I'm issuing one ultimatum after the other to George.

During the morning, once I've taken the kids to school and picked up George's work shirts from the ironing service, I change our bedding and put a wash on. Maria's not in until later and that suits me fine. I don't want to face her again until George has spoken to her.

I did try and lessen her working hours once before but George was having none of it.

'I'm only teaching classes part-time,' I told George when we first moved in. 'I can pick up some of Maria's duties.'

'This house takes more upkeep than you'd imagine. Let's get you settled in first, then we can talk about the help.'

Before I sit down for a coffee, I double-lock the front door and ensure that the gate leading down the side of the house to the back garden is bolted from the inside. Then I rattle the handles of the bifold doors to ensure they're secure.

I've always been aware of security, but never like this. Now I find myself constantly aware of potential opportunities for someone to creep in. I glance out of the window, not to admire the garden, but to watch out for Opal Vardy. George would probably call me paranoid, but he seems to ignore the fact that she stalked us at Christmas and challenged me in the street.

I crank up the coffee machine, make a latte and drink it sitting at the breakfast bar, staring out at the lawn and wondering what I'll do if a figure suddenly appears at the glass.

I scratch absent-mindedly at my hand and when I look down, I see a couple of red scaly patches between my fingers. Eczema. I haven't suffered from it since the day the boys were taken from me and I was admitted to Edge House Clinic.

I can't carry on like this; it's silly. I'll make myself ill. It's just that I know how easy it is to skulk around the edges of someone's life without them being able to do anything about it legally.

It feels like I'm waiting for her next move, when actually I need to put myself more into a position of control.

*

After lunch, on my own Instagram page, I post a picture of the school I find on Google with the simple tagline: 'Looking forward to picking the kids up today.'

Usually Maria picks the children up after school, as sometimes it's too much of a rush for me to get there from my afternoon classes. Of course, Steph or Brenda used to do the honours for the boys a lot, but after yesterday's showdown that's certainly not going to be happening again.

I'm keen to collect them myself today anyway, because my intention, in posting the Instagram status, is to attempt to draw Opal out from the shadows. I scribble Maria a note telling her there's no need for her to go to school, imagining her bitter thoughts when she reads it later.

I collect Romy and Kane first, and then walk around the other side of the building to where the older children's classrooms are. I'm purposely walking in a relaxed manner, chatting to the children, but inside, my guts feel like they've been liquidised.

Contrary to what George would have me believe, if Opal is as crazy as I suspect, she could attack me, try and grab one of the kids… I could literally throw up just thinking about it. But I can't let that stop me from living an ordinary life and ensuring our kids' safety.

I take a deep breath and call to Harrison, who is heading towards the climbing frames that sit on a patch of AstroTurf next to the concrete area of the playground. As usual, he ignores me and begins to climb the tallest frame.

'Can I have a go on there too, Mum?' Kane asks me hopefully. 'I won't climb too high.'

'Go on then.' I nod, and he and Romy scamper off to join Harrison. It's another chance to hang around and see if my bait has the desired effect.

I've been watching the kids for a few minutes, trying to look relaxed and casual, when movement to the left causes me to glance sideways.

A slightly built figure dressed in jeans and a padded coat with a hood, steps out from behind the school building. Whoever it is sticks deliberately close to the wall. I think it's her. I think it's Opal.

The boys are now both swinging like monkeys on the climbing frame and Romy is standing watching them with that wide-eyed look of hers, as if she'd like to join in but is mentally running through all the reasons why she shouldn't. She's worryingly cautious for a six-year-old.

If it *is* Opal, I'm torn between rushing the children home and the possibility of actually speaking to her. Even though I wanted her to turn up, the thought of facing her freaks me out. She's completely obsessed with George, in the same way I've been obsessed with Daniela, but she's far bolder with it. I know only too well the pain such behaviour causes the person doing the stalking. How you battle in vain with yourself to try and stop your negative and destructive actions.

It's the easiest thing in the world, if you've never been through it, to think it's simply a case of choosing to stop. But it's an addiction of sorts, and you don't have to be a mad axe murderer to become obsessed with someone else.

You don't want to necessarily hurt the object of your interest either. In my case, I was always looking for something – *anything* – that made Daniela look slightly less perfect and could make me feel a smidgeon better about myself.

What Opal is after though, I'm not entirely sure. Probably just to be with George.

I stand still and watch the figure. The figure watches me back. Then slowly, cautiously, she begins to walk towards me.

'Hello, Darcy,' she says when she gets closer.

There are one or two parents still around, chatting, but with us being delayed on the play equipment, most of the kids have been collected now. Soon we will be the only ones left.

'Why are you doing this?' I say in the face of her steely glare. No tired eyes and worn expression in evidence today. 'Me and George... we're together now. You've got to accept that.'

'I don't *have* to accept anything,' she says sullenly. 'I'm not hurting anyone.'

'You're hanging around our children's school and you call that not doing anything?' She averts her eyes, stares at the floor, and it gives me the impetus to continue. 'You need to accept that your relationship with George is over and get on with your life. Take it from someone who knows these things.'

She looks as if I'm speaking a foreign language, as if I couldn't possibly understand.

'You think you know him, but you don't,' she says in a monotone. 'You haven't got a clue who George Mortimer is. Only I really understand him.'

Here we go. Here's the bit where she tells me that George loves her and I'm just standing in the way of their happy-ever-after. I almost roll my eyes but manage to refrain from doing so.

'You need to stay out of George's life, out of my life. You need to stay away from our children, or I promise you, I'll get the police involved.' My tone grows colder. 'You're wasting the best years of your life following someone around who doesn't want you. You should deal with it.'

My intention is good, even if I sound like a queen bitch.

She laughs. 'I'd like nothing more than to get on with my life. But first, he has to give me what I want.'

51

She turns and looks over at Romy, and my chest feels as though it's been crushed by a heavy weight. What if she snatches her, right here, right now? What will I tell George... that I lured her out and had a chat to her?

His voicemail from earlier today replays in my mind. His voice was buoyant when he told me about the interview. His lifelong career dream is about to be realised; he'll never forgive me if I mess this up.

'Romy?' She spins around when I call her name, dark blonde curls bouncing, cheeks like shiny red apples in the cold. 'If you put on your gloves, you can have a little climb too. Stay on the lower bars, though.'

'Ha! You've got to use the baby's bars!' Kane calls unkindly.

I scold him and turn back to Opal, relieved now that Romy is further away on the climbing apparatus.

'I know what you have on George.' I lower my voice. 'He's told me everything.'

'Oh, I doubt that.' Opal laughs, and her eyes gain a manic gleam. 'I doubt he's told you *everything*.'

But he *has* told me. He may not be dealing with this in the way I'd prefer, but he has been honest and open and I do see his dilemma even if I disagree with it in principle. If he goes to the police about Opal, she could cause a lot of trouble for him.

I look at her, look through her aggressive manner and I see that she is scraggy and pale, with dark circles under her eyes. For a second, I can see myself, just months after Joel died, when I felt at my lowest ebb. Desperate. Alone.

'You and I, we have more in common than you think.' I soften my voice slightly.

'I'm sure that's not the case,' she says snappily.

She doubts everything. Just like I did for so long.

I don't feel any warmth towards this woman who is making our lives so difficult, but I'm trying really hard to empathise. It's in all of our interests if I can somehow solve the problem that is Opal Vardy. The boys and I are trying to build a new family with George and Romy, and so I regard this approach of mine as a sort of investment for the future.

I'm sure George wouldn't see it that way, but to date, he hasn't had much success in getting Opal off his back and I've issued a genuine threat that I'll be moving out with the boys if he doesn't resolve the situation soon.

She's getting antsy now, looking around, her eyes darting here and there. She's a bag of nerves, and unchecked bags of nerves can be dangerous things to have around.

'How much?' I say without thinking.

She looks at me and frowns.

'How much for you to just walk away and leave us alone?'

She shakes her head incredulously. 'Has *he* put you up to this?'

'Of course he hasn't. He doesn't even know I'm speaking to you.' I'm taking a risk here. If she wants to cause trouble, she could easily make sure George knows about our conversation but I'm willing to take the risk.

The malice suddenly leaves her face and she seems to relax a touch.

I turn and check on the kids. They've stopped bickering now, and Harrison is helping Kane and Romy with their climbing.

'I suppose what I'm asking,' I continue, 'is exactly what is it that's going to get you to move on with your life?'

'Something he will never provide me with,' she says spitefully, turning on her heel. 'I'm here to stay. So you might as well get used to it.'

On the way home, I speak to the kids.

'That lady I've just been talking to… have any of you seen her before?' I keep my tone light, feigning mild interest.

'I think I have,' Harrison says. 'I might have seen her around at the end of school. Is she your friend now, Mum?'

My heart rate speeds up and I think about the stuff he's already told Joel's family. The last thing I want is him logging more fuel for their attempt to discredit my abilities as a mother.

'It's best not to mention anything about her to anyone.' It's hard to find the right words, so in the end I just come out and say it. 'People can get the wrong idea. Like your grandparents, for instance. They worry about things, so we'll just keep this between us, OK?'

'OK,' the boys chime together.

I don't know when they'll be seeing Joel's family again but it's best to talk to them about keeping things private, just in case.

I look at Romy in the rear-view mirror. She's staring out of the window, seemingly in her own little world.

I think about the twin she should have with her, and my heart squeezes in on itself. It's imperative we protect all our children; they've all been through so much already.

George texts to say he'll be home early, so we can eat together. I assume this is his way of showing he wants to work at our relationship and doesn't want me to leave. But I made it crystal clear what

I expected from him. What I want is for him to take some official action, not just pussyfoot around the issue.

I decide to say nothing yet about what happened outside school, to wait until he's back. I don't want him to know I've offered Opal money, but I have to tell him she's made contact yet again and, more importantly, reinforced her intention to carry on with her intrusive and disturbing behaviour.

There's a clenching feeling in my stomach and it takes a while for it to give way to a calmer, more determined mood. I've decided that, no matter what George's reaction is – and I suspect it will be more of the same 'leave it to me to deal with' – I will take action of my own.

Whether that's moving out with the boys or going to the police when George's promotion is out of the way, I will make sure that Opal Vardy is not allowed to continue running the show.

Back at the house, so far as I can see, Maria hasn't been in today. I'd left the note about picking the kids up from school and another saying I'll be cooking George and the children's tea and both are on the kitchen top, exactly where I left them.

I make a quick veggie pasta bake and stick it in the oven, then take out some frozen garlic bread slices to help fill the boys up.

While the food is cooking and Kane and Romy are doing their spelling words and Harrison his science homework, I pop upstairs to freshen up and change my top.

I pull a brush through my hair and dust a little bronzer on my pasty cheeks. My face looks thinner than it did a few months ago, and it suits me. So many things are better now, since meeting George.

In the mirror I can see the reflection of the padded velvet headboard and the peaceful, stylish neutral shades of the walls and soft furnishings.

I love George and I love the life we all have together here. I feel a twist of anger at the thought that Opal will somehow win if we move out, but thanks to George's stubbornness, I'm caught between a rock and a hard place: happiness versus my boys' safety.

It's a no-brainer, and I *will* carry my threat through, if George remains immovable in his attitude.

Back downstairs, I stick the garlic bread in the oven and chop a simple side salad before taking the pasta over to the table and serving the children first.

'Well, this makes a nice change!' George takes a sip of his red wine and beams around the table. 'Daddy Bear is back in time for tea!'

Romy and Kane grin, but Harrison's brow wrinkles as he pushes his pasta around his plate. He won't like the fact that the 'daddy' reference has been applied to them all, although I know George won't have meant it like that.

'So, what have you lot been up to today at school?' George takes a bite of the crisp garlic bread I place on the table and widens his eyes expectantly.

'That funny woman was there again, wasn't she, Mum?' Kane says, loading his fork with food.

I swallow the food in my mouth and lay my fork down, reaching for my wine. I haven't had a chance to tell George what happened after school. I wanted to have a nice family tea together before everything gets ruined.

'Was she now?' George looks at me and I nod.

'I'll tell you all about it later,' I say quickly. 'Romy got a sticker in her art lesson, didn't you, sweetie?'

She beams, and George begins to prise the details from her, as we always have to do. I glance over at Harrison. He's jabbing at pasta twirls with his fork and chopping them into tiny pieces, eating nothing.

*

Later, when the kids are watching their hour of television before bed, George pours us another glass of wine and I tell him what happened after school, and the things Opal said.

'She reckons I don't know the real George Mortimer,' I say, raising an eyebrow.

George snorts. 'I know one thing for sure – *she* certainly doesn't! We were together such a short time, it can hardly be called dating, never mind a relationship.' He takes a sip of wine and then frowns. 'How come she knew you'd be picking the kids up today? It's nearly always Maria.'

I shrug, pushing my status bait from my mind. 'It's obvious she's following us more than we realise. I've decided I'm going to collect them myself from now on. Something has to be done, George. Have you had any thoughts on your choice?'

'Please don't call it that, Darcy,' he sighs. 'Far as I'm concerned, there *is* no choice. You and the boys are my future.'

I fall silent, sensing that nothing has changed in his attitude. Then he surprises me. He puts down his glass and scoots further across the seat cushion, sliding his arm around my shoulders.

'Give me a week and the problem will be sorted,' he says softly, nuzzling into my neck. 'Can you do that? One week, and at the end of it, Opal Vardy will be history. Ask no questions and I'll tell you how I did it once she's gone. Deal?'

'That sounds a pretty impossible undertaking to me.' I frown. 'Deal?'

'I suppose so.' I shrug, displeased at his somewhat cavalier attitude. 'Oh, and there's something else. Maria hasn't been in today and it's not her day off. Maybe she's still smarting from her little outburst.'

'I've spoken to Maria, like I said I would,' George says smoothly, inspecting the clean, short nails on his right hand. 'You won't have any more trouble. I fired her.'

52

I've had a restless night. My mind is just a swirl of worrying about Maria losing her job, but most of all, Opal's words rattle around on constant replay in my head.

I'm here to stay. So you might as well get used to it.

Should I have gone straight to the police? Again, no evidence, no witnesses to hear her words, but I have to take the situation seriously and not give Joel's family any opportunities to say I've compromised Kane and Harrison's safety in any way.

George has promised he's going to finally take action, and for now, I have to trust he'll do that. If not, I have only one course of action. I'll get my boys out of here.

He's showed he's a man of his word by getting rid of Maria. I tried to get some detail out of him about what had been said but I think he's upset about it. Maria has been with him a long time. It's hard to accept that someone you knew well isn't quite the person you thought they were.

The last thing I feel like doing this morning is to run a yoga class. But I've got no choice, and besides, this is a great opportunity to expand my classes.

I slip on some black wide-legged yoga pants and a short T-shirt that rests exactly on the waistband. I've had these garments for a couple of years but stopped wearing them to class when the weight slowly crept on. Now, they fit perfectly again.

I always keep my yoga bag packed and stowed in the car, so I just pull on my grey fleece and a light padded jacket and I'm good to go.

My phone rings while I'm driving and the call comes through via Bluetooth.

'Darcy? I know you're probably on your way to your class, but I just had to tell you something.' George sounds buoyant, excited. 'The interview went great... I mean, *great*! There's one more stage to get through, but I reckon the promotion is mine.'

'That's fantastic, George. Congratulations!' I inject as much enthusiasm as I can into my voice. I just can't process that this promotion means so much to him – on a par with the safety of his family.

He ends the call quickly, as he's off to yet another meeting, and I spend the rest of the journey thinking about where we'll live if push comes to shove and I'm forced to carry out my threat and move out.

I arrive at the gym nice and early. I want to speak to the day manager and get the overview on how things work around here. I can teach a yoga class anywhere. I once ran one in a disused barn when a farmer's wife asked if I'd do a few private sessions for her and three friends.

I used to dream of having my own yoga studio, but gave the idea up a long time ago when I checked out rent and business rates and the cost of creating a calm, serene space. But hiring different places worked out well, and I'm now pretty much sorted with a mixture of classes that I run from various gyms and a couple of church halls.

Getting a spot at the upmarket members' fitness club Lanson's, in Wollaton, was a real boon for me. It's the premier private sports club in the area and great for my local profile. I explained to George how my job worked not long after we met, and he suggested the club, of which he was once a member, right away.

'Manager there is a friend of a friend,' he said easily one night as we sat nursing a coffee after dinner. 'I can put in a word for you if you like.'

I *did* like, and the result was that I'm running my first class here this morning.

Meeting George has given me an insight into a life – a world – I never knew existed. How much easier things can be when you have friends with important jobs in every sector. And if not, then one of them is sure to know someone who can be of influence.

I've had to battle for everything I have. Working hard and making my own opportunities where there initially appear to be none. It's just how it's always been, and I didn't know there was an easier way.

A man in his thirties wearing a suit is waiting for me when I enter reception. He holds out his hand.

'Darcy? I'm Simon Fairbrook, the manager.' He smiles at my surprised expression as we shake hands. 'Your outfit and yoga mat sort of gave you away.'

He leads me through the members' electronic turnstiles and into the club. I'm pleased when I spot a poster in a prominent position promoting the classes with *experienced and qualified local teacher Darcy Hilton*.

'I'll take you to the room you'll be using and I can answer any questions you might have.'

I follow him through the café area with its comfy seats. Everyone here seems to be either looking at their phone or tapping away on a laptop. Through the double doors at the other end, we turn right into the gym.

I see immediately that there are two levels: weights apparatus on the ground level and the cardio machines up on the mezzanine floor. The facilities here are very impressive. I don't know how much it costs to join, but I'm betting it's at least three times as much as the council-run gym down the road.

Doors are dotted around the walls, and Simon leads me over to one. Inside, he snaps on the lights, and I see we're in a large open studio space with walls that are mirrored from floor to ceiling.

'It's a sprung floor, and plenty of equipment for members to use.' He points over to the corner, where yoga mats hang from a rack and a set of shelves are stacked with blocks, belts, cushions and anything else you might need for a class.

The computerised music system is located inside a cupboard on the back wall. Simon touches a button labelled *Yoga* on the screen – one of many different activities – and a list of music loads.

'You'll have time to try a few of these tracks out before your class if you like, or there's a wireless speaker if you prefer to use your own playlist.'

I nod and glance around the ceiling, where there are flat speakers installed for surround sound. Certainly beats the cranky ghetto blaster I have to use at the church hall.

'There's no additional charge for clients to take part in the yoga classes,' he explains. 'They're included in the membership. As you can appreciate, our customers pay a lot of money to use the facilities, and they can be quite demanding in their expectations.' He smiles at me apologetically before continuing. 'I'm required to spell it out to all new freelance instructors, and I suppose the easiest way to put it is that here at Lanson's, it pays to remember that the customer is most definitely always right.'

So don't go upsetting anyone is the subliminal message I'm receiving loud and clear. Things have changed a bit since my days of managing a gym, where we supported and trusted our staff.

'I understand what you're saying,' I reply. I won't be giving an opinion on their policy.

'You'll be fine, I know it. You've got yourself a really good opportunity here, Darcy. If your classes are popular, the area manager will probably want to roll them out to our other branches in affluent suburbs of the city.' He pats me on the arm as we walk into the centre of the room. 'If you have a problem of any kind, you've only to speak to me or one of the other management team here. There's always someone on hand if you get a situation that needs defusing.'

'Well, fortunately I'll be teaching yoga here, not body combat classes. People are usually chilled out by the time I've finished with them.' I laugh, trying to lighten his task, which he seems to appreciate.

'Of course! Well then, I'll leave you to it. Good luck!' And off he strides, pushing the door to behind him. Even the doors have regulated closers on them here, so they can't slam shut. Every detail has been considered lest it offend the sensitive members.

I smile as I unpack my bag. It's a bit different to the draughty church halls with their gurgling ancient radiators that only ever get lukewarm to the touch even in midwinter.

The class starts to fill up: mostly women, but there are a handful of men. Some people smile and come over to say hello to me as the new teacher; others head straight for the mats at the back of the room and claim a spot.

When everyone is settled, I introduce myself, saying a little about how long I've been practising yoga and what my qualifications are. As I glance around, a couple of people smile at me, but most stare ahead looking a bit bored.

'OK, well if there are no questions, then let's make a start,' I say, feeling sick and silently praying the class goes well. I don't think I'll get a second chance in a place like this, where they can have their pick of yoga teachers.

'Let's begin. Everyone lie on your mat in Shavasana. Legs long, feet apart and arms relaxed, away from your sides a little. Perfect.'

I hear the door open behind me as I'm turning the yogic background track up a little before starting the class proper. When I glance back at the room, the participants are all lying on their mats as I've asked, and I see that someone has joined the class late. A woman.

The background music forgotten, I find I can't move as I watch her unroll her mat and take the last place on the front row, directly in front of where I'll be teaching the class.

The woman is none other than Daniela Frost.

53

I force myself to walk to the front of the room and begin the class.

I feel her eyes on me the whole time, and I make a tremendous effort not to meet her gaze. But a couple of times, it's just impossible. I feel myself drawn to look at her like I'm being pulled by a magnet.

She doesn't smile at me exactly, but her expression is pleasant enough. There's no sign of malice or spitefulness in her face. I keep my own expression blank as I scan the rest of the class and turn my body away from her.

It's my habit to walk around while people are in the asanas – the yoga postures – adjusting their bodies here and there when required, praising good examples and encouraging everyone to do their best without pushing themselves too far. As I do the rounds, I try to blank her from my mind, but my plan doesn't work. As soon as I stop to watch someone, my eyes flick up from the person on the mat to the mirror. I manage to view Daniela without her noticing several times.

Slim, lithe and flexible, she looks very well and she's competent in the postures. Her heels touch the floor in the downward dog position, and when we sit up and hold our toes to stretch forward, her torso lies flat on her legs. She's obviously very flexible, the only one in the class who can do it properly, apart from me, and in my opinion, she looks neater and more competent in her asanas than I do.

I quickly remind myself that yoga is supposed to be non-competitive, with the focus firmly on one's own practice, not on other people's. I'm afraid I've already failed to achieve that basic aim today.

I manage to avoid going to check on the people surrounding Daniela. I merely make a few encouraging sounds as I pass, keeping my eyes trained firmly ahead.

And then it's time for the five-minute yoga nidra relaxation, and I silently offer thanks to God that somehow I've managed to get through the class despite my trembling hands and weak knees.

At the end, Daniela leaves her mat where it is and busies herself reorganising her bag. I feel disorientated, as if I can't focus on anything properly. Why can't she just *leave*?

A couple of women have come up to ask questions about one of the postures we covered, and I have to ask each one to repeat what she says because I'm so distracted watching Daniela in the mirror.

I finally get rid of the chatty women and most of the class file out, but I'm horrified when Daniela starts to move directly towards me. It feels like a fight-or-flight moment, yet I can't cause a scene here and I can't allow her to make a scene either, or they'll never have me back.

This is just what I don't need. Another thorn in my side to magnify the worry of Joel's family trying to take my boys away and the issues Opal is causing in my relationship with George.

I crouch down and start rolling up my mat, hoping she'll get the message and turn around again.

'Darcy, could I have a quick word?'

I look up at her, my face burning. I don't say anything but I do feel a sudden bolt of fury at her butting into my life in yet another way.

'I wonder if you and I could go for a coffee and a quick chat? I think this could be a good time for us to sort things out.'

I'm literally speechless. This woman, after trying to rob my sons of their father, turns up out of the blue at *my class* and has the audacity to try and start a dialogue with me? It beggars belief.

What I'd really like to do is tell her, in two choice words, to go away. Sadly, if I do that, I can kiss goodbye to my teaching opportunity here.

'I've nothing to say to you.' I keep my voice level and ensure I don't sound threatening. 'Why did you come here? I'd prefer you didn't attend my class again.'

For a second, she doesn't move, and I think she's going to say something else, but then, thank goodness, she turns around, picks up her mat and water bottle and leaves the studio.

I stand at the side of the room and lean against the wall.

I'm shaking, and people are staring. One or two of the stragglers, still packing up their stuff, take a tentative step towards me, obviously concerned.

I squeeze my hands into fists to try and stop the trembling, but my knees feel like they might buckle at any moment. Finally I manage to grab my stuff and march determinedly out of the studio without saying goodbye to the class participants who are still in there.

Just before the door closes, I look back and see a cluster of women shaking their heads and rolling their eyes. Lanson's instructors are known for their professionalism. They don't behave like this.

I walk through the gym and past the entrance to the changing rooms. I'm just a few paces into the club members' café, next stop reception, when someone calls my name.

Daniela is sitting at a small table tucked away in a corner. I look around. Nobody seems to be taking a blind bit of notice of me, but if I ignore her, she might shout louder and that will draw attention.

I walk over to her and she stands up. We stare at each other for a few moments. She looks so… *together*. I feel like a wreck in her presence.

'Latte OK?'

I give her a curt nod, and she sets off to the counter.

I force myself to take a few deep breaths and look out of the window. The outdoor pool is cloaked in a dark cover, the tables and chairs that members use in the summer months stacked away under tarpaulin.

I can't believe she's had the front to come back to Nottingham and bought the house I was living in. More to the point, I'd like to know *why* she's come back. To make amends with me? I seriously doubt that, and yet it was clear she wasn't going to take no for an answer until I agreed to speak with her.

She'll always be the woman who enabled Joel to live a lie. Because of her, he had less time with his children, and I can never forgive her for that.

I just wish I'd reacted differently to the deceit and betrayal and immediately accepted my doctor's offer of a counsellor. Instead of sliding into obsession fuelled by hatred of Daniela, I could have invested my time and energies into rebuilding a stable life for myself and my boys.

I thought I could go it alone. But when Steph and Brenda offered to look after Kane and Harrison, so I could have a little time to myself, I chose to spend it finding out about Joel's other woman.

I drag my eyes away from the bleak view outside as Daniela returns to the table with two frothy coffees in elegant latte glasses on tiny saucers.

'Look, I know it must be so, so hard still to get your head around what happened.' She holds her cup with both hands but doesn't pick it up. 'I've struggled too. You wouldn't believe what I've been through.'

I bite down on my back teeth as my stomach tenses.

'What *you've* been through? You didn't have two kids to think about.'

Good old Joel, wonderful brother, father and husband, who systematically not only screwed but actually *lived* with another woman in a neighbouring town for half his working week.

'It's not a competition to see who felt the most pain, Darcy.'

I could crack my glass on the top of her head. She's so sorted, so over it. So patronising.

I pick up my cup and force the creamy liquid down my throat. It does help me feel slightly less flaky.

'You don't fool me. I know you've bought the house I was renting. Shame your plan to evict us failed when I moved out.'

But Daniela is not deterred. 'Buying your house wasn't my idea, if you must know, and I haven't actually gone through with it. But I know you've been stalking me online. I saw you outside my house once, about three years ago, just before I moved to Manchester. You were just sitting there in the car, staring up at my window. So please don't pretend this is all one-sided.'

That takes the wind out of my sails. I shift on my seat, cringing at having to face my own behaviour in her presence. I'd made a habit of following her after the funeral. It was easy to find out where she lived.

'Steph told me you were obsessed with me. She's kept in touch with me, as has Brenda. They kept me informed of what you were up to.'

Those snakes. I knew I should never have trusted them.

'They've turned against me,' I say. 'I'd rather you didn't mention them.'

'I know. They're trying to get the boys off you.' Again, I try not to show my surprise, and fail. 'I haven't been snooping; they've been insistent on keeping me up to speed. They even tried to get me to give evidence of your stalking tactics to help their custody bid.'

I swallow hard. 'And are you? Giving evidence?'

'No. Believe it or not, I'm here to try and help you, Darcy.'

I feel like I'm in the middle of a nightmare dreamscape. Daniela Frost is here to *help* me, not to try and ruin my life? Somebody pinch me.

'I moved away because I had to separate myself from what happened. I dealt with what Joel did differently to you. You turned to social media. I closed my old Facebook account from when I was with Joel and opened a new account that reflected my new life. I entered into therapy, refreshed my circle of friends and kept working on my inner thoughts, telling myself that what happened wasn't my problem at all, it was Joel's. And now I've met someone new and I've no need to hold on to old negative feelings.' Her voice softened. 'You took another path. You probably blamed me more than you blamed him. Maybe you still do.'

I lower my eyes, unable to deny it.

'You told yourself that because of the boys, you had more right to be with Joel than I did. But that's just not true and I think you know that deep down.'

'What he did was terrible, but he loved *me*. He loved his sons with all his heart.' I spit out the words like broken teeth. Each one bitter and sharp. It's a strange relief to speak them out loud. 'My boys are Joel's legacy. If it hadn't been for you, we could have—'

'Darcy, your denial has gone on long enough! You've been surrounded by people who've gone along with the lie you've told yourself all these years.'

'What lie? I haven't been lying about anything.'

Daniela juts her chin forward and speaks at me rather than to me.

'*I* was Joel's wife… not you!' Her words pierce my skin like little arrows and I shudder.

Silence falls over us, soft as snow and just as icily cold. I shiver and wrap my arms around myself.

I'm vaguely aware of the two women at the next table giving us sideways glances, but the noise of the café remains a comforting buffer around us.

'He was married to *me*, Darcy,' Daniela says again, each word like a dagger in my heart. 'You came in and broke up *my* marriage. You willingly had children with a man who only lived with you for part of the week.' She sounds breathless. 'But the act of having his kids didn't give you the right to have him. Joel was *my husband.*'

54

My hand flies up to my mouth and I look down so she can't see my brimming eyes. I can't handle it. Hearing it out loud like this. I just... I can't face myself.

All this time, I've dealt with what happened by telling myself *I* was the betrayed one, that I had more right to Joel than Daniela did because of the boys.

But now... her words have shone a bright light on my self-delusion and I'm blinded by the truth. I feel sick, my skull is splitting with a thumping headache and I'm not sure I'm strong enough to feel the pain of it.

It's always been so much easier to suppress the knowledge than to face it, to look at myself properly and see the ugliness of what I did.

It's true. He was married to *her*, not me.

Daniela is his legal wife. The one who got to organise his funeral and inherit his estate.

She kept her own name after they married, but I changed mine to his, even though I wasn't his wife. I did it for the kids. I did it for myself.

Yet still I couldn't deal with it. Couldn't accept it.

I look at her. Daniela Frost. The only person who really understands everything that happened, everything we went through after Joel died. Both of us finding out about his other woman. Both realising we'd been played in the cruellest of ways.

'I'm sorry,' I whisper. 'I… I didn't know he was married. I—'

'You're still young, Darcy. You have your boys and a new relationship but you have to face the truth for your own sake.'

I think of George and whether we'll still be together in a week's time, whether he'll sort out his priorities in time. She bites her lip, as if wondering whether to say something. 'I think you've allowed yourself to be controlled by Joel's family.'

'They helped me out,' I start to say, and then stop, wondering why I'm still jumping to the defence of the people who are trying to take my boys away. 'It was hard, having the boys, and—'

'I know. It must have been horrendous. But what I mean is that you've allowed them to airbrush Joel's deceit out of your personal history.'

'For the boys' sake.' I repeat what Brenda and Steph have told me a thousand times.

'The boys don't need to know until they're adults themselves. But don't you see? You need to respect yourself enough to stand up and say to yourself and to those close to you that you were lied to and betrayed.'

Hearing her say it brings a sob to my throat. I'm shocked that I can be so transparent to her of all people, and swallow it down, embarrassed.

'I sound so clever and knowledgeable, don't I?' she continues. 'But I wasn't at the beginning. I've had to work bloody hard to get to this place. And now, if anyone asks about my late husband – if it's someone I feel quite close to – I tell them the truth of what Joel did to me.'

'You just tell them what happened?' I shake my head, imagining the horror of it.

'Yes. And I do it because *I* did nothing wrong. *You* did nothing wrong. Joel did the bad thing to *us*.' She pauses and stares me right in the eye. 'The truth of it is, however much others have set us apart, you and I have no real reason to hate each other.'

I consider this last statement and find that basically, it's true.

'You know, I asked Joel's family why they've played along with you all this time. Why they've just accepted the fact that you framed yourself as his wife.' To her, the words seem like nothing, but to me they feel like rubbing salt into a raw, festering wound.

I don't want to face myself and my pathetic delusion.

'They seemed to believe it too,' I say, but Daniela shakes her head.

'Your sons are all they have left of Joel. They all agreed between them a long time ago that if allowing you to carry on with your delusion was the price they had to pay to play a major part in Kane and Harrison's life, then so be it.'

I look at her and realise she's discussed all this with them in depth. All of them talking about how crazy they think I am. Laughing about me behind my back.

I stand up, and Daniela's face starts spinning around me like a vortex. My legs are wobbly and I feel her firm grip on my arms.

'Sit down, Darcy,' she says. 'Take some deep breaths.'

She thinks I'm trying to run from the truth, but the reality is, new truths are flooding into my mind.

'I honestly didn't know he was married, but…' I hesitate as I muster the determination to say the words that have hooked themselves into my throat, struggling not to be spoken. 'I'm not sure, back then, it would have made a difference.'

I blow out my cheeks and release the air slowly, together with the shame that's been lodged there for so long. The self-realisation burns my chest like burning oil, but it feels good. It feels cleansing, somehow.

To deal with my choices and what happened, I've blamed everyone else. Everyone but Joel.

My head feels full and my heart feels wrung out like an old rag. I think about George and Opal, about Steph and the rest of Joel's family… the way I let the people in my life control me.

'I've blamed myself and other people. I've blamed everyone but the person who did me wrong. I've buried what Joel did, just like they told me to.'

'We've all done stuff we're not proud of,' Daniela says quietly, studying her hands. 'I've been happy to rest the blame on your shoulders in the past, Darcy, and I know you've done the same with me. But Joel betrayed both of us and he short-changed his own sons, too. Without his lies and deceit, our paths would never have crossed.'

'Why did you come back to Nottingham?'

'Joel's family have fostered hate between the two of us in order to assist them in excusing his behaviour,' she says sadly. 'If what happened was the fault of one, or of both of us, then it was so much easier for them to tell themselves that Joel just got led astray by a woman. All this time you thought they were supporting you and the boys, they've been planning how they could get permanent custody. Then you met this new guy and finally they felt they had enough ammunition.'

I remember the look on Steph's face when I told her and Brenda about my relationship with George. That was her real face, but I failed to recognise it as such. I thought it was just her initial, illogical reaction.

'They've tried to get me onside to destroy you once and for all so they can take your boys, and I couldn't just let that happen, or when would this all stop?'

I process what she's telling me, and it's like someone just lifted a veil from my eyes. The cold core of anger I've held for her shifts inside me.

'Joel's family couldn't face the truth of what he'd done to us. The vile, ugly truth that he was a liar and a cheat... They couldn't handle it, so they told themselves a different story, and they've been doing it for years with my full approval. Steph tried to convince me to buy your house to push you over the edge. In the end I decided not to get into all that.'

It feels good, hearing her say this stuff, like squeezing an infected boil and letting all that hot yellow pus spurt out. I can feel the relief like someone just hit the pressure valve.

And what have I done lately? I've started to get over my obsession with Daniela by throwing myself into stopping Opal from ruining my new start with George, from doing the same thing to me that Daniela did: taking away my man. At least that's what I've told myself since Joel died; that's how I've deluded myself about *Joel's wife*.

My thumping headache seems to ramp up a notch. It's hard to even think it but it's the truth.

What I've never considered is that perhaps Opal is hurting about something I'm completely unaware of; perhaps she feels just like I did when I became obsessed with Daniela. Maybe, just maybe, there are good reasons for her behaviour, from her point of view at least.

It's a long shot, I know, but Opal has tried to talk to me several times and I won't entertain it. Now I see that it's all part of the self-delusion, the way I tell myself my man is innocent and someone else is to blame.

George won't discuss Opal with me, so what have I got to lose?

It's better than this hell. It's better than living with shredded nerves and in fear for my children's safety.

'Well, I must get going now.' Daniela picks up her bag and stands up. She places a business card on the table in front of me. 'If you want to talk some more or need to contact me, you can do so on that number.'

She turns to leave.

I stand up and say her name and she turns back to look at me.

'Thank you,' I say.

55

Back home at last, I unlock the front door and stumble into the hallway. I shrug off my yoga mat bag and sit on the bottom step, head in my hands, thinking about my conversation with Daniela.

Every time I think about it, I cringe inside. The flood of relief when I finally let my true feelings out – the humiliation, the anger, at both Joel and myself – it felt so empowering.

Things have changed. I'm not alone any more, because now I have George and Romy and I'll fight tooth and nail to keep my boys despite Joel's family's deluded bid to get custody of them and to paint Joel as some kind of saint instead of the lying rat he was in reality.

I feel stronger, as though I can confront them and challenge them on their behaviour. If I've been through a period of instability, then they have played a part in that too. They are no more fit to look after the boys than I am!

I make myself a cup of tea and open up my laptop, logging into Instagram once it has booted up. Three notifications, but there's only one there that interests me.

Asking to follow Opal via my false profile has worked. My heart begins to thump as I click on the link. Here I am, still playing games online but this time, I have a valid reason. I truly am trying to set things straight.

From the moment the page starts to load, I have this inexplicable feeling that I might discover something I'll wish I hadn't. But never in a million years do I expect anything like the photographs that now fill my screen.

I run a bath and take my iPad into the bathroom. With the kids running around, it's one of the rare places I can get a bit of peace and my go-to haven in the house.

Fortunately, Harrison has after-school football training, which I don't have to pick him up from for another hour, and Kane and Romy are watching a Disney film in the living room.

I climb into the bath and settle back into the perfumed foam, closing my eyes for a few moments to savour the warmth and peace.

I hold the iPad up above the bubbles and double-click on each photo so it enlarges and fills the screen. They draw me in as much as repulse me.

The one I'm looking at right now is dated fourteen days ago.

It's a picture of the removals van outside my old house, the back doors wide open while it's being loaded. No people are visible, but I can clearly see the boxes I'd packed full of my personal belongings. I can even see the room markings on some of them.

She's typed a narrative for the photograph – *Moving day... the start of my new life with my gorgeous boyfriend and his adorable daughter* – and underlined the words with a row of coloured hearts.

I still can't take in the fact that, at some point during the day I moved in with George, she was right there, outside my house, boldly taking photographs and selecting one to post online.

Then there's the picture she posted this morning. It's of George's back garden. The goalposts are there, and Romy's new mermaid doll is on the patio table so I know it's very recent.

Feel so lucky this is my new home!

I read it again and again and it still doesn't sink in.

I scan through the other photos she's posted since I met George. Curiously, there's hardly anything there before that time.

The photographs aren't all personal to me and George. There are lots of filler pics of coffee and food and animals. But dotted amongst them is the odd image that takes my breath away.

A picture of a car wheel and a partial shot of a door on the exact day George got a puncture at work and had to put the spare on before leaving. *Oops!* she's written.

Some people call lilies the flower of death... but I love them! The front of a flower shop I bought lilies in the day after we moved in.

Further back: *Carrot cake or red velvet? Can't decide!* The window of the coffee shop where George and I met up for the very first time.

And then my breath catches in my throat and I suppress a shriek. I didn't spot this picture earlier.

Two weeks ago, Opal posted a photograph taken from the touchline of a football match at Harrison's school. She must have been standing right behind me, because her view was the exact one I had.

So proud of my boy! she's written, alongside a shot of a few of the players, including my elder son.

Now Maria's gone I'm going to be there to pick the kids up from school from now on even though it's a squeeze, but I've never even considered she'd target their after-school activities.

56

After school, Harrison ran onto the football pitch with the others and started warming up.

'Knee raises! Higher... higher!' Mr Porter yelled, demonstrating raises that were almost level with his chest. 'Faster... faster!'

Harrison scowled as he reluctantly applied more effort. Mr Porter was just showing off to the mums again. At the end of footie practice, they all surrounded him, asking questions, staring into his eyes.

It was annoying, and embarrassing.

Fortunately, Harrison's mum had never been one of those mothers. She didn't usually stay for the whole after-school game, but she always got there in time to see some of it and to pick him up safely.

Harrison looked around the edge of the field as Mr Porter instructed them to pick up the pace. There were lots of adults here watching; some of his teammates had the support of both parents. But it was mostly the dads who came to cheer them on as they trained.

Harrison thought about his own dad, who would never be coming here or anywhere else to watch him play footie again, thanks to that stupid, cruel disease. He pushed himself harder still, trying to focus on the burn in his thigh muscles instead of the ache in his heart.

He liked George, he did. And he really liked Romy; she was OK for a girl. But George could never take the place of his dad. It annoyed him when Kane and his mum sucked up to him.

Yes, George had saved Kane's life at the park, but how many times did you need to thank someone? Marcus Pett's dad was a fireman, and according to Marcus, he saved people's lives every week, because that was what firemen did, wasn't it? It was their *job*.

Would George or Marcus's dad go around saving lives if it wasn't their job? He doubted it. Admittedly, George was off duty that day at the park, but if doctors or firemen saw someone was in trouble, they had a duty to help. Everyone knew that.

His own dad had sorted out I.T. problems for a job, but that didn't make him any less brave. When it came to dying, he'd kept smiling, and when he held Harrison close, he whispered in his ear that it was his job now to look after his mum and brother.

Harrison wanted to make his dad proud. He wanted to step up and be a man, but it was hard. Since George had come on to the scene, he had been waking up in the early hours with a tight, prickly feeling in his chest. He worried that his dad would think he should have stopped his mum somehow falling in love with George.

He sucked in air, feeling a bit faint, just as Mr Porter's shadow loomed over him.

'I said you can stop now, Harry!' he boomed.

Harrison stopped his manic knee raises and looked around. Everyone else had obviously stopped some time ago. The other boys clustered together and sniggered behind their hands. The adult spectators shrugged their shoulders and grinned at each other.

Heat rushed into his cheeks, and he felt a bolt of heat shoot up into his chest like white-hot lightning.

'What are you all staring at?' he screeched, a wave of temper enveloping him in a steaming red mist as his eyes swivelled wildly around the field. 'Get lost! All of you!'

Mr Porter stepped forward and blocked his path like a man mountain, raising both hands in the air like stop signs, but Harrison dodged around him and ran full pelt back to the changing rooms.

He knew that one of the dads who helped Mr Porter run the team would follow him in, try to talk him down and back onto the pitch. They always did that when someone got upset if they'd been sent off for a bad tackle.

But Harrison was having none of it.

He stuffed his school uniform into his training bag, zipped it and snatched it up off the bench. Then he hot-footed it outside again, narrowly avoiding Linford Byers' dad, who was striding towards the changing rooms.

'Harry... hold up!' Linford's dad called, but Harrison kept running.

He didn't know where he was running to. He just knew that anywhere was better than this.

Once he was out of the school gates, he dashed through a series of alleyways, emerging two roads further on. He stopped running then, dropped his bag and leaned back against a red-brick wall, sucking in breath. It crossed his mind that if he suffered from asthma like his brother, he'd probably need resuscitating now.

The awful feeling he'd experienced that day at the park when he saw his brother's blue face and rolling eyes fluttered up through his chest. He *did* feel grateful to George for what he'd done for Kane; it was just that...

A small metallic-brown car crawled down the street and slowed to a stop in front of him. The passenger-side window rolled smoothly down and a lady in a headscarf and sunglasses leaned across and beckoned to him. It was hard to see her face properly. He looked up at the sky and wondered why she needed the glasses when it was a dull winter day.

'Harrison, isn't it?' She smiled before he'd even replied. 'Jump in. Your mum has had a bit of a disaster in yoga class and has asked me to pick you up. I'll explain as I drive.'

Harrison hesitated for a moment. The warning that had been drummed into him since he could walk played on repeat in his head.

Never get into a car with a stranger.

But this was a woman who said she knew his mum, not a creepy-looking old bloke offering him sweets.

Lately, his mum had seemed more scatter-brained and confused than usual. And he'd overheard his grandma and Aunt Steph talking about her in the kitchen the other day, of course. They were worried about her too and he'd overheard his mum and George saying there had been some kind of fall-out because of it.

So it made perfect sense that there had been a problem and she'd had to send one of her yoga ladies to pick him up.

He bent down further and looked into the car again so he could take a closer look but she looked down to glance at her watch and it was hard to see her face.

Harrison stepped forward and opened the passenger-side door.

57

I sit for a moment on the side of the bath with the iPad still in my hands, staring at the condensation on the gleaming white tiles. The steam settles on my face, cloying and hot, and I start to feel a bit woozy.

Then I glance at the photograph of my son on the screen again and come to my senses, standing up too quickly and pressing my hand against the wall to steady me.

Harrison's at football training right now and, after seeing Opal's photograph, I have to get there to protect him as a matter of urgency.

After Joel died, I used to turn up and watch the whole game, because I knew Harrison would miss seeing his dad on the sidelines. But over time, as he has seemed to hurt less, and appears to barely notice my presence anyway, I've taken to going for the last thirty minutes or so. I'm always there to make sure he gets home safely, but in view of Opal's increasing interest in our routine, I'll make sure I'm there for whole thing from now on, even if it means taking Kane and Romy with me.

Shame trawls my stomach. I didn't think anything of it, but now I can imagine that Harrison feels pretty torn up about my obvious waning interest, even if he hasn't said anything.

I'll go there now, get him out of Opal's crazy camera lens, and I'll commit to giving him more of a sideline presence in future games.

I step out of the bath and dry myself roughly with the towel, slipping on my robe and rushing into the bedroom without draining the water.

I feel a rising panic as I pull on my clothes. I need to get to school pronto, make sure Harrison is safe.

I call George and get his voicemail.

'I've got to go and pick Harrison up from football. I found some photos online… I think he might be in danger from Opal. Call me soon as you can.'

I end the call and toss the phone onto the stairs while I grab my coat and stuff my feet into ankle boots.

I can't believe that, after talking to Daniela, I decided to give Opal the benefit of the doubt. No more.

I know first-hand just how hard obsession can grip. It can make you do things that are totally out of your comfort zone. It can make you venture further out than your own moral boundaries ought to allow.

58

It takes me ten minutes to drive to school. Kane and Romy are bickering in the back, both grumpy because I broke up their television viewing.

'Wait here. Don't get out under any circumstances, I'll literally be five minutes.'

They start to complain but I don't hang around to listen.

I lock them in and run through the open gates and on to the big field, relieved I can clearly see the car from here.

I scan the kids playing. I can't spot Harrison, so I walk to the right to view the pitch from a different angle. I can see all eleven players for the school side, and Harry isn't one of them.

I start to run towards Mr Porter, the team coach.

He doesn't see me at first; he's yelling instructions and jabbing his finger at one of his players.

'Where's Harrison?' I ask breathlessly.

Mr Porter takes a step back and refocuses on my face.

'Oh, it's you, Mrs Hilton!' He presses his lips together and I flinch as the title reminds me of my self-delusion that I was married to Joel.

'We've been worried about Harry, his behaviour was totally out of character.'

'What? What behaviour?'

He frowns. 'Didn't you get the message? He stormed off before the match started. I sent one of our volunteer dads after him, but he ran away. The office said they'd called you and left a voicemail.' I pat my pockets down, sweat trickling down my spine. I was in such a rush to get here, I never picked up my phone.

'Where is he now?' I look towards the car.

'I don't know – as I said, he ran away. The volunteer gave chase, but… Well, Harrison's an agile ten-year-old lad, and we have to have a certain number of official bodies present at the match by law, you see, so the dad rightly came back. I checked with the school office, and you'd signed that he's allowed to walk home alone, so we assumed that's what he'd do.' He hesitates. 'He's been gone about forty minutes, I think.'

'But that was before…' My voice rises and I feel sick. I'd completely forgotten about the permission form I signed at the beginning of the school year in September. Back then, I hadn't even met George. Back then, Opal wasn't on the scene.

It's a fifteen-minute walk at the most from school to home, so Harrison should have arrived back at the house even before I thought about leaving to pick him up!

Mr Porter glances back to the pitch and then calls to another man. 'Eric, take over here for a minute, will you?'

He guides me away from the side of the pitch.

'Let's go to the office together now. Hopefully someone will still be there.'

'No! No, I have the kids in the car. I'll drive around to the front of the school and pop in from there. Thanks anyway.'

I rush back towards the car and vaguely hear him calling out to me to let him know when Harrison is home safe, but I don't stop to listen. I jump back in the car.

'What's happening?' Kane grumbles. 'Where's Harry?'

'He's not there,' I say breathlessly, ramming the car into gear and pulling away. We pass by the side roads I know Harrison would have taken if he'd walked home but there's no sign of him.

'Damn and blast,' I curse out loud and in the mirror I see Romy press her hand to her mouth and giggle.

I'm furious I didn't bring my phone to call George and now I've got to call in at the school office, wasting precious time. Right now, literally every second counts.

We're at the front of the school again and I pull over, not turning off the engine but just giving myself a minute or two to clear my head.

This is what it feels like to be utterly helpless. I haven't a clue where my son is… or who he's with.

'Where's Harry, Mum?' Kane whines. 'When can we go back home? I'm going to miss—'

'Kane, pipe down! Your TV schedule isn't important right now. Your brother's missing.'

I hear his sharp intake of breath and I feel guilty panicking him like that.

'I'm sure he's fine but we just have to make sure,' I add unconvincingly. 'We can't go home until we find him.'

The receptionist lets me call George while the kids wait in the car again. Tearfully, I explain everything and I'm not sure it makes sense but George's voice is calm in my ear.

'I've already left work for a meeting so I'll come straight to the school now. Stay put.'

'Can I get you a cup of tea, Mrs Hilton?' the receptionist asks, offering me a box of tissues through the glass hatch.

'It's Miss,' I mumble. I take a tissue and dab at my face. 'Thanks but no tea. My partner is on his way so I'll wait in the car.'

She hesitates, as if she's debating whether to say something. 'If you… if you need to ring the police, we can do that for you here.'

I garble my thanks and rush back out to the car.

'Do you know where Harry is yet?' Kane asks, his voice far from casual now. 'Will he be all right?'

'I'm sure he'll be fine, sweetie,' I say as confidently as I can manage. 'George is on his way and then we can decide what to do.'

I press my back into the car seat. Despite the cold weather and my lack of warm clothing, I can feel a big damp spot at the bottom of my spine, and my hands are clammy and slightly slippy on the steering wheel.

I must go into a bit of a daze, thinking things through, wracking my brains where Harrison might be when a black Audi pulls up directly in front of mine.

'Stay here,' I bark at the kids yet again and rush to George as he gets out of his car.

I fall into his arms.

'It's Opal,' I sob. 'She posted a photo online taken at his football practice. Why would she do that unless she wanted to send me a warning? I know she's got Harry, I can just feel it's her.'

'I'm sorry, Darcy.' George sounds contrite. 'I should have listened. You tried to tell me and…' His voice wavers.

I look at him and he looks terrible.

'Are you OK? Has something—'

'Just work. People making my life difficult.' He frowns. 'But forget that. Harrison's safety is the most important thing and I should have listened to you.'

'This is not your fault, George. Opal's crazy… and frighteningly plausible, as I've found out to my cost.'

George seems to gather himself then, throws back his shoulders.

'Well she won't win. Whatever it takes, we'll get Harrison back.'

'We should ring the police before we do anything,' I say, battling back the waves of fear rolling into my throat.

'We can.' George hesitates. 'But once we make that call, we'll just get caught up in a big tangle of red tape. And I doubt they'll do anything at all unless we can prove Opal has taken him.'

'We can show them the photograph she posted of his football match.'

George frowns. 'But anybody is allowed to go and watch a match, aren't they? It doesn't mean anything, really, only to us. That's how she operates, under the radar.'

I grit my teeth. I can almost hear a clock ticking in my head. Every second, Harrison drifts further away from us.

'Look, it's up to you, Darcy.' George holds his hands up in the air. 'Far be it from me to tell you not to involve the police… and I think we *should* call them. All I'm saying is, let's find out if she has got him before we do, if we can. Then police action will be so much quicker.'

I look at him, see lines of worry etched around his mouth and eyes. He knows Opal better than anyone and is the best person to play her at her own game.

'OK,' I say. 'Anything that will find Harrison. What do you think we need to do?'

'I have a hunch where it is we need to head for.'

I look back towards my car where two small frightened faces are taking it all in.

George thinks for a moment. 'I've got an idea. You wait here in your car, just in case it's a false alarm and Harrison turns up again for the end of the game and his lift. And I'll take the kids somewhere safe. It won't take long.'

59

When George and the kids have left, I get back in the car. But after two minutes of silence, sitting alone with my thoughts, I can't bear it.

'One more thing to try,' I say out loud and I release the hand-brake, steering the car back onto the road. I'll retrace the route I know Harrison should have taken one more time, just in case he's been sulking somewhere in the school grounds and is only just making his way home or back to the match for his lift.

When I get close to the school field again, I spot a solitary figure dressed in jeans and a dark jacket hanging around the corner of the street opposite the school field. I can see the football team clearly from here, I can even see Mr Porter back in coaching mode. Harrison has clearly already been forgotten about.

As I draw nearer, I see that the person is wearing a black knitted hat covering her hair and obscuring her face, but it's not enough to disguise her. I know exactly who this is.

I park the car a little further up the street and run down to the corner.

'Darcy!' Opal looks around in alarm when I suddenly materialise in front of her.

'Where's my son?' I walk forward until I'm really close, inside her personal space. My chest burns with an escalating heat that makes me want to lash out and I silently remind myself not to do anything silly.

'What?' She frowns.

'Don't play the innocent, Opal. I've seen the pictures you've posted online, and I know it was you who sent me those photos in the post. You keep popping up in places you shouldn't be.'

'I… Yes, I admit, I did send those photographs. To let you know I was watching, that was all.'

'That's *all*?' This woman has no grasp on reality. 'Skulking around a ten-year-old boy's football matches, taking photos? And I'm guessing the tomato prank on my car was you too. What's it all about?'

Her cheeks colour. 'Just to unnerve you, I suppose. So that you stay away from George and—'

'And what?'

She hesitates, as if she's debating with herself whether to say something.

'Where is he? Where's Harrison?' I step closer to her, feeling fury coursing through me. 'I'm calling the police. This madness has gone on long enough.' I curse myself again for leaving my phone at home. But this time I'll go to the school office, ring the police from there.

'Darcy, I… I swear,' she stammers, 'I haven't seen your son. I was just standing here searching the field, wondering where he was.'

'Why would you even wonder where my son is? He's nothing at all to do with you!'

Her eyes are wide and she actually looks nervous. In fact she looks awful. Black circles around her eyes, cheekbones popping out under stretched skin. She looks like she might keel over any second.

'I knew something like this would happen,' she whispers. 'I had this feeling… something was in the air. I've been watching things develop, trying to warn you in my own way.'

She's either a fantastic liar or she's telling the truth. But I don't believe the latter, for a second.

'Something might happen like what?' She looks past me, into the middle distance, and I tug at the sleeve of her coat. 'Something like *what*?'

Her eyes refocus on my face, and at last she breaks the silence.

'Something very bad. I want to tell you everything, I do,' she says. 'But can I trust you not to tell George?'

I nearly laugh out loud. Opal Vardy is asking me to trust *her* instead of the man I live with, the man who has given me and my children a loving home.

'But how can I trust *you*? You've been stalking my family, posting pictures of a life that isn't even yours!'

The only reason she can't want George to know is because she still holds hope out of rekindling their 'relationship'. If he finds out she's telling more lies about him, she knows he'll never come around to her skewed way of thinking.

'You won't regret listening to what I have to say,' Opal continues, her eyes growing more hopeful as she senses doubt in me. 'If you truly value your own safety and the safety of your children, then I beg you, listen to me for ten minutes without judging.'

'I haven't got ten minutes!' I snap. 'I need to find my son.'

Harrison might already be home. Maybe he got distracted on the way, took longer than usual. But I can't risk assuming that.

I have to drive the streets and get back to the front of the school for when George gets back.

My stomach is churning and I can feel my heartbeat up in my throat. I never take my eyes from Opal, and the longer I watch her, the more I see.

Her big eyes and pale skin, the dimple to the left-hand side of her mouth. A familiarity I can't pin down.

'I have to keep looking for Harrison. I have to.'

'I think I know where he is, where he's gone. But I've had nothing to do with it, you have to believe that.' She turns and begins to walk. 'Where's your car? I can talk while we drive.'

'If you've had nothing to do with it, how do you know where Harrison is?' I snap back at her.

'Because I've seen things,' she says ambiguously. 'It's a case of putting two and two together if you see what I mean.'

I don't see what she means at all, but time is running out.

The air is damp. There's going to be a heavy frost tonight, and I can feel the nip in the air. And Harrison is out there, somewhere.

Just because Opal is here, it doesn't mean she hasn't already taken my son, locked him up somewhere.

I spin around to face Opal. 'Back off. I don't trust you as far as I can throw you.' I start walking back to my car. 'I'm calling the police.' She doesn't have to know I haven't got my phone with me.

Opal follows me. I can hear her feet pattering behind me. I feel as if my head is about to blow off with the pressure building inside my skull.

'Why have you been watching us?'

She walks beside me, head down against the cold air. 'I haven't been watching you,' she says. 'Not really.'

Her tone sounds surprisingly genuine. I push the thought away. I can't allow her to fool me.

I think about how I watched Daniela in the past, as if it could somehow give me answers as to why Joel didn't choose me and the boys, why he didn't leave his wife. And I remember how long I was able to successfully deny it, even to myself.

'You have been watching us, and you stalked George for eighteen months before I even met him.'

'I've known George a lot longer than eighteen months and it's actually the opposite of stalking,' she says curtly. 'I've been protecting someone.'

'What are you talking about? We don't need protecting.'

I unlock the car and she steps in front of me to stop me getting in.

'I've been protecting someone I love more than anything in the world. Someone I'd die for.' She smiles, pulls off her hat. 'I don't want George; I don't want to hurt you or your children. Look at me, Darcy. *Really* look. Look at my eyes, my smile…'

I pull at the scarf around my neck and relish the kiss of the cold air against my hot, damp skin. What I'm thinking is far too ludicrous. Seeing her features close up, my mind has drawn an impossible line between two faces…

I look away, but her stare doesn't waver. When I glance back, her eyes burn into me like hot coals, her frosty demeanour crumbling in front of me.

'I know you can see it. She looks just like me,' she says, her voice breaking. 'Romy is my daughter.'

60

I slip into the car and Opal gets into the passenger seat. I'm too preoccupied to challenge her. I flick the rear window heater on and set the fans going on the windscreen. My head feels like it's about to explode.

We sit there in the car for a few moments, just staring out of the window. I'm stunned into silence, can't bear her near me, yet a part of me doesn't want her to go until I've processed what she's said.

If I felt as if I were overheating before, I'm chilled to the bone now. I feel as if my flesh is frozen solid.

Opal is Romy's mother? All the instances of George insisting we don't involve the police rush at me. It seems impossible to grasp and yet it's the only thing that adequately explains his continual denial in getting anything official in place to keep Opal away legally.

If it's true.

Why should I believe a thing this woman tells me? Yes, she has a passing resemblance to Romy but… lots of people look alike who are no relation to each other.

'I swear on my daughter's life I haven't taken your son, Darcy. I'm sorry for the things I've done to unnerve you, but I was desperate to drive you away. Not from George… but from Romy. I was terrified you were getting too close to her, would raise her to believe you were her mother.'

I don't acknowledge what she's saying because one thought keeps recurring and it makes me feel nauseous: if Opal hasn't taken Harrison, then who the hell has?

Daniela's face appears in my mind. When we spoke, she was so plausible, seemed so genuine. I accepted without hesitation that what she said was true, that she'd returned to help me recover from Joel's betrayal.

But what if she's just pulled off the biggest betrayal of all?

'Have you got a phone I can use?' I ask. In my desperation I'm ready to plead with Steph to see if she knows anything about Harrison's absence, even though there's a risk she could use it against me to show I'm neglecting my kids.

Opal shakes her head. 'I just need a few minutes of your time.'

She doesn't wait for my reply. She simply begins to speak, staring straight ahead towards the expanse of the school field, where the football team are now leaving the pitch, as Harrison should have been doing.

Somewhere between refusing to speak to her and this very moment, I realise I've given her licence to say exactly what she pleases about George and he's not here to defend himself. I can't verify a thing she tells me.

'I don't want to hear it,' I say. 'Get out of my car, please.'

But it's as if I haven't spoken. She clears her throat.

'My younger brother went to the same school as George,' she begins.

I interrupt her immediately.

'George has told me about his school days, and they were awful. His father sent him away, and he experienced the most dreadful bullying.'

She stares at me.

'It was a hellhole all right. Twenty-five years ago there was none of the protection that's in place in today's schools, no anti-bullying policies or peer support groups.'

So it seems George told me the truth.

'My brother was only at St Mark's for a short time, but he wrote to me at least half a dozen times. His final letter I received a few days after we heard he'd died. He must've posted it just before.'

I glance at my watch, willing George to return.

'My brother was murdered by a notorious gang of bullies at the school called the Panthers. All wealthy boys with influential parents whom even the teachers were afraid to challenge.'

'Opal, where is all this going? Where do you think Harrison is?'

'The leader of those bullies was a teenager called George Mortimer.'

I stare at her.

'Yes, Darcy. *Your* George. The man you live with, the man you leave in charge of your children without a second thought.'

Calm down. She could easily be lying. I can't afford to accept every word she tells me. Her actions have been nothing but unstable and revengeful.

'True to form, George operated from the shadows. He nearly destroyed him and then pretended to befriend my brother when he was at his lowest ebb. He successfully encouraged him to commit suicide. My brother was already terribly depressed, thanks to the constant bullying. George as good as murdered him.'

It's easy to blame someone else when a loved one takes their own life. Understandable, even. But you can't just go around accusing people of doing such a terrible thing.

'So… why didn't George go to prison, if he murdered your brother?'

'Because there was no proof.' She throws her hands up in the air. 'He was clever back then and he's even cleverer now.'

She seems to think I don't know much about her and George when in actual fact he's told me plenty. If she is lying and completely deluded I won't gain anything by reacting aggressively. If she knows where Harrison is then I need to build some kind of rapport with her and quickly.

'He told me he met you online. On a hospital forum, is that right?'

She shakes her head. 'No, though I did work at the hospital, in the archives. I'd searched everywhere for him for years, and then that was how I discovered him. Pure chance… my destiny, even.'

She's starting to sound unhinged, her thought patterns jumping about all over the place. She notices my expression.

'Whatever you're thinking, just hear me out,' she says. 'When I met George, I was a temp in archives and he was the quintessential handsome doctor with ambitions to become a surgeon. He seemed so kind and sympathetic, and everyone in his team looked up to him. The general consensus was that he was destined for great things. At first, I even questioned whether I had the right person, but of course, I had.'

She's not making a lot of sense. I feel like choking her to rush her along, get her to tell me where she 'thinks' Harrison might be.

'We got on so well. Liked doing the same things, eating the same food. We even liked the same movies. I found myself wanting to believe he was the real deal, that my suspicions were a mistake. But when he said that because of his position at the hospital we had to keep our relationship a secret for the time being, I saw a glimmer of his underhand nature.'

I resist the urge to hurry her along and let her tell me in her own time.

'Did you overhear a conversation about an operation he did that went wrong? Did you turn up at the house claiming to be George's girlfriend and demand Maria let you in?'

She actually laughs and shakes her head. 'You couldn't be further from the truth!'

Did George make that up, too… or is *she* the liar?

'It's hard to imagine, looking at me now, but he did seem to find me attractive, which is what I intended, of course. I don't know if he really did.' She looks at me. 'I've asked him a dozen times, and he just gives me this strange smile. After what he did to my brother, I think he's a sadist at heart. I'm certain of it.'

I think about George's caring touch, his butterfly kisses on my eyelids before we go to sleep at night. I think about him saving Kane's life that day at the park. Only a day ago, I'd have called Opal deluded. But now… now I know the truth about Romy – if it is the truth – my whole reality has twisted on its axis.

Yet George has done nothing to make me think he has another persona. Opal, on the other hand, has consistently showed her true colours.

'It nearly killed me, but I had finally found him and so I had to make it count. I pretended I was in love with him, told him I was on the pill and fell pregnant in record time. That was when the real horror began.'

'Why would you do that?' I look at her aghast. 'After everything that supposedly happened with your brother… You knew what kind of a man George was and yet you purposely got pregnant with his child?'

She gives me a look like it should be obvious. 'My only intention was to have his child and take the baby away. I never wanted *him*.' Regret and pain burn on her pale, worn face. 'I wanted him to feel what *I* felt when I lost my brother. So he would know what it felt like to lose the person you love the most in the world.'

I think about this. That someone would go to such extreme lengths, use a tiny baby to exact revenge. It makes me nervous of being in Opal's company all over again.

'What happened?' I'm frightened of hearing what she has to say, but I have no choice. There are three children to think about. Three children living with a possible sadistic psychopath who also happens to be a pathological liar.

Even as I say it, I don't really believe it. And yet… I've suspected something doesn't add up about George and Opal for a long time now. Who should I believe?

'George was furious when I told him I was pregnant. He told me I'd have to get rid of it, that I'd have to choose between the child and him.' She shakes her head in disgust. 'I played along at first, said I'd have a termination. I secretly went for my first scan and found out I was having twins. I wasn't prepared for the strength of emotion I felt towards my babies. Suddenly, hurting George didn't seem the most important thing any more.'

I'm too shocked to make comment.

Opal takes a breath and tries to disguise a sob.

'I had the babies, Darcy. I told George I'd made my decision and he said that because I was completely alone, he would help me and we'd sort out the mess, as he called it, afterwards.' She pauses, steeling herself to continue. 'On George's insistence, I didn't register with a midwife, didn't attend anti-natal classes. He fed me horror stories of the sub-standard care women received and said he would personally look after me.'

She fell silent for a moment or two, thinking back.

'It seems crazy now I never suspected him of having a hidden agenda in keeping me out of the system. I guess it must have been the hormones and I admit, crazy as it sounds, some days I allowed myself to imagine life with George. A proper family. I mean, people change, right?'

I don't respond. Her story is getting crazier by the minute.

'I did what he said and I had a good pregnancy. George was caring and I gave birth at home, just me and George, to two perfect little girls, non-identical twins. I saw them, held them, but I felt so ill after the birth, lost a lot of blood and then post-natal depression hit.' Her voice grows faint. 'He took wonderful care of me and our babies, Romy and Esther; I even began to think he might have changed, that we might have a future together. That's the strength of his hold on people… he can just turn your doubts about him around.'

I think about all the times I've been resolved to take matters into my own hands with the police but the closest I've got is calling 101 for advice. Each and every time I've put up a fight about sorting out the problem with Opal, he's convinced me otherwise. *Turned my doubts around*, as Opal so succinctly puts it.

But I don't trust her. Even though she appears to know so much detail… that there were twins!

'But what happened to the other baby… There's just Romy now.'

Her face contorts into a mask of grief and sadness.

'One of my babies died. George said at the beginning that she was the weaker one and that's normal.' Opal lets out a strangled whimper. 'I was so, so tired but I insisted on feeding my daughters myself, and…' I wait as she fights to say the words. 'I woke up, realised I'd fallen asleep feeding one and I'd rolled on to her… smothered her at just a week old. I was responsible for her death.'

'Oh no!' I press my fingers to my lips against the horror of it. Something new mothers are terrified of doing. I remember vividly the joy and contentment of sleeping with your tiny baby but also the fear that you might crush them or suffocate them whilst sleeping.

'I was hysterical, begging George to help me but he was furious. He turned so cold, said that I wasn't fit to bring up a child and that he had no choice but to take Romy off me for her safety, bring her up on his own. I'd had mental health problems in the past, you see; I was hit very badly by the death of my brother and I had told him all about that as we got to know each other.'

'Having mental health problems doesn't mean you're not fit to be a mother, Opal,' I say.

'I know that now,' she says. 'But back then, I was in the grip of it still. I had an eating disorder and I was self-harming.' She pulls up her sleeves and holds out her arms. I glance away from the road and smart at tangle of both silvery lines and newer, dark red slashes that criss-cross her bony wrists. 'I was already on strong medication for anxiety and depression. He made me believe that what he said was true, that I was an unfit mother.'

'So you accidentally killed your baby?'

She nods, her eyes glittering with tears. 'He said that if I tried to get Romy back, he would kill her and blame it on me.' Her eyes swim with emotion. 'Who'd believe me, with my history of mental illness, against a top surgeon? I knew he had it in him to hurt her.'

She sniffs hard and looks at me.

'But there's more, you see. You're not the only person I've been watching, Darcy.'

61

George had pulled in a favour and dropped Kane and Romy off at the hospital's private crèche which was usually, his colleagues told him, nigh on impossible to get into without a prior booking.

He'd left them happily joining in a singing story-time session and dashed back to the Audi which he'd parked on double-yellows near the ambulance bay. He slipped the parking attendant a tenner as he jumped back in the vehicle.

He wanted to get away from the place as quickly as he could after this morning's meeting. Things were going badly wrong.

But now it was time to get back to Darcy so they could go and find Harrison. It had to be said, the boy had been a bit of an attitude since moving into the house. George had tried hard to form a bond with the child but it wasn't happening. Harry obviously saw George as a threat to his father's memory – aided by Joel's family no doubt – and it had been easier for George to back off.

Harrison excelled at sport and this sometimes gave him an unlikeable air of superiority on occasion. Probably like his father, George thought. From what Darcy had told him, Joel had been a bit of a footballer in his time. Strictly local teams, though, nothing remotely impressive.

'Give him some time,' Darcy had said about the boy. 'He'll come around, I know it.'

When George thought about his own father when he was Harrison's age, any display of cheek was greeted with the same action: a swift slap around the head. He wasn't condoning kids being treated like that but it was frustrating that Darcy never so much as raised her voice to her eldest son when he misbehaved and showed little respect.

When he got back to the school, he'd take Darcy to the remote place where he was certain they'd find Harrison. Opal's place, he'd come to think of it.

'She used to like to go there, for "reflection time" as she called it. It's about a fifteen-minute drive.' As he told Darcy before he'd left for the hospital crèche, 'It's just a hunch but it's the best idea I have right now. If we draw a blank we'll call the police from there, OK?'

And she'd agreed.

He looked down now at his hands, clutching the steering wheel so tight his knuckles were white. He had to convince Darcy not to call the police. Surely she knew there was nothing they could do about what had happened so far?

He needed to know Darcy trusted him, believed what he said about Opal. If she started to see the woman as someone to pity, or tried to help her in some way, it could be disastrous and Harrison would be in terrible danger.

'Please God,' he said out loud to himself. 'Please let everything go well so we can put an end to this madness.'

He gave up a silent prayer that Darcy's faith in him was strong and everything would work out.

62

I just want to get her out of the car now but Opal is still talking about watching someone else.

'Who is this other person you've been watching?' I snap, seriously doubting her sanity. She nearly had me, had nearly convinced me that she was the innocent party in all that had supposedly happened. 'If I find out you've taken my son somewhere, if he's harmed, I'll... I'll kill you myself.'

Steph's face flashes into my mind, her face full of judgement that I could say such a thing as a mother, in charge of two impressionable boys.

Clearly alarmed, Opal slinks down in the passenger seat. Does she think I might hurt her?

Then I see it's something outside that's scared her.

I look up to see the back end of George's Audi as he drives slowly past the side street we're parked on.

'Get out, now,' I hiss. 'I need to find my son.'

'I'm parked on the next road,' she says, opening the passenger door. 'If you need me, I mean. Be careful. When you tell him you know everything, he will turn nasty. And Darcy?'

I stare at her, saying nothing. Her eyes are brighter than I've seen them before. Hopeful. But she is misguided if she thinks I'm going to just blindly swallow everything she's told me.

'Everything I've told you is true,' she says, as if she senses my doubt. 'You have to believe that.' But I'm not sure I do believe it. Any of it.

I reach over and grab the inside door handle, pulling it shut behind her. She stands and watches as I press the automatic locking system. My head doesn't feel big enough to fit in everything she's just told me. I don't want to think about it. I just want my son back.

My hands are shaking so much I can hardly get the car moving but I manage it and after a couple of kangaroo jumps, I drive up the road and around the school to the front of the building.

I don't know whether I want to tell George everything or tell him nothing at all. If I utter one thing she's told me, the whole stack of secrets or lies will come crashing down. All I care about in this precise moment is finding Harrison.

'Where have you been?' George demands when I unlock the car and he wrenches the driver's door open. 'I told you to stay here, outside school.'

'I drove round the block,' I lie, searching his face for some kind of clue of who he really is. 'Looking for Harrison.'

'He's clearly not here and there's not a moment to lose,' he says, hassled. 'Leave your car here, I'll drive us.'

I do as he says and within a few minutes we're driving, quite fast, out of the city.

'Where are the children?' My mouth is so dry I'm going to have a coughing fit soon.

George gives me a sideways glance and wipes a few spots of perspiration from his upper lip.

'There's a bottle of water in the glove compartment,' he says. 'The children are at the hospital crèche. They're quite safe, it's run by qualified staff as you'd expect.'

They're quite safe…

Are they, though? If George is the monster Opal says he is, he might know what's happened to Harrison and have already hurt Kane.

It feels ludicrous to even think it.

I pull out the bottle of still water and take a swig. My hands are shaking, my mind racing. 'I'm a bag of nerves.' I start to cry. 'Where are we going? I really think we need to call the police, Harrison could be… in danger.'

He reaches over and puts his hand on my thigh. 'I know it's hard but try to keep calm, Darcy. We'll find Harrison, I'm sure of it.'

And there he goes again, kind and considerate. I feel a twinge of guilt for doubting him.

'Where exactly are we going?' My voice sounds snappy and I cough and try again. 'Where do you think Harry might be?'

When I say his name, I think about his love of football and how he takes care of his brother. He can be a grumpy so and so at times but has always been an affectionate child and isn't afraid of giving me a hug in front of his teammates.

The lump in my throat seems to swell.

'It's not far. Sit back and breathe. Soon you'll have him back and then I'll do what I should have done a while ago. I'll call the police and we'll sort Opal out once and for all.'

He sounds so… plausible.

I want to believe him with all my heart. I do.

63

Opal calls me in a panic, tells me to be at the end of the street in two minutes flat. I don't know how but I do it, although I look a bit of a state. Unbrushed hair and no make-up.

She frowns when she sees me. 'Good job you're not at work today. Jump in, we need to catch them up.'

'Are they headed to the house?' I ask her.

'Yes, that's where Harrison will be. After all this time, I can read George like a book.'

'And Romy?'

'Darcy told me Romy and Kane are quite safe and we have to take her word for that. Try not to worry, Mum.'

'Stay tucked well behind him. I'm not even sure we should be involving ourselves in this.'

She shakes her head in despair at me but you never stop worrying about your children, do you? No matter how old they get.

'Mum, there's a chance he's going to show his true colours, in front of witnesses. If he does, there's a possibility I could get Romy back. At the very least, if I can get inside the house, I can record what's being said on my phone. This is the best chance we've ever had.'

I hope she's right, I really do. But I gave up hope of getting my granddaughter back a long time ago. The most I could hope for was to see her now and again, even though Romy didn't know who I was.

When George offered me the job as housekeeper, it wasn't a difficult decision. I hated him but I knew he needed someone who knew about Opal, could help control her and be someone he could trust.

I knew he was blackmailing my daughter about the death of tiny Esther, who never got a chance at life. I knew if his wife hadn't died, he wouldn't have let either of us near Romy.

So, when I got the chance to work for him and take care of my granddaughter, I knew it was the best chance of us getting Romy back for good. I had to promise not to allow Opal to see her unless George approved and I stuck to my word… mostly. I told Romy that Opal was my friend and we did get away with a few 'unofficial' visits now and then.

I could just about keep my daughter at bay that way. But when Darcy came on the scene, Opal became terrified she'd take her place, that she'd become Romy's mother. I must admit, seeing Darcy with Romy in the house, every day getting closer and her trying to cut my own involvement down, was a big challenge for me, too.

In the end, I couldn't keep my big mouth shut and I managed to get myself fired.

But I'm here now to support Opal and it's the first time we can stand together against George Mortimer.

Now he's fired me and replaced Opal in Romy's life completely, we've nothing to lose.

64

Five minutes later, there were open fields on either side of the car and yet it was just three miles out of the city's boundary.

It never failed to amaze George how quickly, once he got on the main roads, the city was left behind. There was far less traffic out here too. He'd passed only two vehicles, and one of those was a tractor.

'Are we nearly there?'

'Don't worry, we're just two minutes away. Soon you'll have Harrison back in your arms, I'm sure of it, darling.'

Darcy was a bag of nerves, terrified that if Harrison wasn't here, that they'd wasted vital time in finding out where he was or who he was with. But she should have faith in him. It made him angry that she still doubted him.

At the end of the road, he took a left, then a sharp right, and saw the house up ahead.

'Just wait here.' George turned off the engine, turned to her and touched her hand.

'But… no! I need to see if—'

'Trust me, Darcy,' he said firmly. 'I have to make sure it's safe. You know how crazy Opal is, who knows what she might try if she comes out here? I'll be back to signal to you when it's all clear. OK?'

'OK,' she whispered, on the verge of tears. She mumbled something about seeing Opal near the school but George didn't want to be pulled into a conversation about Opal at this point.

George got out of the Audi and prayed he could put an end to this madness.

65

Daniela was very nearly there: on the cusp of getting the sweet revenge she'd craved for years. It had been a long road with twists and turns along the way.

She'd had a couple of scares, in the early days: one when they'd only known each other a few weeks and had enjoyed a boozy night out at the pub where they'd initially met when they'd both been out with their respective friends. The second time was just a week before they married.

Both times, she'd panicked over her late period and had prayed she wasn't pregnant. She wanted to do everything right, be married, settled, have the right home to bring up their child. Little did she know back then it would never happen.

When Joel died and she found out about his double life, the betrayal of his marriage vows was bad enough. But when she discovered he had two sons by a woman called Darcy Hilton, her heart had literally broken in two.

She'd found out via Joel's mobile phone. Text messages Darcy had sent when Joel had been on death's door and had left unanswered.

Joel's family had convinced her to say nothing, just to take the modest estate he'd left and quietly make a new life. They'd known about the kids and Darcy all along and said nothing to either woman.

But Daniela had called the number and Darcy had answered, and within ten minutes, both their lives were altered forever.

Daniela had been desperate for a baby throughout their ten-year marriage. They'd been through the gruelling medical mill, done all that. Discovering, after tests, that the problem was hers and Joel was perfectly healthy had been a particular low point. Feelings of being less-than, inadequate, incomplete… she'd had the pleasure of them all.

Then there had been two cycles of IVF on the NHS that had failed. And all that time, Joel had been spectacularly neutral about her getting pregnant.

'I love you,' he'd reassured her at the lowest moments. 'I don't care if you can't have kids, that's just not important to me.'

And she'd believed him, that was the worst bit. That was the part she still beat herself up about even now, even though he was long dead.

But now, she'd been thrown a lifeline. Quite unexpectedly, thanks to Steph mentioning where George worked and how she thought someone ought to set him straight about the 'real' Darcy, she'd managed to convince George to speak to her after work one day.

The magnetism of the man was incredible and she felt herself falling for him almost immediately. George felt the same way and as Steph had said, Daniela was a far better match for sophisticated George than Darcy with her hang-ups and mental health issues.

George and Daniela had got close very quickly under George's cover of work meetings and job interviews. Darcy had always been so gullible. But he'd levelled with Daniela, told her the truth about the fix he'd got himself in with Opal and Darcy and they'd schemed together and come up with a viable plan if they could pull it off.

Now, Daniela had the chance to be with a wonderful man and his adorable daughter, little Romy, who was desperate for a mother. Between them, Steph and George had separately convinced Daniela that Darcy was indeed unstable. She was not a good influence on Romy nor on her own two sons. Daniela was convinced that, as Steph had told her, the best place for the boys was with them, Joel's family.

But to do this, they had to lure Darcy, make her vulnerable. Daniela had agreed with George that she would play her part in bringing this to fruition.

The boy whimpered behind the gag she'd applied to him. She pushed away the feelings of revulsion that she'd actually taken a child and done this. George had assured her it wouldn't be for long and the pay-off was going to be wonderful.

'It won't be long now,' Daniela told the boy coolly. 'Be quiet.'

He stared her out with dark, sparking eyes. He was bold for such a young age, she'd give him that. She could see Joel in him in so many ways and she hated it. Looking at the child seemed to magnify her feelings of inadequacy.

But soon, very soon, she'd have her own daughter. Romy was young enough that she'd come to accept Daniela completely as her mother. Given time, she'd hopefully be unable to remember a time when she'd been motherless.

Thanks to George, Daniela's life was soon to be complete. She didn't give a toss what happened to Darcy Hilton and Joel's sons.

66

It was bitterly cold out here and George wished he'd picked up his padded anorak from the back of his office door when he'd left the hospital earlier.

Darcy had been in such a panic when she'd called to say Harrison was missing, everything else seemed unimportant.

George hurried around the back of the house and the kitchen door opened. Daniela stepped out and kissed him on the cheek. She'd approached him weeks ago, when they'd returned from the lodge, got his work address from Joel's sister, apparently. She'd caught him on the day he was annoyed at Darcy for calling the police and the lodge manager about his non-existent complaint.

He'd bought her a coffee and she'd explained everything about who Darcy was and what she had done to her marriage.

'I thought you had a right to know the truth,' she'd said and George had had a lightbulb moment, realising the potential of Daniela's involvement.

She seemed a strong character, but George liked a challenge. Destroying women was his favourite pastime, a reaction to his mother dying and deserting him as a child, psychologists would no doubt conclude. But no, he smiled to himself, he just genuinely enjoyed the power he could wield over them just as he had done with the younger boys at St Mark's. Yet this woman seemed different. She wasn't soft bellied and easy to break and George respected that. Together, he realised, they could finally get rid of the problem that had blighted the last few years of his life: Opal Vardy.

He could even make a new start with a new identity abroad somewhere. Escape the terrible storm that was whipping up around him at the hospital.

'Good job,' he murmured, stepping into the warmth provided by the oil-filled heater. He looked at Harrison, bound and gagged in the chair.

The boy's eyes flashed with fury and he wriggled his torso, kicking out with his feet. The chair wobbled, threatened to tip over.

'Enough!' George barked. 'Stop struggling, you brat.'

Harrison seemed to double his efforts, yelling out a retort from behind his gag that translated as an angry yelp.

'He kicked me when I walked past him just now.' Daniela frowned, rubbing her right knee. 'He's a little live wire.'

In response to this, Harrison let out another aggressive yell and kicked out at George, narrowly missing his leg.

George reached for the pair of scissors on the side next to the large roll of masking tape Daniela had used to secure the boy. Harrison stopped yelling, his eyes wide with fear and trepidation. Quick as lightning, George moved the scissors towards his head, then snipped hard into the soft lobe of his ear. The blood started pouring almost immediately, and he allowed it to trickle down onto Harrison's pale grey sweatshirt.

Colour drained from the boy's face. He pressed his chin down to his chest so he could see the blossoming red patch on his left shoulder and began to shake and sob uncontrollably.

Daniela held a grubby rag to Harrison's ear, stemming the blood flow, and grinned at George. Both of them knew it wasn't a serious cut, just a clean snip about half a centimetre long. But the ear could bleed quite profusely for up to ten minutes, and consequently the injury looked far worse than it was.

George crouched down next to the boy.

'That's one ear lopped off,' he said softly. 'Unless you do exactly what I tell you, I'll take the other one too. Understand?'

Fat, glistening tears ran down Harrison's face and he nodded vigorously, fear rather than fury glinting in his eyes now.

Without warning, George reached up and ripped the masking tape from his mouth, and the boy promptly vomited into his own lap.

Harrison's life would have to be sacrificed, there was no way around that. He was old enough to tell the police exactly how he came to be here and what had happened.

It would be another death he could attribute to Opal's mental illness. She would be here any minute thanks to his message to meet her to finally talk about the future of her child.

67

Opal and Maria watched as George got out of the Audi and hurried inside the house.

'Wait here,' she told her mother. 'Don't call the police until I give you the sign. I have to try and record him for evidence or we might never get Romy back.'

She waited another minute or so before creeping down the path of the old Victorian house sitting in its own large plot. She noted that the front curtains were drawn. Not a usual practice at teatime, she thought.

She was so close to getting her daughter back and exposing him to the world now, she could feel it. With Darcy hopefully on board and knowing about George's lies, she felt sure that between them, they had everything they needed to put him in prison.

Opal believed that Harrison was inside this house and she thought she knew who with. She'd followed George and his new woman here twice in the last couple of weeks. She'd thought it was their love nest, somewhere they conducted their clandestine affair away from Darcy's eyes but now... she wasn't quite so sure. Maybe it was a kind of business arrangement between two people hell bent on getting different sorts of revenge.

Opal had been about to tell Darcy about Daniela when she'd spotted George's Audi returning and so hadn't gotten chance to explain about this place. When she'd got back to her own car and checked the phone she'd left in there, she'd seen George's message asking to meet her. And she just knew something was very wrong.

'Opal!' a voice called out and she froze, looking over her shoulder to see Darcy rushing towards the house. She pressed a finger to her mouth, urged the other woman to keep quiet.

'Is Harrison in there? Is this where you're keeping him?' Darcy stormed towards Opal, her fists clenched and face bright red, as if she might attack her.

'I told you,' Opal hissed. 'It's not me you have to worry about. Now, if you really want to keep your son safe, then be quiet.'

Opal slipped down the side of the house and inched around the corner to the kitchen window. The light was on in there, and as she looked through into the house, she saw a figure walk down the small hallway and into the front room.

Darcy said nothing but she was right behind her and it crossed Opal's mind that she was angry enough to punch her in the back of the head.

Opal crept to the back door and tried the handle. It was open. In their arrogance, they'd left it unlocked, so sure were they of their infallibility.

Very carefully, she applied gentle pressure to the handle until it had moved down as far as it would go, and then pushed the door open, just enough to slip inside the kitchen.

All she had to do was confirm they had Darcy's son here, then she could slip back out and run to the car, where her mother would call the police. With George out of the way and not controlling her any more by threatening to kill Romy and blame it on her, Opal would be free to have a DNA test and prove she was Romy's biological mother.

What a sweet moment it would be when she and her daughter could be together and do all the normal things they had missed out on courtesy of George's wickedness. The thought was pure heaven, and she could be just minutes away from it…

She tiptoed towards the hallway, stopping when she heard low voices. She identified George's deep tones, then Daniela's higher voice. Then a child's cry, a sort of pain-filled yelp. What were they doing to the kid in there?

Opal slid her fingers into her top pocket and depressed a button.

'Harrison!' Darcy screamed and bounded forward through the kitchen.

Opal darted forward behind her and pushed open the door into the front room, then recoiled in horror at the sight of George wielding some kind of stainless-steel implement above the boy's head. That woman who Darcy had been watching for the past few weeks – Daniela – roughly pulled Harrison's head back.

Darcy leapt forward and scooted around George who seemed disorientated for a moment. She smashed the weight of her whole body into Daniela, who toppled, smashing her head on the side of a cabinet behind. Darcy didn't glance at the other woman, she simply pressed her poor son's head to her, absorbing his muffled sobs into her side.

Opal turned to run back outside to alert her mother to call the police, George took three great strides across the room and grabbed her arm.

With just the two of them in the hallway, he pulled her towards him and tightened his grip. In the dim light, his face shone manic and patterned with shadow.

'You can't hold me in limbo any more, George.' Opal spat the words at his smirking face. 'Esther died but I never meant to harm her. I'm no danger to Romy, you know that. I'm her mother!'

'Of course I know that. I also know how gullible you are, doubting yourself all this time.' He grinned and his voice dropped lower. 'I'll let you into a little secret, just between us. I smothered baby Esther. I did it to keep you in check, so I had something to hold over you so you wouldn't fight too hard for Romy.'

Opal gaped. She swayed as the room began to spin, cries and the sounds of struggle emanating from the front room. 'But why... why tell me the truth now? All this time I've hated myself, believed that—'

'I'm a softy at heart. I thought you might like to know with you being on your deathbed and all.' He held a lethal-looking scalpel up in the air in his gloved hand, his crazed eyes gleaming. 'You're about to take your last breath and Darcy will be taking the rap for your murder. With her in prison, the boys will go to Joel's family and you... well, you'll be out of my hair once and for all. Romy will have a new mother in Daniela.'

'My mother, she—'

'Oh, I don't think Maria will be a problem and if she is, she'll probably decide quite quickly to end it all. I'm quite good at convincing people of that, as your brother found out at St Mark's.'

George barrelled forward as Darcy threw her weight into him from behind.

Opal took the chance to wriggle free and flung herself forward, grabbing a long knife from the block on the counter, then turned, pushing back against the worktop. As George charged towards her, she instinctively held the knife out in front of her, faintly aware that Darcy was wailing in the room where Harrison was being held.

Opal felt the warm stickiness on her hand before she realised what had happened. Still clutching the scalpel, George remained standing, staring into her eyes, her very soul, before sinking to his knees, a terrible gurgling sounding in his throat.

At that moment, a figure appeared at the kitchen door. Her mother.

'The police are on their way,' Maria whimpered, covering her face with a hand as she looked down on George's lifeless body.

68

Three months later

After the boys have had their breakfast and allowing them some time in the gaming room, I sit on the sofa watching Romy, together at last with her mum and granny. I feel almost as though I'm intruding on the wonderful love they all have for each other, denied for so long.

'Darcy, look!' Romy holds up the beaded bracelet she's making.

'That's beautiful, sweetie. Well done!'

She beams, her cheeks ruddy and her eyes bright.

She's a different child since she's been reunited with her mother. She never knew what was happening behind the scenes, of course, never knew her own daddy was responsible for the greatest sadness in her life: the death of her twin, Esther. But children can sense danger and tension in the air and it had always been around her as George blackmailed Opal and constantly held Romy as ransom to control her.

We're all living in George's house for now. Sounds a strange arrangement, I know, but I have more in common with these two women than some people have who've known each other for years. I feel relaxed in their presence.

We've all been controlled by George, we're all dealing with our own guilt as we ask ourselves the same question every day: Why didn't I see through him from the start?

But we're finding strength in each other. None of us are stupid people but George was an outstanding pathological liar.

Living here in the house is the easiest solution for a number of reasons. Myself and the boys were effectively homeless having left our own rented home to move in with George. We did so weeks before the *terrible events*, as we've come to refer to the day when Harrison was abducted and George died. I couldn't turn to Joel's family for support when they were fighting to get custody of my sons and that was before I found out that George had helped them in their quest.

But the biggest reason for keeping the status quo is for Romy's sake. She's only ever known this house as her home and been through such already in her short life. Her daddy has died – although for now she thinks he's gone away for a while – and although she loves Maria and has been told she is her granny, Romy still seems to think of her as the housekeeper. Her mother, Opal, she previously knew only as Maria's friend.

Living here has also meant we've been able to talk everything through together... and boy, has there been a lot to talk about. I'm still amazed that the woman George set me up to think of as my greatest foe, Opal, is now someone I trust implicitly.

Likewise, Maria, who I thought hated me, turns out to be someone I greatly admire. A woman who made such incredible sacrifices; she willingly worked for the man who, as a teenager, drove her son to suicide at school. A man who robbed Maria's daughter of her child and prevented Maria from enjoying a close, natural relationship with Romy as her grandmother.

'I was never interested in George, I found out how cruel a man he was long ago and I hated him. But I loved my daughter with all my heart and that's why I shadowed their every move,' Opal explained when we were finally able to talk after all the drama of the terrible events. 'At the end, George inadvertently gave me the greatest gift when he told me for spite that Esther's death was not my fault. I've felt like ending my life so many times because of the burden of that guilt, believing I killed my own child through negligence. It was only my love for Romy and my belief that one day, maybe, just maybe, there might be a chance we'll be reunited.'

'It was Opal's idea for me to take the housekeeper job,' Maria said. 'I had to tell George who I was because I knew if he found out – and he was a very resourceful man – I'd never see my granddaughter again.'

'How did you get him to agree to it?' I asked her, hardly believing that George would allow such an arrangement.

'I put it to him like a business proposal,' Maria said. 'I told him I knew of my daughter's mental health problems and that I thought the best place for Romy was with him. He agreed I could take the position and have contact with my granddaughter but he warned me: the first time I put a foot wrong, he'd make sure I never saw her again.'

'He fired you when you had a bit of a meltdown at me because he thought you'd ruin his plans to set Opal and I at loggerheads?'

Maria nodded. 'He told me I had become too much of a risk and that, if I had another outburst of temper, I might tell you the truth about Romy. He said if I went quietly, he'd consider reinstating me in the future when he'd got some problems "ironed out" as he put it.'

'When I'd attacked Opal for abducting Harrison, he meant. That's what he hoped would happen. He planned to kill her and place the blame firmly on me... with Daniela's help.'

Maria nodded, looked sheepish.

'I admit, when he brought you back to the house, I was terrified you were the one he'd settle down with. When you showed me the diamond bracelet he'd gifted you, I really panicked... it had belonged to Lucy, you see. I knew he was serious about you then, although I never realised you were part of his plan to get rid of Opal.' Maria shook her head. 'When I saw you getting closer to Romy, I became convinced you would end up bringing her up as your own daughter and there would be nothing me or Opal could do about that. Our only chance was to stop that happening in the first place.'

Telling Maria that day that I hoped Romy and I could become closer was probably the worst thing I could have said to her.

'All the stuff I did; watching you, sending photographs, the funeral flowers, messing up your car… it was the only way I could try and warn you off,' Opal said.

'But he'd already told me you were stalking him, so in a way, the actions you took to try and warn me just proved his point.'

'Everything has always seemed to work to his advantage,' Opal agreed. 'Even him meeting Daniela.'

Our conversations spanned over many nights. When the kids had gone up to bed, the three of us would sit with endless cups of coffee, remembering details, ironing out quirks that had puzzled me; lies that George had fed me.

'When he said Opal had come to the door one day demanding to be let inside and you, Maria, alerted him to what happened, he'd made that up?' I asked.

'Of course,' Opal said. 'Mum would never have given me away. Thanks to her agreeing to become George's housekeeper, I got to see Romy so much more.'

'But I could only do so much,' Maria remarked regretfully. 'I couldn't allow Romy to see Opal too much or George would've cottoned on what was happening. So I told little Romy that Opal was my friend and she accepted her as that, seeing her a couple of times a month.'

'It's been so hard to bear,' Opal says softly. 'There have been eating disorders, I've self-harmed… I've utterly hated myself for years. But through it all, I knew that the next best thing to Romy being with me was for her to be with my mum, her own granny. It was the only thing that kept me sane.'

What a terrible, heartbreaking choice Opal has been forced to make.

I looked at Maria. 'What a remarkable woman you are, facing that monster every day. Knowing that, on top of what he was doing to Opal and Romy, he had driven your son to suicide.'

'Rufus was such a sensitive boy. His father had insisted on keeping him at home, he said it was the only way he'd let me take Opal and escape his controlling ways. It was more difficult for women to break free back then. Rufus had been twelve years old, old enough to decide who he wanted to be with and he chose his father. My husband was obsessed with sending Rufus to an independent day school but he sent us away virtually penniless.'

A light bulb illuminated in my head.

'Was it ever proven? That George drove Rufus to suicide?' I asked. 'Because he told me that Lucy, his wife, had also committed suicide.'

'He treated that girl like a dog.' Maria's eyes flashed. 'I didn't know her for very long but George controlled her like everyone in his life. I never found out exactly what lies he spun her to explain turning up with baby Romy one day and telling her she had to pretend the child was hers. But I know she went downhill fast into a deep, dark depression, after he did so.' Maria stares into space, thinking back. 'I know her parents despised George. But they also turned away from Romy and I can never forgive them for that. But I have written to them and told them everything now and I've had a reply.'

'They're elderly, in their eighties, but they're looking into challenging the suicide verdict of the inquest into Lucy's death as Mum is doing for Rufus,' Opal continues. 'Who knows what will come of it? There's no evidence as such but we have to at least try.'

The doorbell sounds, rattling me out of my thoughts. Opal and Maria look up at me from their bead work with Romy.

The moment I've been dreading has arrived.

'Good luck,' Opal says.

'Thanks.' And with my head pounding and feeling like I want to hide more than answer the door, I leave them to it and walk into the hallway.

69

The three figures standing outside merge into one blurry-edged shape through the coloured glass panels. I open the door.

'Hello Darcy,' Brenda says. 'Thanks for letting us come over.'

'Come through,' I say, as they step inside. I hide my shock at Brenda's hollow cheeks and Leonard's pallor. Even in her padded anorak, Steph looks at least two dress sizes smaller than when I last saw her.

I lead them through to the front room feeling relieved that Dave isn't with them. This feels like a close, private family discussion and I'm glad they see it that way, too. They wave away my offer of tea and sit, side by side, on the large sofa.

Leonard clears his throat. 'We asked to see you today because we owe you a very big apology.'

A few months ago I'd have dismissed Leonard's attempt to take ownership of what has happened. 'It's fine,' I'd have said, 'Don't worry about it, it's all in the past now.'

But it *isn't* fine they tried to take my sons away from me. They *should* worry.

So I don't dismiss his plea. I sit and wait to hear what they have to say.

'I speak for all of us, Darcy, when I say we're very, very sorry for what we did,' Leonard continues, his face grey. 'For all of it.'

'We were getting genuinely worried about your ability to look after the boys but now we realise that really, we were just scared.'

Brenda says. She looks so frail and the hand that Leonard isn't holding, her right hand, is shaking despite resting on her knee. 'We were terrified your new life would swallow up our contact with them.'

'I take full responsibility for getting Daniela involved.' Steph's eyes are cast down to the floor. 'Once I'd spoken to her about our plans and she showed interest in helping our cause, it was like a juggernaut started rolling. I knew it was wrong but I couldn't stop it.'

I've promised myself I'll stay calm and reasonable during their visit, but the thought of Steph and Daniela plotting behind my back is testing my resolve.

'Why though, Steph? I thought of you as not just a friend but truly like a sister. We…' I force myself to take a breath. 'We were so close. I wanted nothing more than to share my new life with you but—'

'I know.' Steph looks at me. 'You should have been able to do that but… I couldn't handle it. You'll never know how many hours I lay awake once you'd told us about George. I'd lurch from feeling ashamed, to battling the worst kind of jealousy and need for revenge.'

Her candour is disarming. I'm not sure what to say so I remain silent.

'Dave and I have split up,' she says quickly. 'What's happened has been the push I've needed to re-evaluate my own life. I take full accountability for what I did to you, but it didn't help that Dave was a constant negative voice in my ear spurring me on, telling me I was justified.'

I can't argue with that. Dave seemed to enjoy repeating, to anyone who'd listen, that it was far too early for me to start dating. He reminded me of a barnacle; stuck on the side of the Hilton family, sponging off all the benefits but not really contributing anything himself. I'll probably never know why he disliked me so much.

'We'll never forgive ourselves for what happened,' Brenda blurts out. 'We should have never trusted Daniela, never got involved with her scheming.'

In letters Brenda sent me before I agreed to meet, she explained that they were unaware of Daniela's contact with George.

'She seemed to sense right from the off how worried we were about losing contact with the boys and she played on that.' Leonard shook his head. 'She convinced us you were losing your mind and that you were obsessed with her and neglecting the boys. I'm ashamed to say we believed her. She made us feel we were completely justified in our fears.'

In their own way, they've been victims of George and Daniela just like the rest of us.

There was a time I believed that George, despite being a brilliant surgeon, didn't understand how the mind worked. I told myself that because of my obsession with Daniela, I understood patterns of behaviour in a way he didn't. How wrong I was.

'George was very manipulative. They both were,' I say quietly. 'You weren't the only ones who misplaced your trust.'

It was Daniela who fell for George the hardest. I've read all the letters she's sent from her prison cell. They're upstairs in my bedside drawer. George convinced her he loved her, wanted to start a new life with her and Romy. Her eyes firmly locked on to the prize, she willingly lured Harrison away as per George's plan, not caring what happened to my boy. All this time I've felt the one at fault for obsessing about Joel's wife but it turns out she'd harboured far more treachery towards me than I could ever have imagined. She came back to Nottingham determined to get revenge on me.

Now, in every letter, Daniela asks if I will visit her, speak to her… but so far as I'm concerned, Daniela is as dead as Joel and George are to me. She gained my trust that day after attending my yoga class, pretending to be my friend with the sole intention of setting me up to walk into George's trap.

'We should have seen through her,' Leonard says, driving his fingernails into his palms. 'At sixty-eight years of age I thought I knew all the tricks in the book. How wrong I was.'

'None of us could have known that George's master plan was to kill Opal and lay the blame at my door to get rid of her once and for all,' I say. 'He didn't care how many lives he ruined in the process.'

I can't stop thinking that George helped Kane that day at the park and that could have been the end of it. But I'd chased him down, flush with the possibility of a textbook romance with a handsome doctor. I did all the running in the beginning. But I believe he soon realised the opportunity I gave him; he understood damaged women far better than I ever gave him credit for. And, still reeling from Joel's betrayal, I was certainly that: damaged and vulnerable. Ripe for George to use in his own warped agenda to finally get rid of Opal who'd proved to be far greater of a problem than he'd ever anticipated.

'There's something else, Darcy.' Brenda clasps her hands in front of her. 'I want to apologise for trying to hide our own shame and denial of Joel's betrayal at the expense of your mental wellbeing.'

She blows out air and I feel a twinge of pity. I know how hard this must be for Brenda to face up to and vocalise about Joel.

'He was a good father to the boys but choosing to maintain the lie of two lives, he short-changed them too.' Leonard pats his wife's knee. 'We were wrong to keep his secret quiet when he was alive for the sake of the children and wrong to try and gloss over it when he'd gone. We were lying to ourselves.'

Steph clears her throat and looks at her parents before speaking.

'We'll never forgive ourselves for what happened. For everything,' she says, her eyes shining. 'We should have discussed our worries and fears with you and we're so, so sorry that we chose not to do that.'

I sit in silence for a few moments as I absorb their words.

'As you know, as soon as we heard what had happened, that it was Daniela and George who had had abducted Harrison, we abandoned our custody bid,' Leonard says.

My solicitor had already informed me of this.

'Steph and I have cut all contact with Daniela,' Brenda adds. 'We kept in touch because she'd been Joel's wife and we actually thought of her as a victim too.'

'I suppose what we want to say is, it will be a long road but could you find it in your heart to ever forgive us, Darcy?' Steph's voice cracks and she swallows down a sob. 'We're willing to do anything to be a part of your and the boys' lives again.'

I look at Brenda and Leonard. They look wretched, far older than their years. Their complexions are sallow and Brenda's once snug clothing hangs off her bony frame. They're good people, essentially. Good people who've been led way off the path of decency and truthfulness.

But they're also people who've caused me and my sons a great deal of pain. And if there's one promise I've made to myself after everything that's happened, it's that from now on, I'm going to honour my true feelings. Never again will I allow other people to tell me what I should think and how I should feel. I owe that to myself.

'I appreciate you coming here to apologise,' I say evenly. Inside I'm anything but calm and collected. I'm glad they've come over to the house to speak to me but there will be no big emotional reunion here today. That's just not going to happen. 'I can't say how I feel about everything right now but hearing what you've had to say has helped. It's a start.'

Brenda sobs into a tissue. 'Thank you, Darcy. Thanks for giving us the chance to speak to you today.'

There's banging in the hallway and suddenly the lounge door flies open.

'Mum, can we get some crisps and… Grandma, Grandad!'

Kane lurches across the room and lands in Brenda's lap. She can hardly speak for crying.

Harrison appears in the doorway. He too has lost weight and he's been withdrawn and run down, catching every bug that's going after his ordeal. But his face lights up now at the sight of his relations.

'Come here, lads, let's have a little cuddle,' Leonard booms then looks at me. 'Is that… OK, Darcy?'

I nod. I can see the boys want this as much as they do.

Leonard stands up and Harrison buries his face in his grandad's chest.

When I look at Steph, she's sitting quietly watching her parents and nephews, tears streaming down her face.

'Can we go back to grandma and grandad's house, Mum?' Harrison says hopefully when he finally pulls away from Leonard's embrace.

'Please, Mum!' Kane echoes.

'Not today,' I say softly and the boys groan. Brenda and Leonard visibly deflate in front of me. 'But maybe next week I can take you over to see them for an hour. How's that?'

Brenda's eyes fill up and she places a hand lightly on my upper arm.

'Thank you, Darcy,' she whispers. 'Thank you, from the bottom of our hearts.'

Like I said, it's a start.

70

When Joel's family have left and the boys have disappeared back into the games room for the last twenty minutes of their allotted time, I go back into the lounge and sit quietly for a few minutes to reflect.

I pick up the brown envelope on the coffee table and slide out the piece of paper within it. My deed poll certificate from my name change back to the surname I had before meeting Joel.

'Darcy Ann Sculley,' I say out loud.

That's me. That's who I am. I was never married to Joel and I've never been married. I took his name because I was so desperate to keep a piece of him, to attempt to convince myself and others that I meant something in his life.

I stare at my name in print and find I like the feeling it gives me. I've stripped myself back to the bare bones and generally, I like what I've found there. I don't know where I learned to get my self-value from a man but the game is up.

I finally believe I'm good enough as I am. I always was.

Since the day of terrible events, my learning curve has been very steep.

The whole betrayal by George was a load too much to bear for me and I'm back on medication. The eczema has reappeared on my hands, too. But I don't see it as a weakness any longer, it's a strength so far as I'm concerned. I've faced my demons and I've asked for help. It won't be forever, I just need a bit of a leg-up, right now. My days of smiling through the hardest times and denying my true feelings are gone.

I've suspended my yoga classes. Everyone has been so patient and understanding and I'm relishing the extra time I have to just be with the boys and enjoy the support of Opal and Maria as we travel our shared path.

A press article referred to us as 'recovering victims of George Mortimer'. That, we are not. Bad stuff has happened to us but we don't use *him* to identify ourselves. We are three strong women, with three bright futures ahead of us. We all believe that and it gives us a shared strength on the darkest days.

It has been a long, hard road, but finally we heard yesterday that the Crown Prosecution Service won't be charging Opal with George's manslaughter. Daniela, who suffered just mild concussion from cracking her head on a cabinet when I pushed her away from Harrison, has already been charged with a number of serious offences, including abduction and assault of a child and is awaiting trial in prison.

Harrison is still getting help to deal with what happened, what George and Daniela did to him. He wasn't badly injured and has been left with just a tiny scar. But that day, he truly believed George had cut off his ear and was about to hack off the other one, too. That's the thing that still gives him night terrors. He gets angry and frustrated and I think he holds some resentment towards me for taking us to live with George in the first place.

But with the help of his school counsellor, he's working through his feelings and some days, I'm starting to see a slight improvement in his mood, I think.

With no will in place and Romy being George's biological daughter, his estate, once all the legal wrangling has taken place, will be held in trust for her until she is twenty-one. In the meantime, Opal and Maria are caring for Romy, living in the house and the lawyers say they're hopeful they'll be able to stay there. When the two of them offered us the chance to stay for a while too, it seemed like the right thing to do.

About a week after his death, I found a letter in his briefcase informing George he had been removed from the shortlist of candidates for the promotion he was obsessed with winning.

I made a trip to the hospital to speak to Sherry, the ward manager. She agreed to meet me for a coffee during her break and to chat, if I could promise what she told me remained strictly off the record.

'We're all still reeling from the shock of everything that's happened in *and* out of the hospital,' Sherry told me. 'A couple of week's ago, George's boss, Dharval, uncovered a critical detail George had tried to hide: two incompatible drugs he'd prescribed to a kidney patient, Mr Joseph Hill, that had exacerbated his kidney ailment and left him critically ill.'

I recognised the patient's name from George telling me he had to attend meetings about this particular case and I'd also seen his medical file on the table. Turns out that George was on the brink of being fired from his job in a scandal storm over Mr Hill.

'He'd tried to hide his mistake,' Sherry explained. 'Dharval reported him and George was told he was out of the running for the top job. We all noticed the change in him. He went from being a personable guy to someone who seemed to be teetering on the edge of madness. We heard moves were afoot to suspend him from duty.'

I shuddered when I remembered George's crazed eyes on the day of his death.

It was so hard to reconcile the kind, decent man George had seemed to be with the monster that was finally revealed.

'Don't beat yourself up because you didn't see it in him,' Maria told me. 'George lived and breathed the truth *he* wanted to believe. He convinced himself of a story before he told it to anyone else.

I never heard him speak about Lucy with anything but affection and yet he treated her terribly. He made his lies so real.'

In some ways, Maria seemed to know him best as, in the house, she'd seen him at his most private.

I've found a therapist who is helping me process everything that's happened. That's my starting place in moving forward.

I don't know if I'll ever be able to trust a man again but I'm hopeful I will. Third time lucky... isn't that what they say? Just not for a while. Not for a long time yet.

I hear small footsteps patter across the hallway and the lounge door opens.

'Darcy, look! I made you something.' Little Romy rushes up and grabs my hand, slipping an elasticated colourful bead creation on to my wrist. 'It's a friendship bracelet because you're my bestest friend.'

'Thank you sweetie, it's the prettiest bracelet I've ever had,' I say, thinking about the diamond tennis bracelet of poor, dead Lucy that Maria returned to her parents for me last month.

I hug Romy close, my eyes stinging.

It may have been an ordeal of the worst order and shook my trust in others beyond repair but this hug means everything.

This tiny, precious girl deserves all the love in the world and I'm proud she calls me her friend. Perhaps she is George's biggest victim. He's robbed her of her twin sister and prevented her enjoying a fulfilling and caring relationship with her mother and grandmother for the first six years of her life. And yet here she is, beautiful and bright and full of love.

She is an example to us all.

I've lost a lot but I've made a friend for life in Romy. I still have my world; my boys.

But best of all, I've found someone very special who I thought I'd lost forever. Someone who will never let me down and always have my back.

I've found *me* again.

A LETTER FROM
K.L. SLATER

Thank you so much for reading *Single*, my tenth psychological thriller. I hope you enjoyed reading it as much as I enjoyed writing it. If you did enjoy it, and want to keep up to date with all my latest releases, just sign up at the following link. Your email address will never be shared and you can unsubscribe at any time.

www.bookouture.com/kl-slater

The idea for this story grew from a very simple question that popped into my mind: what might happen if you stepped into someone else's nightmare?

A woman and her children have suffered tragic circumstances but live a fairly ordinary life and manage to get through each difficult day. Then, within a very short time, she meets a man who disrupts her determination to stay single, the sort of man she never imagined she could be with, and she begins to live a life beyond anything she had hoped for.

Once I have that initial seed of an idea that interests and excites me, I try and step into the shoes of the main character. For this story, I asked myself: how far would you be willing to believe this wonderful new person who has transformed your life and lit up your future? Would you rally behind them to sort out a long-standing problem that could threaten everything you have?

We'd all react differently, of course, but I do hope you've enjoyed reading Darcy's story in *Single*.

The book is set in Nottinghamshire, the place I was born and have lived all my life. Local readers should be aware that I sometimes take the liberty of changing street names or geographical details to suit the story.

I know you hear this a lot, but reviews are massively important to authors. If you've enjoyed *Single* and could spare just a few minutes to write a short review to say so, I would so appreciate that.

You can also connect with me via my website, on Facebook or on Twitter.

Best wishes,
Kim x

 KimLSlaterAuthor

 @KimLSlater

KLSlaterAuthor

www.KLSlaterAuthor.com

ACKNOWLEDGEMENTS

Firstly, huge thanks to Lydia Vassar-Smith, my editor, for her patience and immense help throughout the editing process for *Single*. Thanks to *all* the Bookouture team for everything they do, especially Kim Nash and Alexandra Holmes.

Enormous thanks to my agent, Camilla Wray, for her guidance and support in my writing career. Thanks also to Roya Sarrafi-Gohar and the rest of the hard-working team at Darley Anderson Literary, TV and Film Agency.

Massive thanks as always go to my husband, Mac, my Mum and my daughter, Francesca, for their love and support. To my writing buddy and fellow Bookouture author, Angela Marsons, for the laughs, support and the sage advice.

Special thanks must also go to Henry Steadman, who has produced a striking and standout cover for *Single*.

Thank you to Jane Selley and to Becca Allen for their eagle-eyed copyediting and proof-reading skills.

Thank you to the bloggers and reviewers who do so much to help make my thrillers a success. Thank you to everyone who has taken the time to post a positive review online or taken part in my blog tour. It is noticed and much appreciated.

Last but not least, thanks a million to my wonderful readers for their continued loyalty and support.

Made in United States
Troutdale, OR
08/25/2023